SUGAR RUN

SUGAR RUN

A NOVEL

MESHA MAREN

ALGONQUIN BOOKS
OF CHAPEL HILL
2018

Published by
Algonquin Books of Chapel Hill
Post Office Box 2225
Chapel Hill, North Carolina 27515-2225

a division of
Workman Publishing
225 Varick Street
New York, New York 10014

Design by Steve Godwin.

This is a work of fiction. While, as in all fiction, the literary perceptions and insights are based on experience, all names, characters, places, and incidents either are products of the author's imagination or are used fictitiously.

LIBRARY OF CONGRESS CATALOGING-IN-PUBLICATION DATA

Names: Maren, Mesha, author.
Title: Sugar run / a novel by Mesha Maren.
Description: First edition. | Chapel Hill, North Carolina :
Algonquin Books of Chapel Hill, 2018.
Identifiers: LCCN 2018011885 | ISBN 9781616206215 (hardcover : alk. paper)
Subjects: LCSH: Ex-convicts—Fiction. | Lesbians—Fiction.
Classification: LCC PS3613.A7396 S84 2018 | DDC 813/.6—dc23
LC record available at https://lccn.loc.gov/2018011885

10 9 8 7 6 5 4 3 2 1

First Edition

For M.R.O.,
my sugar forever and always

I was raised up from tiny
childhood in those purple hills,
right slam on the brink of language

—DENIS JOHNSON

SUGAR RUN

ONE

July 2007

In the yellow corridor they marched the women single file. Jodi, feeling the worry of the eight at her back, wondered what significance to attach to her position as first behind the sergeant. Not much at Jaxton was left to chance. Oldest, she thought, but that may not have been true; thirty-five was perhaps more of an average age. The rest of the women, all from other units, all nameless and unknown to her, did look more youthful, though. She glanced at the one behind her, reddish bangs combed high and a rose-print blouse tucked into blue jeans. Younger or cleaner or something.

"Stop," the sergeant said, spreading out his arms as if the women might all run on past and taste freedom too soon. Beyond him, at the end of the hall, was a bolted door with a single fogged window in the center.

Perhaps, Jodi thought, release was like diving, or rising rather. You could die from that, she'd heard, coming up from the ocean floor altogether too fast. Something got in your blood.

"Six months," a voice mumbled.

"Quiet," Sergeant called, nodding at the curly-haired guard stationed beside the bolted door.

An arc of warm light cut across the misted window and Jodi leaned toward it; the eight behind her were silent now.

The sergeant looked to the camera in the ceiling, gave a thumbs-up, and the door popped, then swung open to the crash of rain on concrete and the idling engine of a white van. The curly-haired guard lifted a black umbrella and he and the sergeant ran, splashing to the driver's side, leaving Jodi with nothing but the open doorway.

That ground out there—that pen of fenced wet cement—had to have been the same place where she'd arrived at seventeen, shaking, spitting, fucked-up scared. All she could remember of her arrival, though, was walking those endless yellow halls and, before that, the hot chaos of a hotel room in Atlanta—the air heavy with iron-thick blood—the paramedics wheeling Paula's body away, and Jodi stumbling, arms pinned back in silver cuffs, puking all across the parking lot.

The sergeant stepped away from the van. He signaled to Jodi and she felt the distance reel out between them. He looked so small, nothing but a white hand beckoning. Jodi took one step and stopped. She could feel the treacherous edges stretched across that open door. Eighteen years. She'd tried to stop counting but could not. More of her life had been lived inside than out.

"Go on," the redhead behind her said.

Rain streamed down through the double bands of the van's headlights, hitting the parking lot and mixing into the hiss and fog. And above the razor wire, barely visible, the soft swells of green mountains rose. Jodi stiffened. Noises bounced around the doorframe: pulses of words at her back, great waves of sound and under it, a laughter beginning. A rasping laughter—not quite her father's but not her own.

"Go."

A hand slapped her shoulder and Jodi broke free. She ran, soaked wet in two seconds flat. She ran and all she saw were those mountains. Eighteen years at Jaxton and she never knew she was living in the mountains. From the exercise yard she had seen only what was straight above, a sometimes gray, sometimes blue rectangular lid of sky. Mountains were a dream that had ended when the judge said *life in prison*. Mountains were far off, West Virginia, home.

In the van, she bent low and headed for the far-back seat. Her wet clothes steamed and her black braid dripped down her neck, forming a tributary that ran over the edge of the vinyl seat. The other women squeezed in, their voices climbing one on top of the other, as if freedom had expanded their lung capacity.

The van lurched, motor rising steadily as the wheels began to turn. Jodi held her plastic sack tightly in one hand, the other gripping the edge of her seat. She closed her eyes and felt the dizzy, sick-sway motion of the wheels, the heat of close bodies and their faint oniony smell of fresh sweat. Eighteen years since she'd moved this way, moved in any way other than on her own clumsy feet. She leaned her forehead against the window and an arm reached around her, red fingernails grasping the latch, and then the glass tilted open.

She breathed in the cool wind, then turned to face a woman with strawberry lipstick and a tight blue blouse.

Jodi too had changed out of her own numbered jumpsuit but the clothes she wore held the same stink of institutional anonymity and came from the exact same place as that clown suit she'd worn for eighteen years. An XL gray sweatshirt and a pair of stiff unisex jeans held precariously around her hips with a red plastic belt. Her mother—that distant voice that reached out across the telephone wires once a year, curdled with rage and pity and touched over with a strained Christian sympathy—had promised to send clothes. *What all do you need?* Jodi's mind had flooded with a wash of white noise and she'd been unable to pinpoint her pant size, much less a preferred style. The package didn't arrive anyhow. Never sent, most likely, or perhaps not mailed in time. The decision for her release had come so abruptly, there'd been no real time to prepare.

"Hot in here," the strawberry-lipped lady said, fanning her fingers in front of her face.

Jodi mopped the windowpane with her shirtsleeve, and golden spots of light bloomed in the wet air. At the front gates the van paused, the voices inside hushing. A rustle of rearranging feet. A muffled voice called out *go ahead* from the guard booth. And then they were moving. Jodi craned her neck to see the arch of the stone gate, stained black by rain, and the carved words, barely visible: WHOSO LOVETH DISCIPLINE LOVETH KNOWLEDGE.

Proverbs 12:1, she thought, surprised at her ability to recognize it. She had not studied the Bible at Jaxton, as some women had, but as a child her grandmother Effie had taken her to the Nazarene church most Sundays and she had coveted the sprawling, intangible poetry of Proverbs and Revelation. *Whosoever brings ruin on their family shall inherit only wind.*

The van coursed down through low hills of hickory and chinquapin, past sleepy trailers and whiteboard shacks, bald yards bright with discarded ornaments—a yellow tricycle, blue ball, tattered flag, and a Chevy Nova settling in to rust. Out of the rain-haze a cherry-colored car shot free and, behind it, a log truck piled with slabs of orange-hearted wood.

At a crossroads they turned left and the houses grew scarce, nothing out either side but a mountain creek, rain gorged and mud red, and groves of pitch pine, their gray trunks slick as silver against the dark ravines beyond.

"You going to Drina or Simpsonville?"

Jodi looked to the strawberry-lipped lady and shook her head.

"No, I'm done."

"They ain't putting you in a halfway house?"

"Lawyer said I did my time." Jodi rubbed the slippery handle of her plastic sack between her thumb and forefinger. "Eighteen years."

Eighteen years—those words had become an incantation that answered all questions, a measuring stick to hold up against any new or old experience. She herself had wondered at the lack of supervision but the lawyer had smiled and lifted his hands like the whole thing were some kind of a magic trick. Supervised release, he'd said, all excited, Hawaiian-print tie fluttering as he paced the room. He'd been disappointed, it seemed, in Jodi's lack of emotion and tried to make up for it by bellowing on about how the organization that he worked for, something about justice for juveniles tried as adults, had come across her case and realized she could qualify for supervised early release. It seemed so unreal; Jodi didn't truly believe it until they marched her down that exit hall. She *had* filed an appeal, citing her single incidence of violence and the fact that she was only seventeen when she went to prison, but that paperwork had been sent off years back and she'd stopped hoping a long time ago. Life in prison, she kept thinking, minimum sentencing in the state of Georgia. But the lawyer had a million words regarding her case: good-behavior time, nearly two decades of her sentence served, no previous record, and enough of the taxpayers' money spent.

Bus ticket's about all you'll receive, he said. *That and an order to report to your home district parole officer.* And on the phone her mother had choked. *Free?* And then after a too-long pause, a jumble of syrupy *Oh . . . wow . . . well, honey, that's great. Are you coming home? Yes*, Jodi had told her, *soon*, she just had to go down to southern Georgia to help a friend first. *Friend?* her mother said, her voice reaching too high. *Free—home—friend*, like those words belonged to some other language and had no place in conversation with Jodi. She'd wired the money, though, a loan of four hundred dollars borrowed from Jodi's two younger brothers and her father's disability check.

AT THE GREYHOUND station in Dahlonega the van driver shooed Jodi and the redhead out into the parking lot. The rain had slowed to a thin, sifting mist.

Jodi tilted her head back and pivoted left, then right, trying to find east, but the yellow-gray dawn seemed to come from every direction. The redhead started toward the station where a flannel-shirted man hunched under the tin overhang, smoking a cigar. Jodi followed. She couldn't think past this moment or else her mind washed all white again but the redhead seemed to have her feet set resolutely on a path pointed forward.

The station was warm, filled with the calls of departure times and TV chatter. Shelves of colored bottles lined the wall of the newsstand: the rib-boned neck of Grand Marnier, stout-brown Jack, filigreed Wild Irish Rose, and below them, a spinning rack of sunglasses where, in the mirror, Jodi saw her own cavernous cheeks and pit-dark eyes. *Got the worst of both sides*, her grandmother Effie had loved to say. *British teeth and Injun eyes.*

"Can I get you something?" the newsstand man asked.

"Marlboros," Jodi said. Cigarettes, at least, were something solid and not new. When her eyes went back to the bottle of Jack, the cashier set it down on the counter beside the cigarettes.

Out front the wind smelled green. Jodi lit a cigarette, nodded at the flannel-shirted man, and stared through the window to where the redhead stood at the ticket counter.

"Cold for July," the flannel man said.

Jodi glanced back at him. He was small with age, bent deep in every joint.

"Where you headed?" he asked, his breath smelling of cherry Swisher Sweets.

"South," Jodi said. "Chaunceloraine, Georgia."

The man shook his head. "We weren't meant to live in the low places. He tries to show us. Hurriken, flood, malarial fever." The man pursed his lips and turned the corners down. "The Lord resides in the mountains," he said, exhaling a funnel of pale smoke.

THE GREYHOUND WOUND out of Dahlonega and down toward the piedmont, until the hills and ridges were nothing but bruise-blue humps beyond the yellow fields. Jodi had settled herself into the farthest-back seat. The bus was more than half-empty, just a mustached man with a pencil stuck behind his ear, a woman in striped pajama pants, a mother with four kids and a few other sleeping passengers. At Jaxton private space had come only by the inch, if at all. Silence came only in the middle of the night, and even that was often punctured by whispers or screams.

Jodi set her bag on the seat beside her and leaned back but even there, in the quiet of the Greyhound, the voices trailed after her, the roiling noise of the cafeteria. *Last supper?* Tressa had shouted the night before, tucking her hair behind one ear as she leaned across the table. Jodi had looked away and pressed the back of her spoon into her instant potatoes, flattening them out so that the watery gravy spilled into the creamed corn.

They weren't supposed to know one another's release dates but everybody always found out. And once you knew, you could see it, that palpable energy ringing out from a girl in her last week. Some of the women couldn't bear it and they'd steal a girl's date, slip something into her pocket or pay a cellmate to plant it, and next thing you knew she was being kept for another six to nine. The ones who played at husband and wife, they were all the time stealing one another's dates.

"Where you headed to tomorrow?" Tressa had asked, and Jodi had glanced up at her. Neither of them said the word aloud but it had floated around them, that slippery *s* of *release*.

"I've got a little something I've got to move out of here." Tressa leaned in, lover close, lips on Jodi's ear. Jodi had fucked her only once, and that two years before, but they both knew Jodi had wanted more.

"You'll help me right?" Tressa said, and Jodi had smiled, shaking her head.

"No," she said, and it had really hit her then, she was *leaving*. In twelve more hours it wouldn't matter what shit favor Tressa needed or what retaliation she'd dream up later. Another world existed out there, another world that had kept on jumping and skipping and spinning for the past eighteen years.

THE RAIN QUIT but the trees still glistened through the bus window and the clouds sat low enough to hold on to. Just past Dawsonville the bus skirted a lake, the water dark and high to the brim, and from there they raced on toward the shadowed spikes of a city.

The highway ducked straight into the downtown and Jodi watched the buildings emerge, rocket ships of glass and chrome stretching so tall she couldn't see the tops. Streams of people rolled across the sidewalks, clutching newspapers, cardboard cups of coffee, and cell phones. Jodi had seen the new phones on TV over the years but out here they looked even more odd: oversize metallic insects gripped tight in every hand.

"Atlanta," the driver hollered. "Fifteen minutes."

Jodi stayed in her seat, knowing for certain if she got off she'd somehow manage to get left behind. She craved a cigarette but opened the bottle of Jack instead and let the scent burn up all her thoughts.

Three sips in, the door to the bathroom opened, letting loose the smell of cigarettes and a chemical reek. She could have sworn the bus had emptied out but there, right in front of her, was the mustached man. He smiled a false-sweet smile and ducked his head down under the luggage rack.

"Hey, honey."

Jodi pulled the paper bag up around her bottle.

"Hey, now, hey." The man hunkered beside her. "Hey, I ain't like that. I ain't gonna tell nobody."

Jodi shrugged and held out the bottle to him. Men like this were always popping up right in that moment of pleasant silence. Always jumping at you, like the groundhogs Effie taught her to shoot back down into their holes.

"You're going to Jacksonville?"

Jodi swallowed her sip of whiskey slowly. "Chaunceloraine."

Every time she said the name it sounded stranger and she'd have figured she made the place up if the ticket man hadn't nodded and printed it on her slip. The word itself was like something she'd bitten off, too big and complicated to chew. And her plan was nothing but a thin line connected by fuzzy memory dots, an invented constellation that only she could see. Paula's parents' address was gone, stoved up somewhere in her brain with the other memories she'd worked so hard to pack away. All that remained was the name of the town and Paula's little brother, Ricky Dulett.

PAST ATLANTA THE rain-choked rivers gave way to flooded fields. Raw clay banks, limp tobacco plants, and peach trees. The water was a skin pulled tight between long rows, dimpled now and then by a gust of wind. Through the tangled branches the orange fruit glimmered, and around the edges of the groves, men huddled under tarps and stared at the gray belly of clouds.

They stopped in Montrose and Soperton, Cobbtown and Canoochee, and each time the bus rolled onto an exit ramp Jodi's gut pinched and she turned toward the window, searching for road signs, relieved only when she saw it was not her stop. She did not want the ride to end. Once the bus stopped there would be the street and all the new decisions that would come with it. She got the bottle back from the mustached man, took a long swallow, and quite suddenly those eyes—Ricky's blue, blue eyes—hovered in the near distant space.

She knew he must have grown into a man's body by now; still, the only thing she could picture was little Ricky in that wooden chair—hands and legs tied behind him with violet-colored rags. *Been acting the devil again*, Paula's father, Dylan, hollers from the porch, his eyes blue too but sunk deeply into his liver-spotted face. *I had to tie him up. You ain't here, Paula, you don't see how he blows.* Paula cuts Ricky loose and peels his dirt-stained jeans away from the wounds. The lash marks swell red all up and down his legs and while Paula inspects him Ricky sings her a song—*They told us the illusion, the illusion was life.* Paula smiles. *I've got my very own personal jukebox*, she says, and Ricky blushes and ducks his head.

OUT THE BUS window towering trees whipped by, waxy green leaves and wisps of gray moss, and over it all the bleached sky clarified into a seamless blue.

"Chaunceloraine," the driver called, but nothing looked familiar to Jodi and the bus was picking up speed now, passing out of the downtown, past faded beauty shops, blinking tattoo parlors, men on the corners wearing too-big T-shirts, and women in butt-hugging spandex shorts —FREDDIE'S FRIED CHICKEN . . . WE BUY GOLD . . . ROOMS $29.99 AND UP . . . CHECKS CASHED NOW—and there, at the back of a sun-glittered parking lot, the red tents and gilded chintz of a carnival fair.

"Chaunceloraine," the driver said again, and this time Jodi rose and climbed over the mustached man, who slept deeply, cheek resting on his shoulder.

"Luggage?" the driver asked, and Jodi shook her head, stumbling down the steps and out into a face full of sunlight.

The air was thick with the smells of fry oil, gasoline, and hot cement; the rush of tires; and bumping bass. Jodi let it all in, blinking up at a billboard that towered over the station roof, showing a row of blind-white teeth, pink cheeks, and soft, paternal eyes: A SMILE LIKE MINE MIGHT NOT BE A WORLD AWAY. FOR HAPPINESS CALL 1-800-697-6453.

Jodi turned quickly from the smug pink-and-white face but the image of it and those words, *happiness . . . a world away*, stayed with her as she walked across the hot parking lot. She'd never trusted anyone with perfect teeth but until this moment she'd never really thought it through completely. All Effie's teeth had rotted out by the time she was thirty and it hadn't been until years later that she was able to afford a set of ill-fitting dentures. Jodi herself had never been to a dentist until she arrived at Jaxton, where they had filled thirteen cavities and yanked out two molars. And Paula's teeth too had been constantly hurting; for all the money she'd liked to throw around, all she had to do was open her mouth and anyone could have seen where she came from.

THE ROCKLODGE MOTOR Inn advertised air-conditioning but the nicotine-stained unit in Jodi's room could muster only a slight lukewarm breeze. She propped open the windows, splashed cold water on her face, and added ice to her paper cup of bourbon. Unregulated, the hours already dripped like spit, and the cheap floral walls pulsed with indecision—*you can do anything—no one's watching, go out—don't go out, you'll fuck up—what's your plan?* Not since she was seventeen had she made any choice that sprang from her own free will entirely. At Jaxton she'd been preserved, safe from her own self. But now here it was, the weight of decision and consequence yoked about her neck again, making her lungs squeeze tight with each breath. She'd barely managed to order food at the Waffle House. The menu had overwhelmed her, and the waitress talked a string of jargon that made no sense.

At a Salvation Army down the street from the Waffle House, she'd found a pair of scissors and clothes that fit. After an hour of stunned uncertainty she settled on jeans, a navy-blue T-shirt, and a pair of work boots. In the rust-flecked mirror back in her motel room she'd inspected her face, wrinkle lines deep from her nose down to her jaw, cheekbones sharp under pale skin. She pulled her long braid out and snipped off eighteen years of growth, then trimmed the hair that was left level with her chin.

"What do you say?" she mouthed aloud.

Younger, she thought, staring down at the snake of a braid, coiled there in the plastic sink. But there was no one to confirm it, no babble of a cellmate's voice to let in or drown out.

At Jaxton she'd had five cellies over the years and after the first she'd learned the distance necessary for survival. When a new one arrived she'd put her jail face on—a glassy, already-gone look that set the parameters straight. She'd known that all of them, every one, the cellies, the guards, the parishioners, the therapist, they'd all be gone before she would. Only a few girls, like Maritza, the little half Latina with scabbed arms and an overbite, had tried to break through. Her voice—just that morning—banged back and forth between their concrete walls. *You'll write me?* she'd whined, reaching one hand toward Jodi. *Yeah, yeah*, Jodi'd said. *No, you won't*, Maritza said. She'd refused to go to breakfast and refused her morning pills, was winding herself up tight, well on her way to a stay in the hole. *You've got your own money now*, Jodi had told her. *I moved the last of my commissary funds over for you.* Maritza had smashed her fist against the wall. *I don't want your money*, she said. *Kiss me.* She leaned out from her mattress, face sweaty and red. *Kiss me. You'll never see me again. Tomorrow I'll have somebody new in here, somebody that tries to cut me, somebody that fucks with my head.*

Frances was the only one that Jodi had ever really let in. But Frances was different because Frances hadn't wanted anything except to bully Jodi into loving herself a little more. Forty-three years old and serving a sentence for the heroin her daughter kept stored in her basement. *Sure, yeah, you've heard of turning a blind eye*, she said. *Well, I'd carved my eyes all the way out.* When the cops showed up the daughter was nowhere around but the dope and the cash were right there. *It ain't like I'm stupid, I knew what she was doing but I guess I never imagined . . . Forty-three and they're going to reform me!*

Frances had filled out the empty corners of Jodi's days with her easy laughter and bright eyes and it was not until it had already started that Jodi had realized that they were dating. It was six years ago now that Frances was released but Jodi could still feel the way her heart had perked up and her body relaxed whenever she was in the room.

. . .

WIND RIPPLED THE motel room curtains, carrying with it shrieks from the carnival rides and the pitch and dip of a midway barker. Jodi brought over her bourbon and stretched across the bed. The air smelled of dust, cigarettes, and lemon-oil cleaning spray and through the open window she could hear strains of the merry-go-round jingle. The music that always reminded her of first sex, Jack Ambler in the parking lot of the West Virginia State Fair, and the hot vinyl of the pickup seat and the sun setting all glass gold across the railroad tracks.

Outside, a car pulled up and a shuffle of feet walked past. Through the half-closed curtains Jodi watched a blonde woman in a blue bathing suit cross the parking lot and ease herself into the swimming pool. Her head disappeared under the water and Jodi turned from the window, searching for the TV remote. On the mattress beside her lay the contents of her plastic sack, an unabridged version of *Les Misérables* and a brand-new copy of *Real Property Law and Practice*, both gifts from Sonya, the frizzy-haired court-appointed therapist.

Every week Jodi had sat for an hour in that little box of an office, staring at Sonya's bottle-thick glasses and oh-so-earnest face. Jodi told her it was all bullshit, those phrases Sonya taught her: "lack of familial models of self-control," "imprinted patterns of retribution," and "generational intersections of love and violence." Sonya had just smiled patiently, though, and when Jodi told her she'd read the abridged prison-library copy of *Les Mis*, she'd brought her this huge full-volume hardback. Jodi hated it at first, the weight of those fifteen hundred pages killing all the pride she'd built up around conquering the shorter version, and she'd hated that smile that Sonya had gotten on her lips. Jodi could see her already, at some cocktail party with colleagues, sloshing her glass of white wine and telling them all about her brilliant hillbilly client. Sonya stank of privilege and Jodi knew without asking that her life had been just one long stretch of soft, buttered bread.

For a while Jodi only used the unabridged *Les Mis* to keep her feet still while she did sit-ups. Eventually she got caught up in the huge story, though, the little corners of comedy and god arguments. And then, when Sonya found out that Jodi was going to be released, she'd remembered Jodi's talk of Effie's mountain land, the tangle of bank loans and heirs, and she'd given her *Real Property Law and Practice*. The legal language ran all together, overstuffed and thick, but there was hope in the phrases of abators and freehold estates, and anyway, the idea of Effie's land was more than just a need for a place to call home; it was connected to a time nested inside this time, like a grain of sand deep inside the coil of a snail shell. Even when she'd been there, on the farm with Effie alive, Jodi had been bending in her mind toward the memories of before, the time when her parents had lived there too. Maybe, she thought, she'd been like that since birth, filled up with a backward yearning.

MIRANDA HAD HER bathing suit halfway on when the phone rang. Her stomach clenched and she turned to the blinking machine with the note taped to the side: *Rocklodge Motor Inn—Front Desk Dial "o." All Other Calls Yer Expense.* She moved her eyes from the phone to the wall and the brightly colored clothing strewn across the unmade bed. The phone stopped. Miranda eyed it once more and then walked toward the bathroom, the blue one-piece swimsuit bunched around her hips, her tits naked in the musty light. She took a bottle off the shelf above the toilet, palmed it open, and set three capsules on the back of her tongue. She was breaking her "no more than one a day" rule but today would just have to be an exception. She'd already moved down from the Dexedrine-Vyvanse combo to just Adderall and that felt something like a victory.

The phone stayed silent, another small victory, and Miranda turned her attention back to her swimsuit, enjoying the feel of the material as it cupped her ass. *Too tight*, her mother would have said. Her body had been softer ever since the boys were born. It filled everything differently now but she liked it better that way. Her skin gave off a warm ripeness that seemed more fully hers than the taut teenage body that came before.

She'd loved being pregnant. The things that were normally out of balance had aligned themselves during those nine months, her mood swings steadied, and her great cosmic yearnings were traded in for simple, sweet-tooth cravings. She'd cared for herself in a way that she never had before. She'd taken vitamins and planned meals and slept deeply, waking to examine her own body with a gushing eagerness, as if *she* were the new thing being created.

But after Kaleb was born and grew big enough to be away from her for more than a few minutes, it had all returned: the trembling anxiety, the certainty of one day dripping into the next, and her life telescoping into a gray mist. It was only in pregnancy that things got simple again and she was nothing more than a collection of sensations. Cold now, warm later; hungry, then full; horny, sated. The pills, if she balanced them out right, did something similar but not the same.

There were places where her skin remembered, places where, by holding and growing her sons, her body had become dearer. The softness of her stomach and thighs and breasts. But now Lee had taken the boys away. Kaleb, Donnie, and Ross were gone, so far outside of her body that weeks passed when she didn't even see them at all.

She grabbed a towel from the bathroom and stepped outside into the slap of sunlight. Walking the long way around to the pool, she avoided the plate-glass windows of the front office and the cleaning lady's cart. She had told Alfredia that once she got a little cash she would pay extra for the days she owed but Alfredia did not own the place.

As she pushed open the gate the amphetamine jangled in her veins and Miranda slowed, warming to it. The pool was clear and rippleless, shadowed momentarily by a passing cloud that intensified the blue water. She set her towel on a plastic chair and, turning, caught sight of a man on the second floor, staring down at her through the window. She noticed again the smooth line of the bathing suit where it cupped her ass but this time she saw it from the outside, through his eyes, and something in her sparked. She moved toward the pool, aware of every muscle. The water was a little too warm but it softened the dry parking-lot heat. She dove under, stretched her arms wide, and imagined herself from above, a blonde sparkling thing.

She'd always seen herself like this. As if on camera. Under other eyes she moved more smoothly, fully in existence. She'd tried to explain it once, when her mother caught her watching her own face in the rearview mirror. Vanity, her mother had called it, but Miranda thought it was not so much vanity as a way to understand being a girl in the world.

She stayed underwater as long as her lungs would last, then burst up and dipped again, enjoying the strength of her arms slicing and pulling. She'd been on the YWCA swim team in high school but dropped out junior year, too eager to join her future. A future that had now gone on past, it seemed. Still, swimming felt a little like a prayer, or better than a prayer, more like that universal sound the Buddhists made. Everything dropped away, the boys and Lee, the unpaid room, the Adderall. The water was continuous, expansive. Her muscles moved instinctually and when her lungs burned she glided up, took in air, then dove down again.

She felt the man there. Even before his shadow spread across the surface of the pool, she slowed. He knelt at the edge and she surfaced. The camera angled, zooming to catch the drops of water along the tops of her tits.

"You're a good swimmer," the man said.

She would sleep with him eventually. The conclusion was entirely forgone. The interesting thing would be to see how they got from the pool to the room. What set of words would string the distance this time.

"What are you, like captain of the swim team?"

The man was named Daniel, a bricklayer from someplace up north of Atlanta. He'd come down with a crew, he told Miranda, to build a new shopping mall, but now the contractor said he could get Mexicans to do it for half the price and so they were out on their asses while they waited to see if the contract was binding.

"Where are *you* from?" he asked.

Miranda climbed out of the pool, squinting up at him. Midtwenties with bright eyes and a sun-worn face. Small frame and a blond beard.

"Here and there," she said.

"Where's here and there?"

"Well." She smiled and tied her towel around her waist. "Here, I guess, I mean."

"Here, like this town here?"

"Yeah, Chaunceloraine."

He cocked his head.

She glanced over at the motel. "Baby-daddy problems," she said.

Daniel wanted to take her to the carnival down the street but she would need another few pills and less sunlight before she'd be ready for anything quite like that.

She traded the towel for a pink sundress that she pulled on over her still-wet suit, and they walked to the gas station for cigarettes, Seven Crown, and premixed margarita in a bag.

IT TURNED OUT that the words that brought bodies together were never quite as interesting as one might think. Daniel wanted to take her to his room but she knew her own would smell better. He mumbled something about it having been a while since he'd seen a girl as pretty as Miranda and then they were in it: the sweat-smell of his neck and the singularity of his pounding need.

He finished quickly and as soon as he had rolled away Miranda wanted to touch herself, to stay there inside her body. There were times lately when masturbating constituted the high point of her days but she had to be by herself. The images that stirred her seemed not so much perverse as simply a little embarrassing. Alone in a room with the shades drawn and her eyes closed, she touched herself and imagined she was the voyeur. She was the not-so-attractive middle-aged man fucking a girl who looked like her own younger self.

The margarita was too sweet but she drank it anyhow, adding a little Seven Crown every now and then. Daniel sat beside her on the bed, fully dressed, flipping channels and trying not to act like he was eager to leave. Still, it was nice to have someone in the bed with her. Her boys had stayed there that first month and now, whenever she was alone, she could never quite stop hearing their voices in the room. She bummed a cigarette and tried to find the words to ask Daniel about money. Not money for the sex per se, just like how friends can loan money without it having to mean anything. She'd never crossed that line, though, never asked for cash in hand. Maybe he could just pay for her room. She really needed cash, though, needed gas and drink money, but before the words could surface, the benzos she'd swallowed kicked in and she let herself drift.

Lately it was always water dreams. But the water was dark and cold. Her boys were on the other side of the river, Kaleb in the middle, holding tight to Donnie and Ross. She swam toward them, confident in her strength, smiling, but no matter how quickly she moved, there was something rushing faster under her, a current that would reach them before she could.

She woke to the sound of a key and pulled the sheet up to cover herself. A face appeared in the doorway. A tower of frizzy hair in that gash of sharp light. Alfredia.

"Honey, this is it. You gotta get your shit and be out of here tomorrow. I can't hold him off no more. He's talking small claims court now." She raised her eyebrows, showing thick swaths of green makeup. "And if I don't get better at this eviction shit, I ain't gonna have no job."

Miranda blinked.

"You owe me for the six days I done covered."

Miranda's mind reached out for something to say and the sheet slipped from her fist.

"Put some clothes on and bring whatever it is you been taking up to the office, pay me with that."

"Alfredia," Miranda called, unsticking her tongue from the roof of her mouth as the woman turned away. "You'll read my tarot for me?"

"Not again, sugar," Alfredia said, squinting back into the room. "Your future don't change in one day."

As THE SUN melted down toward the horizon Jodi left the motel room and followed the carnival song to the fairgrounds. When her stomach had started grumbling she'd realized that without thinking about it she'd been waiting for the chow bell. She ordered a corn dog and nibbled it as she walked down the aisles of dart and ball games, past a leering Mickey Mouse, garlands of fake roses, and mammoth teddy bears. *Give it a shot here, ma'am—take a swing—whoa, didja see that? As easy as tossing a lima bean.* The barkers leaned against the brightly colored girders with a greasy ease, stubs of cigarettes pressed between their lips, letting their practiced tone carry the pitch far out into the alley, crowded and sawdust thick.

Jodi stopped and watched a row of plastic ducks circling on a miniature conveyor belt. Every once in a while a customer managed to knock one off and it fell backward only to be resurrected moments later, looping along on the same endless track. Here I am again, she thought, popped back up in Chaunceloraine.

The shadows lengthened and the roller coasters glowed with a soft phosphorescence that mixed up into the pink-orange sunset. From the bandstand at the far end of the midway, loudspeakers piped out tinny pop music and over it the single-note ring of guitar tuning and a voice: *Check—check, check.* Jodi felt glad that the long day was dragging itself toward evening. Though she knew she needed to act fast, find Ricky now and then head to West Virginia, it was also a relief to see the sun set and be able to say, *Tomorrow, I'll work on that plan tomorrow.* She felt the struggle of time playing out inside herself, the quick ticking away of her pre–parole meeting days pushing against her overpowering need to be in this moment, beside the bandstand, watching men pace the almost empty stage and a tiny blonde woman painting her toenails on the bench across the way.

When the band started playing she was halfway back up the midway, looking to buy an ice cream. The song began unrecognizably slow but that voice could not be mistaken: *Our land, our land is far through the heart of this snow.* Jodi froze, locked all up in her brain and body, and then she began to run, dodging barkers and families, out of breath by the time she reached the stage. A wire-mesh fence separated the ticketed customers from the general fair but the bleachers were only a little over half-full. Leaning against the fence, she squinted up at the beer-bellied bass player, bearded keyboardist, graying drummer, and there, at the front, a sun-worn Lee Golden. His skin was dry and leather tanned but the guitar glistened and between his lips shone a set of pulsing bleach-white teeth. *She called to me, sweetness, what the fire shows, the truth is set before us or it cannot grow. And with the evening's bleeding I am gone, for our land is far through the heart of this snow.* His pants were purple now instead of the white ones he'd worn on his old album covers but the song was shockingly familiar. A 1989 crossover hit that had threaded all through Jodi's last summer before Jaxton.

"Sad to see him here," a voice said, and Jodi turned to find a man leaned up against the fence beside her. "Weird that he's playing this rinky-dink place. Man, when I was coming up, the name Lee Golden meant, God, you know . . ." He wrinkled his face, searching for the words.

"I didn't know he still played," Jodi said. "I mean, I hadn't heard—"

"Covers. They just do covers now."

"No, he wrote this song."

"That's what I mean, covers of their own songs. They play 'em all weird now. This is the only one Lee can play all the way through, lost the rights to all the others when the Gemini broke off from him. Turns out this is the only one he wrote."

"That's not the Gemini?" Jodi waved toward the stage.

"The Gemini left him back in, like, '95, I think. You didn't hear about that?"

Jodi shook her head.

"Oh, man, yeah, Lee was funneling the band's money straight into Scientology for years and years, telling them they weren't making half the royalties they really were and, shit, sending thousands of dollars over to that cult."

"Well, who are *they* then?"

"He calls them the Jupiter Twins. I think he just hires whatever good old boys he can get to play cheaply in whatever town he's gigging in. They play knockoff versions of all the originals. Get sued again every few years." The man shook his head. "Lee disappeared for a while after the band broke off. He went somewhere out west."

"Joshua Tree," a woman's voice said.

Jodi and the man turned and the blonde woman stared up at them from the bench, her green eyes liquid and huge in her child-size face.

"Joshua Tree," she said again.

"Lee grew up not too far from here." The man looked over at the stage. "About an hour west. I hear he's got a couple of kids too, little boys."

"My boys," the blonde said, her voice punching against their backs.

Jodi and the man turned again. There was something magnetic about the girl, something that made it both hard to look right at her and hard to look away. She was pretty, sure, with a fine and tiny symmetry, but it was something more than that, something about the way she held herself, a strange mix of confidence and unease.

The man chuckled. "Lee's still got somewhat of a cult following but now most of 'em are just drugged up, delusional, and weird."

Jodi glanced over her shoulder again as she walked away, back toward the motel, and the blonde, still sitting on the bench, stared straight at her, a fragile network of emotion behind a porcelain face.

In the dream Jodi's mother stepped from the bathtub, shrouded with steam and thin winter light, reaching for a blue-striped robe. Chin up, she gazed out and over Jodi's father, who knelt on the floor, his face flushed with a pleading need. *Now what?* he said. *You think you're clean? You think you can just wash him away?* She put on the robe slowly, turning so that the shiny, wet front of her faced him. They were always merging together that way or careening apart, messy and pathetic, the wet cotton of regret already filling their mouths. Their fuck-fight need had glowed so hot it obliterated everyone else. Sick, Effie had said, and eventually she'd grown tired of their drunken fights and kicked them out of her house and off her land. They'd taken Jodi's twin baby brothers with them when they moved to town but they couldn't support three children, so they left seven-year-old Jodi to be raised by her grandmother. The dream sped up and flared, images tumbling on top of one another like a film with the projector turned up too fast, the frames clacking by breathlessly. *Stupid cunt.* The volume bloomed and burst. *Spread your legs. . . .*

Jodi sat up and opened her eyes, blinking black to gray to blue, but the voices did not stop.

"I know how you like it."

She flipped her head. She was alone in this room—pale light rippling along the mattress, the corner of a curtain flapping—and the room was so big, walls so far apart, and the glass eye of a TV screen—not a dream, not her Jaxton cell . . .

"See, this is exactly why you can't have the boys, you got no spine, can't never say no. Look, look at you. . . . Close your legs, I don't want no more of that."

A motel, Jodi realized, she was in a motel. The voices echoed on in the room next door.

"What if I was to be recording you?" a woman's voice said. "What if I recorded this and played it for all your God Bless America fans? Huh? You know, I've got stories I could tell about you—"

"Honey, ain't nobody gonna believe you. Just look at yourself, really, come here, look in the mirror here."

"Don't touch me."

Jodi gripped the sweaty sheet.

"Don't touch you? Baby, what have we been doing here for the past few hours?"

"Don't fucking touch me. Lay a hand on me and I'll scream."

Something fell, then the sound of a door opening. Jodi crossed to the window and pressed her face against the curtains as the little blonde spilled out, followed by a tall man in purple pants. Jodi shook her head but the view remained the same, a shirtless Lee Golden in a pool of yellow streetlight.

"I'm taking the boys away from here," he said. "Can't have them growing up in this corpse of a country. Look around, we got gays and wetbacks all over the place. Give me your tired, your poor, yeah, send 'em on over here, come suck on mama's big fat titties." He spoke slowly and quietly, though the blonde was disappearing across the parking lot. "It's a rotten, fucking whore of a country."

The blonde did not look back. She walked barefoot, her pink dress fluttering down the street until she ducked into a neon-lit doorway.

THE ALI BAR was older than the buildings around it, made of stone, with shuttered windows and a wrought-iron balcony. As Jodi opened the door music spread out before her, something singular and antique—piano notes—a deep and trembling sound, churning up like colored leaves. Jodi blinked. She could make out two men in a booth along the wall and two more up at the bar. The room was longer than it was wide, dark, with a carved wooden counter and green glass lamps. The warm air smelled of billiard chalk, whiskey, and cigarettes and the music, she realized slowly, came not from the jukebox but from the far end of the bar where the blonde sat, at an upright piano, her back to the rest of the room.

The door thudded shut and the bartender looked up.

"Don't worry, Miranda," he called over the music. "It ain't him."

Jodi took a seat at one of the stools and ordered a well whiskey, glancing at the men beside her, one with silver chains and the other sporting a Braves cap. When they moved over to the pool table, the barkeep closed his eyes and leaned into the music that surged on, something like a mountain creek now, a spring stream with the ice breaking up. Jodi had never quite heard anything like it, except for perhaps bits and pieces on the radio and an old phonograph her second-grade teacher had played in class.

When the song ended, the breath went out of the room. In the rising silence the bartender applauded and as Miranda stood and walked toward the bar they all began to clap, hesitantly at first and then louder. Miranda shook her long pale hair and kept walking and a soft circle of light followed her; though the room was full of shadows, she carried with her a certain spotlight of shimmering.

"Ah, no, it's nothing." She waved her hand in front of her face. "Good old Rachmaninoff," she said, the end of the name drifting off under her accent. "Always helps lift the mood."

Sliding onto the stool beside Jodi, she smoothed out her pink cotton dress so that it covered her knees. "Hey, Alister, give me a gin and juice, babe."

She swallowed half the cranberry-colored liquor in one go, then wiped her lip with her cocktail napkin. "Hey," she said, her eyes brightening. "I know you. You were over there at Lee's concert. I guess you thought I was lying?"

Jodi wanted to reach out and touch her, right there where her neck curved elegantly up toward the back of her skull.

Miranda shrugged. "I don't carry their birth certificates around with me but I grew all three of those boys right in here." She rubbed her hand across her stomach and scrunched up her face thoughtfully, as if she herself found this fact nearly unbelievable. "Didn't I, Ali?"

"Irish twins," Alister said, winking.

Jodi watched as Miranda swallowed the remainder of her drink. She thought of her own younger twin brothers, Dennis and A.J., those two tousled blond heads. They would be thirty now but Jodi had no way to envision them past the age of twelve, sunburned with skinned knees and oversize egos, their first cigarettes hanging too cool out the side of their mouths.

"Alister didn't actually see me pregnant but—hey, hey, don't skimp me on the gin there, babe."

Alister rolled his eyes.

Miranda retrieved her glass and drank deep. "Alister's seen my boys."

"Spitting image." Alister nodded, wiping the counter with a rag that gave off a smell of bleach and old beer.

"Spitting image of who?" Miranda asked.

Alister paused. "Truth-truth?"

"Truth-truth."

"Spitting image of Lee Golden."

"Ah, shut up." Miranda raised her glass as if to throw it at him. "You owe me another drink for saying that."

Alister shook his head. "Truth-truth," he said.

"Hey, what's your name?" Miranda spun suddenly on her stool so that her knees knocked against Jodi's.

"Jodi McCarty."

Miranda pumped Jodi's hand three times before letting go. "Let me buy you a shot."

Jodi looked down to her empty glass.

"Oh, I'm Miranda Matheson." Miranda paused and narrowed her eyes. "Well, legally, I'm Miranda Matheson Golden but I like the sound of just the double *M*'s."

Alister set two whiskeys on the polished wood and Miranda put down her gin glass and picked up a shot. "To Jodi, for believing."

Jodi clinked her glass and swallowed quickly but the whiskey caught somewhere in her throat and insisted on coming back up. She turned away, face flushed, and tried not to cough. Miranda wasn't paying attention anyway.

"We need some music," she said.

"Well, you're the piano girl. Before you come along that thing was just something too big for me to carry away."

"I'm not talking about music like that." Miranda stepped down from the stool and moved off toward the jukebox.

In the glow of the lights, she swayed, blonde hair shiny all down her back and her face so serious and concentrated on those little record covers as they flipped by. There was something about the way she held herself and the way the men in that room treated her that gave her an air of near royalty and made Jodi feel significant, as if she'd achieved something major simply by being included in Miranda's circle.

"Where are her kids?" Jodi asked.

"Over in Delray. Living with Lee's aunt Nina." Alister folded his bar rag and shook his head. "Miranda come up in here about six months back, I guess. She had all three boys with her, bought 'em a bunch of maraschino cherries, and set herself down at that piano. I'd never heard anything like it." He unfolded the rag and wiped a spot on the already shiny counter. "Lee's the one who taught her to play like that. Her daddy hired him—can you imagine hiring somebody like Lee Golden to teach piano to your little girl? Course he got her pregnant." Alister looked over at Miranda. "I give her a job here 'cause she said she needed one. I didn't know she was leaving those boys alone over at the hotel."

A trembling blast of Michael Jackson's "Smooth Criminal" burst into the room. Miranda stepped back from the jukebox and spun, eyes closed and arms out. *So, Annie are you ok?* Her pink dress lifted and the men at the billiards table locked eyes on her. Jodi watched the way the room tensed and focused and she pictured her own sixteen-year-old self perched on a barstool in the Wild 'N Wonderful Casino. Back then she'd been trying for something, not even knowing what it was she wanted, reaching out blindly for her future like sticking her hand inside a grab bag. And now, she thought—seeing her older self here on another barstool—not that much had changed. She'd been pushed out into the world again, feeling just as lost and seasick as she had after her grandmother Effie's death. And all she had to cling to was her need to find Ricky.

"Hey, Ali, ain't Fairchild Road out there by Shady View?" Miranda tucked her legs up underneath her on the stool.

Alister was in the back of the bar, sweeping up, trying to close, but Miranda was boozed—chatty and breathless. "I'm going to help Jodi go find her friend tomorrow."

"Fairchild Road," Jodi whispered, her words bumping all funny out from between her lips. The room swirled and tilted into a blur of green lamps and polished wood. Jodi closed her eyes. The phone book in the motel room had said Dylan and Anna Dulett lived at 211 Fairchild Road.

"Yeah," Alister said, "out there past the Shady View Mall." He looked up from his broom and nodded toward the counter. "Now you better hurry up and finish that drink."

Miranda picked up the glass and took it with her as she walked, hips swaying, toward the bathroom. The door clapped loudly and then a silence filled the room, nothing but the soft scratching of Alister's broom and his feet crossing over the wood floor. Jodi gripped the edge of the barstool. She'd overstayed.

The room sloshed as she stood up. She kicked herself mentally. Three drinks in and her jail face had dropped entirely. Just got out of prison, she'd said, back in town for a few days, searching for an old friend. She'd rattled on, twisting some facts and omitting others. It seemed that out here nothing stayed in place. In Jaxton she'd managed to make a neat package of most emotions—especially the thoughts of Paula, that ache-rage of a tattered beast inside her heart, all teeth and claws and need. Out here, though, the walls were slipping. The thing to do was to have a plan. Ever since Effie had died, when Jodi was sixteen, the future had felt to her like one of those fogged-over mornings where you could never see where you were headed until you were already there.

She walked across the floor, past the piles of dust and cigarette butts, cringing at the memory of her own voice, gushing, boundaryless. Miranda had encouraged it, telling her she'd drive her out the next day, help her find her friend. But Jodi could see that Miranda was one of those who rotated on her own axis, center of her own gravity. She pulled you to her but cared only momentarily.

"You ain't gonna walk Miss Miranda home?"

Jodi stopped and stared back at Alister.

"You know what?" Miranda's voice called out from the hall. "I've been looking at this thing all wrong. All Lee's got are his threats. I ain't lost custody yet and he ain't going to the cops 'cause he knows what I could tell them."

Alister came out from behind the counter. "Randy, honey, go home and get you some rest."

Miranda spun to face him. "Do I look crazy?"

"Truth-truth?"

She nodded.

"You look hungry, baby."

THE SKY OUTSIDE was thick with stars. Miranda gripped Jodi's arm and together they shuffled across the pocked concrete and into the empty road.

"You're walking me home?" Miranda moved her hand down to Jodi's elbow as they made their way up the drive to the Rocklodge Motor Inn, dark now save for a shaky neon VACANCY.

"I'm staying here too." Jodi patted her pants pocket for the room key. "I heard you earlier. You and Lee."

Miranda let go and stepped back. "Oh," she said, looking like she'd just been slapped, and then, fixing her eyes on something over Jodi's shoulder, she smiled. "You want me to tell you something else you won't believe?"

Jodi turned and caught sight of the billboard up behind her: A SMILE LIKE MINE.

"That's my daddy. Dwayne Matheson, the Denture King." Miranda laughed, turning and heading back across the street.

Of course, Jodi thought, she's not only Lee Golden's wife but also the heir to perfect teeth.

Miranda stopped at the base of the billboard and tilted her head back, staring at the ladder that ran up the side of the pole.

"I really have been looking at everything wrong," she said. "I've been so weak. You know when you get so tired sometimes . . . it's like every little thing can just make you wanna sleep. I haven't legally lost them yet and already I'm acting like it's over." She reached up and grabbed onto the lowest rung of the ladder.

Don't follow this one, Jodi told herself.

"I like the way you do things." Miranda glanced back at Jodi. "You show up in town with nothing but conviction and an old address and I have no doubt you'll find your friend."

She hoisted herself, swinging her bare foot until it caught on the second rung. Her legs were smooth under the tent of her pink dress. The daughter of that smug smile. Jodi almost laughed out loud. Here she was, breaking all her own self-commandments and somehow it felt good. Maybe what the billboard was meant to say was something about second chances, *new beginnings are not a world away.*

Jodi stepped closer to where she could see the lace of Miranda's panties and the plump curve of her ass. There was something different about this moment, she thought, from any lust she'd felt in Jaxton. Not that those times had not been real. Out here, though, on her own, Jodi felt the heat of her desire and her chest filled up with adrenaline. *You can choose your sins,* Effie reminded her, *but you cannot choose the consequences.*

"I got off track, that's all," Miranda said.

And evil comes to one who searches for it.

Jodi jumped and caught hold of the rusted ladder, the chipped paint and flaking metal sharp under her palms. A breeze blew past and she felt it all liquid across her skin. So much air, she thought, picturing the dead-grass square of the prison yard with the flat sky above. Here the wind moved loud in the trees and in her hair and she filled herself with it, with the whiskey and the height and the fact that she ought to be in bed right now, resting for tomorrow.

"I'm gonna get clean." Miranda had poked her head up above the catwalk and only her legs were still visible.

"Other than getting drunk off your ass and climbing billboard signs, what kind of shit do you usually get into?"

"Oh, just some pills."

Up close the Denture King was frightening, his smile big enough to bite off their heads.

"All right, we climbed up here," Jodi said. "Now let's get down before the cops see us."

Miranda motioned her toward the end of the grated walkway, past the beaming bulbs. She tucked herself into the corner, legs dangling, and pointed out into the blue-black night. As her eyes adjusted, Jodi saw the sleeping carnival, the giant dormant rides, and beyond that, a sprinkle of streetlamps and yard lights. The outline of the Ferris wheel was visible above the other rides, and though completely dark, it still seemed to be turning.

"I'm gonna do it," Miranda said. "I just got to find the right path again."

Jodi looked down at the small blonde woman seated at her feet. Miranda smiled and pulled a pack of smokes from the pocket of her dress.

"This *is* your path," Jodi said. She could feel the alcohol moving inside of her. It always seemed to come like this; after the drunken doubt and self-deprecation the whiskey brought on a loose-tongued philosophical stage.

"Like fate?" The flame of Miranda's lighter pierced the air.

Jodi inhaled and tapped her cigarette on the railing. "If we're here right now, it's because we were always going to be here now."

"Well, that's real uplifting," Miranda said. "So you're saying we could just not do anything at all and everything will turn out the same?"

Jodi shook her head leaned out over the rail. "No." She flicked her cherry and watched it dance in a shower of sparks on the concrete below.

"What about going to find your friend? You think it's written in the stars for you to find your friend?"

Jodi glanced at Miranda and then lowered herself until she sat on the metal grating beside her, staring out over the empty parking lot, past the carnival and strip malls and streets to where a train wound its way south.

THOUGH HER OWN room was quiet and apparently empty, Miranda insisted it was not safe. She crouched on Jodi's bed, finishing the last of the bottle of whiskey.

"I'll drive you out to your friend's place first thing."

Jodi took the empty liquor bottle and carried it to the trash can. The room seemed softer now with someone else there but Miranda's presence was sloppy too and Jodi kept her distance.

"It seems like there ought to be a law," Miranda said. "Like a law that nobody could ever take away something that you made with your own blood and cells, something you carried inside for nine months."

Jodi caught herself in the mirror, face framed in the unexpected haircut, skin milk white and eyes too big, too sad. Looking like a bad joke, like a scapegoat, she thought, just waiting for somebody to use me.

"Please? I can't sleep by myself."

"You can have the bed, I'll take the floor," Jodi said.

"No, come up here with me, I can't sleep," Miranda pleaded, but already her eyes were softening. Jodi sat down on the end of the mattress, back stiff against the wall. Miranda took hold of her hand and Jodi looked away.

Headlights tracked paths across the peeling wallpaper, and through the open window came the rush and whir of traffic on the highway. At Jaxton it had never been totally dark. Darkness was too dangerous and fluorescent bulbs buzzed in the cells even in the middle of the night. Some women tried to dim the lights by covering them in sheets of toilet paper stuck on with chewing gum or even smeared layers of their own shit. Jodie had closed her eyes and tried to will a darkness, deep and clean, a velvet closeness she remembered from the way-back corners of caves.

There had been three linked caves down below Effie's land, and Effie had loved to tell Jodi stories about them. Tell how her uncle's sow wandered down over the cliff one fall, hunting for horse chestnuts, and when a freak storm dropped three feet of snow the pig got stuck. Stayed the whole winter down in those caves. Effie and her uncle came out to the cliff every few days, wading through waist-deep snow with a pail of slops. They lowered the bucket over the edge on a long rope, fed the sow that way till spring, when she come back up over the ridge with six new babies. It was a wonder she wasn't killed, because come winter, all the good-size caves were claimed by bears, Effie said, and Jodi had loved to picture that, all the crooks and crannies of the land under her feet filled with sleeping bears.

The Lady Cake Caves, Effie called them, for the formation in the middle of the biggest cavern, a mineral deposit shaped just like a big white cake. The mouth of the cave was shallow, not much more than a shale overhang, but if you followed it back, you'd see it kept going. Lying as flat as a dog, you could wriggle through and out into the first chamber. Effie claimed that if you looked closely enough, you could see cave paintings. Jodi never did see them but she liked to hear the stories. Effie told her how the land was precious, older than old, but with every generation they lost a little of its essence, even when they were right there in the middle of it. Every generation, she said, grew more and more distant until the land itself was nothing but an encumbrance, nothing more than the thing in the way between your trailer and the nearest shopping mall.

WHEN JODI FIRST brings Paula up to the caves they have known each other for only four days. Paula doesn't believe Jodi, says she must be pulling her leg, telling her they can push through that split mouth into a room big enough to stand up in. Jodi goes on ahead, burrowing in between the muddy rocks. Paula is hesitant but stubborn too, and though Jodi has known her only briefly, she can already see how she hates to be left behind.

The cold air laps up against her, a heavy black, darker than the dark behind her, an air full and wet with shifting invisible proportions. She can feel the space in that circle-room adjusting to her, the hole her body makes in that mineral thickness, and it feels safe. The rest of the world out there is far away.

"Jodi?" Paula calls, her voice small.

Jodi stretches her fingers in front of her face, feeling without seeing, eyes frantic at first but soon settling. "Come on," she hollers.

When Paula tumbles, finally, into the cavern, she sucks up half the air and Jodi feels everything flip. The room loud now with the jumble of both bodies.

"I've got a lighter here somewhere," Paula says, but Jodi silences her.

"Shshsh, no. You'll ruin it. You turn on a light and our eyes'll never adjust."

Adjust, just, just, ust, us, the rocks whisper.

Jodi can see without seeing that all Paula's cocksureness is gone. She is scared and it tastes to Jodi like an ice-cold sweetness. She drinks it in, keeps it there on the back of her tongue.

"This way," she says, inching forward toward the arch into the next room.

Their eyes do adjust and they quit falling, eventually, over every bump and start seeing the outlines of the stalagmites under their feet, the long white drips of icicle rocks, and green lichen glowing on fallen slabs of stone. They leave the second chamber and bend again, bowing to their knees as they make their way into the throne room.

The cake sits in the very center, as tall as Jodi's waist and perfectly white. Paula's breath sucks in. Stepping up, Jodi pulls her close, the warmth of their bare skin tingling against all that wet air. And just above them, in the arched dome of limestone, a small hole lets in two pin beams of light, bright at the surface but bluer below as they fall and spill across that slick mineral.

When they emerge everything is fuzzed up with the soft mauve of evening and lightning bugs just beginning to glint along the edges of the trees. Jodi can feel Paula beside her, taking it all in, and she wonders if the heart of this place is visible to her, if anyone else can ever love it like Jodi does.

Out of the dense grass, a few feet in front of them, a whorl of dark motion streams up, flapping and chittering. Paula falls back—*What the fuck?*—stumbling into Jodi. Jodi is stunned but laughing too.

"Bats," she says. "They come up this time of night, out of the crevices and caves."

. . .

THE MATTRESS SHIFTED and there was a rustling in the blankets. Jodi twisted up out of her dreams and drew back instinctively, blinking, confused and then slowly remembering. Miranda was huddled in the bed beside her, sniffling.

"Hey." Jodi touched her pale shoulder.

"I'm a fuckup."

Jodi bent over her and in the dark she could just barely see the tears on Miranda's freckled cheeks and her eyes swollen with crying, droplets caught in the long curl of her white lashes. As a child Jodi had never been much interested in playing with dolls but she could see now the joy it could bring. All the whirling, purring energy Miranda had carried with her earlier seemed to have leaked out and now she looked to Jodi like a small fragile jewel, something to be kept in a little velvet box, something worthy of adoring.

"You'll be fine," Jodi whispered.

"I'm such a fuckup," Miranda repeated. "I can't believe I let this all happen to me."

"It's gonna be okay." Jodi brushed a strand of hair off her cheek and Miranda opened her eyes. They were wet but steady. She gripped one small surprisingly strong hand behind Jodi's neck. Her lips were salty and insistent. Hungry, Jodi thought, as Miranda pulled up Jodi's shirt and pinned her against the bed.

August 1988

"Check," a voice calls out through the swarm of smoke and ping of slot machines. The voice is distinctly female in a room full of the deep vibrations of men.

Jodi glances over her shoulder, past the Triple Rose, Crazy Eights, and penny arcades, to the far corner where a poker game is under way. In a cocoon of smoke at a green table sit a trucker, a bearded dude in a hunting cap, one thin, pale-suited man, and a woman dressed like a redneck boy. The woman leans forward, elbows on the table and black hair slicked back under a cap. She's been there for three days, winning more than half the hands she plays, and her presence carves a space in the room disproportionate to her size.

"Here you go, sweetheart." The bartender pours a long stream of reddish-orange liquid into a frosted glass, lifting the shaker high and dripping in the last drops with a flourish. Jodi nods and swivels toward Jimmy Lauder on the stool beside her. His eyes jump to her face and she can feel his pride swell over the fact that she is sitting here with him. Jimmy was hired on at Render High only months before, taking over the junior- and senior-year chemistry classes. He has not started balding yet, though his body is softening into middle age. He is grateful, nearly pious in his appreciation of Jodi's tight flesh, and his chemical-stained fingers move electric when they touch her.

In the weeks after Effie's death, while the bank men and lawyers stalked her grandmother's land, Jodi had escaped her parents' house and lost herself in the pulse of Jimmy's fingers and those long chalk-dusted afternoons. She is enamored with his need for her, the lost-dog look he gets in his eyes, and the way she can, simply by removing her shirt, cause him to tremble and beg. She is secretly astounded that this body of hers, with its bony angles and pale, chigger-bit skin, can have such power. She carries this knowledge around with her throughout her days and it makes her feel colossally tall.

"You want more vodka in there, you just tell me." The bartender, Jimmy's older brother, is pathetically proud to be serving Sex on the Beach to a six-teen-year-old. It is in his pickle-green trailer, in Wheeling, that Jodi and Jimmy are staying, blinding themselves all day with alcohol and the jittery screens of slot machines. Four days at the Wild 'N Wonderful Casino but this woman at the card table is the only interesting thing Jodi has seen.

"Raise twelve hundred," the woman says.

She could be beautiful if she didn't look so strange, dressed in the same worn flannel and work boots that all the men in Jodi's family wear, a web of blue-black tattoos sleeving the skin of both arms. She is softly familiar but altogether different, a mixture of beautiful and ugly that wavers, like a holo-gram. Sharp cheekbones and a full pout of a mouth. She's built like a country boy too, broad in the shoulders, thick biceps, and narrow hips.

"Hey, baby, what do you want to eat?" Jimmy leans in close, his hand against Jodi's back.

Jodi shakes her head and takes a sip of her drink, the cold crystals catching in her throat.

At the poker table the suit flicks four orange chips from his stack. Beside him the trucker looks at his hand, then sends his cards sailing in the general direction of the dealer, who collects them swiftly and points at the woman. She adds orange chips to her purples and pushes them forward.

The bearded hunter folds, slides his cards to the dealer, and sits small in his chair as if losing to a woman has made him physically shrink.

On the stool beside Jodi, Jimmy spins, turning his attention to the game. His fingers find the clasp of Jodi's bra under her shirt and he plucks it in a rhythm of one-two-three.

The suit matches the woman's stack.

"Showdown," the dealer barks.

For a moment, neither the woman nor the suit move.

"Gentlemen," the dealer says, then glances at the woman and starts to correct himself.

She lays her cards on the felt and the dealer then pivots to the suit who throws his hand facedown. The dealer nods and rakes the pot toward the woman, chips jumping and clattering. She gathers them and then stands, mouth set hard, staring straight at Jodi.

"What a game." Jimmy laughs a laugh-track laugh and brings his hand down to Jodi's waist. His sweat hangs between them, smelling of fast food and anxiety.

IN THE BATHROOM mirror under the sharp overhead lights, Jodi is too skinny, with too many freckles and all that stringy black hair. She smoothes her tank top and pulls it low across her tits. The light flickers and the door swings in. Jodi freezes. Behind her the woman stands so close she could stretch her fingers out and touch her, so close she can smell her. Bourbon and cigarettes and something sweet. Jodi looks up and meets the woman's eyes in the flecked glass, and her breath jackknifes, a sharp heat forming between her legs.

"How much is he paying you?" the woman asks.

Jodi blinks and shakes her head, a line of sweat trickling down her chest. "We're just friends."

The woman's lips break into a wide smile. Jodi stares down at her feet. She can't really explain, even to her own self, the hunger inside her and the way that Jimmy's lust can make it temporarily evaporate.

"You like those fruity drinks he buys you?"

Jodi moves away, scuffing her sneaker along the tile floor.

"You don't even *know* what you like, do you?" the woman calls, and then, as Jodi opens the door and the flush of casino music filters in, "My name's Paula," she says.

BY THE TIME she has resumed her place at the poker table Paula has attracted a flotsam-jetsam audience: the bartender, a silver-haired business-man, the hunter, who is sitting out a round—everyone but Jimmy, who rests heavily in the low-slung seat at the Triple Rose machine, feeding it quarters. Jodi watches from the bar and every time she looks at Paula her breath goes all funny in her chest.

"Bet." The suit flicks his orange chips. "Five thousand."

Paula matches him, and the game rolls out in a repeating shuffle and snap. All Jodi understands of poker is the tight, angry wrestling of egos. The games she's used to are a jumble of dog-eared cards and sweaty bills on oil drums out back of the Gas 'N Go, insults and compliments traded between neighbors and cousins while the girls nurse beers and stretch out on the hoods of rusted Chevys, showing off their newly shaved legs.

"Jesus fucking Mary." The trucker sends his cards up into the air in a bright flurry. "The way she's watching the dealer, she knows what's coming her way."

Jodi blinks and tries to focus. Something is happening and she doesn't understand. The energy in the room has shifted and she tries to parse out what has just gone on but the vodka is heavy in her head.

The suit says something that Jodi can't hear and sets an orange stack of chips on the table. Paula tightens her eyes. "Raise," she says.

The suit nods and a tickle of a smile crosses his lips. He reaches for his chips. It's just the two of them left in the game now.

Jimmy has gotten up from the Triple Rose machine and he is pacing between Jodi and the poker table.

"All in," Paula says.

The suit moves. He bucks across the table toward Paula and a slurry of words spills from his mouth. ". . . fucking bitch."

Paula doesn't flinch, the air smooth around her like a shield. The room is a sweating, beating organ. It constricts in low, instinctual rhythms: voices from the TV and the music of the slot machines.

Paula stands.

All eyes on her.

Jodi leans forward but Jimmy is blocking her view. She pushes up off her stool but she is too drunk. She sits back down and wills Jimmy away, wills them all away, everything but the clean strength of Paula. She brings her cigarette to her lips. From the speakers overhead a song fogs out: *Our land, our land is far through the heart of this snow.* Jodi closes her eyes and focuses on the sad lilt of Lee Golden's voice on that radio—*far through the heart of this snow.* She takes another drag and in her mind's eye she sees Paula reach into her jacket and retrieve a silver pistol. She pictures Paula raising it high above her head.

A shot roars out and then a white rain of plaster filters down over the table.

Paula brings the pistol level with the suit's forehead and then, smiling, she pulls back and smashes it into his face. The suit lets out a long wet noise as bright blood runs out his nostrils and into his mouth, blooming in great dark spots all down his white shirt.

Jodi's pulse thrums and she opens her eyes. She blinks and the room tips a little, readjusts: that song is still playing, Lee Golden's lullaby fuzzing out through the speakers, but there is no gun, no blood, no hole in the plaster above. No Paula.

Her stomach buckles. She looks at Jimmy, slouched back into his cockpit chair, and panic shatters open inside her. *Focus.* Did she dream her? The bartender is there behind the bar and the men are standing around the table, the dealer, the suit, the trucker, and the rest. *Focus.* She's been doing this too much lately, ever since Effie's death, letting her mind run into wild dreamscape universes. *Focus.* She pivots on her stool, turns toward the back of the room, and there, shadow-cast under the red EXIT: a black-haired figure.

Jodi jerks. She feels the sweaty pressure of her own fingers pushing her body up, her blood suddenly buoyant, and though it is too fast to know, she does know. Everything else smudges out as she focuses and she sees herself choosing. She sees her own legs unfold, her body turn and release.

Our land, the radio croons, *our land is far through the heart.*

She tumbles into the hallway, past the brass elevators and on toward an exit door so heavy she has to slam her hip to open it. The sunlight scrapes her eyes and she stands there, breath ragged and blood still hurtling, until the black dots diminish and she can see: Paula, halfway across the asphalt lot, head turned and eyes on Jodi as a hot wind flaps around her, filling her shirt and lifting it like a billowing sheet.

July 2007

J odi woke alone, the yellow heat of the morning floating around
her.

"Alfredia needs to see you," a voice called from outside the
door. "She says, are you gonna stay another night?"

Jodi was naked and the air held a faint tang of sex. Below her the sheets
were scrambled, the top one drooping onto the floor and the bottom untucked
at the corner to expose the dimples of the mattress.

Day two, already it was day number two. Jodi's head would not lift from
the pillow. She tested other parts. Her legs stretched fine and her arm rose,
disrupting the falling pattern of dust motes and sending them gusting off
away from the window. But her head stayed there on the coarse pillow. The
digital clock blinked: *11:32, 11:32, 11:33*. No sounds came from the room next
door.

Jodi managed, without moving her head, to find a cigarette on the nightstand. The wheels of the maid's cart squealed outside the window, and her muffled radio called out, *On this, the Day of Our Lord, July 25, 2007* . . .

A car drove fast through the parking lot, sending a slice of reflected light against the floral wall, and Jodi remembered the spasm of electricity every night in lockup. They'd kept her in the holding tank in Atlanta for three weeks, shit scared at seventeen, clinging to her metal bed, surrounded by DTing hookers and puking junkies. Every night, after the guards quit their rounds, a quiet had set in. A silence like you'd never hear a single sound again. And then, from somewhere in the concrete tunnels, would come a scream.

Jodi never knew who the screamer was, or maybe there were multiple screamers, all she knew was that it happened every night there in the holding cells, and she would wait up for it; through the guards' pacing, their talk of the new lemon-cream-flavored donuts down at Stella's, and the size and plumpness of the new nurse assistant's ass, she waited, and once the quiet set in she began to count. She counted the tiny glow dots that appeared when she blinked her eyes. She counted the rhythms of the other girls' breath. She closed her eyes and counted the length of the darkness and in the blackest black she saw lights. She'd see the orange glow of Effie's cigarette—her tobacco smell richer than the scent of the store-bought slims that Jodi's mother smoked—and her face, the wrinkles etched as deeply as knife wounds, and her dentures, white between thin lips.

Jodi counted, sometimes all the way to two thousand, and then, finally, it would come. The scream—more animal than anything she'd ever heard in the wild. The scream and then the loudspeakers blaring and a spasm of electricity as the whole bank of lights flipped on.

ALFREDIA'S OFFICE WAS deeply cool. A cluster of bells bounced against the glass door as a blanket of cold air reached up and pulled Jodi in. The shades were drawn, covering nearly the entirety of the front windows, just a whisper of movement from the passing cars. The air smelled of clove cigarettes.

"You gonna keep staying in two thirty-two?" Alfredia's eyelids were defined with thick green swooshes.

Jodi nodded. "Tonight, at least."

Alfredia brought her pencil down to her records book. "Thirty-seven dollars with tax," she said.

On the corner of the oak desk sat a stack of cards, three of them faceup: a drawing of two naked lovers, a lightning-struck tower, and a dazzling moon. Alfredia caught Jodi's eye as she took her cash. "A reading'll cost you fifty."

Jodi shook her head. "You know that girl staying in two thirty-three?"

Alfredia counted the limp bills twice. "Miranda checked out this morning," she said.

Something kicked in Jodi's chest. "Checked out?"

Alfredia didn't even try to hold back her smile. "Wait, don't tell me—she promised you a ride."

THE TREES IN Forrest Park were lacy and thin leafed, sending scattered bits of shade over the sandy ground. From the green bench Jodi watched the buses come and go on Wauteegan Street; every thirty minutes she saw the red line, number 30, the one Alfredia told her to take, but she wasn't ready. That fine alchemical body balance that would give her the courage to face Dylan had yet to be met and so she stalked the scant shade, drinking vodka from a carton of orange juice.

The one evening that she had spent with Dylan—when Paula brought her there, the day they were supposed to rescue Ricky, back in June of '89—his presence had sucked up all the air in the house. He was not a very large man but violence hung on him like a second skin so that everything about him, even the handsome beauty of his features, was soaked in it. His wife and children had moved about him with a skilled deference, not so much cowering as presenting themselves as if they were not really there. They managed to be the hands that brought him beer and food, and the mouths that laughed at his jokes while their true selves were off somewhere, watching it all from afar. The only moment when Jodi had felt their presence, all together there in the room, was after dinner when Dylan took out his fiddle and played some slow, lovely tune. And as they sat there silently listening, Jodi could sense them—Paula, Ricky, Anna, and herself—all wrestling with the strangeness of that beautiful song coming out of that man.

THE BUS RIDE to the Shady View Mall took nearly an hour. Out the window tract houses spread across parched fields: cream-colored siding and immaculate black roofs, no fewer than two cars, and every three houses there was the sparkling blast of an inground pool. Jodi slept through most of the ride and woke with a terror cementing in her throat. *What the fuck are you doing? You really thought that girl would help you?* Laughter exploded inside her head as she remembered the night before: Miranda's nipples stiffening under Jodi's lips and the cry she gave, her fists clenching as she came.

By the time the bus reached the mall it was almost empty, the only other passenger a teenage girl with hoop earrings that pulled the lobes of her ears low. Jodi stood in the scrambled heat of the parking lot and watched the girl walk toward the gleaming building.

Out past the mall the blacktop lost its shine and crumbled into dusty ruts. Half a mile away the subdivisions hovered on the horizon like props, with puff-painted clouds and too-bright light. And there, at the head of Fairchild Road, the peanut fields resumed. A memory jumped in Jodi's mind, something familiar but not quite surfacing.

It would have been that field over there, or this one right here. This land that she and Paula had sped past on that June night. *We'll be back soon, Ricky, real soon, okay?* The fields had been planted with melons then. Under the quarter moon Jodi had seen their smooth, green forms, like pregnant bellies all up and down the field. *We could have just taken him, I've got a gun,* she'd said, staring at the empty backseat of the sedan. Paula had insisted they weren't ready, that Ricky needed more than they could give him right then, but watching her drive away, white knuckled, Jodi had seen in Paula's face not forethought but shit-scared cowardice.

. . .

THE HOUSE WAS a two-story clapboard, dusted in red clay and choked with kudzu. The vine looped across the power lines, down the walls and out across the yard toward an empty driveway, the place where Dylan's Skylark had gleamed hot silver, the car that had been driven only on Sundays but cleaned or waxed by the children every day of the week.

Jodi studied the house, blinds drawn tight against each windowpane, the porch set with a glass ashtray and a metal folding chair. The air did not move. She glanced again at the empty driveway and felt her thoughts and emotions scrambling over top of one another. Perhaps, with a little luck, it could be true that Dylan was not home right now, but then, what about Ricky? Maybe none of them lived here anymore?

"Hello?" she called, walking up the drive.

Above in the flat blue sky a red-tailed hawk dove straight toward some invisible prey. Jodi followed its movement with her eyes and was reminded of Ricky, on that June evening, whispering to her about his highest hiding place. Anna had been in the kitchen, cooking, while Dylan and Paula talked and smoked on the porch. *You're Paula's best friend?* Ricky had asked, and Jodi had smiled and nodded. *You wanna see something secret?* he'd said, reaching for her hand and leading her out the back door and along the fence row to a towering live oak. *You can't tell no one,* he said as he climbed up into the branches. Jodi had followed, scrambling from limb to limb until she heard, somewhere above them, the flapping of wings and looked up to see a huge crow peering down from the top of the tree. Ricky held out his arm, his wrist still swollen and bloodied from where Dylan had tied him to the chair. The bird skimmed down to land on his shoulder. Seeing him there in the tree with his strange pet, Jodi was reminded of her own younger self, wild and lonely on the mountain with nothing but her solitary grandmother and animals for company. *This is Darling,* Ricky said. *I found her in the tall grass when she was a baby and now she brings me things.* The crow balanced on his arm as he scrambled the rest of the way to the top to show Jodi her nest full of shiny trinkets: strips of foil, beer tabs, a watch chain, glass marbles, a few rings. From the top of the tree Dylan and Anna's house had looked small and far away and for the first time since arriving there Jodi felt like she could breathe. *Every day she brings me new things.* The huge black bird lifted up off Ricky's arm and swooped away across the open field. Ricky had watched, smiling as her strong wings beat against the sky. *She'll go off like that,* he'd said, *but then she always comes back to me.*

"Hello?"

The front door opened just a crack.

Jodi froze in the worn dirt, below the porch steps.

"What you need?" It was Anna's voice, smoke tinged and raspy.

Jodi's tongue stuck to the inside of her cheek. She tried to find the kick and surge that the vodka had put in her veins but it was all gone.

"Car break down?" Anna offered, her voice a bit softer.

Jodi shook her head. "No, ma'am, no. I'm with the Georgia Department of Human Services." She stepped onto the porch.

The door opened just the tiniest bit more but Jodi still could not see inside. She waited to hear Dylan's footsteps but when no sound came she took a deep breath and barreled on. "This is the residence of Patrick Dulett, correct?"

"Yeah."

"Then you must be his mother, Anna Dulett?" Jodi's voice marched out and she listened to the tone of it, so disconnected and confident. "I'm Ricky's new caseworker. I'll just need to speak with him for a moment."

"He's not here."

"Oh." Jodi paused and licked her lips, trying to recalibrate her plan. She shifted her weight from foot to foot and the porch boards squeaked. "May I speak to Dylan Dulett?"

The door opened a little more and then swung back, almost closed. "You ain't the same worker Ricky had last time we come up to Human Services," Anna said. "And they never sent nobody out to the house before neither."

"Ma'am." Jodi looked back over her shoulder, scanning the road for Dylan's Skylark. "I'm sorry to bother you but—"

"I know what you're doing. You're trying to steal his identity."

"No, ma'am."

"Happened to a man down in Sarita Springs. And I says to myself when I seen that on the TV, I says sure as the day is long they're going to try to get me. I've been waiting for you." She paused, overcome by a deep, phlegmy cough. "I knew you'd pick somebody like me. You ought to be ashamed going after people's identities like that."

"Ma'am," Jodi said. "Ma'am, that was not my intention. I just need to verify the whereabouts of my client."

"I know how to protect myself." Anna stopped, no more words, just a small wheezing breath in the crack of the doorway. At the edges of the frame the chipped paint revealed layers of past colors, powder blue and faded mint.

"I don't put none of our mail in the trash. I keep it all in here. Ricky'll carry the bags up to the attic for me and—"

Jodi stepped in closer. "Where *is* Ricky?"

The door opened then, just enough for a small, perfectly round face to fit. Anna's white curls stuck to the sweat along the edges of her cheeks. Her eyes swam fast, all up and down.

"Wait," she said, letting go of the door. "That ain't it at all, is it?"

She stepped out onto the porch, her purple housedress giving off gusts of talcum scent. Something moved along the floor in the hallway behind her and Jodi leaned in to better see but Anna's words snapped her attention back.

"I know who you are." Anna's eyes met Jodi's and then flitted off to a point just over her shoulder. "Oh, God, I remember you."

Breathe, Jodi told herself. Just breathe.

The therapist always said *count and breathe and follow your breath* but Paula was on the floor and the blood would not stop coming. All the hotel towels were wet and yet the blood kept coming.

Breathe.

"Why ain't you in that prison?" Anna leaned out toward Jodi.

"Where's Ricky?" Jodi said, glancing again over her shoulder, sure now that she heard the rasp of tires on gravel, but when she turned, the road was empty.

Anna's hands fluttered, her handkerchief shaking, and Jodi grabbed her arm.

"I need you to tell me where Ricky is."

Anna's skin felt dry and too thin under Jodi's fingers, her bones brittle and body as light as a child's.

"I'll scream," Anna said. "I'll scream till somebody comes."

Jodi pressed her hand against Anna's mouth. She felt the wet heat of Anna's breath and something stirred in her—the old ache-rage.

"How come you never screamed before?" she said, the anger rising like a drug in her veins. "How come all these years you watched Dylan beat them and you never once thought to scream?"

Anna thrashed and bucked and Jodi pushed her back into the house.

The hallway was shadowed inside and the heat hung thick and mixed with the smell of urine and curdled milk. As her eyes adjusted, Jodi noticed a movement all about their feet. Cats. All up and down the hall, the constant movement of slippery, long-haired cats . . . ten, no, twenty or more of them.

The sickness of their smell and the sickness of the house flared up in Jodi and she smashed Anna backward, up against the wall. "Where is he?"

Anna trembled and then relaxed, submitting to Jodi's grip. Dylan must have beaten her too, Jodi realized, a senseless anger pulsing in him just like this.

"Off at that museum." Anna looked down the hall.

Jodi loosened her grip. "Where's that?"

"The music museum."

Jodi let go of Anna's arms and smoothed the sleeve of her housedress down over her shoulder. "In Chaunceloraine?"

"Dylan's got him working full-time."

"Uh-huh, and where's the museum at?"

Anna closed her eyes.

Jodi looked past her, down the hallway and into the half-lit kitchen where three cats lay on the wooden table, asleep among scattered dishes.

"Dylan don't tell me much of nothing," Anna said.

Jodi glanced back at her. Even with all her wrinkles and white hair, she looked every minute more and more like a confused child.

"How old were you," Jodi asked, "when you married him?"

Anna did not move.

"Did you ever try to leave?"

She blinked her eyes open and stared straight at Jodi.

"Get out," she spat. "Get out of my house now."

August 1988

"All it takes is just one great hand," Paula says between swallows of beer. "Just one night, with one sweet sugar run, and you're hooked."

She sits across the booth from Jodi, arms resting on the scarred wooden table, hands wrapped around a bottle of Bud. Jodi listens to her speak of sugar runs and thinks of the runs she knows—flashing mountain creeks that appear out of nowhere after a good rain—and she smiles at the appropriateness of this phrasing: luck like a creek that glistens and then disappears, leaving only swirled leaves.

Paula glances over her shoulder, then pulls her flask from her hip pocket and tips it into Jodi's glass of Coke. Between them, in the strips of sunlight that sneak through the wooden blinds, dust motes glimmer.

The bar is called Blue Mine, a long narrow shack, the only business open in a one-road river town. The place is full of sleepy midafternoon heat but Paula's energy fractures the lull. She is laughing now, telling a story about a dog that eats paper money. Jodi watches her, absorbing every gesture and inflection, grateful for how Paula's presence shakes off the gravity that's settled on her over the past few years, the weight of her future. She has not pushed herself to excel in school and she is not beautiful and the pieces of her life are very plain to see. But Paula seems to her to be weightless, free of all normal responsibilities and constantly on the verge of something dangerous and great. There is a velocity to her that pulls you close. Her life lived like the coil before the strike.

"You're so damn cute." Paula reaches out to touch Jodi's chin.

Jodi ducks her head. Being wanted by Paula is completely different than being wanted by Jimmy. This is something rare and magnificent. She is afraid it is a mistake somehow and will soon be taken away.

"You win a lot?"

Paula shrugs. "I'm saving up to buy a piece of land. Gonna build a house and move my little brother in." She pauses, pulling the wet label off the bottle of Bud. "He needs a good place to live."

Jodi sips her spiked Coke, her tongue bristling under the bubbles and alcohol. *A good place to live.* She pictures Effie's house, the row of three small rooms, long porch, and the garden with beanpoles pointed sky high. For the past few months, since Effie's death, she's been living at her parents' place in town but there she still feels like an awkward guest and she has not stopped dreaming about returning to the mountain, has not stopped needing to feel needed by someone.

"How old's your brother?"

"Ten," Paula says, then knocks back her beer in one long drink.

THE ROOM THEY find at the River Rest Motel is nothing more than a linoleum-floor box but it has a little balcony and a claw-foot tub. Paula fetches a quilt from the trunk of her sedan and she and Jodi settle on the balcony to watch the sun set over the shallow water. The air smells of thick bottom mud, fish rot, and algae. It hasn't rained in two months and the streams are crawling away from their banks, leaving catfish skeletons, old refrigerators, and piles of trash and dirt that give off a sweet stink.

"Look there." Paula points to where the last rays of sun catch in the neck of a green glass bottle. The world seems so bright suddenly, flush with beauty, and Jodi can't remember the last time she really looked at anything. Paula lays her hand on Jodi's thigh and stares off across the water toward a dock jutting out from the far bank. Her hand kneads circles into the soft skin just below Jodi's skirt. Jodi shifts and moves toward Paula but Paula pulls back, stands up, and disappears inside.

Jodi hears the *hsst* of a beer bottle opening and then the sound of water running in the porcelain tub. Dusk settles around her, fuzzy with the blue of night seeping in, and after a while Paula calls.

The room is dim but Paula grabs Jodi's hand when she reaches for the light. The air is full of the wet heat of bathwater, and Paula undresses her slowly, piece by piece from the top down. Jodi feels every inch of her skin: bony arms with too much black hair and thin legs. She reaches for Paula and Paula leads her to the tub.

Paula washes carefully between Jodi's toes and runs the cloth up each leg. Through the open balcony door Jodi sees the lights of the bar, just downriver. The cicadas have gone quiet but the voices of the katydids rise in the branches outside. Paula smoothes the cloth across Jodi's stomach, then brings it up to her chin. She lifts Jodi's face and, bending close, kisses her. Her mouth tastes of salt and smoke and beer.

"Nobody's ever made you cum before, have they?"

Jodi's throat tightens. In the dark she cannot see Paula's eyes. She pushes away and turns toward the smooth white porcelain, her face hot with shame, but Paula pulls her back. She brings her hand down between Jodi's legs and the feel of it catches in Jodi's stomach, throbbing. She lets her head fall back into the water as a breathless pleasure shimmers under her skin.

July 2007

The jelly donut oozed onto the china plate as Miranda watched, coffee cup gripped in two hands. Her first bite had punctured the side of the pastry and now it was leaking obscenely and she couldn't bring herself to eat any more. Powdered sugar stuck to the back of her throat, and her stomach, though empty, did not seem to welcome anything.

"More coffee?" The waitress leaned over the counter, gold necklace swinging.

Miranda glanced up. She liked this diner with its narrow row of Formica tables and one long counter with a TV at the far end, dark enough to be anonymous but friendly all the same.

"Uh, yeah, um, do you think you could fix me a screwdriver too?"

"Screwdriver?" The waitress paused, coffeepot halfway to Miranda's cup.

"Yeah, you know, like some orange juice and—"

"Oh, honey, I know what a screwdriver is." The waitress was still laughing when she reached the end of the counter and nestled the coffeepot back on the heating ring.

Miranda looked away. There were horses racing on the TV, all that weight pounding on those spindly legs. Though the sound was turned off, she could hear their rhythm in her head.

She flipped her pack of Camels open. She had only three cigarettes left.

Shit, fuck, what am I doing?

She'd tried to stay there in bed with Jodi but mornings were the hardest. With too much sunlight and no extra chemicals, her self-doubt exploded until she was afraid it would permanently cripple her. She had to move fast. She'd taken a cold shower, hauled her suitcase out to her car, and brought the remainder of her pill stash up to the front desk to give to Alfredia. Now she needed this one drink and then she'd shove off and go find Lee. Somehow in all their arguing the night before, she'd never managed to get any money from him and the ten-dollar bill curled inside her cigarette pack was all she had left, that and her EBT card.

She inhaled and focused on her cigarette, trying to coax her mind away from her boys. She should have stayed there in bed with Jodi. Last night was the first time in a long while she'd actually felt happy. She pictured the two of them up on the billboard platform and then later in the dark warmth of the bed, Jodi's whiskey-tinged kisses and her small, perfect breasts. Miranda shivered and looked up to see the waitress walking slowly toward her, beautiful yellow-orange cocktail on her tray.

"Screwdriver for the lady." The waitress whisked the gruesome donut away and set the cool drink before her and Miranda nearly wept. The waitress would not make eye contact. Whatever. Miranda lit one of her precious cigarettes and lifted the drink. Glory hallelujah, Christ is risen.

THE FAIRGROUNDS WERE deserted and heat snug over everything, the air unmoving. Miranda climbed in through a cut in the back fence and picked her way past signs for the Exotix Petting Zoo and Pig Races and on toward the little trailer that served as Lee's greenroom. His greenrooms had gotten smaller and smaller over the years of receding fame but this was an all-time low, more of a camper than a trailer, made of some flimsy material like the surface of an old mattress.

Miranda hesitated at the door, filled suddenly with the fear of finding someone else in there with him.

"Lee?"

She turned the handle and was met with a wall of hot silence. The trailer was empty. She glanced over her shoulder, off past the stage. The tour bus was gone. *Shit, fuck.* She'd stayed on too long at the diner, chatting with a retired army commander who'd come in when she was finishing her first drink. He'd bought her two more and apparently time had kept on ticking.

She stood there on the steps, smoking her last cigarette, the rush of highway traffic and the sound of the midway music looping behind her. She felt herself rising up above this particular moment, pushing away from the jagged edges of reality. She was not as drunk as she would have liked but she'd tipped just enough to feel halfway free.

The faucet in the trailer was dripping. She ducked inside, crossed the room in three steps, and found, there on the counter beside the sink, a single nylon stocking, brown and warm to the touch as if just discarded. She gripped the countertop, feeling sick and unsteady.

It was she who had left him, technically, but not really, only after too many weeks of being abandoned—she and the boys pushed aside and dumped at Lee's aunt's cul-de-sac bungalow in Delray—until she realized that leaving him would be the one way to get his attention. She hadn't run far, only here to Chaunceloraine, and he'd found her almost immediately and taken the boys back. Miranda herself refused to go with him and now they played this I-love-you / I-hate-you game, her calling him every few weeks but most of the time not answering when he called back—either that or answering just long enough to tell him she needed money. He always found her whenever he was in town, and in hotels and dressing rooms after his shows she flung her pain at him until she was clean and empty.

Inside the trailer the air was unbreathably hot and smelled of leftover barbecue. Miranda dropped her cigarette in the sink and lifted up the stocking and quite suddenly she saw, very clearly, a memory of Lee's mother and herself, at age seventeen: A long sash of buttery light fell through the kitchen window, across the table and down along Lee's mother's legs. From where she had lain, on a blow-up mattress on the floor of the living room, Miranda could see nothing but legs. The legs of the man in the black suit and the legs of Lee's mother, encased in panty hose.

"You know, Bella, for the auditing to work, you have to be completely truthful with me," the man said. "Can you recall a time of change?"

Miranda had been sent to live with Bella, to finish up her pregnancy there while Lee completed his tour.

"I need you to retrieve the memory more fully."

Bella brought her heels together, the white leather of her pumps rubbing against each other. Inside the shoes her feet slid up and down, the panty hose sparkling a little each time they crossed the band of light. These auditing sessions were important, Bella had told Miranda, a sort of cleansing, a way to go clear.

"Either pink or blue," Bella was saying. "Pastel definitely."

Miranda had three pairs of Bella's panty hose stashed in a wooden cigar box. She had other things too, a nearly empty bottle of eau de toilette, a cotton ball Bella had blotted her lips with, the peel of a Cara Cara orange they'd shared that first day in LA. Miranda's sadness over being separated from Lee was almost completely eclipsed by her joy at spending time with Bella. She'd been homeschooled her whole life and had never really had any close girlfriends.

"Stop, stop, go back. It's that moment."

The first thing Miranda had noticed was how different the light was in LA. When she'd stood on the tarmac in Georgia the fat hand of the sun had smothered her and she'd felt she couldn't breathe properly with Lee there hugging her too tightly and promising he'd join her soon. The light in LA, though, was thin, sifted like cake flour so that it fell always at oblique angles.

Some days Bella took Miranda to the Celebrity Centre down on Franklin Avenue. She'd kiss Miranda on the cheek and send her up to the terrace while she met with important people. The rooftop terrace was white on white: pale wicker furniture on a tiled courtyard, the tops of the palms reaching just over the roofline like tufts of stiff hair, and beyond them, the scabbed backbone of the San Gabriel Mountains where wildfires sometimes licked, emitting columns of furious smoke. On the big fire days people gathered there on the roof, Bella telling anyone who would listen how the smell of char and smoke turned her on.

Other days Bella left early and Miranda woke alone in the apartment, the rooms nearly bare and the walls quivering with that pale LA light. On those days she lay on the linoleum floor, hands against her belly, feeling the water-song of her baby and staring up at the clothesline tied across the kitchen window, over which were draped two rows of Bella's panty hose, the feet still pressed with the impression of her skin. Miranda loved the strength Bella took from her own beauty, even now as she aged, the way she commanded any space she stepped into, not demanding attention so much as simply, naturally eliciting it.

"Again," the man said. "Tell me again."

That first day, after Bella greeted Miranda out on the landing strip, the wind from the blades gusting her curls all across her face, after the man, who maybe was but probably was not *this* black-suited man, drove them up into the hills later, in the evening, when the heat had soaked out, they'd walked together, just the two of them. They left the apartment carrying oranges, Bella scattering the peels like a trail of crumbs to follow later. They seemed to be walking in no particular direction, the gulls flying overhead like little paper planes, and children screaming in the street. Bella's sandals slapped the sidewalk confidently, until they reached the sea. A smell before it was a sight. A salt and fish-rot mist that lay over the whole neighborhood, and then there, on the corner, a two-story-tall painting of a young Bella. She said nothing but looked up casually at her own long legs, bare all the way to where the white skirt began, and on the wall, her lips: as large as a window, pink and parted with a word bubble: SIPSA COLA, THE LADY'S DRINK!

THE BOOTHS AT the Ali Bar were long enough to lie down in, wide and deeply leather scented. Jodi was the only customer in the whole place but

Alister pretended not to remember her until she wandered up to the bar for her third drink.

"You find your friend?" he said finally.

"Miranda?"

"No, out by the Shady View Mall."

Jodi shook her head. "You ever heard of a music museum around here?"

"This woman I was seeing drug me along up to a museum in Savannah." Alister shrugged. "Something-Something of the Fine Arts. It looked to me like any two-year-old could've made those paintings with his eyes closed."

On the wall above Alister's head were shelves and shelves of antique clocks with little owl faces, images of suns and moons, and gilt hands stilled under fuzzy coils of dust. The quiet timelessness of the bar and Alister's ramblings felt like they could trap Jodi eternally and so she finished her drink and headed back across the street.

Her motel room was still also but the weight of time was not so enormous there. She settled into a chair beside the open window and listened to the wind flap a foam life preserver against the swimming-pool fence. There goes day two, she thought. An airplane tore up from the horizon and smeared a bleached trail across the sky. Someone headed north, flying up toward the mountains fast.

She took a swig from her whiskey bottle and felt the alcohol gliding inside her veins. She closed her eyes and pictured her mountains and how before the mountains were mountains they were a sea. An ancient weedy sea, crawling with centipedal beings. And water over all of it. The rush and purr of giant waves.

"IF I'M NOT back in fifteen minutes," Paula says, "that means they let me in." She pushes the car door open and slides away across the seat.

There is nothing but the tick-tick-tick of the cooling engine and the chemical smell of warm vinyl seats. Sweat forms on Jodi's upper lip, damp patches on the backs of her knees. Day by day she is evolving, slimming and straightening, turning to salt.

"You love me?" she calls out.

Paula turns toward her, mouth breaking open into a full grin. "Love with a capital *L*," she says, holding out a wrinkled ten-thousand-peso bill.

Her voice hangs warm and full inside the car even as she walks off, shoulders tense under a starched white shirt, hair slicked back and attention fixed on the four stories of colonial brick at the far end of the lot. Even the gravel here is immaculate, white stones bordered by pale sand. In the windows, on the third floor of the hotel, thin lace catches and swells with the wind.

Jodi fingers the velvet paper of the peso bill and listens to the slap of a broom on the old boards. A small brown man in loose blue clothes sweeps and resweeps the front porch. She flattens the money against her wet thigh. Despite all those zeros the bill is worth less than a dollar back in the States. She feels it fold under her fingers and calculates what they have spent, do spend, are sure to spend—fish soup, 24,000 pesos; bread, 2,000; fruit cocktail, 5,000; sweet rice milk, 4,000; flask of rum, bottle of tequila, hotel room, two grams of cocaine, a bottle of Dexedrine, valium. . . . They are hemorrhaging.

Mexico was supposed to be a warm, cheap place to pass the winter but none of the expat resorts will let Paula into their games. Here she has no history, no name. Her savings, their land money, is almost gone and in the smaller local games it's just inflated pesos and no one bets enough.

They'd driven south from Texas and at some point the white crosses they were taking had lost their peak and Paula started crushing up the Dexedrine, first to snort and later to shoot. Jodi was sick with fear the first time they shot it—the headlights of passing cars raking across the dashboard as Paula mixed the hit and drew it up through a cotton ball. That first time, she couldn't look at the needle or at Paula's face but soon it was all a part of the rarefied joy of it, the anticipation coming on in a rush from the moment Paula ties off her arm.

Jodi reaches into the backseat and opens their carpetbag; all their belongings are stuffed inside that orange caterpillar—clothes and shoes and, somewhere among the jumble, a little leather purse with Effie's .38 tucked inside. The pistol frightens Paula, which makes Jodi smile just a little. It keeps Jodi company too; she polishes, cleans, and oils it during the long nights of poker games when Paula is gone and she is alone in the backseat of the car, sweating and zipping along her own brain highway.

She folds the ten-thousand-peso bill in beside the pistol and, slipping the purse over her shoulder, climbs out of the car and follows a dirt path along the edge of the building and on past a wooden sign that says PLAYA. The heat rests in layers around her, shifting as she moves through the smell of something burnt and something deeper, the musk of too-ripe fruit.

The crisp disk of the sea meets sand that is as clean as sugar. Unbroken except for one tan woman with a shock of bronze hair and a boy under an umbrella with a table of coconuts, cigarettes, and bottles of blue and white liquors.

Down at the water's edge the salt breeze spins around Jodi. Lifting her arms high, she feels the weight of the leather purse against her hip and closes her eyes, listening for Paula to call her name. *Love with a capital* L. She needs to hear those words over and over again. Every time that Paula says them, the hunger-wound inside her ebbs away a little. Still, she is unsure how to picture their future. She has never felt that she could properly see herself. There are the basics—her age and weight and schooling—but Effie was the only one who could ever really see her. Her parents couldn't, she is sure of it; otherwise why would they have left her? She seems out of focus to herself most of the time; only now, with Paula, do things feel a little clearer. The way she sees it, she is always staring out from her own center but she is yet to master the trick of looking in. If she could just line up the way the world must see their love with the way this all feels, then everything would come into clearer view. If she could push back the words—*dyke, queer*—then everything would make sense and turn out all right. Sometimes, though, the terror of it grips her, the knowledge that she is not seen at all, or seen only backward and out of focus. It is a feeling she is sure will crush her someday.

A SOUND THAT was at first a bell—an alarm, a car horn—reached Jodi and she startled. The phone rang out loudly from the small table beside her, barely visible in the shadowy room. She grabbed the receiver.

"Your name's Jodi?" a woman's voice shouted.

Jodi held the phone a few inches from her face.

"This man keeps calling the front desk, saying he needs me to tell you to come over to Alister's. I didn't patch his calls through 'cause he don't know your last name or room number."

Jodi stared at the earpiece of the phone where the woman's voice leaked out.

"You've got to go over there and tell them to quit calling."

OUTSIDE, THE PARKING lot still held the heat of the set sun, and Jodi walked as if she'd never left her dream, the air all the same except that it lacked the salt of the sea.

Before she even opened the door, she could feel the beat of the bar, a packed bass rhythm of Friday night, a shift in chemistry. Alister looked up as she walked in and pointed down to the end of the room where Miranda stood on a table, spinning, the edge of her skirt skimming the tops of three men's heads. Jodi felt a panic rise inside her at the sight of Miranda's skin. She thought of her, naked in the motel bed, the arch of her back and her heavy breasts.

"Hey." Alister motioned Jodi over to the bar. "Miranda's feeling wild tonight," he said. "I thought maybe you could hang out with her for a while. She was asking around for you earlier."

Jodi rolled her eyes. She barely knew this woman and already it seemed she was somehow responsible for babysitting her. But the truth was, she'd been happy for the phone call, happy that there was someone in this world who would bother trying to find her.

"Hey, Randy," Alister called out over the bar. "Your friend's here."

Miranda stopped spinning and her dress fell down to her legs. One man ran his fingers up her thigh, catching hold of the skirt, but she flinched and pushed his hand away. "Hey," she said to Jodi. "Why'd you leave?"

"Why did *I* leave?"

"I come by your room this afternoon, looking for you."

Jodi shook her head but helped Miranda down and led her toward the bar, holding her hand high and light as if she were about to curtsy to the crowd.

"What happened to going clean?"

"I'm not taking the pills anymore, it's those pills that distract me."

Miranda widened her eyes. "Hey, baby," she called out to Alister. "Pour me a good one."

She clinked their glasses together and when she leaned her head onto Jodi's shoulder Jodi felt a humming inside her, a special current of electricity.

"God," Miranda said, "I'm so glad you're here. I love you."

Jodi laughed. "Yeah, right, me and every man in this bar."

"No," Miranda said without lifting her head. "You."

Jodi laughed again but she did not pull away. Miranda's overfamiliarity felt strange but also somehow comforting. She looked down at the blonde head on her shoulder, smelling of sweat and coconut shampoo, and she wondered when exactly those words had lost their meaning for her. Those sparkling declarations of love turned as bland as unsalted butter. She heard her own voice, clawing and begging with those same words. *I love you. God, I love you so much.* And Paula's passive face. *You've got to quit saying that. You know those phrases stop meaning anything when you repeat them like that.* But how else to explain that instant, dizzying bond?

"What's his name?"

Jodi swallowed and focused on Miranda.

"Your friend. Alister said you couldn't find your friend today."

Jodi was tired and already too drunk. She gripped the bar, trying to remember exactly how much she'd had to drink. The bottle back at the motel was nearly gone but how many hours ago was that?

"You didn't find nothing?"

Jodi shrugged. "His mother told me he worked at some music museum but there are no museums here and—"

"What about the Folk and Country?"

"Folk and Country?" Jodi shook her head.

"Over in Delray, the Georgia Folk and Country Musicians Museum. They've got a big Lee display."

Jodi narrowed her vision, tunneled it in on Miranda's flushed face. "Why didn't nobody else tell me about this?"

"Well, it's over in Delray."

"You'll take me there?"

She nodded.

The room swayed unevenly. Jodi gripped her glass of bourbon. Miranda was still talking but Jodi was only half-listening.

"I knew when I met you," Miranda said, "we had a special connection."

Jodi shook her head. She wanted to laugh off Miranda's gushing "I love yous" and "special connections" but at the same time she wanted desperately to believe in them. Despite herself she liked Miranda's high-pitched reactions, the way she poured it all out so openly. It reminded her of a painting she had once seen through the window of an art gallery in Dallas, layers of pink and ranges of corals and roses that were globbed onto the canvas in thick streaks, growing darker until, in the middle, they formed a gash of raw-heart red.

"A meteor fell from the Alabama sky once," Miranda said. "Hit a woman in her sleep."

The noise of the room seemed at once too close and very far away. Jodi got half her shot down and felt a little steadier.·

"A meteor what?"

"Out of all the places in the universe it could've hit, it came through the roof and landed on her hip." Miranda pushed her empty shot glass across the countertop. "Talk about coincidence, now that's a coincidence."

Jodi smiled, watching the green glass lamplight play over Miranda's shiny hair and the cigarette smoke building in layers above her. She turned slowly, fresh drink in hand, and Jodi pictured her as a bright ball hurtling through the universe and coming to land, violent and precise, on someone's sleeping skin.

"Where is this music museum again?" Jodi leaned against the bar.

"Over in Delray, same fucking place where Lee's got my babies."

THEY DROVE THROUGH Hazeville, Tifton and Willacoochee, nothing but one-pump gas stations and single-story ranch homes with cotton growing right up into the yards.

"My boys were all born in the afternoon," Miranda said, taking one last drag on her cigarette and flicking it out the car window toward a billboard that cautioned FOR THE GREAT DAY OF HIS WRATH SHALL COME AND WHO SHALL BE ABLE TO STAND?

"I read in an astrology book once all about birth times. I think being born in the afternoon gave my boys a head start. They're all smarter than most kids their age."

Jodi lit one cigarette off another and repeated Miranda's boys' names like a newly learned prayer.

"Kaleb, Donnie, Ross—"

"You really only have to find Kaleb," Miranda said, lifting her hair up off her sweaty neck and piling it on top of her head. When she took her hand away the hair fell down again, tumbling across her shoulders. "He'll be out there by the bus, and if he don't already have Donnie and Ross with him, just tell him to fetch them."

The air smelled of gasoline with a sugary undertone of Miranda's bubble-gum. The heat and lack of sleep weighed on Jodi. They'd stayed at Alister's until closing again, spitting stories at each other—Jodi enthralled by the coincidence and the smallness of the world and Miranda shrugging it all off. Jodi still had not told the whole truth but she'd explained that Ricky was Paula's brother and she had said the words *dead girlfriend* and *gun accident*.

Truth or no truth, it hadn't mattered to Miranda; she wasn't really interested in Jodi's past. What she wanted to talk about were her own experiences with Lee, long stretches of hot LA streets, seven-hundred-dollar dresses, and bare feet. It wasn't until Jodi spoke of the land in West Virginia that Miranda had paid attention. Could she and the boys come stay there for a bit, she had wondered out loud. *We just need somewhere to rest for a while, somewhere outside of all this, so we can live together the way we're supposed to, away from Lee and his aunt and their judgment.*

Jodi had closed her eyes. Her heart picked up at the request but she knew she ought to say no. This was in no way part of the plan but here was this girl with her pretty little face, the soft apple scent of her skin—her knowledge of where Ricky might be and a car that could drive them all out of the state. And somehow she seemed to understand precisely what the land in West

Virginia was for, exactly what Jodi and Paula always dreamt it would become: a refuge from judgment.

"You gotta guess." Kaleb rattled his *Toy Story* lunch box for emphasis. "If you don't guess how many steps, Ross won't walk."

"One million two hundred and thirty-seven trillion, eighty bajillion, kadillion, ten thousand and one!" Donnie shouted.

He was already almost half a block ahead of them, throwing his *Spider-Man* backpack up the sidewalk and then running to catch up. But Ross hung back, standing on the corner, staring down at his shoes.

"Not like that," Kaleb pleaded. "A for-real guess. He knows when it's not real."

The boys had been together in the bus line when Jodi found them, Kaleb carrying his own lunch box and backpack along with Ross's. Ross was tiny, even for a six-year-old, tired and stunned looking with Donnie bouncing constantly beside him. Jodi had waited for the teacher to do a last count before she'd approached.

"Where is Mom anyway?" Kaleb glanced back to the redbrick school and long line of yellow buses.

"Right up here." Jodi pointed. "Just like four blocks up here."

She'd gotten them to cross the street by telling them that their dad had sent her to pick them up and take them to eat ice cream with their mom. *You know Dad?* Kaleb had said, and Jodi had smiled big and nodded, feeling the lie lodge tightly in her chest.

"Where's your car?" Kaleb looked up the road and then back again, toward the playground with its shining sheet of metal slide and empty swings.

"Two hundred and four steps," Jodi said. "I bet you a double-dip ice cream that it's just two hundred and four steps."

Ross smiled and started walking fast, mumbling numbers under his breath.

Jodi pressed her hand to Kaleb's back and hurried him, pushing him almost on top of Ross. She swore she heard sirens, shouts, and concerned voices trailing them, and looking at her hand there on Kaleb's red T-shirt, covering the entirety of his small shoulder, she wondered what the hell she was doing. The idea of helping a mother reunite with her children had sounded good—and Miranda claimed up and down that she still had custody—but now the whole situation felt rumpled and dirty. Three days out of Jaxton and already her life was careening.

"Donnie, sweetie!" Miranda's voice pitched out from the alleyway and up through the buzz of afternoon traffic.

In the gravel lot next to a boarded-up car wash the Chevette sat with all four doors open and beside it stood Miranda, grinning. At the sight of her smile Jodi let her mind unclench; it was a smile so pure and huge that it rang out from every inch of her body.

Miranda held Donnie to her, his legs dangling just inches above the street, head tucked under her chin, but he was gone from her arms in a second, backpack abandoned as he vaulted himself into the backseat.

"No seat bets," he yelled. "There's no seat bets!"

"Belts," Kaleb said, more to himself than anyone else. "Seat *belts*. There have to be seat belts, it's a car."

"Rossie!" Miranda squealed, bending toward her son.

Ross kept moving without looking up until his nose touched the maroon metal of the Chevette door.

"Four hundred and thirty-six steps," he announced.

"Ross, baby, come here." Miranda squatted and pulled him toward her but he held his body stiff.

"Wrong," he said, looking back over his shoulder at Jodi. "It was four hundred and thirty-six steps. You were wrong."

"Uh-huh, yeah, let's get in the car." Jodi pressed her hand against Kaleb's back but he wouldn't move.

"Hi, Mom," he said, turning toward Miranda. "Neenee says we're not supposed to go anywhere with you."

Miranda blinked. "Hey," she said. "Nice to see you too."

Donnie was right. There were no seat belts in the backseats.

"That's not safe," Kaleb said.

Jodi nodded. "Come on, just climb in," she said, glancing over her shoulder.

"I love you guys so much." Miranda settled herself into the driver's seat, studying her boys' faces in the rearview mirror.

"I scream. ICE CREAM. I scream," Donnie chanted as Miranda drove.

Kaleb practiced his protective reflexes, throwing his arms out across his brothers' bodies every time she braked.

"Where are we going?" he asked. "We can get ice cream at the Freez-E. It's on the way to Neenee's house."

Miranda shook her head and turned the radio on. *Stock prices rose today by 1.3 . . . Crimson and clover, over and over . . . Unidentified arsonist in downtown Albany . . . And the Delray Church of Christ Choir took top spot in the state championship today. . . .*

"Neenee says it's cheaper to buy in bulk," Kaleb said. "We could get ice cream at Walmart and eat it at her house."

"Don't worry, it's my treat," Miranda said.

"That way Neenee could have some too."

"I'll eat Neenee's ice cream," Ross offered.

"I'll eat *Neenee*," Donnie yelled, rocking his head back and forth, hitting his face against the window.

Kaleb slashed his arms across his brothers' stomachs. "Watch out," he said. "We might have to stop real fast."

At the Dairy Queen, Miranda seemed to panic. "You don't want ice cream?" she said, turning to Jodi.

"I gotta go look for Ricky."

"Yeah, but you could still eat with us." Miranda spun around in the seat to face her boys again. "You guys want Aunt Jodi to come eat ice cream with us, right?"

"Jodi?" Ross cooed, squishing his body into the corner. "Who's Jodi?"

Donnie grabbed the door handle and pushed his way out of the car.

"Get back in here." Miranda stretched her arm over the seat as if she could simply reach into the busy lot and snatch him back to safety.

Kaleb slid out the door and grabbed Donnie by the hem of his shirt. Miranda let her hand droop but did not move to follow them, and Jodi wondered again what exactly she was doing here with this child-mom and all her problems. She'd let the convenience of the car and blonde brilliance of Miranda's beauty get to her.

Effie would not have approved. Effie said you had to take note when God threw you curveballs and you had to be quick on your feet and get out of the way. But Miranda had a force about her, an urgency that could bring the Ricky plan up to date and pull them all into the present; and Jodi had a fear, or maybe more than a fear, maybe it was knowledge of a real and possible danger that if she and Ricky were to do this thing alone, they might slip through the fabric of time and get trapped somewhere between dream and memory.

"I'll be gone one hour, max," Jodi said. "You've got money, right?"

Miranda stood up and opened the back door, reaching in for Ross. "You want me to order you something?"

Jodi shook her head and slid over into the driver's seat.

In front of the car Kaleb held tight to Donnie's blue-striped shirt while he ran in place, arms stretched toward the Dairy Queen.

THE GEORGIA FOLK and Country Musicians Museum was located in a former Woolworth's storefront on Main Street. The name was written in a big neon script and behind the plate-glass windows stood a huddle of dusty mannequins, the men in sequin-studded suits and the women in faded miniskirts, each one holding a cardboard guitar.

The street was nearly empty, one white Honda in the lot on the side and a Winnebago parked out front. Jodi pulled up behind the Winnebago and turned off the car. She'd stalled the engine twice before even leaving the Dairy Queen lot, her hands shaking on the steering wheel and her mouth dry with fear, but by the time she'd reached downtown she remembered that she liked driving. She listened closely to the cooling engine, closed her eyes, and tried to picture Ricky's face: the hope in those blue eyes. She counted to three and pushed herself up and out into the fuzzy heat.

The air inside the museum was slightly cooler but too still; the cavernous room was lit by banks of trembling fluorescent bulbs and partitioned off with beige wall dividers. In the quiet Jodi began to make out the jump-rope tones of a tour guide's voice from the back of the room.

". . . have reached the Lee Golden display, the largest and most central display in the Georgia Folk and Country Musicians Museum, not only because Delray can claim the fame of being Golden's hometown but also because Lee Golden is an ideal conclusion to your Georgia Folk and Country experience, as his musical style truly blends a bit of all the styles we saw in the other displays, from mountain music to country and even rock."

Jodi followed the voice toward the back, peeking into the sectioned-off areas she passed. Each one was set up as a diorama with name plaques, mannequins, and photographs. She passed an exhibit with ancient gray pictures of Fiddlin' John Carson and a wooden table full of old whiskey bottles; a hawk-eyed man called Gid Tanner; a short-skirted, big-haired Brenda Lee mannequin; a huge photo of a handsome curly-haired Jerry Reed with a shiny red guitar and a woman named Hedy West playing clawhammer banjo at the Newport Folk Festival; Gram Parsons in a bedazzled suit; and then a snapshot of the Allman Brothers.

". . . raised here in Delray by his maternal grandparents while his young mother pursued a career in Hollywood. Golden's vocal talents were recognized early on by the minister at the Baptist church his family attended."

Jodi followed the voice back into the Golden section: a display showing a modest living room with an orange shag rug, a green velour couch and gold-framed oval photos of a blond-haired family, and then a chapel complete with a choir of mannequin singers.

In the tenth display room, she caught up with the group. A tall, broad-shouldered man with an unkempt shock of black hair stood before a graying couple in matching blue visors and sweatshirts. The room was equipped with what seemed to be a six-foot-tall dollhouse—a replica of a totally white turreted and many-windowed building, the wall behind it painted with palm trees, and a sign affixed to the roof that read SCIENTOLOGY.

"December of 1978, thirteen-year-old Lee Golden met Tamara Monti of the Monti Singers at the Celebrity Centre International in Los Angeles,

California. Monti, who liked Lee's abilities in the area of oral sex, invited Lee to accompany her on a worldwide tour as her backup singer and harmonizer."

Jodi stopped in the doorway, hand to her mouth, unsure if she had really heard those words—*oral sex*—blended in so nonchalantly with the rest of the pitch. But Ricky—for it *was* Ricky, a big life-size, grown-up version of Ricky—kept right on rattling names and dates like he hadn't said anything unusual at all.

". . . broke off from Monti when he was eighteen and started making his own records. Folks called him the new Gram Parsons."

"July the eleventh of 1986 he was married to Chelsea Jean Miller, in Los Angeles, California."

Jodi ducked behind a partition when the group exited the LA part of the exhibit, then trailed after as Ricky described the breakup of the original band and Lee's marriage to Miranda Matheson. There was a Tamara Monti–Lee Golden Reunion Tour poster with the names of various European cities and an image of Lee and Tamara on stage with a girl in a minidress who looked very much like a young Miranda. Then there was a framed cover of *Star* magazine featuring an exhausted-looking Miranda with one baby on her hip and the two others clustered at her feet. *Family life doesn't settle well with the Golden Boy*, the caption read. Then a photo of Lee at the Grand Ole Opry, another photo of him on a bucking bull, and a display of the Gemini dressed as cowboys pointing pistols at one another.

Ricky's voice faded in and out of the displays up ahead, weaving away from Jodi. She stared down at the splotched brown carpet, feeling heavy with some sort of dread. She wasn't sure exactly how she had thought this whole thing would go but certainly not like this, with him giving tours in some strange, musty museum and looking like an insurance salesman or a Jehovah's Witness, buttoned-up shirt tucked into wrinkled khaki slacks and talking about oral sex. This most important moment, this glorious instant of triumph that Jodi had played over and over again in her head was, she now realized, fairly dependent on the image of that little blue-eyed boy's joy at her return.

This was all moving a little too fast. She just needed some air, she thought, keeping her eyes on the floor as she walked out the front door, where she was hit with a climbing wave of noise and heat.

At the edge of the parking lot the yellow-and-black boxcars of a passing freight train flashed through a stand of maples and the rhythm rocked under her feet. She lit a cigarette and leaned against the Chevette. She'd played out this moment in her brain so many times now that the little mind movie she'd made of it seemed more real than this present moment. This present moment in which she'd come here with stolen kids, a probably stolen car too, a car that she couldn't even really drive, and now she was, what, going to swoop up Ricky and carry him off?

She'd never really known how to understand Ricky. *Simple*, that's how Paula had always explained him, and when Jodi had asked more she'd said that Dylan and Anna had taken him out of school because they claimed he couldn't keep up well and his temper flared. Seeing him now, though, it occurred to Jodi that he seemed no different from any other undereducated small-town country man.

He was still living there, though, in that stinking house with Dylan—a prison worse in some ways than Jaxton had been.

Jodi pinched her cigarette between her teeth. *I like the way you do things*, Miranda had said. *You show up in town with nothing but conviction and an old address.* She took a last drag and dropped her cigarette to the concrete. If it was too late for Ricky, then it was too late for her, and it couldn't be too late for her. She looked up as the sweatshirt couple walked out of the museum and toward their Winnebago.

From the far end of town the train engine sounded out one long note as it turned the corner, picking up speed. Jodi pushed herself off the Chevette and toward those plate-glass doors.

"Ricky," she called. "Ricky Dulett."

He stood in the front window among the mannequins and as she came in he turned slowly, his hunched shoulders and black hair silhouetted against the soft afternoon light.

"Ricky, do you remember—"

He held up his palm to stop her.

"Jodi," he said.

Her throat drew in tight and she squeezed her eyes shut for a moment to keep back the tears.

He stepped down off the lip of the display window and walked toward her and there he was, after so many years: Ricky, three feet away.

"I came back for you," Jodi said.

The air in the room sounded huge, sucking in and out with the rhythms of the air-conditioning units.

"Oh, yeah?" Ricky said.

Jodi nodded and looked away. Out front the Winnebago drove off, scattering slices of light all up and down the walls. Jodi glanced back at Ricky.

"Dylan's got you working up here full-time?"

"Most days, yeah."

"You just give tours?"

Ricky stared at her from under his shaggy bangs. "I get a little tired of saying the same things sometimes. Sometimes I'll throw in something extra."

"Oral sex?"

His mouth twitched into a tiny smile. "Sometimes."

"You're still living with Anna and Dylan, huh?"

He nodded and turned to walk toward the front glass doors, pulling a pack of Winstons out of his shirt pocket. "Mama and Daddy says I can't smoke cigarettes." He looked back at Jodi. "Says I can't be trusted with fire but the angel of the Lord appeared unto him in a flame of fire out of the midst of a bush: and he looked, and, behold—"

"The bush burned with fire and the bush was not consumed," Jodi said.

Ricky smiled fully now.

"I went out to the house," Jodi said, following him through the double doors. "Went out looking for you yesterday."

Ricky glanced at her, then down at his cigarette. "Can't hardly breathe in that house," he said. "Too many cats. Daddy says breeding those special cats'll bring in the money. The cats breed but there ain't no money."

Jodi lit her own cigarette and dragged deeply. "Remember how Paula and I said we'd come back? Said we'd get you out of that house?"

Ricky did not look at her.

"My family's got land in West Virginia, we can go there. I'm driving up there tonight."

Ricky held his cigarette out at arm's length, then brought it back to his mouth. "I can't go nowhere."

"Sure you can," Jodi said.

Ricky inhaled and blew smoke out his nose as he stared off across the parking lot. The air outside was hot but moving now with a wind that stacked the clouds up thick across the horizon.

"You like working here?" Jodi asked.

"I get paid." Ricky brought his digital watch up close to his eyes. "First Friday."

"You mean Dylan gets paid."

"He'll cash the check, yeah, and I'll buy a new CD."

"He's got you working full-time and he gives you enough money to buy one CD?"

Ricky pointed to the Chevette. "That your car?"

"A friend's," Jodi said, unsure whether to mention Miranda and the boys and the fact that they would be in West Virginia too. It seemed to her that Lee didn't think so highly of Miranda anymore and she couldn't tell if Ricky would see her connection to Miranda as a good or bad thing.

"How fast'll it go?"

"As fast as I need it to, I guess." Jodi shrugged. "You wanna try it?"

Ricky froze, cigarette halfway to his mouth. "I can't drive."

"Don't matter," Jodi said. "I'll teach you."

It began to rain nearly as soon as they'd gotten in the car, big pearls of water that snaked down the dusty glass. In the empty parking lot Jodi pressed her fingers into the back of Ricky's hand and guided the stick shift as they drove in circles. "Up into first, now wait—you'll feel when it's ready for second."

After a while Ricky got the hang of it enough and Jodi could sit back and watch fat raindrops drip down the windowpanes and the red neon of the

museum sign glow with a smeary light. On the second floor of an apartment
building across the alley, a door opened and two little girls scampered out
onto the balcony. They stood under the eaves and played a singsong hand-
slapping game, their little voices barely audible over the Chevette's engine.

Miss Mary Mack-Mack-Mack
All dressed in black-black-black

Jodi glanced over at Ricky with his stubbly chin and bent shoulders,
hunched over the steering wheel, his hairy hand cupping the gearshift.
Looking at him for too long gave her a cool, disquieting shiver of a feeling.
She could not square this large, quiet man with the ten-year-old she had met,
who was all shining eyes and pure voice. She thought of her own younger
self—that wild, sad young woman with her giant hopes of healing all their
lives. This Ricky here, in all his grown-up strangeness, was physical evidence
of the gap between the plan then and the plan now. But he was also the only
remnant of a life map that Jodi had left. If she could not convince him to
leave, she would be failing them all—her own younger self, Paula, and that
ten-year-old boy with his pet crow—and then it would be true, that thing he
must have thought all these years: that she was not coming back, that he was
not worth saving.

"How about when you go to Dylan and Anna's place tonight . . ." Jodi
tried to keep her voice level as a nervous blood rhythm drummed inside her.
"How about you get whatever it is you want to keep out of that cat-piss house.
I'll stay in a motel here and you think about it. Whatever you want for a new
life, bring it here with you in the morning."

Ricky pressed his foot on the brake and slowly looked over at Jodi but his
expression was too complicated to read clearly.

"Dylan comes for me at six," he said. "I oughta get going before he shows
up." He nodded good-bye and stepped out into the wet parking lot.

Jodi couldn't resist the possibility of seeing Dylan. It felt like both the
worst idea and also perfect somehow and so she stayed there, motor running
and radio on low, in the back of the parking lot. The rain picked up. She

could barely see anything through the flashing windshield wipers but a few minutes after six a car pulled in and she rolled down her window to see the Skylark, old now with rust along the front bumper, and behind the glass, a pale face distorted by the rain. Her stomach flew up and the tattered beast uncurled inside her. As she gripped the steering wheel Ricky ran out the front doors of the museum, hunkered against the slanting storm, and disappeared inside the car.

WITH ITS STAINED carpet and dripping sink, the Belmont Motel wasn't the most uplifting place to bring Miranda's little family together but the boys occupied themselves immediately, Ross studying the phone book, Donnie sliding headfirst off the bed, and Kaleb watching a TV show about water moccasins.

Jodi headed across the street for a six-pack and bottle of bourbon and when she came back into the room she was stunned by their ease and familiarity.

Miranda lay on the bed, smoking a cigarette.

"Do you want a drink of Coke?" She held a pop bottle out toward Donnie, who slithered across the carpet, arms tight against his sides, legs stuck together, pumping the air.

"I'm a guppy," he said. "I'm a guppy, gup-peeee!"

"You must be thirsty, flailing all around like that," Miranda said as he flopped his way up onto the bed and snuggled beside her, nuzzling the pop bottle. She set her cigarette in the ashtray and ran her hand through his hair.

Jodi smiled, warm and buzzing before she'd even had one drink. They were not yet on the road and time was running out—if she didn't make it up to West Virginia for her parole meeting the day after tomorrow, she would be in violation—but, finally, everything seemed to be almost coming together and her anxiety was offset by the joyful disarray of Miranda's family. There was something unspoken, she thought, a kind of proprietary confidence and ease that parents and children seemed to carry with them. The way these four people could make this room home in a matter of minutes, claiming the space and settling in, so self-contained that the world outside seemed unnecessary.

She'd seen it with her own family, first between her parents and then between her parents and the twins. An inwardness that changed the space around them so that the corner of a restaurant, the sidewalk, or the park was suddenly unquestionably theirs. Somehow Jodi had never been on the inside, though. The link between her parents was so tight they could hardly fit anyone else, but A.J. and Dennis, with their own special birth bond, made space for themselves while Jodi was always outside, circling.

"Gup-peeee!" Donnie heaved himself off the mattress again and thumped his way around the perimeter of the room, following the baseboard.

Jodi poured generous shots into two Styrofoam cups and carried one to Miranda.

"You really think they won't find us here?" Miranda said, leaning close to Jodi.

"We haven't done anything wrong. You're just visiting your children and you've still got custody, right?"

Miranda nodded.

Jodi settled on the bed beside Kaleb, who watched intently as the TV screen blurred with baby snakes.

"You know the only reason he hasn't already taken them somewhere far away is because of his mom," Miranda whispered in a stiff but not-quiet-enough voice. "He won't go without her and she won't leave the country."

The female water moccasin will give live birth, the host on the TV announced, *sometimes having as many as twenty young moccasins in late summer or early autumn.*

"It's like every minute of his sleeping and waking life she's got his balls cupped right there in her hand. You know how hard it is to respect somebody like that?"

Donnie had completed his circle around the room and managed to squirm his way back up onto the bed. He lay down beside Miranda and butted the bottle of Cherry Coke with his nose.

"Use your hands, sweetie," Miranda said.

He grabbed the bottle with his mouth and, gripping the neck in his teeth, shook his head back and forth viciously.

"Use your—"

"He can't," Kaleb said.

Miranda glanced back and forth between her sons.

"He's a guppy," Kaleb explained. "He don't have hands."

Jodi saw the lick of satisfaction in his eye as he said it, the joy of correcting his mother.

Donnie reared up, bottle still in his mouth, delirious with his brother's recognition. He leaned back and ricocheted off the headboard and toward the nightstand. There was the smack of contact and then a long silence before the scream.

He curled on the floor, his face blank white except for the curtain of red all across his chin and neck. The pop bottle, wet with saliva, lay beside his head.

"Oh, shit," Miranda said.

Jodi bent and helped Miranda gather him up and carry him to the bathtub, his screams blasting so loud now they blotted out all other sound.

"Oh, shit," Miranda cried again, turning on the faucet. "Oh, God."

Donnie flailed, choking on snot and blood.

The cut was deep. Small but deep and pulsing.

"Let's get him down to the car," Jodi said.

Miranda thrashed her head back and forth. "I can't take him to the hospital," she said, her own tears distorting her voice.

"What do you mean?" Jodi leaned over the tub as Miranda held Donnie's face under the faucet. He bucked and squealed, his screams building up and then bursting out in wet gasps.

"Uh-oh." From the other room Kaleb's voice rose over the TV. "Let's call Neenee."

Miranda wiped the blood away and pressed the edges of the cut together. It looked to be a little longer than half an inch and the edges met just fine but blood rushed up to part them almost instantly.

"Talk to me," Jodi said. "Are you lying about having custody?"

Miranda inhaled. "No, but this won't look good," she said, and the fact hung there, loud and indisputable in the too-warm air.

Jodi stepped back and watched mother and child wrestle at the edge of the bathtub. As the bright blood built and pooled down across Donnie's jaw, dripping off his tiny ears, she remembered her father's calloused hands, one palm pressed against her baby brother's chest, pinning him to the kitchen table, and the other hand working carefully, stitching closed his busted lip. *People waste a lot of money paying doctors to do this,* he had explained to six-year-old Jodi, *but as long as the cut ain't too big, all you really need is a steady hand and a clean needle.*

"Hey, just hang on a minute," Jodi said as she turned away from the frantic scene. "I'll be right back."

When she reached the front office it was empty. Just a glass room, fogged from the rain and smelling of cigarettes and chlorine.

"Hello?" Jodi yelled.

Her voice echoed and mixed in with the drip of water from the drainpipes.

"Shit, fuck," she said, turning away just as a face appeared in the doorway behind the desk, a pretty brown face framed by long black hair.

"Oh, Jesus, thank God, I need a first-aid kit." Jodi leaned across the counter.

The girl set a stack of towels on her cleaning cart and stepped toward the desk, then drew back, eyes big. Jodi looked down at her own hands and saw the bright trail of blood there, smudged from her fingers onto the countertop.

"Oh, shit, sorry." She wiped her hand across her pants. "It's no big deal really, just a small cut."

"Nine one one?" The girl said, her words heavily accented.

"No." Jodi's voice came out fast and breathless. "Uh, no, we just need a first-aid kit or whatever you've got, really. A sterilized needle would be great but a butterfly bandage would help."

The girl shook her head. "No," she said, "no English."

"Oh . . ." Jodi closed her eyes for a moment and concentrated. *"Ayuda."* The first word came easy but the rest tumbled just out of reach at the back of her brain. *"Ayuda. . . . Necesito . . . ayuda."*

The girl's mouth opened just a little and she blinked and then nodded. *"Sí."* She moved quickly toward the desk and grabbed the phone from its cradle. *"¿Quiere que llame una ambulancia? ¿Y policía, señora?"*

"No, no." Jodi stumbled and reached across the counter as if to snatch the phone from the girl's hands. "*Telefono no. No*," she repeated helplessly. "I just need, oh, shit, I need . . . *¿una venda?*"

The girl continued to hold the phone even after she understood that what Jodi wanted was a first-aid kit. She retrieved the white box from a shelf, snapped it open, and pushed it across the counter. Jodi glanced at the plastic-wrapped packages, nodded, and then looked at the phone in the girl's hand.

"*No telefono*," she said again, hoping she sounded firm and not pleading.

Back in the room she found Miranda on the floor, cradling Donnie between her legs and holding a washrag of ice against his chin.

"Blue jean, baby queen," she sang.

Jodi spread the contents of the first-aid kit across the dresser. Everything inside was yellowed with age but apparently untouched, the needle still sealed in its plastic pouch. She thanked whatever there was out there to thank, the universe, she guessed, and poured out three bourbon shots. One she drank, another she passed to Miranda, and the third she mixed, three parts whiskey to one part flat Coke, and poured down Donnie's throat. He twisted and bucked and tried to spit it out but Miranda pressed his mouth shut.

"It's just juice," she cooed. "Good juice."

They laid him across the floral bedspread.

"Just two stitches," Jodi said. "Just keep his arms and legs down while I get in two stitches."

She gripped his small jaw with one hand and tried hard not to look into those wild green eyes. A steady hand and a clean needle, she thought. She wanted desperately to be the kind of person who could handle a situation like this but her heart was jumping erratically and her hand was not feeling particularly steady. She took a deep breath and wiped the wound with a sanitized towelette.

The needle met the skin and slid through with an ease that turned her stomach and Donnie screamed. Our bodies, Jodi thought, doubling back and stitching once more for good measure, oughtn't be so pliable like that. From the inside the edges of your own skin seemed so firm and sealed but that's all it took, a little pressure, and you were open to the world.

She snipped the string and stepped back. "Done," she pronounced, staring at the dark thread that marked the little chin.

The moment they let him go, Donnie's hands flew to his face and Miranda scrambled. "No, no, no, don't touch it," she said, bending close. "Put your hands down here, sweetie. Remember, you're a seal!"

He tossed his head back and forth. "Nuh-no-o," he choked out. "I . . . I . . ."

"He's a guppy," Kaleb reminded them.

MIRANDA SETTLED DONNIE and Ross in one bed with her, and Kaleb in the other with Jodi. Watching her set up the sleeping arrangements, Jodi thought of Miranda's tears and insistent kisses and the expanse of her naked body in that motel room in Chaunceloraine. She wondered just how drunk Miranda had been that night and how much she could even remember. Last night they had slept and cuddled in the bed together and the night before that—Jodi swore, although maybe she'd just dreamt it, but no—she *had* woken up naked, she knew that for sure, and now she felt a stinging shock at the thought that Miranda, in all her lush beauty, could ever have wanted to be with her.

She lay in the dark and concentrated on the soft breath of the boys and told herself it didn't matter, she didn't need anyone like that right now; but half an hour later when Miranda tiptoed over and carried Kaleb around to sleep with his brothers, Jodi's pulse tripled. Miranda slid into the warm place where Kaleb had lain and drew close, fingers cupping Jodi's hip, and Jodi tried to quiet her heart, careful not to lean too far into Miranda's embrace and careful not to stay too stiff.

"I'm scared," Miranda whispered.

The heat of her hand pulsed like a bull's eye on Jodi's hip.

"Donnie'll be fine."

"No, it's not that. I feel . . . I don't know if I can stay off the pills and take proper care of my boys. I don't know, I . . ."

"Of course you can," Jodi said. It felt good to comfort someone else; she could muster a certainty about Miranda's future that she could not claim for her own yet.

Miranda nuzzled her chin against the back of Jodi's neck and they listened to the rain dripping on the metal railing outside.

"You know," Miranda whispered, "when I was little I thought the universe had an order that was waiting for me. I thought there was a space, a me-shaped space, and when I found it I'd know it. Like when a key fits into a lock, I'd click into place and move through into a new future. There were hundreds of millions of spaces, I thought, holes in the universe, and you had to find the one that was right."

Jodi let her body relax into Miranda's embrace, and her eyes moved over the lumpy shadows of the room, the bedside table, the alarm clock leaking cherry red up toward the ceiling and there, where the curtains were parted, the liquid light of reflected puddles dappling the fabric.

"After school I used to go on these walks," Miranda said. "We lived in this subdivision, one of those with the houses with fake shutters glued up beside all the windows, and they were always building new homes. But down at the end of my road everything turned into fields, just big, blank, muddy fields. And I used to walk. I'd go to the dead end and find a leaf or grass. I'd hold it up and let the wind take it, and whatever direction it blew, that's where I'd go. I knew if I kept walking long enough, eventually I'd feel it. Something would click and I'd fit."

Jodi let Miranda's words roll over and around her, and there, in that dark anonymous room, she knew that what Miranda said was true of her too. *I'd fit*, she thought, and pictured the land in West Virginia, the smell of wheat in the field and sunlight scissoring through the trees, the way the rhythms of the days and even the air around her had always felt right there.

August 1988

Paula drives the car up into the yard and Jodi is silent, too hot to talk. The whole world is trapped inside a fever haze, the air thick and drowsy. The cabin, only five months empty, is already a husk. And so small, Jodi thinks. It seems impossible that those three rooms once held her father, mother, two brothers, Effie, and herself.

She climbs the stairs, the tin roof popping overhead. There is no lock. A stack of plates sits on the drain board, pile of cookstove wood in a basket by the door, can of coffee on the shelf, and there, in the center of the table, a wren's nest woven from horsehair, dry grass, and a single blue ribbon.

Under Effie's bed she finds the .38. She hadn't thought to take it with her before, but then, she'd hardly thought to take anything. It had all happened so quickly, first the stroke that twisted Effie's legs, leaving her limp and depressed in a wheelchair, and then the second stroke that stole her voice. Jodi had argued that she could care for her, that Effie would rather die than leave her land, but Jodi's father and uncle had signed the papers and moved her off to the county home, and only three days later a nurse's aide had found her slumped in her wheelchair, wrists slit.

The pistol needs oiling but it feels good in Jodi's hand, smooth and compact with a certain magnetic kind of weight. She carries it into the back bedroom where Paula is napping on the dusty mattress.

"What you got there?" Paula turns and blinks.

"Effie's .38," Jodi says, spilling the gun and bullets onto the bed.

Paula sits up quick and scoots back to the edge of the mattress.

"What?" Jodi laughs.

"Why are you bringing that gun in here?"

Jodi tries to tamp down her smile but her lips twist. "You're scared?"

Paula shrugs and narrows her eyes.

"Come on," Jodi says, "you're really telling me you never shot a pistol?"

BACK BEHIND THE cabin there is a dump pile, generations' worth of glass jars. Jodi and Paula select the prettiest, the old teardrop perfume bottles and liquor pints printed with pheasants. They carry them out to the cemetery, where they arrange them across the tops of the family stones.

"It's all about keeping your mind with your body," Jodi says.

"What if I hit the stone and the bullet bounces back?"

"Well, don't aim that low," Jodi says, delighting in Paula's uncertainty.

The wind hush-hushes all around them.

"Keep your eyes and body connected. You'll feel it."

The first bullet flies high over the gravestones, and Paula looks back at Jodi. The second bullet is no closer and Jodi's hands itch.

"Here," she says, "let me see it for a second." The wooden handle is smooth under her fingers. She narrows herself, breathes out, and the bottle explodes, shiny fragments of blue quivering through the dry grass.

July 2007

B y the time Jodi arrived at the museum, Ricky was digging his
nails into his arms and leaving half-moon marks on his skin
as he paced the front of the room. Jodi glanced about to see
if he'd brought a suitcase or bag with him but she saw nothing.

"Hey," she said, "I got you something," and from her back pocket she
produced a pack of Winstons. "For you." She held them out.

"I can't be trusted," Ricky said, but when he looked up he was smiling.

They stood silently under the awning out front, lighting cigarettes and
staring off across the street. The rain had stopped in the night and the sky
was clearing.

"You ever left this state?" Jodi asked. Ricky glanced at her, then brought
his eyes back to his cigarette. "You know." She leaned toward him. "Paula
always talked about the places she wanted you to see. She said when she got
the money saved she was going to take you to the mountains, and the desert
and the ocean."

Ricky dropped his cigarette and stepped on it. "That's your friend's car?" He gestured toward the Chevette.

Jodi nodded and drew on her cigarette.

"What's your friend's name?"

"Miranda Matheson," she said slowly.

"I met her." Ricky eyed Jodi. "She come in a while back with her boys, said they belonged to Lee Golden. But then she come back again and when I asked after them boys she said he'd taken them away."

Jodi exhaled a blur of smoke. "I helped her find them again," she said, a flicker of pride in her voice.

Ricky reached for another cigarette and nodded his head toward the car again. "There's room for me in there?"

MIRANDA WOKE TO Kaleb softly patting her arm. She stirred and was surprised to see his face, so serious there beside the bed. Jodi was gone. Miranda closed her eyes again.

"It stopped raining," Kaleb said, "and Donnie and Ross are hungry."

For as long as Miranda could remember, Kaleb had separated himself from his brothers. She worried what the future could hold for a skinny boy who always put the needs of others before his own.

"Okay," she said, lying there and watching her boys through half-closed eyes. Sunlight washed in through the front windows and turned the room all soft. Donnie and Ross were jumping on the other bed, their laughter swirling up with murmured words. *Snake-eyed cheese monster—you old blooty-fatooty—naw-uhhh.*

"Hey, be careful," Miranda mumbled. "Don't jump, you already busted your chin."

Kaleb watched his brothers with his arms tucked across his chest. Miranda wanted to touch all of them, Kaleb's bony seriousness, Donnie's rolling giggles, and Ross's silky, still almost baby skin. She was delighted just at the simple joy of being there in a room with them again, like the feeling after recovering from a sickness, that brief time when even the tiniest moments of normal life are treasures. Some of Jodi's sincerity, her earnest straightforwardness, had rubbed off on her, Miranda thought, and anything seemed possible now. She pictured Jodi's freckled face, her slightly gapped teeth and big eyes, and she felt sure that taking the boys to West Virginia was the right idea. She knew almost nothing about Jodi and what little she did know—something about a gun accident and recent prison release—was not perhaps the most heartening but more than anything Miranda needed to believe in fresh starts and any second thoughts she'd had disappeared when Jodi so confidently stitched up Donnie's chin.

These past few months Miranda had been waiting, for what exactly she didn't even know. For Lee to grant her a divorce and give her custody? That, she saw now, would never seriously happen. In the eyes of the law she was not stable enough but what she and the boys needed was just a little time together, time to reconnect. Mother and sons, out in the country, somewhere pretty. Anything was possible. You just had to put your mind to it.

"Hey," she called to her boys, propping herself up on the pillows, "come here and snuggle."

Kaleb held back, sitting on the edge of the other bed, swinging his legs impatiently.

Miranda tucked Ross's head under her chin, breathing in the smell of his soap-scented curls, while Donnie burrowed under the blankets by her feet.

"Hey, Kaleb, honey, come here."

Kaleb's legs swung faster, thud-thudding against the mattress.

"Hey, Kale, baby."

Thud-thud, the swinging pendulums of a sped-up cuckoo clock.

"All right, okay, I see." Miranda rolled off the bed, holding Ross tight to her chest. "We just need a little sound track for this party."

She shifted Ross to her hip and made her way around the bed, past piles of dirty clothes and snack wrappers, over to the clock radio. She sped the dial past BBC News, Bible talk, a rupturing bass-filled rap song, and when it hit on Barbara Lynn's trembling *If you should lose me*, Kaleb called out, "Stop."

The horns lifted under Barbara Lynn's voice. Kaleb had quit thumping his legs and was watching Miranda intently. She walked over and reached a hand out toward him and he took it, staring up at her while she swiveled her hips, Ross's drowsy head bouncing on her shoulder.

When the boys were little babies and cried constantly—Ross, colicky; Donnie, teething—and Lee was gone all the time, Miranda used to get Kaleb to put the radio on and turn it up loud. *It's a party!* she would scream, smothering the baby cries with classic rock and swooping Kaleb up for a dance.

If you should lose me, oh yeah, you'll lose a good thing.

Miranda lifted Kaleb's arm high over his head and he spun in a clumsy circle and she smiled. The sweet self-righteousness of the lyrics mixed up in her mind with Kaleb's unswerving eyes and she felt weak with emotion.

"Donnie and Ross are hungry." Kaleb broke Miranda's gaze and lowered his arm.

Miranda smiled. "Oh," she said, "yeah, let's go get some food."

She set Ross on the bed and sifted through her suitcase, searching for something she hadn't already worn during the past three days.

"How long are we staying here?" Kaleb followed her as she walked to the window. She hated to leave the room. Jodi managed to diffuse some of the tension but outside—alone with just the boys—she felt like an impostor, some shoddy caricature of a parent whose skills came from daytime television. The boys were uncontainable and she knew that everyone could see that she didn't have the upper hand.

"Come on Donnie, Ross, put your shoes on."

She pulled the curtains all the way open. The parking lot was almost empty. No white Mercedes. Lee only ever drove white cars. It was the first thing Miranda remembered noticing about him, that long white car with gold rims parked at the end of her father's driveway.

She'd met him when she was sixteen and her father had been in the midst of his training plans for her. He had homeschooled her all through her childhood and as she grew older his techniques had become more elaborate—oil painting lessons, violin, and of course, piano. He held on strong to some strange, dated image of his daughter's future as an eligible southern lady. What exactly her adult life was supposed to hold in store for her was never very clear but he had used any and every tactic to cultivate her toward it, including enlisting the help of one of his dental patients, Lee Golden, who took one look at Miranda and agreed to give her lessons whenever he wasn't away on tour. The piano lessons had not interested teenage Miranda half as much as Lee's stories of LA and Paris. His every word and move seemed to her to carry with them a delicious foreignness and she was pregnant before six months had passed.

JODI PULLED THE Chevette into the Belmont Motel parking lot, looked over at Ricky in the seat beside her, and then kept driving toward the far end of the lot where Miranda, Kaleb, and Ross stood, staring up at a tall chain-link fence.

"That's a little boy up there," Ricky said.

At the top of the fence, behind a green Dumpster, Donnie clung, his hands gripping tight to the metal.

Jodi opened the car door and climbed out. The trees all along the edge of the lot were neon green, their leaves wet and quivering in the slight breeze.

"Sweetie, can you climb back down?" Miranda cried.

"Ouch," Donnie said. His fingers were turning white.

"Miranda?" Jodi walked closer, eyeing the nearly ten-foot distance between Donnie's dangling feet and the concrete below. "What's going on?"

"Oh, God," Miranda said. Her hands shook. She dropped her cigarette. "I let him out of my sight for one second." She fumbled in her pocket and pulled out a fresh cigarette. "I told Kaleb to watch him."

"Mom?" Donnie cried, and his chin trembled, the line of stitches looking monstrous there. "Maw-um?"

"Can you reach your arms down?" Jodi called to him. "Like you did to get up there but backward."

She could not stop staring at the stitches on his tiny chin. That, she thought, would have been the moment to turn things around, take him to the hospital and straighten everything out, but no, she'd decided she wanted to try to be some kind of rugged hero and now she was implicated.

She looked over at Ross's tiny body and Kaleb's worried face. It was all coming on so fast and at this pace the decisions seemed to have already been made. There was so much about life outside of prison that she had forgotten or maybe never really known.

"We need to help that boy down," Ricky said, and Jodi turned toward him as he moved past, squeezing in behind the Dumpster and reaching up to grasp Donnie's legs.

Donnie squirmed and pumped both arms high. "Iron Man and Captain America take on the Trash!"

THEY DROVE EAST, Miranda navigating in the front seat, a map spread across her lap, and Ricky squished in the back with the boys.

"Mom, there's not enough *seats*," Kaleb said for the tenth time.

"Wait, wait, that was our turn," Miranda yelled. "Yeah, turn around, we need 82 East."

"There's only *three* seats."

Jodi slammed on the brakes and swung the car around, turning up the radio.

We're all about big, a woman's voice trembled through the speakers. *Big savings and big readings. We want you to save big with Miss Lia of the Magic Hand and her ninety-nine-cent psychic palm readings!*

They passed dirt roads with crumpled mailboxes, defunct gas stations, and vegetable stands with signs announcing tomatoes, cantaloupes, and peaches. When Miranda fell asleep, cigarette smoldering in her right hand, Jodi took the smoke and rested it between her own lips. She drove the same route they'd taken just two days before but it all looked different now, more hopeful. Rain washed and green, towns with names like Enigma, Alapaha, Axson, and Reaching Branch.

"No, four hundred and thirty-six," Ross mumbled.

Miranda stirred and blinked awake, the impression from the doorframe pressed into her face.

"Mom?" Kaleb said. "When are we gonna go back to Neenee's?"

Miranda rubbed her eyes.

"I want a story," Donnie said. "When Neenee drives us she tells stories."

"Fuck Neenee," Miranda said.

In the rearview mirror Jodi watched Kaleb's lip tremble. "You should tell us a story," he said to Ricky, who sat rigid beside him, one hand on each knee.

"I don't think I know any stories." Ricky stared at the windshield, his black hair curling down over his left eye.

"But you've got books and papers." Kaleb pointed to the folder resting on the floorboard between Ricky's feet.

"I don't know," Ricky said, but Kaleb had already grabbed it and started pulling out bits of newspaper.

"Atlanta," he read. "All five members of the Rounder family of 1609 Daylily Drive passed away last night in their sleep. A natural gas leak and lack of vent-ee-lat-shun are to blame."

"What?" Miranda sat up taller in her seat.

"Bright Beach, Georgia." Kaleb gripped a new clipping. "The Hunt family from Turner, Georgia, were vay-cat-shun-ing in Bright Beach when a traffic axed-id-dent cost them their lives. The Hunts pulled to the side of Route 2 to consult a map when an eighteen-wheel semitruck carrying a shipment of oranges coll-ee-ded with the family car."

"What is that?" Miranda turned around in her seat and grabbed the folder, little pieces of paper sifting out.

Jodi glanced back at Ricky. He looked away.

"Mom!" Kaleb squealed.

"Look at this." Miranda lifted handfuls of papers out. "Whoa, look, it's all clippings about dead families. Oh, this is so sad."

Jodi kept her eyes on the road.

"Except this one. Look at this one."

She held up a ripped page with a photograph showing a giant pig laid out in clean straw and suckling at her tits, one orange-and-white fox kit, one brown-and-black puppy, and three pink piglets. The caption read *1984 Guinness Book of World Records: The world's strangest family.*

"Those"—Ricky's face rose up behind Miranda's head, his eyes flat and distant—"are my personal things."

"Mom, Mom, Maw-awm." Donnie vaulted his voice high over the others.

Miranda turned so that Donnie could see the pig picture and in one quick motion Ricky lunged over the seat and grabbed the photo and then the whole folder. "I said, my *personal* things." His voice boomed louder than Jodi had imagined possible.

You ain't here, Paula, you don't see how he blows.

Jodi gripped the steering wheel.

"Mom?" Kaleb moaned.

"Be quiet now," Ricky said. "You'll like this story better anyway."

He put the folder back down between his feet and opening his Bible he bent his face close and read, "The Philistines stood on a mountain on the one side, and Israel stood on a mountain on the other side: and there was a valley between them. And there went out a champion out of the camp of the Philistines, named Goliath, of Gath, whose height was six cubits and a span. And he had a helmet of brass upon his head, and he was armed with a coat of mail; and the weight of the coat was five thousand shekels of brass."

"What's shickles-a-brass?" Donnie leaned past Kaleb to look at Ricky's book.

"Quiet," Ricky said, moving his finger along the thin page. "And he had greaves of brass upon his legs, and a target of brass between his shoulders. And the staff of his spear was like a weaver's beam; and his spear's head weighed six hundred shekels of iron and—"

"What's shickles-a-aaron?"

THEY JOINED I-95 North at Brunswick and the Chevette's engine strained as Jodi urged it up the entrance ramp. The highway shuddered in front of them, semi after semi, the whole flow of it, moving impossibly fast. She pressed the gas deeper, her heart slamming as she pushed in to merge, but the stream of traffic did not break and she was forced off the road, drifting to a stop on the side of the highway. The trucks buffeted by in booming flaps of wind.

The story in the backseat had stopped.

"I haven't driven on the highway in a long time," Jodi said, looking off at the frantic traffic.

"Let me do it." Miranda opened the passenger's door and stepped out.

She drove them up to I-26 and then I-77, through the Carolinas, past Columbia, and on toward Charlotte. They stopped for dinner at a Bojangles' and then again for ice cream. At eight fifteen the sun set all orange red through a forest of tall pines, their thin branches outlined like claws against the bright sky. The boys fell asleep, all except Kaleb, who sat with his brothers' heads in his lap and stared straight ahead, eyes wide and white in the dark night.

In Statesville Jodi drove again and let Miranda rest. Miranda had wanted to find a motel where they could stay but Jodi said she'd drive on through the night, not wanting to mention her dwindling money and mandatory parole meeting.

Even before they hit Virginia the mountains began, a soft rising at the edges of the sky. The car was all quiet, save for the ripple of sleep breathing. Up ahead the lights of the semitrucks climbed, as if ascending into the night sky, the road wreathing the ridges gradually.

After Wytheville the highway narrowed and dipped into the Big Walker Mountain Tunnel. The squat block face of it was like some huge institutional building and then the tunnel itself was so suffocatingly narrow, with streaks of overhead light slashing across the windshield and those concrete walls mocking Jodi's memories of Jaxton's endless yellow halls.

On the far side the view was nothing but ridgelines, the craggy silhouettes rising up against the night sky like the body of some dormant god. Jodi felt her breath go tight in her chest. This road went only one way, it seemed, in under the mountains until you were circled, the broad backs of the Appalachians blocking out everything. As much as she had desired to return here this place was itself a prison of sorts and she could feel herself dissolving into it. Coming home was like disappearing in a way, she thought, slipping back into the past. Until a week and a half ago she had thought she would not return here until death—a body shipped to a family that barely remembered it, a body to be laid back into the mountains to rest—but now here she was, not just a body but a jumble of wild thoughts and emotions, coming home. She glanced at Miranda in the seat beside her and Ricky's sleeping face. She told herself this was different, this was new, but still she could feel the weight of those mountains, even unseen, the heaviness of all that familiarity.

September 1988

Paula pushes the Cutlass up to ninety, ninety-five, one hundred, and the air gusting in the window chills Jodi's arms. The sun is strong but the day has changed in that special September kind of way; they went to sleep in summertime and woke this morning to a cut of cold breeze.

WELCOME TO VIRGINIA whirs by in a burst of bright sunlight. Jodi turns in her seat and squints back after it.

"What you thinking?" Paula asks.

Jodi watches the sign grow small. The land looks all the same on this side of the border, ditches of thistle and milkweed, mountains spotted with yellowing birch trees, huddles of wood houses, and a coal tipple there on the far bank.

"You're in a whole new state now," Paula says, smiling.

Jodi likes the smile on Paula's face, the way she seems to take pride in each of Jodi's new experiences. Already Jodi can see the two of them, years down the line, Paula's hair gone gray and both of them talking and looking back on the speed and beauty of this day.

THE FIRST PALM tree comes just after the South Carolina sign, and Jodi makes Paula pull over in the McDonald's parking lot. She climbs from the car, her legs wobbling. In southern Virginia the mountains had disappeared but it only looked like an absence and not something truly new. Jodi presses her hands against the scaly skin of the palm tree, listening to the wind in the reedy branches until Paula hollers and lays on the horn.

They eat drive-through food and keep on moving, the burger papers drifting around between them and blowing into the backseat. Farther south the day warms and Jodi props her feet in the window, feeling the wind run up her legs and under her skirt.

Randy Owen belts out "Song of the South" on the radio. *There ain't nobody looking back again.*

There are peach orchards in Georgia, advertised on giant orange-and-yellow signs. But Paula says they shouldn't stop, wrong season. She says they can't stop in Salamanca Springs for the snakeskin belts or palm-frond baskets. They've got to keep going because they're headed to a place with luck in its name.

"Bee-luck-see?" Jodi pronounces, tapping her feet against the air vents.

Paula sucks on her cigarette. "*X*, it's spelled with an *x*."

Jodi thinks she might climb in the backseat and sleep but Paula says she needs the company and something loosens up inside Jodi at the thought of Paula needing her there. She doesn't really understand it—the giddy lifting in her body—and it seems a little fragile, one of those things best left unexamined. She is happier than she ever remembers being. Happy just to be here in the car with someone who wants her beside them. The kind of someone who wakes up in the morning and says *let's go to Mississippi* and then puts her hand on the wheel and does it.

"Here," Paula says, "take these." In her outstretched palm she holds two salmon-colored capsules.

Jodi lets them lie on her tongue too long and the pills open up. Their bitter shock covers the inside of her lips. Paula stops for gas and Jodi goes to pee. When she gets back in the car someone has turned the volume up on the whole world. The windshield is a movie screen all lit from behind and she doesn't ever want them to stop driving; the rhythm of the wheels matches the patterns in her brain and suddenly she knows that what her life has been lacking is motion. She looks over at Paula's sharp face and the beauty of it hits her like a fist; she's only known her for one week but already she sees that she won't ever be able to let Paula go, already she has become the prism through which Jodi wants to experience everything. Before Paula, even the wildest decisions she made—like fucking the new chemistry teacher—felt utterly predictable and somehow without consequences. With Paula, though, each moment takes on a texture of delicious unfamiliar risk. With Paula each moment itself feels roomier, as if the two of them are moving about together inside each second, generating possibilities.

They drive into a sunset that lasts for over an hour. Smears of pink and gobs of red turning down to purple. When the dark stumbles in, the mile markers tick by, perfectly spaced in the tunnel of headlights, pulling the future toward her.

They stop finally, in a parking lot, under a shining tower of lights that spells out BAYOU QUEEN. The world is still moving at eighty miles an hour, even here outside. Jodi breathes in the scent of parked cars, old oil and gasoline. It is 3:30 a.m. and black dark. She stretches and walks toward the lights but Paula grabs her hand and pulls her back the opposite way.

"Hey, wait," she says. "I want to see your first-time ocean face."

PAULA STAYS AT the poker tables through the rest of the night and in the morning they keep driving. They drive and talk and they do not stop until the gas gauge hits the orange marker.

"You know that moment," Paula says, "when it really, *really* sinks in and it's so much more than just the planetary models and all that—that moment when you *feel* it, how fucking tiny we all are in comparison to the universe, and your stomach drops right out and so do your lungs."

Jodi does not want to take her eyes off Paula. She is the most capable and crazy person she has ever seen. She drives without watching the road at all. She is demonstrating something, turned sideways in her seat, her arms stretched to show the breadth of a bear or the length of a snake.

In the middle of the night outside of Omaha Jodi looks at Paula and realizes that she will never know the difference between the things that Paula has told her about herself and the things she has dreamt about her, in snatches, in the backseat, at half-lit rest stops and gas stations: how at fourteen she followed a man she saw in Tupelo, Mississippi, a man who won poker games with his eyes only half-open. She shadowed this man for two years until he broke down and taught her, trained her to count cards out on his ranch in Nevada. When they weren't playing poker he took her up in his prop plane, flew her over the desert, and pointed out the silent, hooded mountains that would one day be stuffed full of nuclear waste.

A dry grass wind hits the side of the Cutlass with an ancient rhythm and when Jodi opens her eyes she cannot tell if the sun is setting or rising.

In Dallas she eats a steak so thick it swallows up her whole knife. Out the window, buildings stretch into the smog and she has to keep reminding herself that she is not just watching this on TV.

They drive and talk and Paula's father's name etches its way into their conversations like a poison. She tells how Dylan beat them, how she promised Ricky she'd be back to take him away. *Dylan.* It's a strangely pretty name, Jodi thinks. *Dylan.* She watches Paula's face and wonders how you can possibly protect someone from their own past.

TWO

July 2007

"Miss Jodi." Ricky's voice licked up out of the darkness of the backseat. "I gotta take a leak."

Jodi glanced in the rearview mirror. The boys were piled on top of Ricky, Kaleb's head resting on his shoulder while Donnie and Ross lay stretched across his lap. It was impossible to tell where one brother ended and the other began. *The world's strangest family.*

"Okay," Jodi said. "I'll stop here in just a minute."

The sky was beginning to lighten, a slate-gray fade across the mountain peaks, and the headlights sketched a weak trail through the greenery. Vines and tree branches crowded thick on both banks of the road and half-hidden among the bushes a sign flashed by.

MALONGA COUNTY, WEST VIRGINIA

Render	12 mi
Painter Creek	16 mi
Salt Sulphur Springs	23 mi

The words repeated themselves in a flash of reflective paint, over and over behind Jodi's eyelids as she blinked. *Render 12 mi.* This was it. This here, and there and there. The turnaround where the school bus always stopped and looped back toward Painter Creek, the junkyard there where the Weinshotzer kids lived, all of them wearing knit hats, even in the summer heat, hiding the shame of lice-shaved heads. The little brick house that belonged to that princess, Mallory Estep, the doctor's daughter, her ankle socks adorned with white lace all through elementary school and, in high school, her hair attended to in the back of the bus by no fewer than three handmaids, a cloud of Aqua Net hairspray perpetually frosting the air around them.

Render was still sleeping, just a few bare bulbs glowing above front-porch swings and strings of Christmas lights in the windows. Jodi sped through town, ignoring the Exxon station and Ricky's need, heading instead for Bethlehem Mountain Road, a one-lane track that jutted up between limestone boulders as pale and exposed as sun-bleached bones and then wound on into the green immensity of oak and hickory. But just before the turnoff for Bethlehem a neon sign caught her eye, the yellow letters arched above an arrow pointing downriver. SLATTERY'S GIRL, it read, OPEN 24 HOURS. BEER. MUSIC. BOOZE.

Jodi slowed the car and stared at the sign. Through most of her childhood Malonga County had been dry. It was only in '86 that they began to sell gas station beer and even then there were no bars. If you wanted to drink, you did it at home or on back roads in half-wrecked cars.

The mountain showed other changes too: a new gravel road, cut hastily through the old Jessup apple orchard, spread out across a shale cliff, giving way to a perfect bird's-eye view of the town below. A tower rose there now, a tall metal grid looming over the trees, and as she slowed for the steep turn Jodi caught sight of a huge mud-splattered truck moving like some giant dinosauric creature down the ruts of the new-made road and, on a tree, there beside the entrance, a hand-painted sign: FRACKING = PERMANENT THREAT AND DANGER = OUR WATER IS OUR LIFE!

"Miss Jodi," Ricky called from the backseat. "I can't hold it much longer."

"Shit, sorry." Jodi stopped the car. "You can just piss in the ditch here."

The boys whined as Ricky unearthed himself from under them, and Miranda stirred too, blinking awake. Jodi reached over and brushed away the blonde hair matted against her sweaty cheek. "We're almost there," she said, and then, as Ricky climbed back in, she turned and she smiled at him too and said, "Just call me Jodi, okay? I don't need the 'Miss.'"

EFFIE'S LAND WAS ripe with disuse. The Chevette could barely fit into the mouth of the lane, clogged as it was with multiflora rose and goldenrod.

"We'll walk from here," Jodi said, opening the car door to the smell of honeysuckle and a darker fungus scent.

Up ahead the contours of the road were visible in a ghostly way under the swells of jimsonweed—it was a little like looking back and forth between a much younger photograph of a woman and her now aging face; the bone structure was still there but the surface had all but completely changed.

"Watch out for snakes." Ricky's voice boomed at Jodi's back.

"I wanna see a snake," Donnie said.

Jodi quickened her pace, her head buzzing with worry as she came around the bend. And then there it was: the little off-kilter cabin with the metal roof curling up from the frame. Jodi didn't realize she'd been holding her breath until she let it out and took off running, greenbrier vines snatching at her jeans as she rushed forward, expecting every moment for it to all ghost off into a dream.

Time did not separate here. The past ran parallel and you could catch a glimpse if you turned quickly enough. Nineteen years ago she left the cabin, in the paling light of gray-green storm clouds, receding through the dirt-smudged glass of a rear windshield. For all those years the hologram danced. But now it was real: the porch creaking under her feet, the front door open, and a slice of light pointing across the pine floorboards straight to the cast-iron woodstove. The window above the sink was shattered, triangles of glass still clinging to the frame, and on the back wall a rack of copper pots hung untouched.

Jodi stepped inside, dry leaves and acorns crunching underfoot. She moved slowly toward the kitchen table, that unforgettable oak slab with the heart of the tree running down the center in a single stripe. Three chairs were set on each side, pushed back at an angle, as if a card party had just ended.

She opened the china cabinet and pale moths lifted up from among the cups and flapped blindly against her face. A calendar hung on the wall. December 2002—Jodi's thirteenth year in Jaxton. It featured a blonde girl with boobs bursting out of a camo hunting shirt. This was the only sign that anyone had been inside since Effie died back in '88.

Jodi moved over to the sealed-off fireplace where on the mantel sat a mason jar of tiny bones and fingernails.

These, Effie had explained to ten-year-old Jodi, *are the three important things*. The first was her Smith & Wesson .38 with a smooth wooden handle and LADY SMITH engraved in cursive on the side; the second, a Remington 721; and the third, the mason jar with the remains of Granddaddy McCarty's right hand.

The Ladysmith .38 had been a wedding gift from Granddaddy to his bride and the best thing, Effie said, she ever got out of that marriage. The Remington was an inheritance from the uncle who took Effie in, and the bits of bone and fingernail were the result of Granddaddy's affair with a lady, or two, from town. When Effie had heard about it she'd turned her wedding gift on him and he lost the hand before he got out of their cabin. Their older son, Phillip, went with his father, following the blood trail down the rutted lane, leaving Effie and Andy, Jodi's daddy, with the land to themselves.

"He's telling you to *be careful*." Kaleb's voice carried up the porch steps.

Jodi turned to see Donnie burst into the cabin, carrying a tall stick and jabbing it out in front of himself. The others crowded in the doorway, Ricky eyeing the log walls, Miranda on tiptoe, peering over his shoulder, and Kaleb pressed in behind her.

"It really is like *Little House on the Prairie*," Miranda said.

Jodi laughed and shook her head but she was relieved to see Miranda smiling.

THE TRIP TO Beckley took an hour and Jodi drove it alone, leaving Miranda, Ricky, and the boys at the cabin. Half a block from the South Central Regional Parole Office she realized she didn't quite have a license yet and probably shouldn't be seen driving so she stashed the Chevette in the shade of a white pine and approached the redbrick building on foot, preparing on her face a look of earnest compliance.

Officer Ballard hardly glanced at her, though. He was sleeping at his desk when the young receptionist cleared her throat and called out *Benny* twice before he finally stirred and looked up at Jodi.

"You've got a new supervised release here," the receptionist said, then left quickly.

Benny Ballard's head was too big for his neck and his face was stamped with an expression of deep annoyance. He ran his hand through his graying hair and then turned in his swivel chair and reached for the coffeepot that sat, burning, on a hot plate behind him, filling the office with a dry, bittersweet smell.

"Now I suppose you expect me to shake your little hand and do the whole how-gee-do-gee bit," he said, pouring the dregs of the coffee into a mug that read SARCASM: MY GENEROUS GIFT TO THE UNIVERSE. "But let's cut that crap and see if we can't get this over with and get me out of here a little early today."

Jodi sat down quietly in the folding chair. This wouldn't be hard, she thought. She knew the type. There were the ones who took their jobs too seriously, believing they were personally responsible for helping reform criminals and then there were the ones like this who only counted the hours until they were back home in front of the TV. As long as you gave them the proper respect they ignored you ninety-nine percent of the time.

Ballard set his coffee mug on a stack of papers and pulled out a manila folder. "You must be Jodi McCarty, 611 Murdock Street, Render?"

"Yes, sir."

"All right, then, here we go." He let his eyes slide halfway closed and stared over Jodi's shoulder, rattling off a litany of regulations, fast and breathless, his rote voice reminding Jodi of Ricky's tour guide shtick. "You *shall not* leave the geographic limits fixed by the certificate of release without written permission from your supervision officer. You *shall* make a complete and truthful written report to your supervision officer between the first and third day of each month and on the final day of parole. You *shall also* report to your supervision officer at other times as your supervision officer directs, providing complete and truthful information. You *shall not* violate any law. You *shall not* associate with persons engaged in criminal activity. You *shall* work regularly, unless excused by your supervision officer, and support your legal dependents, if any, to the best of your ability." Ballard looked up at Jodi. "In other words, *get a job* and keep it."

Jodi nodded and looked away toward the pea-green bookshelf with a dead plant on top. In prison you were never really allowed to be an individual human being, responsible for your own life decisions, but once they'd released you it was like you were suddenly supposed to know how to do it all effortlessly.

"There ain't much in the way of jobs in Render," Jodi said.

Ballard cracked the knuckles of his left hand.

Jodi took a deep breath and glanced back at him. He raised his eyebrows.

"I was thinking," she said, looking not at Ballard but at a fly that had landed and was now cleaning its wings on the rim of his coffee cup. "I'd like to raise some yearlings, build up to a little cow-calf operation eventually."

Ballard lifted his cup and the fly moved to his hand. He did not seem to notice. "Gotta be legitimately employed." He put the cup down and the fly returned to it. "Where you planning on raising 'em anyhow? In the backyard in Render?"

"Oh, no." Jodi squeezed her eyes shut. *Shit, fuck.* How could she have come so close to admitting to this man that she didn't plan to live at her official given address, that she would instead be squatting on land she owed who knows how much taxes on. *Shit, fuck.* "No, I guess I didn't think that one through."

Ballard barked out a laugh. "You gotta be *employed* and *paid* by somebody."

Jodi looked up at him. "Who's gonna hire me when they see the Class B felony?"

Ballard shrugged.

"Some of the girls inside said even McDonald's won't take felons."

"Mmm-hmm, well, yeah." Ballard cracked the knuckles of his right hand. "What do your parents do for work?"

"Disability." Jodi looked down at her lap. "Before that, Daddy was a guard over at the prison. Federal prison camp's about the only place in Render that's got steady jobs."

Ballard laughed again. "Well, shit," he said. "All right, well, you prove to me that you're looking. You don't find nothing after a while and you might consider getting a CDL. Long-haul trucking companies'll sometimes hire on felons."

Jodi stared at him. He raised his eyebrows and then the corners of his mouth turned up into a small mocking smile. "You submit to me a written report between the first and third of each month. If I'm not here, you leave it with the secretary. You report punctual and factual and we should have no problems but you cause troubles for me and I will make your life hell."

He blinked at Jodi.

"Is that clear?"

Jodi met his eyes. "Yes, sir."

"All right, that's it, that's my side of the responsibility." He tossed her folder onto the desk among the other papers, all those other typed reports of crumpled, bruised-up lives. "You are officially a supervised release parolee. Now get the fuck outta my sight."

JODI'S PARENTS LIVED at the back end of Render, in a small blue house on a dead-end street, tucked behind the county jail and a baseball field.

When they reached the block Jodi slowed the car to a crawl and the boys climbed one on top of the other to see out the window.

"You're not gonna say Lee's name, right?" Jodi glanced at Miranda.

Miranda was distracted, picking bits of red polish off her nails.

They'd gone over all this back at the cabin, sending the boys out to play in the yard while they incubated a story to tell Jodi's family that did not include Lee Golden's name. They'd settled on the idea that Miranda's husband had died in a car wreck last week and so she'd moved to West Virginia with Jodi.

"Lee's too chicken," Miranda said, inspecting her cuticles. "He won't really send the police after me, with some of the shit that he knows I could tell them."

Jodi felt a pang of deep irritation. She tried and tried to keep the boys from knowing the full mixed-up reality of their situation but Miranda seemed to undermine her every chance she got, flinging out her words with disregard for the audience.

"Well," Jodi whispered, turning the stereo higher to cover her voice, "somebody's gonna be looking for them, right? What about their beloved Neenee?"

Miranda looked up, her eyes suddenly bright.

"We could dye our hair," she said, and Jodi laughed out loud.

"What do you think, red or black?" Miranda pulled the sun visor down and snapped the mirror open.

Jodi watched her making faces at her reflection and thought of the billboard with the blinding white teeth and Miranda's pride. *That's my daddy!* This girl really had never done anything on her own; she'd gone from her Denture King daddy straight into the arms of her husband and all of it, even poverty and losing her children, was a game of sorts, a dramatic musical that always starred her.

"Are we there?" Ross asked.

Jodi let the car roll to a stop across the street from her parents' house. A dog ran out from under the porch, eyed the car, and then paused to sniff an empty margarine tub in the middle of the yard. Jodi hadn't called, hadn't said a word to her parents since Jaxton, but Andy and Irene were there, she knew, day in and day out, their lives a flat road with repeating scenery. At the beginning of the month they would be flush from the government check, indulging in a week of excess followed by three weeks of wheedling frugality.

She cut the motor just as the front door opened with a clamor of bells and wind chimes. Irene appeared on the stoop, squinting.

"Hi!" Miranda called as she stepped from the car and opened the back door for the boys. Jodi watched her move and despite her frustration she found that she was, more than anything, overwhelmed by a relief that Miranda was there, a seeping gratitude for the fact that she didn't know and couldn't care that she was not expected here, a thankfulness for the way she filled up all the awkward spaces so effortlessly, snugly drew in all the attention with her children, her problems, and her shining hair.

"Hello?" Irene said, skinny arms crossed at her chest.

Jodi stepped out of the Chevette and stood there in the leafy shade of an oak tree.

"Goddamn," Irene said, "if it ain't Jodi Marie."

The concrete between them was scattered with sticks, a broken matchbox car, and a deflated basketball.

"Hey." Irene's mouth split into a grin.

She was still so pretty, Jodi thought. Small features, big eyes, and long red-gold hair. Behind her in the doorway, Jodi's father, Andy, stood, a few inches shorter, and lovely too, in an unexpected way, with a fierce but delicate beauty that emanated from his high cheeks, thin nose, and girlish mouth. There was something strangely sad about their beauty, there in that rundown house at the end of Murdock Street. Their loveliness, it seemed, had always taunted, promised them something, but nothing came, and oddly, no matter how drunk, how fucked and crooked they went, the beauty stayed.

"You brought babies!" Irene crowed, and they all tumbled into the house together, into those rooms stuffed with the noise of daytime TV and the smell of off-brand cigarette smoke. Irene directed Andy to the kitchen to get sandwich fixings, the boys into the back bedroom to nap, and Miranda into the master bedroom to rest and get clean.

"Take a shower or bath if you want, feel free, please," she said, then grabbed Jodi's elbow and pulled her close. "That your boyfriend?" She jerked her chin toward Ricky where he stood in the kitchen doorway, staring down at his feet.

"God, no," Jodi said, pulling her elbow free. "No, no, no."

Irene raised her eyebrows. "Oh, well, sorry, I just—"

"He's the brother of an old friend." Jodi tried to calm her voice. She'd reacted too violently and made the whole situation seem stranger even than it really was.

"He just needed to get out of a bad situation," she said, glancing at Ricky.

"He ain't *her* boyfriend?" Irene nodded toward the bedroom.

"Her husband passed away last week," Jodi said.

Irene shook her head slowly, a little almost smile playing across her lips. "Looks like you got out of prison and went straight to finding yourself a heap of folks needing your help, huh?"

Jodi shrugged and turned toward the kitchen.

It was midmonth, not yet quite into the panic but just past the excess. There was still beer in the fridge and lunch meat on the counter, bread, and deli spreads. Jodi opened a beer and joined Andy by the back door where she could see, on the far side of the yard, the Little League kids milling about the baseball field.

After a while Miranda came out of the bedroom with a towel wrapped around her head and busied herself fixing a plate of sandwiches and carrying them over in front of the TV. Jodi watched as she and Ricky sat there eating on the living-room couch and she couldn't help but marvel at the ease with which they made themselves comfortable in this house. Even when she had lived there, during the months between Effie's death and Paula's arrival, Jodi had never been able to shake the feeling that this was the place where she *wasn't* raised. Andy had tried to care for them all with just his disability check, but what with the way they drank and baby Dennis so sick, Effie had insisted that it was better for her to raise Jodi.

"So they let you out." Andy turned toward Jodi and lifted his can of High Life as if to toast her but then brought it to his lips instead.

Jodi nodded and lifted her own beer. The haze of the night road—no sleep—and nineteen years away grew thicker with each sip.

"Irene says you'll be living up at Mama's place?"

Jodi glanced at Andy. From his tone she could tell not tell what he thought.

"Yeah," she said. "I need to see a lawyer and figure out what's the taxes owed, and the place needs a new roof too."

Andy brought his lighter up to the tip of his cigarette. "Ain't worth a new roof."

"I'll rig up a tarp for now. Keep us dry, at least," Jodi said. "I'm gonna get us some chickens, plow up the garden plot in the spring, and then once we're steady, I'm thinking we can get a couple a heifers from auction, get into raising yearlings. Start off small, you know, but then—"

"Acreage is grown over mostly," Andy said. "Ain't no good for grazing, full up with locusts and greenbrier."

Jodi nodded. It was true that in her dreams for the place, the fields had been far less choked but she could not let go of the vision of raising cattle up on the mountain. It was the only part of her future she could imagine succeeding at and so she went on repeating the plan over and over, holding tight to those words like a railing up some shaky flight of stairs.

She took a drink from her beer and stared at the lunch meat laid out on the counter. The pink folds of pig looked suddenly wicked in their similarity to her own skin.

"Yeah," she said, more to herself than anything, "I'll have to see about clearing the pasture."

The kitchen was cooler than the rest of the house, a shadowed blue hemmed in by quilted drapes. Andy cracked a fresh Miller and the sound stayed there, loud in the silence.

The Andy that Jodi remembered couldn't wait to tell you a story, didn't much care if you cared, he needed to tell. But maybe now, Jodi thought, he couldn't square his stories with the fact of his daughter, just released. Most of his tales were from his prison guard days. He'd worked at the federal women's penitentiary in Render until he dislocated a disc while restraining some inmate. He could tell you all about the bull dykes with swastikas

carved into their shins. And the Manson ladies—he was there when Squeaky
Fromme escaped and caught a ride to the bus station with a man from Painter
Creek. A man who, depending on who told the tale, either did or did not
enjoy a little fellating on the way. On his drive home, though, the man heard
a warning report on the radio and pissed his pants before he could pull over
to call the cops to say he'd just given a ride to a young lady much like the one
they'd described.

Jodi looked over at Andy. "What are they building up in Jessup's orchard?"

"Fracking," Andy said, stubbing his cigarette out in an ashtray shaped like
a miniature frying pan.

"What's that supposed to mean?"

"Pulling gas up out of the shale. They paid good money for that land.
Your cousin Robbie's working up there now and they pay him good too. I
told A.J. he'd be smart to get himself a job with them but fuck me if he ever
listens to a thing I say."

As the afternoon wore on, Irene made phone calls and devised
a slapdash party with neighbors, cousins, brothers, and in-laws, forgetting in
her haste to play good host that she and Andy preferred to spend their time
getting drunk alone and pinning each other down with arguments that led
inevitably into sweaty, early-evening sex.

As the guests arrived the men gathered out back, taking turns poking a
pair of metal tongs into the charcoal grill while the women perched on various surfaces in the kitchen, the air opaque with their cigarette smoke. Ricky
sat in the living room watching TV until Irene shooed him out with the other
men. Jodi felt strange and uneasy as she watched him standing out there
beside her brothers under the walnut tree, their lips moving in a conversation
she could not make out.

Dennis and A.J. had grown heavier around the middle, and their faces
were free of teenage acne, but other than that they seemed not to have changed
in the years that she'd been gone. They'd both arrived stoned, their eyes distant and shaded. Despite their sameness, there had always been something

about Dennis that A.J. could never quite attain, a confidence that Dennis exuded even from a distance. On Dennis, the thick lethargy of weed seemed like a smooth and boundaryless ease. A.J. just looked too high to speak.

"Be glad you've got all boys," Irene said to Miranda who sat in the middle of the kitchen, bouncing Dennis's newest baby on her knee. "Boys are easiest, the sweetest, none of that meanness." Irene looked to the other women for confirmation but multiple conversations were circulating, something about Jell-O molds and that slut who was always sunbathing down by the municipal boat slip.

The women moved about the kitchen as if they'd rehearsed every step, pushing past one another to grab the Saran wrap, pausing to light a new cigarette. Jodi couldn't quite place their faces or remember specific names but she knew these women well. They had always been there in the background with coffee and sticky, starchy foods. At the scene of every disaster and celebration they filled out the edges of the room with their pillowy housedresses and clouds of smoke. By the very generosity of their bodies they comforted the children and men. In their midst, Miranda looked fresh and peaceful. Her damp hair hung down over the back of the chair and she wore a white tank top, borrowed from Irene, and cutoff blue jeans. Jodi found herself filling again with a gratefulness for the way Miranda put everyone at ease, giving herself over to each new moment. You couldn't help but feel that everything you did with her—fixing a macaroni salad or driving to the grocery—was special and exciting.

It was early evening by the time they were ready to eat and the beer was gone; someone was sent to fetch more but had not come back yet and Jodi was beginning to feel sober. The voices around her grew louder like radio stations coming into range and she edged away from the picnic table spread with orange salad, mayonnaised tomatoes, barbecue, and corn bread. She was relieved to find A.J. hunched over and stupefied under the oak tree, even more relieved when he flashed her a handful of pills.

"You want some Dex?"

Jodi nodded, glancing around for Miranda. She was busy, though, carrying stacks of plates out from the kitchen and laughing with Irene. Jodi closed
her fingers around the peach-colored tablets. It would be another month
before she had to meet with Ballard, almost certainly enough time for the
Dex to leave her system, and anyhow Ballard hadn't seemed like he'd be too
intent on drug testing. She swallowed the pills and settled herself on the roots
of the oak, listening to the twang and curl of accented voices all around her.
It warmed her, the familiar sound of those words, shortened and pulled out at
intervals by tongues that had never left these hills. She had never entirely lost
her own accent but over the years it had begun to seem to her like a strange
leftover burden, something that only made sense here.

As the sun sank, the evening light glowed around the edges of everything,
forming hazy halos, and Jodi looked at A.J.'s profile and wondered how many
times she had waited just like this, with him, in the silence and the heat. In
her earliest memories, before her parents moved to town, it seemed she was
always in the backseat with her brothers on long drives. The three of them
tumbling with no seat belts, a jumble of chigger-bit skin and sharp elbows.
Where they would have been going, Jodi had no idea. Except for the few rela-
tives who'd gone up to Michigan, everyone her family knew lived in Malonga
County. Maybe her parents had just needed to drive, Andy trailing the smoke
of his cigarette and Irene's hair spilling out like red-orange ink.

Later, for Jodi, the point was definitely the driving. Dennis had tagged
along with the boys who gave Jodi rides because even at eleven he'd known
how to talk to the old hippie guys and get them to part with their weed
for cheap. And A.J. was innocent looking enough to buy a whole case of
canned whipped cream. In the backseat everything was much the same as
when they were babies, a flurry of wind and sunlight in their laps. And then
the sharp rise and tingling warmth of whippets, and the driving. Moving,
rolling. A.J. and Dennis had always wanted to get out of the state. They had
hopped a freight once but it was the wrong line and the train just wound
deeper into the mountains and halted in Anjean, at the mouth of the slope
mine.

"You been this whole time in prison?" A.J. leaned toward Jodi.

She nodded.

"They call it a Bible cake," a woman at the edge of the porch was saying to Ricky. "One cup Proverbs 30:33." She gestured with her thin arms, the skin transparent with veins, a snarled, blue circuitry. "Two cups Jeremiah 6:20."

Ricky's eyes opened wide. "And the sweet cane from a far country?"

"I heard you turned queer." A.J. looked at Jodi.

She turned away, fingers curled into fists. She should have known it was impossible that none of them would mention it. She let her mind fuzz out from this present moment but she could still smell the stink of her own shame and hear the bitter drawl of that word.

She pictured A.J. reading the newspaper stories and laughing. Back in '89 her case had gone a little famous, temporarily. It had all the thrilling elements the newspapers craved: kidnapping, violence, sex. Her first few weeks at Jaxton, she'd received piles of letters from sicko strangers who had read about the trial and wrote her fucked-up fan mail, twisted, dark wet-dream madness, or else letters from lesbians everywhere: San Diego, Boston, New York, all of them acting like they knew her just because she and Paula were lovers. They'd wanted Jodi to be their poster child for an ACLU lawsuit attesting to the homophobia of the Georgia court system. A public awareness campaign. Alone in her cell she'd felt so far from their talk of solidarity, so far outside their supposed community. She'd thrown away their letters. They reeked of privilege, the clean white pages soggy with their "compassion," perfumed with their need to "understand." Their willingness to forgive nauseated her.

As THE SUN set mosquitoes came out and most of the party guests left. Those who did not reconvened in front of the small TV inside. Dennis wanted to stay but his wife followed him around, repeating her words like a trained bird. *We've gotta get the girls to bed and you've got work tomorrow, Dennis, work tomorrow.* Finally Irene told them both to shut up and get out.

Dennis looked back at Miranda as he got up to leave but she was six beers deep and intent on watching the TV, where someone had put on *Trenchknife III*. Ricky sat on the couch beside her, and the boys sprawled across the floor.

"Mom?" Kaleb's voice snaked up through the darkening air. "Mom, where are we?"

Behind the couch, Jodi paced, counting and recounting the last four cigarettes in her pack. Tomorrow, she kept thinking, trying to concentrate on "next steps," but her brain cut back each time and looped to the dwindling cigarettes.

"You'll ruin your eyes like that," Ricky said to Donnie, who'd inched himself up two feet in front of the screen.

"Move your head, sweetie," Miranda mumbled.

The girl on the TV was using a skeleton key to open the creaking door to some abandoned castle.

"I wouldn't go in there if I were you," Ricky told her.

Ross had found a phone book and he sat inspecting it in the light of the TV.

From the kitchen Irene and Andy's staccato whispers echoed out. *I told you I never . . . Oh, yeah? Not once never? . . . Then why don't you just make me wear a fucking chastity belt?*

Through the mesh of the window screen Jodi could see the lights of the baseball field out across the yard. Behind her the TV screamed and Ricky mumbled a *told you so.*

Once they had all fallen asleep, Jodi carried the boys into the spare room, nestling them in bed under a framed photo of some gap-toothed ancestor of hers and a giant poster of Jim Morrison's face. When she came back into the living room Ricky was standing in front of the couch where Miranda lay dozing.

"There ain't a lot of room in this house," he said.

Jodi stared at him, feeling suddenly defensive. "It's just for tonight—"

"I'll go on out and sleep in the car."

"No, no, you and Miranda take the couches."

Ricky did not move. "Where'll you sleep?"

"There are plenty of blankets." Jodi turned away and busied herself gathering an armful of crocheted afghans from a wooden trunk and dumping them on the floor by the end of the couch.

"A.J. says you just got out of prison."

Jodi looked up. Ricky stood tall over her, silhouetted by the spastic TV light. She had nearly forgotten that they had not yet spoken of Jaxton.

"Yeah," she said. She could not see the expression on Ricky's face. She looked down and fussed with the blankets, straightening them, and then stood and moved toward the door, her pulse jumping in her throat. "I'm going down the road to buy some cigarettes. You need anything?" she said without looking back.

Out on the front stoop she stood still and let the screen door close slowly behind her. The broken neck of a beer bottle shone dully on the bottom step, and under the porch she could hear her parents' dog shuffling in the dirt. After a minute, when she did not hear any reply from Ricky, she took off across the yard, pushing away thoughts of what all he and A.J. and Dennis might have talked about.

It was cooler out now and the wind had picked up, scudding a pile of papers along the road. Jodi bent and grabbed one. They were little folded "Come to Jesus" tracts, a black-and-white photograph on the front showing a teenage boy in a Hail Satan T-shirt. She stared at the sad-eyed teenager, feeling the tug of Dexedrine and the slurry of beer in her veins.

When she looked up again something was flashing through the trees, a tall beam of quivering light. She stepped onto Front Street and eyed it. Up on the side of Bethlehem Mountain, a spike of orange gas flame lit up the metal tower and showered light over a patch of scraped ground. And there, at the base of the mountain, the blinking sign announced SLATTERY'S GIRL.

THE BAR WAS nestled on the riverbank, so close to the water that the first thing Jodi thought was *flood*. But perhaps the establishment didn't plan to be around long enough to face disaster. The walls were made of plywood covered over with a collage of beer advertisements. The music was turned high, some wailing saxophone, but the room was almost empty, just three men in dirty work clothes and a girl seated at a bar lit by a series of bare bulbs.

"The well's running low now," one of the men said. "That's why they're spiking her, let it flame and finish it, move to a new spot, up the mountain."

The girl sat silently, face turned up, intent on the huge TV. None one of them looked at Jodi as she crossed the room.

The bartender was a tall brown-haired girl in stonewashed jeans and a tight T-shirt. Jodi ordered a Budweiser and the girl filled a plastic cup from the tap.

"Five dollars."

Jodi froze, hand halfway to her pocket. "I could buy a six-pack for that."

"Yeah, not here."

"Why the hell's it so expensive?" Jodi counted out six ones from the fifty dollars she had left.

"Prices gone up on everything since the frackers come into town." The bartender nodded toward the men at the end of the bar. "They come from out of state and I think they're used to paying more." She lowered her voice. "My boss says he could probably charge 'em twice this much and they'd still keep coming. We're the only bar around." She tucked Jodi's money into her pocket and then resumed inspecting the tips of her hair, lifting sections up toward the light and biting off the dead ends.

Jodi took a seat halfway down the bar and sipped at the foamy piss-colored beer.

After a few minutes the back door opened and a girl stumbled into the room wearing only a ratty Mickey Mouse T-shirt that did not quite cover her soft white stomach and ball of brown pubic hair. Behind her the fluorescence of video lottery screens lit the doorway. "So you couldn't come? Sorry," she declared. "I don't care."

The bartender looked up, flicking her hair over her shoulder. "Put some clothes on, Sylvie," she said. "Nobody wants to see that."

Though the music pounded loud, there was a silence throbbing through the room too. Something was happening in this place, Jodi thought, something that turned to liquid all accountable space, a furious stop-time boredom that existed only in places so far away and buried that even sex stopped meaning anything. It was something to do with distance from the center of things. Everything that had ever mattered had happened somewhere else. There was that saying about the effects of the single flap of a butterfly's wing but in places like this time and distance smothered everything.

November 1988

"You know I love you," Paula says.

It is a command.

You know I love you. You have to know I love you.

Jodi stands before a beveled mirror and stares at her own skinny nakedness and Paula behind her, laid out across the bed. The room is dark but already she hears a rooster crow somewhere down the road and, through the wall, the whisper of Spanish words. She is weightless with alcohol and speed, comfortably situated at the edge of the present moment, watching everything from the eaves.

"What are we?" she says.

In the mirror, Paula's face contracts a little. "You want me to say girlfriend? Is that what you want me to say?"

Jodi brings her hands up to her own breasts, to feel the warmth of them and the sharpness of her rib cage under tight skin.

"I mean, what are we doing?" She turns toward the bed.

Paula lights a cigarette and in the glow her face appears, soft and beautiful, big eyes and that lush mouth. No amount of shit-life can beat that beauty out. Jodi thinks of Paula's father's hands on that small face, and her pulse quickens.

"There's some part of this plan that's bigger than us," Paula says. "There's something inside us that makes the world treat us like it does but that's all just training wheels. We're ready now, we're building." She smiles and inhales long. "We'll make a new family."

She slides across the bed, stretches her arms, and reaches out for Jodi. Jodi looks at the bottle of rum in her hand and its emptiness makes her inexplicably sad; in her dead-drunk head it proves something, shows that everything must end. Yesterday, tomorrow, this night. The wooden shutters on the window are latched but she knows that if she opens them she will see that it is already there, the flat, broad heat of another morning.

"Come here," Paula says, and Jodi hears the pleading in her voice and she thrills at it. She needs Paula to want her, needs her to keep on needing.

July 2007

Over the phone the lawyer's voice sounded tinny and very far away. "Public auction," he said. "The land was sold for taxes owed in 1990."

Jodi stood in her parents' kitchen wrapping the yellow phone cord around and around her wrist. She felt the word more than she heard it, *sold*, slamming like a fist into her face.

"Went for thirty-five hundred to a Ron Leonards of Jacksonville, Florida."

Through the open window she could see her father and brothers tossing horseshoes in the backyard, each one landing in a puff of red dust. She wanted to speak, to say something—anything to stop the flow of the lawyer's words—but it seemed that someone had stuffed feathers down her throat.

"Unpaid land tax going back two years," he added.

This same lawyer had made out big when he won Jodi's father's workplace injury case against the prison and he'd assured Jodi that he'd be happy to take a look at the legal status of the land.

"You must have received the eighteen-month notice."

"My family." Jodi's voice barked out louder and angrier than she had expected. "My family has owned this land for five generations."

When she closed her eyes, she could smell the dark green scent of cut alfalfa in the back pasture and see Effie's chickens following one another across the yard, climbing up into the arms of the apple tree, out of reach of sharp fox teeth.

"The legal notice would have come back in '89, then, eighteen months later—"

"You're saying a man from Florida has my land?"

For five generations, they'd scrabbled and struggled and fought to keep their land and then Jodi had managed to lose it in a matter of months. It had been gone all this time and she had only imagined it still there like some sort of phantom limb. She felt the anger at herself mixing in with images of her high-cheeked, upright ancestors, their gunmetal bright eyes slashing her with contempt.

"There has to be something I can do."

"When the tax is not paid the land escheats to the state, which then sells—"

"I was in prison in 1989 and I got no notice. I wasn't even legally an adult yet." There was too much self-pity in her voice; she wished it would come out steadier than this spinny, pleading thread of *stop, stop, stop.*

"Could argue that the land was bought illegitimately and should be sold back to you at the auction price. But we're talking eighteen intervening years here."

A mosquito bumped dumbly along the wall beside the phone, and through the open door of her mother's bedroom Jim Morrison urged Jodi to *break on through, break on through.*

She stayed there in the kitchen after the lawyer hung up, holding the silent phone and watching her father and brothers out in the yard, her anger ebbing and then spiking back up. A man from Florida? How in the hell did a man from Florida even know to come here looking for land? For so many years the mountains had protected this place, the landscape keeping it safe for those willing to scrape out a life, but now it seemed that a man from Florida could drive up and buy your ancestors' land on a whim.

She set the phone back in its cradle. The legal notice had likely been sent to Andy and Irene, for though Effie had left the land solely to Jodi, she had not yet been eighteen. And they had not paid attention to the impending auction, not had the money to pay the back taxes—or not cared? Andy had never been fond of the farm.

As a child, examining Effie's few photographs of the older generations, Jodi had imagined that she would have fit in better with them. The black-gowned women and deadly serious men in those sepia prints had reflected her own dark eyes and hair. She was a changeling, she'd thought, slipped through time somehow but better fitted among those dusky-eyed ancestral men who, in Effie's stories, carried slabs of oak on their backs down off the mountain to the sawmill to build their brides high-backed beds, men who saved newborn babies, keeping them alive in the warming ovens of cookstoves through terrible snowstorms, and men who loved those thin-soiled, hog-backed ridges and tilled at night, planting their acreage by the light of their headlamps after full days spent down in the coal mines.

THAT EVENING, AFTER she got Miranda and Ricky and the boys settled in the cabin, Jodi walked Effie's land with the new knowledge that it no longer belonged to her. Ron Leonards began to take form in her mind: green polo shirt on a stocky Floridian body, round face, a little like the KFC colonel, no, not like that, more sinister—well oiled, well sunned.

After the phone call she had asked Andy if maybe official mail had come for her from the state. *Back in '89?* He'd shaken his head and said he couldn't rightly remember how it had all happened after she left. *Even if I did get them papers, I didn't have that kind of money.*

His words mixed in Jodi's mind with images of Ron Leonards and Officer Ballard's warnings about parole violations but even these worries couldn't truly ruin the beauty of the woods as she walked among the sapling locusts until the voices at the cabin faded and there was nothing but the flush of bird wings in the trees. She came out into the back pasture where a family of wild turkeys fed. The little ones were awkward in their new feathers, spilling through the straw at the sound of human movement and their mother chortling a warning, her wings flapping frantically against the high grass.

The sun set but the evening light stayed on, a smudgy glow draping over the trees, and after walking for a while Jodi looked up and realized that she had no idea where she was. Had she wandered off Effie's land? There were no points of reference, nothing but two white-tailed deer flickering through the shadows in a spring of muscle and hoof. Jodi stopped short, her heart taut, and in her fear she felt her distance from the land.

As a child these woods had been as familiar to her as the cabin. Everything else—school and town—had seemed difficult and confusing. From blue dawn, when she stepped onto the school bus, until late afternoon, when the doors opened to set her free, she'd moved in a kind of daze, the way she imagined someone who needed glasses must feel, only to her it was not about vision but interaction. She never quite understood the connections among the other kids, the TV shows they watched that she had never seen, their trips to the skating rink and football games. If she'd even half-cared, surely she could have made friends but they all felt like a distraction, a hurdle between her and the hours of long after-school walks: the soft hills of orchard grass, neon toadstools spiking up through rotting stumps, the perfect palm-size smoothness of horse chestnuts, and the celestial patterns of oak leaves in the pond ice that split with a bright cracking sound under the pressure of her boots.

The teachers had worried. She'd heard them whispering too loudly. *Just her and her granny living up there . . . enough to eat? Smells funny.*

She'd taken on the habits of an old woman, early to bed, early to rise, suspicious and quiet, always with some other story playing in her head. She had not gotten her first period until nearly two years after the other girls in school and in that time she had decided she would never menstruate, that her body was already too old, but then it came, all at once, with a smell of iron and wet earth. Even so, she was marked apart, wrapped in a cocoon of wood smoke and damp wool. One morning she'd risen earlier than usual and gone with Effie to help deliver a Hereford calf and then run on down the lane to the school bus. Under the fluorescent lights of the classroom someone pointed out the wine-rust streaks that stained her sleeves and arms. It wasn't that she was the only girl with farm chores—plenty of them were up before breakfast, feeding chickens and yearlings—but they were careful then to change into clothing that approximated the stonewashed styles of music videos. In the buses and hallways they huddled with siblings and cussed their rural lives.

One spring, after the Milk River had risen and spilled itself out into Render's streets and buildings, the middle-school students were tasked with cleaning up the library. The highest shelves were dry but the lower levels were caked with mud and silt. In the back corner Jodi found a swollen collection of Tennyson poems splayed open to "The Lady of Shalott." She'd wiped the sand away and read about the solitary woman who, from her tower room, captured the lushness of the world around her—*Long fields of barley and of rye, / That clothe the world and meet the sky; / . . . Little breezes dusk and shiver / . . . unhailed / The shallop flitteth silken-sailed / Skimming down to Camelot*—until one day a man came along and ruptured the lady's simple life. Something ecstatic entered Jodi as she read those words, some quicksilver reflection of self that she had never experienced before. She tore the pages from the book and carried them with her, chanting the phrases under her breath as she paced the concrete halls of school and the pine-needled paths of Effie's land. It was not just the slick imagery of the natural world that made her ache in a singsong, melancholic way, though the descriptions of how *the sun came dazzling through the leaves* and *the stormy east-wind straining* and *the pale-yellow woods . . . waning* could captivate her for hours; it was more than that, though, it was about being hidden right in the middle of things, with a sucking hunger inside. It summed up everything Jodi felt but could not name, everything in her high-strung teenage heart. Tennyson was writing about *her*, she thought. A *bow-shot from her bower-eaves / He rode between the barley-sheaves*. She ached for someone to enter her life like that and shatter all the simple things that had once satisfied her.

MIRANDA STEPPED ONTO the sun-bright porch and lit a cigarette. A breeze tickled her nightgown against the backs of her knees. She sat down and stretched out her legs, watching Kaleb push Ross on the tire swing at the bottom of the hill where the shadows of the leaves crisscrossed their skin. Every day here she woke feeling brand new and confused. It wasn't a bad feeling, much better than the strangling quiet of that lonely hotel room in Chaunceloraine. She just wasn't quite adjusted yet. The boys' voices wove their way into her dreams and she would wake for a moment and then turn to fall back asleep but find Jodi there in bed beside her, and opening her eyes wider she'd see the Lincoln log walls of the cabin and hear Ricky's voice whispering *hush up now, your mama's still sleeping.*

The surprise of it all, of waking in the midst of this rare scene, canceled out her usual self-doubt and internal bickering. The mornings were relentlessly beautiful—mist-filled green dreams that unfurled into sharp yellow afternoons. Fog crept under the tarp roof and hung in the kitchen, wet against the cheesecloth-covered windows, as Jodi prepared coffee and stoked the cookstove.

The first morning there Kaleb had padded out of the bedroom and asked sleepily what Jodi was doing. "Making breakfast," Miranda said, showing him the open firebox. He'd approached slowly as if the flame were some skittish animal he might scare off. "Neenee just makes breakfast in the microwave," he'd said, his face filled with awe. Miranda had smiled and crouched beside him, watching the orange flame as a small persistent joy unfurled inside her. Truth was, she herself felt a childish wonder at this strange place. It was beautiful here in a way she'd never really experienced, a simple kind of green-on-green splendor that was all enveloping. She liked to picture how it would look from up above, an aerial view of blanketing trees with a small clearing carved out and the six of them inside. That first day she'd said *Little House on the Prairie* but really it was much more *Snow White and the Seven Dwarves.*

"Mama, mama, lookee." Donnie was practicing cartwheels in the side yard. He could barely get his feet up off the ground but he seemed positive that his movements must look like pure magic.

"Watch out for bees," Ricky called from the kitchen window. "Yellow jackets love to nest in grass like that."

Miranda nodded in agreement, though really she knew nothing about where one might find bees. "Careful, Donnie," she echoed.

It was so much more fun caring for the boys when it wasn't just her and them. It was really the way it ought to be done, she thought. No one should live so isolated. She herself had been raised all alone and it had set her up for a life of anxious desperation. Her mother was sick throughout her childhood and then she passed when Miranda was thirteen, and from that point on it was only Miranda and her father and occasional social interactions with his dental hygienists. Her world had been wrapped in plastic, the house sealed to preserve her mother's things; dust covers encased all the furniture, and blinds were drawn down tightly. She'd have given anything to live like her boys were living here; even with cut chins and probable bee stings, a contagious current of happiness was fairly pulsing out of them.

And they deserved it with the kind of shit they'd been through. Let the rest of their childhoods be nothing but long afternoons of fresh-cut grass and ice cream. Maybe that could obliterate some of the bad memories. They seemed genuinely unfazed by almost anything, though, and really it was she who carried the weight of memory: their little faces in the window of that hotel room where they stayed while she worked her bar shifts after running away from Lee and, before that, the image of Lee passed out on the bedroom floor and baby Kaleb beside him, playing patty-cake and dipping his chubby toddler hands in a bag of cocaine.

That was in those flailing years between Kaleb's birth and Donnie's, when they lived in an imitation plantation-style house outside Delray—after Bella had refused to let Miranda live in her apartment anymore and before Lee's career plummeted and he moved her and Kaleb in with his aunt. The house was large and sat on top of a manicured hill with a winding drive but the construction was shoddy and the materials cheap. The sliding glass doors stuck in their tracks; the swimming pool leaked steadily. When Miranda went to replace the toilet-paper roll, the fake gold contraption came loose from the wall and left a hole in the Sheetrock. The jagged mouth of the hole scared her somehow, as if proving that everything were just waiting to crumble.

They bought a TV for every room (though there were rooms on the second floor that Miranda hardly ever even set foot in), and comfy couches and thick rugs, and then the rest was all just stuff they thought Kaleb would love:

bouncy horse, rocking boat, model train, antique gum-ball machine, and a mechanical bubble blower.

Sometimes Miranda felt as if she were on a set, like she might turn the corner any minute and see that the house didn't really exist, or that it existed only inside the lens, only enough wall and window and floor to fill the frame. Bella had let her tag along one time to watch the filming of a commercial she was doing for an age-defying facial cream. Miranda had loved the vertigo feeling she got from watching everything whirling around the outside of the shot, how *inside* the frame everything was perfect and seemed to extend endlessly. When you saw it on TV, your eye drew out the lines and assumed no edges to the world, but *really* it stopped right there. Just past the floral curtains there were the giant lights and cameras and cranes. They'd only needed half of a kitchen for the shot, so that was all that existed. Just three feet from where Bella stood, beaming and leaning against the counter, it was nothing but rough cut boards, the jagged edge of that tiny universe.

The day Miranda came home to find Kaleb playing with cocaine was the same day that she had gone to the doctor and confirmed her second pregnancy. The house, when she returned, was strangely quiet. She found a note from the cleaning lady on the kitchen counter:

Miss Miranda,
   Your husband told me I was not to clean upstairs today, sent me home early.
—Julia

"Lee?" Miranda screamed.

He'd been fine that morning, giddy in that just-home-from-tour and I-don't-wanna-be-anywhere-else-in-the-universe kind of way. When she left for the doctor he'd been up in their bed with Kaleb, cuddled into a sea of fluffy pillows, eating Cool Whip straight from the container and watching *Ghostbusters*. She'd imagined coming back home and crawling into bed with the two of them, telling Lee the news of the new baby and watching his face light up with love.

"Lee?"

She could hear Kaleb's burbling bird voice now. She was racing up the stairs. Their bedroom was at the end of the hall but she didn't even make it that far before stopping and then lurching forward again. The door was open and it framed a scene that looked like some grotesque distortion of Renaissance painting: golden sunlight across a huge white bed, the shafts of light caressing the yellow curls of her husband who slumped, half-naked, against the mattress and, beside him, glittering sunbeams playing on the perfect skin of her smiling child, hands dusted white.

She grabbed Kaleb and ran to the bathroom, holding him so tight he cried. She ran his hands under the water and tipped his head back, thank God there was no white on those rosebud lips and fat little tongue.

"Lee!" she screamed again, but her voice made Kaleb cry more, tears dangling from the end of his nose. She kissed the salty drops away and carried him to the bouncy horse, strapped him in there. "Mama will be right back."

She raced up the hallway to her husband's body, bent and pressed her fingers against his neck. He had a pulse. She let her breath out and leaned back. A part of her itched to slap him right across the face but another part of her was not sure she wanted him to ever wake.

Kaleb was crying on the bouncy horse, his hiccupy sobs competing with the squeench-squeench of the coiled springs. Miranda left Lee and went to him. She carried him outside, away from those too-quiet rooms and into the shaky chatter of cicadas, the midday Georgia heat.

They followed the white pebble path around to the backyard. There was no one else around, no neighbor close enough to have heard her screaming, no one to tell or not tell, nothing but the rush of wind in the trees.

The pool had drained itself again.

"Ool! Ool!" Kaleb pointed and laughed, clapping.

The pool had been leaking so much that Kaleb didn't even know it was supposed to have water in it.

"Ool!" he insisted, and she hugged him against her chest and climbed down into the deep end.

The chalky blue concrete was hot but Kaleb didn't mind; he wriggled out of her arms and took off crawling. Miranda lay back. The walls sloped up and met a sky that nearly matched them. Blue above and blue below. Sealed off, she thought, and when panicky questions rose in her head she pushed them out. Not in here, she said, spreading her fingers across her stomach, one hand for her new baby and one for her perfect boy who lay beside her, blinking and cooing.

AT THE RURITAN Club thrift store in Render Jodi found a few rugs and curtains for the cabin and they set up the two bedrooms, Ricky in the back with the boys and Jodi and Miranda in the middle room.

Miranda seemed to take to the rustic living with a fervor that surprised Jodi. There was no way to get the electricity reinstated so they used oil lamps and the old hand pump that drew rainwater up from the cistern to the kitchen sink. Jodi waited for the moment when Miranda would protest the lack of an indoor toilet and hot water. She could picture her already, packing her kids into the car and driving away, and panic filled her at the thought of waiting there in the dark cabin with Ricky, wondering if Miranda would ever return. So she tried to shield her from the worst. When they cleaned out the cookstove they found that mice had made the oven into a giant nest, and beneath the layers of stinking insulation Jodi unearthed the tiny bodies of a dead litter, little perfect paws tucked up under their chins. She turned quickly before Miranda could see, dumped them into a bucket, and carried it outside, gagging.

Every morning she woke with the intention to go buy a newspaper and look into jobs. But she was afraid that leaving the land would break the spell and wake her from the dream of Miranda's night-warm body, so open, there in the bed beside her, the crackle of twigs laid on banked-off coals, and the smell of wood smoke. Tomorrow, Jodi thought, tomorrow. She'd have to find some way to make steady money eventually but the thought of begging for work sickened her, knowing that she would likely not be hired anyway, not after anyone saw her GED and Class B felony.

As long as she stayed there on the land her days were full of a nebulous distance—the tawny fields and arched blue sky, like some carefully preserved memory. They really could be safe here, she thought, in this most distant of all places; not only did Lee have no reason to think the boys would be here but also the land itself seemed to possess a special kind of force that kept it separate and abiding. Up here it did not matter that she had no real life skills and as she walked through the fields nothing outside the beauty of the present moment seemed consequential, not even hunger. Only when the boys complained did she notice that it was time to eat.

Irene had brought them a couple of boxes of food-bank goods and Miranda took trips to town for whiskey and beer. She'd managed to convince some store clerk to ring up the alcohol as "miscellaneous" on her EBT card. Jodi wondered just how much money she had on that card but she hadn't yet dared to ask. Her own dwindling cash was worrisome but only when she went to town; up there on the mountain, there was nothing to even spend money on.

One afternoon she had gone down to Render with Miranda and called the lawyer but he was out of the office; though she knew it was foolish, she'd felt relieved. He had said that he would look into refuting Leonards's claim, since Jodi had been in state custody and never informed of the auction, but the less she knew about the proceedings, the more she could dream. She had the sense that she was teetering, just barely managing to balance between the sweetness of the summer days and the dark reality of the lawyer's words. Ron Leonards's fictive face kept looming up, smug and sun creased. His presence hung over the land like acrid sweat, but if Jodi pushed back, he receded into a haze of spritzed green grass, palm trees, golf courses, and tennis courts.

The present moment beat loudly around her with the drone of deerflies and the saw-call of the cicadas in the trees. She watched the yellow grass wave above her from where she lay, sprawled on an old quilt in the back pasture. Up in the branches of the sweet gum she could see Miranda's pale, brier-scratched legs. She was perched on the thickest branch, swinging her feet and holding her Pabst can high to cheer for the boys who were playing a makeshift game of baseball with Ricky as the pitcher. Watching her, Jodi was filled with a rush of giddiness, that certain simple joy of new beginnings. It was not unlike the feeling she had gotten with Paula but with less of the trapped and circular logic. She couldn't think of her months with Paula now without seeing how Paula had been looping through her win-lose cycle for years, and Jodi, caught in the swing of it, had thought it was actually leading somewhere. She remembered something Frances had said to her once. Jodi had brushed the comment off—Frances didn't know Paula, could probably never understand a love like theirs anyway—but her words had stayed with Jodi. *Did you ever think that maybe she wasn't worth any of it? Your love or your hate?* The thought hit Jodi's stomach with a snare-drum rhythm. If their brief love wasn't worth everything, then both of their lives had been wasted, shaken out like a sulfur match—that quick—for nothing.

January 1989

The morning is a thudding red sun in Jodi's face, a heat that matches the fierceness of her headache. Paula stands over the bed, bending close and tucking a wisp of hair behind her ear. "Wake up, princess," she says.

The room they've rented is as small as a closet, just one twin bed with faded Donald Duck sheets. Through the open window Jodi hears the cloock-cloooock of chickens in the dusty yard, the dip and rise of Mexican radio voices—*Ahora en Radio 88.9*—

"Come on." Paula pulls her up. "I've got a surprise for you."

The taxi takes them past the downtown market—women in plastic sandals arranging piles of green bananas beside displays of electric alarm clocks and bottles of oily parasite cures. They drive around a man on a bicycle with a bundle of firewood piled so high it hides his body and then out past the resort hotels and beach condos to where the buildings taper off into thatched shacks and concrete bunkers. Jodi wants to stop for coffee, a bottle of water, but Paula says they have to hurry. She leans forward, staring over the driver's shoulder until finally they turn off onto a sandy road that leads to a tin shed with two tiny propeller planes.

Jodi eyes the planes, glances at Paula, then back to the planes. There is absolutely nothing else around.

Paula smiles and pulls her close. "I wanna see your first-time flying face."

The propellers are so vibrational Jodi thinks their rhythm will never leave her body. She is squished in the tiny cockpit, sitting on Paula's lap, waiting to die.

Paula has to keep reminding her to open her eyes. The land glides below them. She is surprised at how slowly they seem to be moving. The concrete landing strip is still visible, flanked by trees, and a dog has come out from the tin shed to trail after them, his head lifted, barking. Jodi hears the wind snatch at the banner that is right now wafting behind them, an advertisement for a new hotel at some place called Isla Holbox.

The tops of the trees are a deep tangled green and among them Jodi spots a row of bungalows, half-collapsed back into the earth but the yards still sprinkled with plastic chairs and umbrellas. If she squints her eyes, she can imagine a mother out back hanging sheets on the line. It's nothing more than junk, really, but somehow its placement there makes the land dearer, some stranger's intimate past displayed so openly. As a child on the mountain she would come across rusted tin buckets and chimney stones, or a head of a baby doll, the plastic cracked and thin as an eggshell. Effie had shrugged it off as trash but Jodi turned around each time they passed to see the lonely way those objects looked among the winter trees.

"See," Paula says, whispering into Jodi's ear and pointing out to where the ocean begins, clear and heavenly, like a wrinkled extension of the sky. "I knew you'd love flying."

And then they are over it, water expanding below them, and though there is air everywhere, Jodi cannot get enough of it into her lungs. It is stupendous, this vast blueness. She needs other words for it, something more than just aquamarine, turquoise, navy. None of those names catch the heart-wild magic of it.

"Thank you," she says, laughing and gripping Paula's leg.

What luck, she thinks, what staggering luck, to have found someone who wants to give her *this*.

THE CUTLASS LEAKS a long trail of gasoline, like spilled blood beading and clumping in the sand. The man who is supposed to be fixing it does nothing but cuss and squint and drag on his cigarette. A rooster scurries between the man's feet. Paula says she could probably fix it better herself but she doesn't have a welding torch, so they leave the car and hitch a ride into town to eat. All they have had all day are tortillas from the shop around the corner where the air is wet with the steam of warm corn dough.

The man who lets them ride in the back of his pickup is old, his skin crisp under the noon sun, his eyes like raisins. The wind blows around them the smell of fish and diesel fumes, and Jodi watches Paula as she raises her arm and points straight above them at the rippling rainbow of a hot-air balloon. The little woven basket is dwarfed by the glowing cloth and flames shoot straight up the center.

"You wanna try that next?" Paula says.

Jodi smiles and lies flat in the bed of the truck to watch the painted puffball.

"How about we go up in one of those and watch the sun set and then a fireworks display?" Paula stretches out beside Jodi, their heads knocking together every time the truck bounces. She grabs Jodi's hand and they are staring at the cloudless sky and laughing, their laughter lifting up around them into the hallucinatory blue.

August 2007

"Miss Jodi?"

Jodi startled out of a dream and turned to see Ricky in the doorway behind her.

"You plan on taking care of that hornet's nest?"

She squinted across the dim room. The cabin was entirely silent.

"Where are Miranda and the boys?"

"I tried not to wake you but standing here, watching, I got to worrying, it's right outside the window by the boys' bed and with the roof peeled up like it is and all . . ."

Ricky filled the doorframe and as Jodi stepped toward him he did not move back. She glanced out the window and saw that the car was gone from the lane.

"Miranda went to town?"

Ricky nodded.

"How long was I napping? I didn't even know I fell asleep." Jodi rubbed her eyes and looked around the room. There was an empty whiskey bottle and a couple of cans on the table beside the dirty dinner dishes. Why hadn't Miranda woken her when she decided to go town? Jodi stared at the filthy floor, scattered with leaves blown in through the front door. What was she going to town for anyway? If she kept ringing up booze on that food-stamp card, they'd soon have nothing left to eat.

"I figured you'd knock it down," Ricky said, "but it keeps growing and—"

"All right." Jodi turned back to Ricky. "Okay. Where is it? Let's take care of it."

He led the way around to the back of the house and Jodi followed, searching her pockets for her cigarette pack. She lit one and paused, waiting to hear the drone of hornets. Ricky approached the bedroom window slowly but Jodi saw nothing.

"There." He pointed and she came closer. Instead of the monstrous gray funnel of doom she had expected, there hung from the upper pane of glass a small cluster of papery cells with three hornets hovering.

"That's it? You've been worry watching that?" she said. "Why didn't you knock it down when you first seen it?"

Ricky stared at her like she'd said the most obviously stupid thing. "I didn't think it to be my place, Miss Jodi."

She looked closely at him, blue eyes blank but mouth crimped with worry, and she could not unwind the thread of his thoughts or make sense of his expectations. She had found it hard recently to look straight at him for very long. She'd glance up and find him staring at her from across the cabin and a quiver would lick through her as she turned away. It was something about the distance between the boy of her memories and this large, quiet man, something about the way she sometimes saw Paula in his face, and something else too in his overdone respect for her. Back in Delray, at the museum, he'd seemed so competent but now that he was free of Dylan he seemed scared all the time, or angry, Jodi couldn't quite tell which.

"Come on," she said, "just call me Jodi, please. I don't need the 'Miss.'"

He bobbed his upper body in a sort of nod, sort of shrug. "Well, this being your house and all, I figured you'd be the one to take care of the nest and—"

"It's your house too, Ricky," she said, "and Miranda's. We'll all take care here." She watched his face but nothing about it seemed to relax or change and so she looked away, dropping her cigarette into the grass and stamping it out. "Go on and knock that nest down now, all right?"

She was halfway up the porch steps when he called out again.

"You and Paula lived here?"

She stopped and turned back toward him but he was not looking at her. He stared off instead across the field toward Randolph Mountain. Her mind jumped and tangled in itself and she had to calm her breath before she spoke.

"We were coming back," she said, watching his face closely. "We were gonna bring you here."

Their eyes met and Jodi did not look away this time and she saw in his face some sharp spark of pain or hate before he turned and walked toward the hornet's nest, his footsteps flattening the high grass.

THE INSIDE OF the phone booth was thick with dust and Jodi had to wipe her fingers across the glass to get a clear view of Miranda leaned up against the Chevette, her pink dress sticking to her sweaty thighs. It was only the beginning of their second week in West Virginia and already Jodi's money was gone, nothing but ten dollars left. They were eating grim little food-bank donation meals of boiled hot dogs and canned corn and still Jodi hadn't quite managed to tell Miranda the whole no-money truth yet. It was part of a larger conversation about the future that she felt sickly ill prepared for. Their relationship was best kept in present tense.

She pushed her quarters down into the machine and squinted at the numbers in the phone book. It was hot inside the booth, the sun blazing all its strength at that little cube, and Jodi's brain was swathed in gasoline fumes and last night's whiskey.

"Thank you for calling Walmart."

The sun felt personal and vengeful in its intensity.

"Hello?" the Walmart voice said.

Focus, Jodi thought, then realized she'd said it out loud. "Oh, sorry, I was wondering . . ." The words were there but backward. "Do you all, uh, well, would having a criminal record stop me from working at Walmart?"

"Would what?"

"I'd like to apply for a job."

"Well, honey, you can't do that on the phone."

Jodi drew an *X* on the dusty glass. "No, I know, I was wondering, what if I have a criminal record?"

The voice paused and there was a rolling boom in the background, voices on top of voices. "Let me transfer you to management."

The line beeped and then rang again. Jodi drew an *O* around the *X* on the glass.

"Thank you for calling Walmart."

A shirtless man had come out of the gas station and was walking across the lot toward Miranda. Jodi dragged her eyes back to the pay phone. "Hello, I was wondering, if I happen to have a criminal record, would that disqualify me from a job?"

"Criminal record?" It was a man's voice this time. "Well, yes, we run background checks on all applicants. What are we talking about here, a felony or misdemeanor?"

Jodi closed her eyes and an image sprang up, something from a movie she must have seen as kid: an astronaut, pulling himself, hand over hand, back toward his ship by a line tied around his waist, a line that, as she watched, unhitched itself and floated slowly up so that the astronaut in his puffy suit was left spinning, utterly alone, against the pulsing black forever of space.

Kmart and Magic Mart had the same policy. Jodi deposited the last of her change into the phone to call her brother Dennis. He'd lent her money before and could do it again but the words necessary for begging felt so cripplingly embarrassing that she only managed instead to ask him if he could lend her his weed whacker and help her clear out around the cabin. In person, she told herself, she could ask him better in person.

He came up the next evening after his work shift, eight hours on the line at the chicken factory, and Jodi—watching him walk across the yard with his chain saw and weed whacker, babies, wife, and a bottle of bourbon—felt the thawing warmth of gratitude spread through her.

"You didn't have to do all this," she called from the porch. "I just wanted to borrow your weed whacker."

"Ain't no trouble," Dennis said, hefting his younger daughter up onto his hip.

The small house filled with the flurry of six children and Jodi hung back, smoking on the porch until Dennis's wife, Veeda, called her name.

"What's up with Donnie's chin?" Veeda poked her head out the front door.

"He fell down and then—"

"No, I mean, you planning on leaving those stitches in there until his whole face gets infected?"

Jodi turned away from Veeda's sharp eyes. Truth was, she had noticed over the past week how the skin around the stitching had grown puffy but she'd hoped . . . hoped what? That the stitches would just disappear?

"Lord," Veeda said, shaking her head and exhaling loudly. "Dennis, fetch my first-aid kit from the truck."

Jodi paced the porch while Donnie screamed inside. She pressed her fingernails into her palms until she couldn't stand the pain. What must they look like, she and Miranda? Fuckups, she guessed. No matter how much Jodi cared about those boys, she didn't know anything about how to raise them.

Dennis came outside and gave her a smoke. "He'll be fine. Veeda's been working down at the VA hospital for almost a year now, she knows what she's doing," he said. "And, hell, we got hurt worse than that all the time when we was little. Remember? We was always cutting each other up, shooting each other full of BBs."

Jodi smiled weakly and followed Dennis as he picked up his chain saw and headed off toward the overgrown road.

As they crossed the yard she cleared her throat. "I need to ask you for a favor."

"What's that?" He glanced back at her but kept walking.

"I need to borrow some more money."

"Really?" His voice was soft and almost teasing.

"Not even Walmart will hire me with the felony and—"

Dennis stopped walking and turned, raising his hand to cut her off. "Yeah, you know, I was just thinking on that the other day, wondering how y'all are making do."

Jodi looked down at her feet.

"I got to thinking." Dennis shifted the chain saw from one hand to the other. "It just so happens that I need a favor too."

Jodi glanced up.

"I need somewhere to store something and I was thinking, now that you're staying up here, you could keep an eye on it for me."

"Store something?"

"Yeah."

"What something?"

"A few pounds of sinsemilla." His eyes skirted off toward the trees.

Jodi's laughter cracked out louder than she'd meant it to. "You do know I just got out of prison, right?"

"It'd only be for just a little while. I got a guy I'm selling it to but he can't take it off my hands just yet. I'll give you a cut for holding it for me. I just can't have it at the house."

"I'm on supervised release."

"You got Ballard, though. You know that fucker's just sleeping his way to retirement. I've got friends who've done way crazier shit than this while they was on parole under him. He ain't even gonna check anything. Hell, he don't even know this place exists, does he? As far as he knows you're living with Mom and Dad."

"Dennis, I'm not having nothing to do with—"

"How the fuck else you plan on making money then?"

Jodi turned away. Across the hoof-scarred pasture a group of cattle stood out blackly against the deep green trees.

"Look, if you can help me out with this, don't even worry about the four hundred I lent you before."

Jodi breathed deeply and looked back at Dennis, his nose and cheekbones hawkish in silhouette.

"No, I'll pay you back," she said, "soon as I get settled and get a job. I swear—"

"I ain't asking for that money back. I'm proud to help you. That's what family does, Jodi, they help each other out."

Dennis pulled the cord on the chain saw and the machine barked to life as he cut past her in two quick steps, the blade only inches from her leg. He set at the thicket of sumac and chinquapin, slashing the branches, trampling the feathered leaves and fuzz of ocher-red berries. Jodi watched him, his muscled arms tanned and inked with a five-pointed star, an Indian war bonnet, and a blue-black bird whose wings spread like a cloak over his shoulders. He turned toward her and she startled and lifted up the weed whacker.

Halfway down the lane they came to a fallen sourwood tree, the crooked trunk nearly thick as Jodi's waist. Dennis worked at it, cutting it down to stove-size chunks, his chain saw bucking against the green wood. Jodi hauled the logs over to the edge of the lane, sweat beading all across her skin. The sun had sunk below the ridgeline but the heat still clung in the air.

A quarter of the way down the log, Dennis stopped and shut off the chain saw. He left it lying beside the tree, the air booming with the new silence.

"Hey," he said, looking straight at Jodi. "You and Miranda got some kind of sick shit going on up here?"

Jodi froze.

"Are you fucking her?" There was a flint edge to Dennis's voice that buried itself deep inside Jodi.

"No," she whispered, the word coming out before she even had time to think, a slap of a reaction that left her dull and defeated. She hated that this was her first response and tried to tell herself that she only wanted privacy but there was something else there, the scent of self-hatred as ripe and familiar as her own shit.

"I can't stand to think of those boys growing up around something sick like that." Dennis dragged his eyes up and down Jodi's body.

"No, it's not like that between us," she said again, feeling the lie, heavy and ugly on her tongue, as she waited for the chain saw's scream.

BACK AT THE house Miranda had set up a bar. She'd gotten Ricky to haul over a couple of logs and balance them between the porch railings and she'd lit candles along the edges and laid out the cans of Budweiser and bourbon and Coke in little teacups.

"Aww, shit, would you look at this?" Dennis said. "Now that's neat."

Donnie, recovered from the removal of his stitches, was chasing Dennis's girls, five-year-old redheaded Dana and her white-blonde three-year-old sister, Janelle, back and forth under the rotten beam while Kaleb frowned at them from the corner of the porch.

"No, it's nothing," Miranda said. "We don't even have ice."

Veeda rolled her mascara-rimmed eyes and blew out a thin stream of smoke. "There's hot dogs on the stove," she said.

"Hot dogs again?" Donnie cried.

"Don't talk like that." Dennis leaned down toward him. "My wife fixed you food, now you be grateful."

"Bluh-uh-uh." Donnie pretended to vomit into his own hands and Dennis set his beer on the bar and grabbed Donnie's arm.

"Don't touch him," Jodi said. Their eyes met and stayed but Dennis's hand loosened and he let the boy go.

"Fine," he said. "Spoil the sonofabitch."

They brought oil lamps out onto the porch and the light flared over the tired faces, Dennis drinking fast to keep himself awake and Miranda waving her cigarette all around to drive away the mosquitoes. Ross and Janelle, playing waiters, hustled back and forth between the porch steps and the bar.

"Can I take your order?" Ross's eyes were so serious.

"I'll take whatever is in that teacup," Jodi told him.

"Whiskey," he said sternly, "and Coke-Cola."

"All right." Jodi smiled. "I'll take that."

Miranda stirred the drink with her finger, licked it, and added another drop of bourbon before handing it down to Ross, who carried the blue-and-white china reverently, not spilling a drop. He served cups to all the adults all the way around and when he brought one to Ricky Veeda turned toward Jodi.

"He supposed to have that?"

Jodi studied Ricky, twenty-nine but hunched like an old man, silent there on the steps beside Kaleb.

"Yeah, sure, why not?"

Dana had a bag of sparklers that she counted and recounted carefully before passing them out among the boys.

"Go on out in the yard with those," Dennis said, handing her a lighter.

They clattered down the steps, leaving only Dennis's one-year-old son licking his blanket and working up a good cry. Veeda looked at the baby wobbling there, naked except for his rumpled diaper. She eyed him as if he were a mildly irritating drunk, a man she wished she could stop from coming over and talking to her.

"Refills," Miranda said, stepping out from behind the bar and splashing the last of the whiskey into their cups.

Dana could not get the sparklers lit. Donnie pushed his up his nose and Dana screamed at him until Ricky came down off the porch steps and took it. He gathered up all the sparklers, then pulled out his lighter and cranked it up high. Watching him, Jodi felt a pinch of worry. *Says I can't be trusted with fire.* She wanted more than anything to believe that Dylan and Anna were every bit wrong about him, but still, sometimes his moods seemed to shift unexpectedly, like something large and silent moving underwater, and the way his eyes caught and stayed on that flame worried her some.

The children leapt at his legs like yappy dogs. He passed out the sparklers but kept his lighter on high, only inches above those little heads.

"Hey, Ricky," Jodi called. "Watch that flame there."

He looked over at her, his eyes unreadable, and kept the flame turned up high, pulsing so that it singed his thumb. No one said a word and the moment stretched long, the children bouncing in a circle around him while Ricky stared at Jodi and Jodi stared at the flame. Then, just as Jodi stood up, he took his thumb off the lighter and dropped it back into his pocket.

"Look at all those stars." Miranda leaned out over the railing, her hair rippling.

Jodi watched Dennis watch her.

"Seek him that maketh the seven stars and Orion," Ricky said, sitting down on the steps. "And turneth the shadow of death into the morning, and maketh the day dark with night."

"It's already night." Donnie stomped up onto the porch with his burned-out sparkler, marking a black trail across the sagging boards.

Ricky continued on. "There is one glory of the sun and another glory of the moon—"

"And another glory of the stars," Jodi said, the words coming back to her from some far corner of her memory. "For one star differeth from another star in glory."

Ricky glanced at Jodi and smiled. "And the third angel sounded and there fell a great star from heaven, burning as if it were a lamp, and it fell upon the third part of the rivers, and upon the fountains of waters."

Jodi closed her eyes to better see the wild pictures painted by those ancient words.

"And the name of the star is called Wormwood and the third part of the waters became wormwood; and many men died of the waters, and they were made bitter."

"Oh, hey." Dennis startled up out of half sleep. "Jodi, I almost forgot, Mom said to tell you that lawyer's been calling and asking for you."

Jodi sat up straight. "What did he say?"

"Hell if I know. Mom just said he's been calling."

April 1989

"No, I *know* you can do it. Really, it's simple, just about timing," Paula says. "The guy goes to take a piss, you drive up to the door, come in with the gun, grab the money, and we're gone."

They are sitting across from each other on the narrow bed at the Hospedaje Familiar while Paula rolls a joint and explains her plan. She's been playing poker with the same group of men in the back room behind a butcher shop in Tampico for two weeks now and the plan has come into shape slowly. There is a man who guards the door, she says, checks them all for weapons and won't let anyone in or out after the game starts, but once each night he leaves his post to step into the bathroom. The bathroom is right beside the poker-playing room but its door is on the outside of the building, facing the street. All Jodi has to do, Paula explains, is wait until he is inside and then drive the Cutlass up to block the door. He won't be able to do a thing until they have the money and are driving away.

"But I don't know hardly any Spanish," Jodi says, taking the lit joint that Paula passes to her.

"Doesn't matter, the only word you need is *dinero* and probably not even that. I think it'll be obvious."

Jodi gets up from the bed and rummages around inside their duffel bag until she finds her purse with the .38. She stands and faces the mirror, stretches her right arm out straight, and holds the pistol steady as she walks slowly toward her reflection.

"God, you look sexy like that," Paula says, smoke coiling out the corners of her mouth.

They practice that evening, in a sandy, abandoned lot out past the municipal dump. As the sky melts from orange to coral to gray, and the bats come out, flitting and dropping spastically, Paula stands with her back to the dunes and smokes, watching Jodi rev the Cutlass's engine, then slam on the brakes, leap out, and run, pistol held tense and high, nylon panty hose pulled down over her face.

THE NIGHT IS hotter than usual. Or maybe not, Jodi thinks. Maybe it's just her nerves. She tried, for the past twenty-four hours, to decide if she should do up before this and finally she realized she could not possibly accomplish it sober. Now, though, she is not sure the speed was such a good idea. Instead of the usual rush of supersexed power and holiness, it is just making her feel itchy and paranoid.

Paula has been inside the back of the butcher shop for over an hour now and all Jodi has to do is wait. She has a clear view up the street to the gray door of the shop and the pastel-green door beside it that is the bathroom. Maybe the guy has changed his routine, though. Maybe he took a piss before the game started and now he won't have to go all night.

She lights a cigarette and tries to concentrate.

There is the smell of frying meat coming from one of the apartments on the street, and the scent makes her stomach bunch up like a fist. If she leaves the car windows down, mosquitoes land all along her arms, but if she rolls up the windows, it is too hot to breathe. She blows out her cigarette smoke, directing it toward her arms, and the insects lift up momentarily.

A song comes on in the house across the street, something fast and jumpy with lots of accordion. Jodi finds that her feet and hips are bouncing along with the rhythm. She thinks this is a good thing. See, she says, I'm not nervous.

The door swings open.

Her heart drops straight down into her lap. She remembers to crank the car and press the gas. She cannot remember to breathe but she steers the car up the street, bucking over the sidewalk and roaring into the green door. She is out. Panty hose pulled down over her face, blood pulsing loud in her ears, pistol steady.

It is only five steps to the door but they have heard the car and are already on their feet when she enters. The room is patchy, everything blurred by the hose on her face, just dodgy spots of light and dark and her own voice, spiking, panicky. The men move back, a chair topples; their hands go to their belted waists instinctively, though they have no weapons there. Only Paula is still sitting, looking back and forth from the men to Jodi.

Jodi is suspended, watching the men's attention, fixated on the pistol in her hand. It thrills her, this moment of pure concentration. She feels their energy pulled toward her, and though this was not a part of the plan, she thinks now that they should see her shoot. None of them have gotten out any money and she is not sure how to go from this moment to the next. She turns the pistol up to the ceiling and pulls the trigger.

The sound breaks open and pours down on them and the men are all movement now, hands flying to pockets and billfolds. Jodi can hardly breathe inside the panty hose but *this is it*, it is all happening. She grabs the bills from their shaky hands and stuffs them into her bag. She looks toward the door and Paula rises beside her. They are moving together now.

Jodi looks back just once and this is when she sees first the chair and then the man lifting it up over his head, lunging toward her. She spins, tumbling against Paula, and holds the pistol out.

"Stop," she says, not sure if she is saying it to the man or herself, but already her finger has squeezed the trigger and the man falls backward. The chair and the man land and break apart, the chair hitting the wall and the man rolling, curling in on himself. His shoulder is dark with blood and the blood is moving, spreading out quickly across the concrete.

Jodi stumbles and is jerked back. Paula's arms are around her and she is moving, turning. Paula is pushing her. *Run, run, RUN.*

THEY DRIVE FOR eight hours straight, Paula at the wheel and Jodi staring out the window, watching shadow shapes. When Paula tells her to, she counts the money and finds it to be several hundred dollars less than they had expected. She cannot stop seeing the pool of blood.

"Do you think—"

"It was only his shoulder," Paula says, without taking her eyes off the road. "He'll be fine."

They cross the border at Matamoros just before the sun rises. The lamps at the guard hut spill thin green light into the dusky air. The guard tells Jodi to get out of the car. She hands him her passport and stands there, trying to calm her pulse, listening to the bug zapper on the corner of the building. The guard looks from the passport to Jodi. She stops breathing. He looks back to the passport and then to his watch.

"Happy birthday," he says.

August 2007

Route 3 wound in from the south end of the county toward Lewisville, where the ridges dropped back and the Milk River valley opened wide, the jagged paths of ancient icebergs visible in the huge boulders, tipped as if still in midmotion. Jodi drove up from Render in the late afternoon. Trailers and two-bedroom ranches gave way to three-story Greek Revivals with Suburbans in every drive and nausea bloomed inside her at the sight of all that wealth. Lewisville was at least twice as large as Render. It was the county seat and had been the local Union headquarters during the War between the States, a strange pocket of liberal ease.

Just past the redbrick courthouse, she parked and found the young lawyer, pacing and staring down at his phone.

"I thought we could grab a cup of coffee at the Milk Mermaid," he said, pumping Jodi's hand. "You been there?"

Jodi shook her head.

"You live over near Render?"

"Bethlehem Mountain."

"I guess that end of the county doesn't have quite as many cafes, huh?" The lawyer walked ahead of Jodi, his sandy ponytail bobbing against the back of his pink neck, blue dress shirt working its way up and out of his chinos.

"It's a little weird, maybe," he said, turning down a side street, "but it's also kind of cool that you can get a hand-dripped cup of organic free-trade Guatemalan here in this little town in the middle of bumfuck nowhere."

This man, Jodi thought, carried with him a nearly visible halo of money-education-confidence-ease, a gauzy light of protection, and even as he spoke kindly to her she could barely stand to listen.

"When we visit my family they're always remarking on how deprived we must be. But it's not really so true anymore. I mean, in this day and age, where else could I live where I would feel safe letting my kids walk home from school?"

They passed the Moon Goddess Yoga Studio and a boutique selling hand-dyed silk scarves. At the red light a pickup idled, the bed filled with garbage bags and the windows open, leaking out the chorus of "The Night They Drove Old Dixie Down." A tiny brunette woman holding a purple yoga mat glanced up timidly at the truck before crossing the street.

"It can be just a little claustrophobic at times, though, I guess, especially down your way." The lawyer looked back over his shoulder. "I imagine that growing up here must really set your way of looking at the world. A little like an island, huh? Safe but probably also stifling."

Ahead of them the sidewalk was blocked by a teenage boy stapling glossy posters onto a telephone pole. The lawyer stepped out into the street and passed around him.

The teenager moved on up the sidewalk and Jodi stared at the poster.

THE ONE AND ONLY
—THE GOLDEN LEE—
Live at the Roanoke Coliseum on September 10.
Buy your tickets NOW.
Box office opens August 1 at 8 a.m.

Lee's face leered at her, the crisp blue and white of his eyes glowing above his leather-tan cheeks. Jodi reached out and touched the poster, her heart speeding. The paper felt smooth under her fingers. She glanced at the lawyer, half a block up the street. She gripped the corner of the poster and ripped it off the pole.

THE MILK MERMAID Cafe smelled strange, a mixture of farts and old flowers, and the music was up so loud it pulsed the floor. The lawyer sat close to Jodi, balancing his coffee and file of papers on a tiny round table but she couldn't pay attention to anything he was saying, distracted as she was by the posters and the thought of Lee coming so close.

"As it turns out, Ron Leonards has your piece of land listed with Davis and Davis Realty for forty grand." The lawyer flicked his eyes up to Jodi's face.

She looked past a dread-headed man and out the back windows to the parking lot where a couple of kids practiced kick flips. She felt herself falling, sinking backward toward despair and the snaking certainty that victim was the only role she was ever really meant to play. She closed her eyes. Ron Leonards's polo shirt was as green as the lawn that flowed out behind his house, as green as the chlorine-tinged hair of his white-blond children.

"Looks like he bought up a bunch of plots at auction back in the early nineties."

Ron Leonards touched his toupee constantly, checking the positioning with his fingertips, his pinky ring glinting in the noon-high sun.

"The people over at Davis and Davis said he's from around here originally, living down in Florida now. Eye on development."

Ron Leonards's green polo shirt hugged his distended gut. *Bun in the oven?* his wife teased. *How many months?* The girls at the Fox Den ignored his stomach. They dipped their sleek skin close, grinding hips and asses into his crotch, their eyes skimming but never really landing on him. He closed his own eyes, breathed in the smell of them, a heady, synthetic coconut beach party.

"Even at those prices, some of them have sold." The lawyer shook his head and stirred his coffee, spinning the spoon three times in one direction and then three times in the other. Jodi watched the precise movements of his spoon, trying to narrow and calm her mind. She should never have come here; now she had the Lee poster and further knowledge of the hopelessness of the land. At least up on Bethlehem she had not known.

"Can't we explain that I was in prison?" she said, an edge of desperation in her voice. "I could start to pay off the taxes now."

The lawyer's face pinched as if Jodi's words had hurt him physically.

"The notice was sent," he said, "in September of 1989 to the address listed for Andy McCarty."

She could feel him waiting for her reaction.

"No, but—"

She pushed herself upright in her chair, forcing back the self-pity.

"I can pay him the amount he bought it for. You said he only paid thirty-five hundred. I can save up and pay that."

The lawyer tapped his pen against his notepad and ignored her illogical plea. "There's a fracking operation on the western end of Bethlehem Mountain, right?"

Jodi nodded.

"Fracking is a pretty hot ticket around here, pretty divisive." The lawyer stirred his coffee again. "You know much about it?"

"I saw that piece of land down near Render. Looked like they tore it up pretty good."

"Yeah, it's big money for some folks but it's also pretty clear that those operations contaminate local drinking water, among other things. There's a woman here in town, Lynn Bower, she runs a group, Don't Frack with Us, I think she calls it. Anyway, they've been trying to buy up land before the gas companies can get to it. If there's enough Marcellus shale under your acreage, I think she might help."

Jodi stared down at her cup of coffee and ran her tongue along the back of her teeth. "Help how?"

"Well, the conservation group would own the land and—"

"Own *my* land?"

"Maybe you could buy them out eventually or pay it back or—"

"How's that supposed to help me? I'll never have that kind of money."

The lawyer's phone beeped and lit up on the table between them, the screen flashing a photograph of a blonde woman, her face squished between two plump, pink-cheeked kids.

"Sorry," he said, pulling the phone closer to him. "Deirdre keeps messaging me, they're down at Virginia Beach this week."

"We'd have an agreement?"

The lawyer was already piling his papers back into his bag. "Agreement?"

"That the land really belongs to me? That I'll just pay it off, like a loan?"

The lawyer wrinkled his eyebrows and smiled a little as if Jodi had just performed a small, mildly amusing trick. "Well, of course the land would not belong to you *legally* any more than it does right now but"—he lifted his cup and swirled the coffee, tipping it to his mouth—"we're putting the horse far before the cart anyhow. I'll contact Lynn, and if she's interested, she'll give you a call and will probably want to meet with you."

Walking back to the car, Jodi tore down every Lee Golden poster that she could see, as if this would somehow stop him from coming near. When she reached the Chevette she dumped the pile of them onto the passenger's seat and drove out of Lewisville.

Hot wind roared through the open windows and as she picked up speed the posters fluttered, Lee's gleaming face flapping around the stick shift and down by her feet. *Well,* he mocked her, *of course the land would not belong to you* legally.

Along the edge of Route 3, just past Cold Creek, a row of red-and-white signs, NOW HIRING: CASHIERS, were stabbed into the earthen embankment. Jodi slowed the Chevette and looked at them, buckling under the wind of the passing cars, and then up the hill at Harry's Superette, flanked by an abandoned Biscuit World and the River's Edge Motel. She wanted badly to return home with something more than just Lee's grotesque face and the news about the land.

She pulled into the parking lot and stopped the car in front of Harry's. A teenage boy pushed a line of shopping carts past her window, his head thrown back and face tilted up. The light was beginning to leave the sky and jet trails stood out like scars against the deepening blue. Two girls came out of a motel room wearing boxer shorts and worn-out bras, a mustard-colored towel thrown over one shoulder. They crossed the parking lot and headed toward the river, passing between them a single cigarette.

Jodi stood and lit her own cigarette. Maybe, she thought, walking slowly toward Harry's, maybe because it wasn't a chain store, they wouldn't have the same policies as Walmart and Kmart. The RC Cola vending machines blinked in the growing dusk and beyond them the store shone with a bright fluorescent hopefulness, full of bold primary colors of encouragement: red cashier aprons, blue plastic sacks, the yellow of a dish detergent display.

A girl with leopard print pants handed Jodi an application and led her to a back room.

"You can fill it out here," she said, motioning to the break room table, scattered with Styrofoam cups and ketchup packets.

Jodi thanked her but the girl did not leave. Jodi stared at the blank lines on the paper. The girl poured a cup of coffee and stood in the corner picking at her fingernails. Jodi filled in her name and parents' address. She wished the girl would leave. Walking in here, she hadn't realized just how embarrassingly unprepared she was for this moment, having arrived at age thirty-five without ever applying for a job.

Donovan's "Mellow Yellow" came on over the loudspeakers.

Jodi moved down to the next line.

Educational Background and Degrees: _____

She scratched *GED* in small letters.

Driver's License Number: _____

Work Experience:_____

Her pen hovered. The only possible thing she could ink in was "janitorial labor at Jaxton Federal Correctional Facility." Or what? The six months she spent washing dishes at a diner in Render back in 1988?

Professional References: _____

Her hand froze.

"I'll go fetch the manager," the girl said, and Jodi startled.

The room shifted and closed in. How did it get to this? How the fuck had she become someone whose hopes were all pinned on landing a grocery store cashier position?

She flipped the paper over.

Have you ever been convicted of a felony or misdemeanor?_____

Jodi stood. All around her was the ticking fluorescence and windowless concrete block of an interrogation room. Not enough air. No exit.

There were footsteps in the hallway.

She balled up the application and walked out fast, head down and eyes averted as she crashed past the manager.

WHEN SHE ARRIVED at the cabin, a truck was parked in the yard. A dust-covered black pickup. Jodi sat there, squinting at it until slowly she began to recognize: Dennis's. She twisted the Chevette's keys and jerked the car door open, all her focus thrown forward toward the cabin.

She rushed the front-porch steps but the house was empty, matchbox cars strewn across the floorboards, the pitcher pump dripping. She stepped back onto the porch. The evening air was full of movement, a cooler wind sluicing under the dry heat and crows massing in noisy bunches in the black oak trees.

"Miranda?" she called, making her way around to the side steps, splintered porch boards aching loudly under her feet.

In the powdered dust of the woodlot she found them: Miranda, standing,

arms crossed, watching Dennis as he stalked about under the shed roof, a
black duffel bag slung over his shoulder.

"Dennis," Jodi said, and when he and Miranda both turned to look at her
Jodi's heart slammed up between her lungs.

"Hey," Miranda said, her mouth teasing into a smile at the corners.

Dennis set down the bag and stared straight at Jodi, moving his right
hand around inside his pocket until he found a crumpled pack of cigarettes.

"What are you doing?" Jodi said, but even as she pronounced the words
she knew the balance had long ago been tipped and whatever kind of older-
sibling authority she might have once had was gone.

"I was thinking up in the woodshed rafters might be an all right place,"
Dennis said, the orange end of his cigarette neon in the gloaming light.

Jodi closed her eyes. She felt a tug inside her and wanted to run, not
so much from Dennis as from herself, the self that seemed, recently, to be
increasingly thin and weightless, ill equipped for any choice or decision. She
sensed that something hung before her now that she ought to grab ahold of
but her mind just spun.

She walked across the woodlot without looking at Miranda, then knelt
beside the black bag and unzipped it. The smell bit her nostrils, a dense, oiled,
almost animal scent. It reminded Jodi of the hide odor of a horse after a long
run, that hard musk, so different from the simple stink of cows. She lifted one
of the plastic packages out and fingered the buds, miniature Christmas trees
furred over with long red-brown hair.

"You make a lot of money with this stuff?"

Dennis stomped his cigarette out and shrugged.

"I need more than just a few hundred dollars if I'm agreeing to keep this
shit here on a regular basis," Jodi said, her voice trembling a little.

Dennis's face cracked open with a look that might have been sympathy.

"I'll give you some up front and then we'll see what all I get for it," he said,
grabbing the bag and walking past the bow saw and a cobwebbed posthole
digger into the back corner of the shed.

. . .

RAIN CAME THAT night in a great enveloping movement. Jodi heard it arrive just as she and Miranda were getting into bed, raindrops on the tin roof like so many spilled marbles, rattling the trees against one another, stripping the leaves. She sat up and pushed the blankets aside to go check that the windows were closed but Miranda pulled her back in. The warmth of the blankets and the heat of Miranda's body had no edges to them. She pooled across the bed, smelling of whiskey, her hair tangling among the pillows as she slid her hand up Jodi's chest, under her T-shirt, to find her nipples. All evening Jodi had been waiting for the boys to go to bed so she could tell Miranda about the Lee Golden posters but now she felt nervous to bring it up. She'd drunk too much again and everything was slipping. Miranda kissed Jodi's ribs one by one and pressed her face into the dip of her stomach.

"Hey," Jodi said. "I meant to tell you, I saw the weirdest thing when I was in town earlier."

Miranda lifted her head, her hair falling down into her eyes.

"There was posters all over Lewisville for *Lee*." She whispered the name as if to say it out loud might conjure him.

Miranda nodded but did not say anything.

"Like advertising for him playing a concert, just over the border in Virginia."

"Okay." Miranda sat up. "So?"

Jodi looked away. A flash of frustration pulsed across her brain. Apparently no one took her seriously. Dennis showed up and left drugs at her house without permission and now Miranda looked at her like she wasn't making any sense.

She took a deep breath. "Don't you think it's a bad sign, him coming so close to here?"

"He plays concerts all over the place."

"But we haven't been doing such a good job of hiding. I mean, we're driving around with a Georgia license plate. We gotta get rid of that. What if there are missing-persons papers out on the boys? Anybody around here could put two and two together."

"You're just paranoid." Miranda shook her hair out of her eyes and stared at Jodi, her face looking placid and stupid.

"Paranoid?"

"Him playing near here doesn't mean anything."

"Oh, really? I bet you miss him, is that it?" The words seemed to have launched themselves from Jodi's lips before she had even conceived of them. "I bet it was real nice being with him, huh? He gave you money and drugs? Is that it?"

"Well, yeah, but—"

"You want somebody that'll take care of you like that? You hate it here, don't you?" The muddied force of all Jodi's worries seemed determined to flow straight out of her mouth. "I'm sorry, I can't provide for you like that, you know, I really am. But all you care about is yourself, you know, sometimes I think I care more about those boys than you do. You wouldn't really mind if Lee found the boys, would you?"

Miranda's eyes snapped into focus. "What the fuck?"

Jodi thought for a moment that Miranda might hit her but she just rolled off the bed and stood, shaking, in the doorway, looking back, her eyes wet. "You have no fucking right to say that."

Jodi saw then that she had reached her, she had truly hurt her, and this ability to cause her pain opened something in Jodi, a gushing return of love, and as Miranda walked out of the room she looked suddenly ineffably beautiful again.

Two days later, Dennis came back, his truck grinding slowly up the dirt road toward the cabin. At the sound of his rusted tailpipe, Jodi came out onto the porch and watched him leap from the cab and dart through the rain around to the passenger's side. He pulled the door open and stood there, dripping, as a dark-haired woman stepped down and turned to gather her things.

They walked across the grass together. The woman—Mexican, maybe, or Cherokee—wore a short, shiny dress and hugged to her chest a pink child-size backpack but her face looked over thirty. Dennis squinted as he walked up the steps, rain running down the creases of his cheeks.

"Hey, how's it going?" He glanced toward the cabin door where Ricky stood, his eyes following the movements of the dark-haired woman.

Jodi shrugged. "What's up?"

"Not a whole lot." Dennis shifted his weight between his feet.

Jodi raised her eyebrows and clenched her cigarette in her teeth.

"Hey, look," Dennis said. "I need you to do me a solid."

"I already did you a solid."

"Well." His voice pitched up in the middle of the word. "I need you to do me another."

Jodi jerked her chin in the direction of the woodshed. "Are you taking that shit out of here today?"

"Look"—Dennis pressed his hand to his breast pocket for his cigarettes— "this is Rosa. She just—"

"Ros*alba*," the woman said, the name rolling, half-soft, half-staccato, off her tongue.

Dennis paused, cigarette raised to his lips. He looked over at the woman and her body tightened, muscles tensing visibly.

The rain rang heavy on the roof.

Dennis turned back to Jodi. "I just need you to keep Miss Rosa here for a little bit."

"Keep her here?" Jodi looked up and caught a glint of fear in the woman's black eyes before she glanced away.

"I got this friend, Cruz, who runs a little, uh, you know, bunny ranch." Dennis's eyes met Jodi's and his mouth twisted up into a smile, his whole face itching with a tamped-down gleefulness, and for a moment he looked no different than he had as a twelve-year-old making up stories about getting laid. "Most of the time the cops take a little cash on the side and turn their eyes, pretend it's just a trailer park. But now there's talk that state police want to investigate, turn Cruz's whole place inside out, and Rosa here ain't got papers."

He exhaled smoke in two thin streams and stepped closer, pressing into Jodi's palm a limp one-hundred-dollar bill.

Jodi stared down at the crumpled money, a buzz not unlike nicotine rising in her brain.

"Why are *you* helping her?"

Dennis was halfway down the porch steps already. "I told you, it's a favor. I owe Cruz."

Jodi looked back to the money and there she was again, tipping over the edge of some precipice of decision making, but it still did not seem real and she wondered now if she had somehow managed to carry the floating, choiceless world of prison here with her into this unreal place.

"I'm gonna need more than this."

"It'll just be a few days."

"You *need* me to do this, right?"

Dennis squinted at her through the rain.

"Then I'm gonna *need* a little more money. You think you can just—"

Dennis tugged his wallet out and freed another hundred-dollar bill, tossing it at her, and then he was gone, his truck tires sucking loudly at the mud until the rain-haze swallowed him completely.

ROSALBA SMOKED HAND-ROLLED cigarettes like the ones that Effie had favored, and though Jodi had told her she could smoke inside the cabin, she seemed to prefer one particular spot down at the end of the porch where the gutter spat the rainwater out into the flat dirt.

For a while they all crowded in the cabin door and studied her, the boys poking their heads through Jodi's, Ricky's, and Miranda's legs. Rosalba seemed not to notice them. She sat there, looking distant and utterly self-contained, watching a gray squirrel cross the yard, flicking its tail against the rain. Eventually everyone wandered off except for Ricky. He was fascinated by her; he'd trailed around the cabin as Jodi introduced her and he moved in closer now as Rosalba measured a line of tobacco onto a paper rectangle, licking the edge and pinching it closed.

It didn't seem right for someone who had been forced into hiding—dropped off in a totally unfamiliar place—to spend the afternoon smoking cigarettes and watching the wildlife. Someone illegal, someone running from the law, and here she was acting like this was a bed-and-breakfast. She pricked at something in Jodi, some old Jaxton instinct that made her want to force the girl to show her pain.

"Is Dennis in love with you?" Jodi asked, stepping around Ricky and walking toward her down the porch.

Rosalba's laughter was rough and phlegmy. She shrugged, pursed her lips, and let out a thin stream of smoke. "I don't really know your brother."

The wind blew in sideways now and the trees all leaned.

"Your English is real good," Jodi said.

Rosalba pulled a loose strand of tobacco from the end of her cigarette. "In Mexico I taught at the university."

Jodi looked up and Rosalba met her gaze. The skin around her eyes was hatched with soft wrinkles, her mouth full and bow shaped.

"You could teach me?" Ricky said, leaning past Jodi and pointing to the tobacco pouch in Rosalba's lap.

Rosalba smiled. Her left front tooth was rimmed in silver and it winked when she opened her lips. "Here," she said, holding out the half-smoked cigarette. "You can have it."

"But you could teach me how you do your trick?" Ricky said, moving his fingers in a mime of Rosalba's rolling action.

Rosalba clamped the cigarette between her lips and brushed the loose tobacco off her lap. "I will show you any trick you want if you first just tell me where is a bathroom."

Ricky nodded and stepped to the edge of the porch, pointing toward the outhouse at the bottom of the yard.

Rosalba froze, half-sitting, half-standing, her eyes wide with shock.

Ricky looked at her and laughed, still pointing down the hill. He laughed and Jodi turned to face him. She heard his laughter and everything spun out slow as she watched him tilt his head, smiling broadly.

"Oh, okay, wow," Rosalba said.

She set her bag on the chair and headed toward the outhouse without noticing the magic alchemical shift of the moment but Jodi was paralyzed by it. She heard Ricky's laughter and something loosened inside her, some rearrangement of particles that opened up room for more air. She didn't know that she had been waiting for this, didn't know until that moment that she had not heard Ricky laugh, ever, and had not really seen him fully smile, not since Paula.

IN ADDITION TO her tobacco, Rosalba kept in her backpack playing cards decorated with images of Catholic saints and a bottle of tequila. What began as a demonstration of card tricks and then a round of rummy between Ricky and Rosalba turned into a full-tilt poker game by early evening. Miranda joined the table, gathering up her cards into her hand and watching intently as Rosalba wet the web of her thumb, poured on salt, and licked it before drinking down a shot of tequila. The boys crowded around, Donnie climbing up onto a chair for a better view. The room was loud with laughter and shouted instructions, the lamplight drawing their silhouettes tall against the log walls.

"Hey, Jo, come play," Miranda said, but Jodi hung back, feeding kindling wood into the cookstove.

She couldn't shake her feeling of irritation at Rosalba for acting so easy and comfortable. This is my place, my people, she found herself wanting to say, as if Ricky, Miranda, and the boys were a finite resource that might get all used up. *My people.* But, truthfully, she and Miranda were yet to ever use the word *girlfriend*, and Ricky, well, she wasn't sure exactly how to quantify her connection to Ricky. Already, in just the four or five hours that she had been at the house, Rosalba seemed to have inspired in him more of the sort of awe and trust that Jodi herself had hoped to spark when she'd walked into the Georgia Folk and Country.

"For you." Rosalba passed the tequila to Ricky, who sniffed the bottle and shook his head.

"It cleans you out," she told him. "Brightens you inside."

"He doesn't need to be drinking," Jodi said.

The table went quiet.

Miranda looked over at Jodi, confused, and Jodi felt sorry for having so resoundingly smashed the good mood. She stepped out from behind the cookstove and watched as Ricky locked eyes with her and lifted the bottle slowly to his lips. Somehow, when Veeda had questioned his drinking of a whiskey-coke, it hadn't seemed like a big deal but now Jodi realized that she had no idea how he reacted to alcohol or if he had ever had much to drink before at all. Her own mother was not what you would call a happy drunk and it worried her, thinking about that possibility of an unpredictable personality shift.

Ricky closed his eyes as he swallowed the shot, then blinked and set the bottle on the table but kept his hand around it.

"All right, that's enough now, leave some for me!" Jodi stepped closer, wishing her voice sounded more playful.

Rosalba raised her eyebrows and looked back and forth between Jodi and Ricky. Jodi took the bottle and drank a too-long swallow that caught and burned at the back of her throat. She felt them all watching.

"Kaleb," she said, setting the bottle beside Rosalba. "Come help me fix dinner."

Kaleb stood on his tiptoes, his face peeking up above the table, lips pinched into a pout. "Why?"

"Don't sass me," Jodi said, hearing the sharpness and wanting to take it back already, hating the way that Kaleb's face crumpled. "I need your expert advice," she added, "your opinion on the seasoning."

He sighed loudly and Miranda giggled. "Is she working you too hard, little chef?"

Kaleb nodded but slipped his hand into Jodi's.

The thing was, she realized, she knew almost nothing about Ricky. She knew he loved Paula and that Dylan had beaten and abused him for all those years. She knew he was obsessed with music but when she thought about it now it occurred to her that she hadn't heard him sing once over the past two weeks.

She dumped three cans of chili in a pot and handed the spoon to Kaleb.

None of this not knowing had seemed like a problem until now. Back in Jaxton she'd assumed that freedom would be enough, both for her and for him. She had pictured Ricky safe, out of Dylan's reach, but beyond that all she had was some image of him fishing. Did Ricky even like to fish? She couldn't decide if this was something Paula once said or just something she'd invented and she felt an ache now, a yawning sadness at this not-knowing and all the distance it implied.

"Rummy."

Jodi looked up as Ricky held an ace high above his head and shouted again, "Rummy!"

"Wrong game." Miranda was laughing breathlessly and reaching to snatch his card.

"One moment," Rosalba said as she stood and walked out onto the porch.

Jodi left Kaleb at the stove and followed her.

"Hey," she called.

Rosalba turned to face her and there was a current there, a measuring and waiting that was, to Jodi, so familiar. She waited as the silence tripled between them.

"I am sorry about the tequila," Rosalba said finally. "He does not drink?"

"If he wants to." Jodi shrugged, realizing suddenly that she did not want to be cast into the role of the one who held Ricky's leash. She stepped closer. "What happens to me if you take off and Dennis comes looking for you?"

Rosalba's eyes were blank. "Take off?"

"I don't care what he pays me, I'm not going to keep anybody locked up here. But if he comes back for you and—"

"No." Rosalba shook her head. "Do not worry about me." She managed a better jail face than Jodi ever had—so quiet she was not there, just the whisper-crinkle of cigarette paper as she rolled a fresh smoke—and yet her presence was somehow loud also, proof of how little control Jodi had over anything.

April 1989

Paula came back to their hotel room last night, Jodi thinks, but then again, maybe she only dreamt her. The hotel room is empty, thin yellow light seeping in under the curtains. Jodi checks for the .38, feels the curve of the handle there under the corner of the mattress, and relaxes back onto the lumpy pillow. This is San Antonio, Texas, but the voices outside are still Mexican.

Paula leaves these days without saying anything. Sometimes she brings Jodi to the games, in the backrooms behind pizza restaurants, in white-pillared houses or smoke-thick clubs, but most of the time Jodi does not want to go. Once, she stayed naked, alone in the hotel, for three days straight. She smokes cigarettes and paints her toenails. She drinks Carlo Rossi and adds water to make it last. She plays solitaire. She masturbates. She cuts her hair.

She had thought that the money from the poker game in Tampico, though it was less than expected, would make them ready. Ready now to go get Ricky and return to Effie's land. But Paula says that is just the base layer, they have to keep building.

When Paula is gone, Jodi is desperate for her to come back—the emptiness ravaging inside her as the Paula-less hours pass—but when Paula is there Jodi experiences a creeping sort of irritation at no longer being alone. In her solitude she feels she is getting somewhere, burrowing deep into a new and unexplored self.

Lately she's found that she can't fix Paula's face in her mind, even when Paula has just left the room. She thinks of Effie's land—pulls up the image, full and intact—the house with the sloping porch and black oaks out back. She closes her eyes and forces herself to concentrate until she can see Paula's face just as clearly. Those sharp cheekbones and full lips, how her mouth pinches at the corner at the mention of Ricky's name and the way her eyes rake a room, consuming, filtering, putting it all to use—a look that Jodi thought at first was the thrill of a vision, the beginning of a plan that wrapped around to satisfaction. It was that look that gave Jodi the idea that Paula could lead her to live inside a life bigger than anything she could manage on her own. Lately, though, Paula looks more desperate than powerful.

Sometimes Jodi thinks of taking money from Paula while she sleeps. She thinks of ticket counters and a long bus ride back east. But the thing of it—the great, oozy, uncontrollable thing of it—is that she's grafted her happiness onto this life with Paula, the flash and burn of it, the somewhere new each night and we don't need anything but each other.

In the beginning, when they first headed south, she'd called her parents a few times, proud to report on her travels. No one else in her immediate family had ever crossed the state line. In Mexico, though, the phone calls were too expensive and she hasn't spoken to them in months. And now, she thinks, Paula is her family and the idea of herself without Paula is like the thought of amputation. She is reminded of certain evidence, studies that have shown how crack saturates the senses so that nothing quietly delightful will ever be satisfying again.

August 2007

With Rosalba there it made seven of them in the three-room cabin, and the storm kept on, hurtling against the tin roof. At first Miranda told her boys to play inside games but soon she gave up and let them tussle in the mud while she sat on the porch, smoking and tipping whiskey into her coffee cup, joined sometimes by Ricky, sometimes Rosalba or Jodi as they paced in and out and peered up at the cloud-dark sky.

All the aimless, forced proximity reminded Miranda of life on the tour bus, when Kaleb was six months old and she had started performing and touring with Lee. It had been the manager's idea—fresh blood, a way to perk up the show—and Miranda had been ecstatic for the chance, though really she was nothing more than a backup singer with a spotlight. They had done mostly local shows at first, not too much hard traveling with such a little baby, but then Tamara Monti booked a reunion tour with Lee and insisted that he bring Miranda along with them to Europe. Miranda was dazed with excitement and worry. There was no way she could bring Kaleb and she knew she ought to say no but this was her chance to see the glittering Old World that Lee had always spoken of. She weaned Kaleb and left him with Lee's aunt Nina, telling herself that it would be *just six weeks*.

Tamara invited Miranda up to New York a few days before the tour to learn her songs and in her sleek steel-and-stone apartment they drank martinis and stared at each other, a reflection of blondeness. Most people took them for mother and daughter, though with her surgeries and hair dye Tamara could almost pass for Miranda's sister.

"When I die, when I die, Daddy don't fret for me," she sang as she paced the window-walled room, cradling her guitar. "For the one who comes from the still and the quiet will surely know me."

Miranda looked away and watched the olive bob in her glass.

"Come on," Tamara said. "I want to hear you try out the melody."

Miranda closed her eyes. "When I die, when I die, Daddy don't fret for me."

She opened them. Tamara was staring straight at her, fingers picking quick over the metal strings and yellow hair falling long and straight across her shoulders. "Fear," she sang, "is the driving wheel but flesh from the blood He will conceal."

"You wrote that song?" Miranda leaned toward her.

Tamara smiled. "The universe gave it to me."

MIRANDA ENTERED THE tour grinning ear to ear and leaking breast milk down the front of her minidress. No matter how much tissue she stuffed in her bra, the warm milk leaked through in quarter-size circles by the end of every show and her breasts ached fiercely but there was the Eiffel Tower, all lit up and looking, well, looking just like it did in postcards, but there it was for real! And the thrill of performing! She knew no one really cared about her, they were there for Tamara and Lee, but it didn't matter, the whole experience was electric: her own voice rising and turning in with Tamara's—*when I see you coming across the Beulah Land*—and the heat of the stage lights on her skin. Lee seemed disappointed with the tour, the musty old theaters and coffeehouses they'd been booked to play in and the small size of the audiences. Miranda had little to compare it to, though, and the applause sounded thunderous to her, a roar like a wave breaking over her head.

Tamara was sweet, telling Miranda she was beautiful and asking her about motherhood. *I never even considered having children. I guess my career is my baby.* She smiled and tucked Miranda's hair behind her ear. *Good for you, doing both.*

Lee was distant and as the tour continued he grew more so. Slowly the glitz of traveling wore off and Miranda began to notice. The days and places all blended into one another. She was constantly hungry. There was always another drink but never anything to eat. Never enough time to sleep, to bathe.

In a dark stone city somewhere—Budapest, maybe—Lee filled their room with new friends, a plump bag of coke, and bottles of champagne. Miranda passed out on the couch eventually and woke to a strange man kissing her hair. She pushed him away and stood, blinking, calling out for Lee, but the room was full of strangers. No Tamara and no Lee. She picked her way through the crowd and wandered down the marble stairs to the front desk, where she demanded a different room.

The air in the new room was thin and blue. She slept deeply until she woke to a sobbing Lee crawling into bed. *Don't leave me like that, baby,* he cried, his breath full of warm cognac and cigarettes. *You let me fuck her.* His cries were jagged, wet holes. *Don't let me do that to you, baby, don't let me.* Somewhere, in a room above them, a violinist was practicing, the notes like a soundtrack to someone else's dream. Eventually Lee quieted and the music rose, building into something Miranda could make sense of: Rachmaninoff's "Vocalise."

In Istanbul they took a wooden boat up the Bosporus. There the seasons had already changed and the wind blew smoke and leaves. On the deck of a teahouse, they huddled close, the wicker chairs creaking as they leaned against each other. They hadn't spoken of the night in Hungary and both

Lee and Tamara acted as if it hadn't happened and so Miranda preferred to remember it only as a bad dream.

After their show in Athens they took a break from the tour and split up, Tamara staying in Thessaloniki with an old lover while Miranda and Lee went to Crete. In Heraklion, though, Lee went out alone to the fisherman's bars, often not returning until morning.

One night in Barcelona the three of them went to the hotel bar after dinner. Lee and Tamara were discussing some old mutual friend whom Miranda did not know. She sipped her wine and watched a young couple standing by the elevator, their hands running over each other's bodies. The girl brushed a speck of dirt from the boy's face, smiled, and turned, bending over her suitcase. Her peach-colored dress slipped up her white legs and the boy placed his hand there, smoothing the fabric against her skin until she laughed and pushed his hand away. Miranda watched the twinness of them, faces so young, the desire coursing equally between them, and something in her ached, a burning lodged behind her sternum. She was seventeen. They were most likely her age but to her their dance-dream of love seemed impossibly, childishly naive.

"I'm going to buy cigarettes," she announced, walking out of the bar without looking back. She could have bought them there at the hotel but she needed a moment alone, away from Tamara and Lee.

Rain began to fall while she was at the kiosk. The season was changing here too, a damp cold leaking in from the sea. Fall, Miranda thought, but the word seemed strange, connected only to some other part of her history. These past four weeks had been the longest of her life.

The rain fell harder as she ran across the narrow street toward the yellow lights of the hotel. Through the bright window she could see Tamara and Lee up at the bar ordering again, and as she watched, a bearded man approached Tamara. Through the fogged glass, she could see him speaking silently and see Tamara turning, her hair swinging out in a single blonde sheet.

Miranda clattered in out of the rain and stood, shaking her boots off in the doorway. Behind the bar a waiter polished wineglasses, wiping the huge delicate globes deftly, then holding them up against the light.

"No, I'm not lying," Tamara said. She sat on a stool facing the young man while Lee stood behind her, propped up against the bar.

"But why not tell your audience where the song came from?" The bearded man's English was strong but accented. "Why not simply say the song is 'Fear Is the Driving Wheel' by Cissy Jackson? You wouldn't conceive of singing one of Bellini's arias without giving credit to him, would you?"

Tamara shook her head and ran her fingers through her hair. Lee leaned in closer and placed his hand on her shoulder.

"No, no, it's not the same at all," he said. "With these traditional songs it's, well, it's part of a tradition more than an individual. She's just channeling that—"

"But it's not a traditional. Cissy Jackson wrote and recorded that song in April of 1939."

"No one can prove that she wrote it." Tamara grabbed her glass of red by its impossibly thin stem. "She was probably just performing something she'd heard other musicians around her play."

"No," the man insisted, rocking back and forth on his stool. "No, that's very unlikely, no one has ever heard that song sung by anyone but Cissy Jackson. If it were a traditional song, it would have surfaced somewhere else as well."

"Fine." Tamara set her glass down and the liquid leapt up the sides. "I'm inspired. Her song inspires me, so I sing it."

"It's called art," Lee said.

"It doesn't bother me that you sing it." The man would not look at Lee but directed his gaze back at Tamara instead. "I just don't understand why you can't attribute."

"It's not about where you get your inspiration." Lee tried again to catch his eye. "It's what you do with it."

"And who's listening for her name?" Tamara said. "She's dead. I sing it now."

"But the truth in that song is Jackson's truth, not yours."

"Truths don't belong to any one person."

The man smiled and his smile was surprisingly warm. "That's good but stealing someone else's truth, even if it mirrors yours, is still stealing," he said, raising his glass of beer. "Why not do like Hedy West? She has no problem admitting where her lyrics come from."

"What makes you such an expert on American music?"

The man nodded toward Miranda. "Your friend, I believe, is waiting for you."

Tamara spun on her stool. "Oh, you," she said, and she sounded exhausted. "What are you doing?"

Miranda found herself smiling a little. She didn't know what to say. She looked to Lee but he seemed suddenly absorbed in his drink.

Tamara's eyes narrowed and snapped. "Why are you smiling?"

Miranda stepped closer, shaking her head. "No, no. It's just interesting, he's talking about that song we sing—"

"'Fear Is the Driving Wheel' by Cissy Jackson." The man nodded.

"That one she says the universe gave her." Miranda really *was* smiling now.

"Fuck you." Tamara rose up off her stool. "Fuck you, you little fucking bitch." She streamed across the room and out of the bar.

Lee closed his eyes, pressing his fingers against his temple.

Miranda stared down at the parquet floor and squeezed her pack of cigarettes in her fist. "I'm sorry," she said.

Lee pushed himself away from the bar and headed out without looking at her. "I knew it wasn't a good idea to bring you on this trip," he said.

Miranda felt her tongue swell inside her mouth, filling up with all the things she couldn't say. She couldn't move and she couldn't say a thing. The elevator doors closed behind Lee.

"Hey," the bearded man said. "Sorry about all that. Can I buy you a drink?"

THEIR SHOW WAS in Bordeaux the next night and Tamara and Miranda still had not spoken. Miranda also refused to talk to Lee, who had spent most of the previous night in Tamara's room comforting her but apparently not really helping because all day Tamara was still sulky, curled up in the corner of the greenroom couch, blue-gray smoke trailing out of her mouth.

On stage Tamara skipped "Fear Is the Driving Wheel" and dove straight into "Patchwork Heart." Miranda stood two steps behind, squinting at the audience—a small and distant hurdle between herself and the end of her night.

Halfway through the song Tamara's breath came short, the words escaping only half-formed. She stopped midverse. The band continued for two measures until she sliced her hand across her throat.

"Bordeaux," she called out to the audience. "Bordeaux, what do you know of friendship?"

Her voice was deep and smoky.

"Do you know who this is?" She was smiling, waving her hand at Miranda.

Miranda's heart sped up.

The audience was nothing but a dark, rumpled mass.

"You know who this is?"

Lee's wife, a small voice called, joined then by a few others. *Miranda Golden.*

"Yeah." Tamara's voice was strong now. "You know who this fucking kid was when I met her? She could barely sing."

Miranda's head throbbed and the lights burned her eyes. She looked toward Lee.

"You know who invited her? Gave her a chance?"

Miranda felt the audience move in. They were invited now, in the conversation.

"Who trained her and showed her that she had a voice that could sing? Me." Tamara spat the words out fast and the audience bellowed.

Miranda watched as Lee turned slowly toward Tamara but did not say anything.

"And you know how she fucking repays me?"

The audience was hungry now and Miranda could feel herself shrinking. She should have seen this moment coming, ever since her first interactions with Tamara, the catlike circling and sizing up. It always seemed to happen like this with the women she looked up to; with Bella also, things had suddenly shifted inexplicably. She could feel tears forming, clogging her throat. She could not cry in front of this audience, they would eat her alive. Run, she thought, feeling the heat of the lights shift to the back of her head as she turned. Run, run, she urged herself.

The backstage was dim and full of movement but Miranda pushed through into the greenroom—a blur of sconced lights and table of half-eaten food—and out the emergency exit. The night was cold but brilliant and the fire escape led down to the back parking lot. The puddles in the lot were scabbed over with thin crusts of ice and Miranda tracked her way between them, crunching the brittle crystals under her heels. At the edge of the lot was a low fence and, beyond that, the highway, glistening.

SHE WAS PICKED up by the first rig that passed, a Spanish trucker on his way to Santander.

"You are traveling alone?" the man said, looking at her there in her yellow floral dress in the open doorway of his truck.

Miranda nodded and took him in—square jaw, bright eyes, and a beer belly. He had a kind face. She climbed up into the cab.

"You are cold?" he said, pulling the rig back onto the road.

Miranda shook her head. She was too astonished to feel cold. She liked the comfort of the cab, though, the cushioned seat and spread of dashboard lights, and everything else black, just the trail of the road ahead and, up close, a darkness so complete she could not even see her feet. It comforted her, this bodilessness.

"You are going where?" The trucker was nothing but a thick voice, his rough silhouette barely visible, reflected spectrally in the glass.

"I gotta get back home to my baby boy."

"In Spain?"

Miranda shook her head. Though her breasts had quit throbbing weeks ago, she felt a new ache now, a full-body I-must-hold-him-right-now kind of pain.

"You have problems with your husband."

It was not a question and so Miranda did not feel obliged to answer. The statement just sat there between them until the trucker spoke again, quietly.

"You like France?"

Miranda let her answers come slower and slower until they were both comfortable with the silence.

She slept and the seat held her, cupped close, until she woke to a bright spread of outdoor lights spilling across both sides of the road.

"We stop here," the trucker said.

They were at the Spanish border, the Pyrenees rising up around them in the moonlight. The air had turned sharp with cold but the parking lot was full of voices and engines, steam rising off the hoods of the trucks and mixing with the smoke of cigarettes, drivers leaning in to talk close over the grind of gears and blast of air brakes. Outside of his rig, the Spanish trucker looked different, old enough to be Miranda's father. He wrapped his coat around her shoulders and led her past the diesel tanks and over to a huddle of restaurants. The other drivers hushed as she walked by and the Spaniard put his hand lightly on her shoulder and herded her straight for the building with a blinking red sign that said LA SIRENA.

"I know a girl here, will let you stay with her. The little sister of my wife," he said, pointing to the counter inside where a black-haired girl was pouring a huge stein of beer. "Come, first we get a hot shower?"

Alone and naked in the shower Miranda began shaking. The tiny room was as blank as a cell: tiled ceiling, tiled walls, tiled floor, and a shower activated by coins. Miranda gripped her fist of metal money and shook. The water was warm but something inside her convulsed, wrenched out a jagged, uncontrollable shiver. She pictured baby Kaleb and she pictured the distances, the ocean between her and him, the hundreds of miles between herself and anyone who loved her, if anyone still did. She thought back to those months she'd spent living with Bella, watching and admiring her. She had always wanted a mother like Bella, a woman so shimmery that even her bad choices were beautiful, a woman you could write songs about, like Gram Parsons's "Brass Buttons," not a quietly bitter, death-smelling mother like her own. And Bella encouraged Miranda's adoration until that last week of her pregnancy when Lee had joined them in LA and Bella accused Miranda of stealing her jewelry and, worse, called her cloying and pitiful. *Lee, baby, see, look how she follows you everywhere. She does that to me too, nearly smothers me, she can't do anything on her own.*

When the shower cut off, the noise from outside the room rushed in and Miranda pressed more coins into the slot, focusing on the splatter rhythm of water falling. She used all the coins but she did not wash herself or loosen the grip of her fists.

When she walked into La Sirena the trucker was halfway through a tall beer.

"Ah, my American girl!" he called, waving Miranda toward the bar. He slapped the stool until she sat down. "Cristina!" he said, pointing to the woman who was stooped over a bucket of ice. *"¡Cerveza!"*

"My American!" he proclaimed as Cristina set down Miranda's beer.

Cristina's lips parted to show a dark gap between her front teeth. She had a soft round face, with huge luminous eyes.

"She speaks no English," the trucker said.

The trucker ordered pork and green olives, eggs and soup and mounds of white bread. Miranda was shaking less but she still could not eat. The trucker insisted, though, pushing toward her a plate piled with cheese, and after the first few bites it went down easily. The room was warm and dim, lit only by a row of small lamps and blinking pinball machines. Business was slow and when the trucker invited her Cristina came around to their side of the bar. She ate quickly, licking her fingers, stuffing her cheeks, and glancing up at Miranda.

"I tell Cristina you are having husband problems," the trucker said. "Cristina, she knows husband problems."

Miranda smiled and nodded at Cristina and offered her some beer. She took it in both hands and drank, the huge stein nearly covering her entire face, and in the quiet Miranda heard her teeth clink against the glass.

After his third beer the trucker stood and stepped away from the bar. Miranda moved to follow but the girl called out to her.

"*Espere aquí,*" she said, and then to the trucker. "*Dile que espere aquí.*"

"Wait here," the trucker said, bread crumbs trembling in his mustache. "She will take care, just wait here."

Cristina cleared the plates from the counter, disappearing behind a swinging wooden door, and Miranda listened to the pinball machines bleating out some looping tune and, outside, the constant engines rolling like a tide. She was grateful for the fact that she and Cristina spoke no common language, grateful for the easy silence that came with it. She didn't want to speak anymore, didn't want to say a word until the next morning when she would call Lee and tell him she needed to go home.

At 3 a.m. Cristina flipped the sign on the door and took Miranda's hand. She led the way to her room, a tiny closet around back of the restaurant that reminded Miranda of images she'd seen from monasteries. The single bed was made tight with striped cotton sheets, and the wooden dresser was laid out with a metal washbasin, porcelain pitcher, comb, brush, and mirror. Miranda was overcome with the perfect simplicity of the moment. She wanted to stay there, she thought, in that little room forever, to climb inside this other life and disappear.

"*Venga,*" Cristina said, slipping her shoes off and moving toward the bed. "*Y cierre la puerta.*"

JODI WOKE ON the morning of the fourth day of rain to the sound of Ricky's frantic voice.

"The tarp's leaking," he called from the bedroom doorway. "Water's coming in."

Eyes half-open, Jodi dragged herself up and into the next room to see the tarp hanging above the bed like a giant blue bladder. Miranda had painted yellow stars across the fabric and they quivered now as it drooped from the beams, so low that Donnie could bounce on the mattress and touch it.

"Hey," Miranda called to him from the doorway. "Hey, sweetie, no, get down from there."

Rosalba helped and together they all hauled the mattresses out and lined them up beside Miranda and Jodi's bed. While the boys ran back and forth across the one big mass of mattress, Miranda pulled Jodi into the back room. She pushed the door shut and leaned against it, pressing Jodi's hand up between her legs.

"Hey," she whispered. "I'm sorry I called you paranoid. I'm glad you care so much about my boys."

Jodi bent down to Miranda's neck and smelled the turning-apple scent of her sweat but she could not stop thinking of Rosalba, so close there in the next room, and her connection to Dennis and his judgments. Since Rosalba had arrived, they had not had sex once.

Miranda pulled her nightgown off over her head until the whole glowing paleness of her was naked there in the wet room, the air around her colored by the watery weight of the blue tarp. The rain roared, battering the trees outside and against the white cloth of the windows where dark leaves spattered and stuck. Miranda set a chair in front of the door and bent over it, pulling Jodi close, and though she obliged her, Jodi's mind stumbled forward out of the moment. Even with Miranda's perfect skin right there under her hands, she felt herself drawing away, looking back as if remembering this. She had managed, for a little while, to ignore the tenuousness of the land and the boys' custody but now that she was tangled in with Dennis and all his problems she could feel the instability in the very air around them, the fragility of this life they were trying to build.

She lifted her gaze up to the swaying tarp where water gathered and began to spill, perfectly, as if poured from a pitcher, down onto Ricky's papers and books.

She left Miranda on the chair and rushed to the corner, pulling the papers up into her arms, Ricky's folder of clippings, the faded squares so thin and soft: *Cardona, Nev.: Ten-year-old Naomi Gibbs, sole survivor of a trailer park fire that killed her entire family . . . Three-month-old baby found alive amid rubble, the sole surviving member of family killed by Tuscaloosa tornado . . . Bismarck, S.D.: Six-year-old brother kills four-year-old sister in shotgun accident . . . Waukeegan, Ill.: Dr. Lemuel Luther killed by 11-year-old son who claims his father "let the ghost in again."*

From among the little clippings a larger square of folded newsprint fell.

It drifted down to Jodi's feet. DULETT TRAGEDY UNDER INVESTIGATION, the headline read, and below it was a schoolbook-style photo of a tiny wide-eyed boy and the caption *Patrick Dulett, six, accused by his father of murder.*

"What's that?"

Jodi turned to see Miranda standing behind her, still naked.

"Ricky's clippings." She tried to keep her voice steady and emotionless but her heart was beating high in her throat and her hand shook as she folded the paper.

"Oh," Miranda said. "You don't think I'm sexy anymore?"

"What?" Jodi felt her mind skid sideways. The newspaper clipping was fairly pulsing in her hand. She stepped toward Miranda, trying to make eye contact. "Jesus, Miranda, look at me. I'm overwhelmed. Okay? We gotta get this roof fixed now and—"

Miranda tucked her tangled hair behind one ear and looked up. "You like the way I painted it?"

Jodi leaned in and kissed her. "Put on some clothes, we gotta make breakfast," she said, and when Miranda turned away she looked once more at the Dulett tragedy headline and then tucked it into her back pocket.

May 1989

Jodi wakes in the night to the rhythms of Paula's body convulsing beside her under the thin sheets. Her shoulders shudder but when Jodi bends over her Paula's face is dry. It is something deeper than weeping.

Jodi presses her palm into the middle of Paula's back and feels the heat trapped there under the trembling skin. She imagines she can lift away the pain, draw it out like a stain, and the thought of this makes her feel solid and necessary.

"Please, don't touch me," Paula says.

Jodi removes her hand.

"We have to go for Ricky." Paula struggles to stand, the sheet tangling around her legs and the mattress springing up as her weight lifts from it. "We have to go get him. Now."

Jodi watches Paula gather their things—a red T-shirt, purple panties—and stuff them into their carpetbag. When she turns on the light, a thudding sound begins at the window, a small, steady beating. Jodi slides off the bed and steps closer, squinting into the red eyes of a moth the size of her hand with dusty yellow orbs on each wing. It clings and shakes itself against the metal screen over and over again, desperate to reach the light.

Paula moves quickly down the hall and into the hotel lobby, tossing the keys onto the counter. There is no desk clerk in sight.

Off to the south the carpet of lights of some not-so-distant city shine faintly. They drive past the slick blackness of the night sea, oil derricks, and shrimp boats sheering up into view and then disappearing. Jodi watches Paula with a fresh intensity, aching with the thirst to touch her, to transfer some of the pain.

She passes out eventually and wakes to a sudden spray of car headlights that illuminate Paula's face. She drifts back into dreams then and when she opens her eyes again the car is not moving. Paula sleeps with her forehead against the steering wheel. They are stopped in an enormous parking lot, the highway overpass pulsing up above, thickening now with traffic as the sun begins to rise.

They eat breakfast at a place called the Yellow Bird Diner and Jodi watches Paula over her plate of scrambled eggs, trying to figure the direction of her thoughts from her face. Paula has not spoken of Ricky since waking and her movements are languid, all the frantic panic of the night before now faded.

Back on the interstate Paula points the car south and Jodi's words tumble out unbridled.

"Aren't we going to get Ricky?"

Paula does not unfasten her gaze from the horizon.

Jodi turns to her. A silent distance yawns open between them and it guts her, the fact that she can feel this lonely with Paula there, only a few feet away.

"We're not ready," Paula says. "You don't know him, Jodi, you can't see how it is."

She grips the steering wheel and the muscles of her shoulders tense and then release.

August 2007

═══════════

J odi was wet with rain before she'd even left the yard but the
air outside was good and clean, and walking was all she felt she
could do right now, just walk and walk and keep on walking
with Ricky's newspaper clippings in her hand.

She'd kept them in her back pocket while she made the fire and prepared
breakfast, questions fuzzing up her brain so she couldn't quite look at Ricky.
She'd excused herself after the meal, and out in the woodshed she'd unfolded
the paper.

DULETT TRAGEDY UNDER INVESTIGATION

May 25, 1985

LOCAL 911 OPERATORS RESPONDED to a call last Saturday evening
from Ms. Paula Dulett of North Chaunceloraine, who reported that
her infant son was dead and her younger brother in severe condition.
Upon arriving at the house, police and paramedics found Ms. Paula

Dulett, 21, with her infant son Jamie Vaughn Dulett, her brother Patrick ("Ricky") Dulett, six, and her parents, Mr. and Mrs. Dylan Dulett. The infant was pronounced dead at the scene, and Ricky Dulett, who appeared to be suffering from head trauma, was transported to the Deauvont Regional Children's Hospital in White Cane.

In her report to the police, Ms. Dulett stated that around 3 p.m. Saturday afternoon she and her mother had left the children, Jamie and Ricky, in the care of Mr. Dulett while they went to the grocery store. Upon returning, Ms. Dulett said that she heard screams coming from the backyard and found Ricky lying on the ground and bleeding from his ears and mouth. Mr. Dulett, who was present with Ricky in the yard, told Ms. Dulett that "the little bastard killed your son and then jumped from a second-story window." Inside the residence, Ms. Dulett found Jamie Vaughn on the floor beside his overturned bassinet. The infant had no pulse and was not breathing.

Mr. Dulett, in his statement to the police, explained that he had been out in the garden for "a good hour" and when he came inside he found that "Ricky had killed the baby." When pressed for details Mr. Dulett said that he found the bassinet turned over and Ricky beside Jamie Vaughn, who lay lifeless on the floor. Mr. Dulett stated that when he approached Ricky, the boy ran, and when he chased him upstairs, Ricky jumped from a back bedroom window.

Dylan, Anna, and Paula Dulett were all initially held in police custody but Ms. Paula Dulett has been moved to the state psychiatric hospital and Dylan and Anna have been released on bail.

And folded behind that report there was a second article.

DULETT CASE UPDATE
June 10, 1985
POLICE INVESTIGATION INTO THE death of infant Jamie Vaughn Dulett has come to a close. Sheriff James Dulett, at a press conference in Chaunceloraine yesterday, stated that after thorough investigation

it became apparent to him and his men that the death of the infant
boy was an accident.

The sole apparent witness to the death, Patrick ("Ricky") Dulett,
the six-year-old uncle of the infant, remains in critical condition
in the trauma ward of the Deauvont Regional Children's Hospital.
According to Sheriff Dulett, "Whatever the little boy did that caused
that baby's death we may never know but a six-year-old child cannot
be held responsible nor legally punished for such an accident."

Ms. Paula Dulett is currently undergoing treatment at the state
psychiatric hospital and charges against Dylan and Anna Dulett have
been dropped.

Jodi looked up at the trees as she walked, moving her feet in no particular
direction, just away—away from the voices jabbering in the cabin, away from
Ricky whom she could not face right now.

All around her the limbs of the oaks bucked under the weight of the rain,
and the once-gray trunks of locusts glistened with green lichen. She walked
and the words shuddered through her: *infant son . . . the little bastard killed
your son . . . bleeding from his ears and mouth.* She felt the words breaking
apart and moving inside her like shards of ice. *State psychiatric hospital . . .
critical condition.* They crashed over her head and threatened to drown her
with their enormity, this shadow she had seen on both Paula and Ricky but
never understood. She wanted to hug Ricky to her but almost equally as
much she wanted to never have to see him ever again. She found it impossible
to convince herself he could have killed that baby, though it would explain
the way that Dylan treated him.

In her hand she could feel the crinkled newsprint and it sickened her, this
proof of all that she had not known. She had to recalibrate everything: that
memory of little Ricky up in the oak tree and all that Paula had ever said
about him. *You don't know him, Jodi, you can't see how it is.* She thought of the
mountains back at Jaxton, those green swells that she had never even known
existed until her last day. She'd taken that flat sky over the exercise yard to be
everything but she'd known so little.

A spike of anger tongued its way up between her ribs and she crumpled the papers. *Fuck you, Paula, fuck you.* How could someone carve their way into you and yet give you so little? She remembered those first few weeks with Paula, their buzzed days of driving and talking. Talking and talking until their words ran all together, but what had she really known of Paula? *Not enough*, Frances would have said. *Love is a give and take.* But who the hell made Frances the authority on love anyway?

Jodi felt Paula's absence now more strongly than she had in years. *I need you here*, she thought. *I need to ask you things.* The more she thought about the articles, the more her mind twisted, and over and over again she came back to the name in the second clipping, *Sheriff James Dulett.* Brother to Dylan? Uncle? Cousin?

She stopped at the base of a black oak and sat down, her back against the riven bark. She opened her fist and stared at the newsprint squares, damp now. She wanted to bury them here in the leaves but surely Ricky would notice that they were missing, and anyhow, they weren't really hers to keep or destroy. She folded them over carefully and tucked them into the pocket of her flannel shirt and as she sat there she felt a shiver move through her, a dark rush that was not entirely fear and not entirely sadness.

June 1989

The fields spread out on either side, tangles of vines limp in the clouded moonlight, and among them Jodi sees the globes of ripe melons. She hadn't noticed them on the drive in and now she wonders how she could have missed them, so full under those green skins.

"Soon," Paula says, "soon."

She repeats the word like a magic pass code, a special, perfect phrase. She has been repeating it since they fled, since they left Ricky singing "Far through the Heart" in that grease-splattered kitchen.

Jodi turns in her seat and looks back the way they came. The house is still visible, a tiny patch of light across the field, but it seems different now. It looks warm, the yellow porch lamp fogging out soft into the night. It looks like any house on any road, not like the place that turned Paula so weak and ugly.

"We could have just taken him," Jodi says.

She wants Paula to argue, wants Paula to spit and swear and have some good reason for the way that she is acting, but all she says is *soon*, Ricky needs more than they can provide for him right now but they'll come back *soon*, and as she talks Jodi sees her again the way she saw her back there, standing on the porch with Dylan's fingers in her hair. His hands—those same hands that tied Ricky to that chair—moved on Paula's bare arms and she was gone, her face blank. She hadn't spoken a word about taking Ricky, hadn't hardly said anything the whole night, just chased peas around her plate while Ricky's wrists bled and on the radio Chuck Swindoll preached of heathens and end times.

"We'll come back," Paula says again, and then a silence settles in, sucking up all the air.

Jodi reaches under the seat and pulls out her purse with the pistol in it. The gun glints in the dashboard light and she runs her finger along the barrel, thinking of Ricky with his bird in the oak tree. *She always comes back to me.*

"What are you doing with that?" Paula says.

Jodi smiles. All evening, through dinner and the rest of it, she'd kept thinking of the warmth of the pistol in her hand and the way it had focused those men in Tampico and made her strength visible to them. She ought to have had it there with them in Anna and Dylan's house, she thought, but Paula had forbidden it. Now, though, she realizes that she ought to have just told Ricky to go out and wait in the car and dared Dylan to do anything.

They drive through the night and Jodi sleeps eventually. She dreams of melons and babies and the pure trust in Ricky's eyes. She dreams and wakes with Paula's hand up her skirt and in the haze of the dashboard lights Paula's face is distant again, vacant.

August 2007

O ut in the pasture the creek had sprung its banks and blended in with another stream. Jodi stood, brushed the oak leaves from her pants, and walked along beside the water, off toward the Phillips family cemetery and then on past the edge of Effie's land and down the mountain to where the trees changed, wax-green rhododendrons clogging the undergrowth. Over the rhythm of the rain there came a louder sound, a grinding of motors and chank of clattering chains, and then there, at the edge of a steep bank, the forest stopped and trees were tipped over sideways to make room for a tire-scarred road.

Jodi followed the mud lane toward the sound of drill blasts and coming out from around a curve she was met by the tall outline of the fracking tower. The structure was set on a flattened patch of land, a raw, muddy mess surrounded by seven trailers. Fire whipped out from the metal bars like a flag, oily smoke pillowing around the frame.

She left the road and climbed up the bank, ducked behind a laurel bush and peered down at the scraped ground and the line of trucks moving from the well to the road. This quick, she thought, feeling the drill rhythm in the earth beneath her feet. It could all change this quick. First Jessup's orchard, then what next? She should call the lawyer to see if he had talked to that antifracking group about buying Effie's land. Anything was better than her woods being scalped and singed like this.

"That flare's illegal."

Jodi flinched and turned to see a man, right there, not more than ten feet behind her. He had thin white hair and stood with his hands shoved into the pockets of his camouflage coat, lips clenched around a hand-rolled smoke.

"They ought to be fined over five hundred thousand dollars. Been flaring that thing for more than eighty-six days."

Jodi looked back toward the spout of flame.

"You're staying over at Ephigenia Phillips's place," the man said. His voice was gravelly and when he pulled his hand out of his pocket to relight his cigarette Jodi noticed he was missing his right pinky and ring finger.

She glanced at his face and tried to discern threat or question. In the brush behind him a blue-gray dog hunkered, eyes steady on Jodi.

"You kin?" the man asked.

Jodi nodded.

"Need to get you a roof over that back room. A piece of plywood, at least. You got kids staying there."

Jodi looked up at his face again. "You've been watching us?"

The old man squinted and spat. "Been watching the land," he said. "Been watching it lay fallow for near about twenty years now."

He turned then and when his coat swung open Jodi saw the butt of a handgun tucked up inside. She felt her blood pulsing in her veins and she steadied herself against a tree as he walked away.

When he was gone she followed his footprints to a well-worn path that snaked along back up the mountain. She searched for a shack or trailer the old man might be living in but saw nothing but a deer stand tacked up in a black walnut tree.

By the time she got home the rain had stopped and a mist rose from the yard where Donnie stood, naked from the waist down, aiming his stream of pee at the grass near Kaleb's feet. Kaleb sat on the bottom porch step with his face in his hands. When Donnie saw Jodi, he let go of his penis and a trail of piss dribbled down past his knee.

"We found a dog," he said.

"What's that?" Jodi came toward him, scanning the yard and porch for Ricky.

"And we named her Butter!" Donnie smiled and grabbed his penis again, gripping the foreskin between his thumb and finger and stretching it delicately.

"But Mama won't let us bring her home." Kaleb lifted his head and Jodi saw that his face was smeared with tears.

She walked up the cabin steps, worry washing over her. A worry that when she saw Ricky she would not be able to stop herself from saying something, a worry that he would have noticed the missing clippings already, but maybe most of all, a worry that she would not be able to look at him in the same way.

From the porch she could hear Rosalba's voice and Miranda's laughter and as she blinked into the dim room she saw only the two of them standing at the kitchen sink, Miranda priming the pitcher pump while Rosalba squirted dish soap onto a pile of wet laundry.

"Where's Ricky?"

Miranda glanced over her shoulder. "Hi," she said.

"Hey." Jodi peered past the woodstove and into the back bedroom. "You seen Ricky?"

"He was splitting some of that wood y'all cut. Why? What's wrong?"

Jodi shook her head. "What's this about a dog? Kaleb's out there crying on the front steps," she said, edging over to the bookcase where she slid the clippings quickly back in among Ricky's papers.

"Oh, yeah," Miranda said. "You know that little gas station down over on the other side of the mountain? We went to get some beer and Popsicles and the boys found a skinny old mutt there that they wanted to bring home."

Jodi found Ricky out behind the woodshed, not chopping kindling but lifting Ross up onto his shoulders instead.

"They're so loud!" Ross said, squirming in Ricky's arms and leaning out toward a maple tree.

Jodi could not tell what was happening until she got close enough to hear the desperate bird voices and then see the nest perched in the crux of the limbs.

"And their mouths are *so* big!" Ross said.

Ricky bent his knees a little and repositioned himself, holding tight to Ross's legs. "Don't touch 'em," he said. "The mama bird don't like the smell of humans."

Jodi stepped back, not wanting to interrupt the moment, and as she watched from the porch the glut of worries inside her loosened a little. Alone, out there in the woods, she had half-convinced herself that rescuing Ricky was the stupidest decision she'd ever made, but now, watching him lower Ross to the ground and brush the leaves from his hair, she thought it might be just the opposite.

Still, she could not stop watching him, staring at his tall, angular body and soft face across the dinner table, waiting to notice something she had not seen before.

"God, I'm tired of canned food," Miranda said, poking at her plate of instant potatoes, peas, and corn.

"I think it tastes pretty good," Ricky said, stirring the vegetables into his potatoes until they formed a rainbow slop in the middle of his plate.

What would he have been like without the accident, Jodi wondered, or did it even matter? She might as well have asked what she herself would have been like without eighteen years in prison. Somehow, though, she felt a little closer to him in his possible culpability. Maybe neither of us is innocent, she thought, watching him light a cigarette and walk outside into the grainy light of evening, but surely neither of us knew we were capable of causing such pain.

AFTER THE DINNER dishes were done Jodi crouched at the woodstove, coaxing the damp wood that flamed and then sputtered out, and after a while she heard a sound like singing coming from the porch, a shaky but rising lilt. *Far through the heart of this snow.* She crossed the room and looked out the front door to see Ricky, blushing and singing while Rosalba hummed along.

"That is a beautiful song," Rosalba said, and Ricky blushed deeper.

Jodi retreated back to the woodstove, knowing she should just be happy that he was singing, knowing she should not care who it was that he was singing for. But the tattered beast of old emotions lurched up inside her.

When Miranda asked her to fetch buckets of water for a bath Jodi insisted that Ricky help her, and Rosalba and the boys followed along. They walked in single file toward the springhouse, down a path littered with wet leaves and freshly sprung mushrooms and then up out of the hardwoods and into the dense coolness of a white-pine grove where the air hung heavy with the smell of sap. Jodi looked back at Ricky and the boys, their feet making a soft padding sound against the carpet of pine needles, and Rosalba, in line right behind her, looking sad and far away.

"Why did you leave Mexico?" Jodi said, the words spilling out before she had time to swallow them.

"Leave?"

Jodi turned to her. "You said you taught university."

Rosalba's shoulders tightened and she slowed her pace. "Everything was gone."

"Your family?"

Rosalba stopped and tipped her face up toward the tops of the trees, eyes closed. "The land I grew up on, the way we used to live." Opening her eyes, she looked straight at Jodi. "Now it is, if you do not grow for the cartel, you do not farm at all."

Jodi stared at her sad eyes and she wanted to apologize and tell her it didn't matter, she didn't even know why she'd asked. She ought to be kinder to Rosalba, she thought, for really Rosalba did fit in here, running from her past just like the rest of them.

"I came north because I had the education." Rosalba's smoky laughter lifted up among the pine branches. "Here I am not teaching but at least I am sending money home."

Jodi nodded and looked off, watching as a shadow-movement flitted behind a shagbark hickory.

"Hey!" Something was happening in Jodi's dream and she could not untangle herself from it or the words she did not fully understand. *Out in the yard . . . a man . . . in the yard.*

A hand slapped her cheek and suddenly she was there, in the cabin, with Miranda's face inches above her own.

"Jodi, there's a man with a fucking shotgun in the yard." Miranda's cheeks were red and her eyes puffy.

Jodi sat up and her breath choked in her throat. "Stay here," she said, reaching for her pants.

In the front room she pressed her face against the cloth and there, in the yard, she could see the old man and the dog out in front of the house, still and silhouetted in the morning fog. They did not move, even when Jodi stepped onto the porch, and for a moment she doubted. Eyeing the tall shotgun, she felt fear settle inside her.

"Hello?" she called, sighting the distance between them.

"More rains coming," the man said. "Need to get you some boards over that back half."

Jodi walked down the steps slowly. The fog was so thick she could not see past the nearest trees.

The man slung his rifle strap over his shoulder. "I've got some deer meat in the freezer too. You can't just feed them boys on canned food. Gives 'em a bad temperament."

Jodi nodded, wondering if he'd been keeping track of her nocturnal additions to the neighbors' trash pickup bins.

"How's y'all's water? You don't have a well here, do you?"

Jodi shook her head.

"You wanna see what them gas men have done to my well?"

Jodi cocked her head.

"You won't believe your eyes. I'll show you water that turns to flame."

He introduced himself as Farren and as he talked Jodi felt a whisper memory of Effie out there in the yard with them. Farren was younger than Effie would have been but not by much and Jodi remembered his name, remembered Effie talking about a man who folks had told stories about, living alone with no company besides his hogs; children had spooked each other with his name and parents scrunched up their faces, trying to hide their laughter, saying he'd come home from the war not quite the same, whispering that they'd heard he sometimes wore his sister's old dresses. When Jodi had repeated the stories, Effie had slapped her cheek, told her to quit, that he was a good neighbor, steady and dependable.

Once she knew they were safe Miranda had fallen back asleep, and Rosalba too lay curled in dreams, but Ricky and the boys tagged along behind Jodi as Farren led her across the field and out onto the paved road, down by the Nazarene church. He walked ahead along the gravel berm, his feet dragging a little, shotgun strapped to his back and his shoulders hunched under the camouflage fabric of his coat. The dog followed closely, glancing hopefully at the old man's hands as he rolled a fresh smoke.

"See, he's got a dog," Kaleb whispered, tugging on Jodi's sleeve. "Why can't we have a dog?"

"He's got a gun too!" Donnie yelled. "Boom-boom-boom!"

At the head of a long gravel lane, Farren paused. "Got some wood in the shed," he said, nodding toward a cluster of buildings out past the pigpens. "We ought to be able to find you a piece that'll fit your roof."

He walked on up the lane but Jodi hung back, pricked with shame over not having already fixed the roof herself and feeling also a nameless childhood fear as she eyed his mutilated right hand. "Hey," she called to him, "hey, how come you're doing this?"

He turned slowly and tilted his head.

"I mean helping us like this?"

Farren shrugged, or maybe he was just adjusting his rifle. "You're the first young ones up on this mountain in more than twenty years," he said, staring off down the road. "Rest of us is just a bunch of old-timers, be dropping like flies before too long. It'll take new ones to save and keep this place."

He kept walking then and after a minute Jodi and Ricky and the boys followed along past a little brown house with water barrels set under the corners of the roof.

"My well's contaminated," Farren said. "Got to drink rainwater now."

He nudged a skinny white cat out of the way and waved them all over to an outdoor spigot.

"Watch," he said, pulling a lighter from his pocket. He lit it and held it under the stream, and the water leapt, spurted, and then burst into flame. Jodi jumped back but Farren held steady as water poured down between his feet and the fire puffed up into his face.

"Boom," Donnie yelled, leaning forward on his tiptoes.

Farren looked up. "Methane. Them gas companies have piped it up from the middle of the earth." He stared down again at the clear stream circled by a juddering ball of flame.

It was Farren who reminded Jodi how to find the Lady Cake Caves. She was out on the back end of Effie's property, picking blackberries with Farren, Ricky, and the boys, the six of them carrying cutoff milk jugs heavy with dark fruit, when she felt some old sense of directional memory.

"There are caves near here, aren't there?" she'd asked.

Farren nodded. "Right over yonder's the old road."

They left their jugs of berries in the field and followed him down the foot road that hugged the cliff edge, the boys running ahead.

"Hold on," Farren called as they rushed down the rocky path covered in poison ivy and wild grape vine. "Hold on, it gets snakey down in here."

"Snakey?" Kaleb turned and looked back at Farren.

"That's your entrance right there," Farren said.

Jodi came to a stop. She wouldn't have even seen the mouth of the cave except that Farren had slowed and squinted, brushing away the weeds with his walking stick.

Jodi entered first, crawling flat on her stomach, the darkness blinding her immediately. Behind her the boys' voices bounced but each of them, as they slid into the cool, open room, went silent, one by one. Nothing but the sound of shallow breathing.

Farren told them to sit still until their eyes adjusted and slowly they found their voices again.

"There are snakes in here?" Kaleb asked.

"They're more afraid of you. Just don't go sticking your hand in any cracks or holes."

Farren led them farther than Jodi had ever gone before, past the huge white mineral cake and on into a fourth cavern. The entrance was narrower than the others, nothing more than a three-foot gap, but halfway through, Jodi began to see a bright band of light. She dragged herself forward with her fingers and elbows, the roof of the tunnel only inches above her head. She breathed into the pressure of all that rock, the narrowness of the tunnel that led to a deeply rounded room.

The air smelled wet and full of the fungus-scent of plants that need no sun, the silt and sandstone, and something ranker, layers and layers of unseen earth. The band of light before her grew until she pushed out into a circular stone room with one wall completely open to the cliff face. The sunlight blinded worse than the darkness and she crouched with her eyes closed, feeling the rock at her back and the air before her. The wind flew in at them and funneled around, shuffling the dry oak leaves.

"Is this the house," Donnie said, "where baby Jesus lives?" His voice bounced off the limestone and mixed in with Farren's laughter.

Jodi opened her eyes to the billowing treetops, the miles of valley spreading below, and the timbered mountains extending endlessly like a wind-chopped sea.

"I never knew this part of the cave," she said.

"Most folks expect a crack of a tunnel like that won't lead to nothing." Farren paced the limestone edge. "My daddy showed me here. He liked to tell how the Indians used caves like these in their ceremonies, for their boys when they were coming of age. They had to stay out here for a good number of days with no supplies and then make their way out the tunnels to the other side."

This, Jodi thought, must have been what Effie meant when she complained of distance from the land, that children were no longer taught to test themselves against the earth.

She stood and joined Farren at the rock ledge. Below them the shadow of the cliff stretched across the shivering treetops; farther out, patches of cloud shade skated over the pastures. A cluster of blackbirds landed, bowing the branches of a tall oak, and above them, out of the clean blue, heavier wings lifted and dipped. Up from the flat glass river a pair of vultures skimmed, their circle ever tightening.

THEY WERE HALFWAY back across the field, headed home, when Jodi noticed the brown sedan parked under the dogwood tree. Her heart jerked, though she had no specific hope or fear. Miranda had gone to town for groceries and no one else was expected.

"You've got visitors," Farren said just as her father came around the side of the Oldsmobile.

Jodi let out a breath and watched him walk toward her, looking strange and small out there in the grassy yard with no beer can and no TV light spilling across his face. He pinched his cigarette between his lips and raised one hand in a noncommittal greeting.

"You been getting a lot of phone calls," he said. "I figured I'd come up here and let you know. That lawyer called and then this woman's been calling all week. I've been taking down her messages, something about land conservation. She's anxious for you to come by her house and meet with her, says she wants to talk this evening." Andy reached into his back pocket. "I got the address."

Jodi took the scribbled slip of paper from his calloused hand: *614 Taylor Drive, Lewisville.*

"Your car's gone," he said.

"Miranda's at the grocery."

Andy dropped his cigarette into the grass and stepped on it. "I guess I'll run you on over there then."

Jodi glanced up at his face. This was as close, she guessed, as she was going to get to an apology for his part in losing the land.

THE TALL WHITE house at 614 Taylor Drive had stone gateposts and a long, smooth-paved lane. Andy pulled up front, squinted at it and nodded, then lit a fresh cigarette. From the driveway Jodi could hear music warbling out of the house.

"You must be Joanie?"

The voice seemed to come from the porch but Jodi scanned it and saw nothing until she tilted her head back to take in the balcony and a woman draped in what looked to be silk scarves.

"Jodi."

"Oh, yes, come on up."

The carpet inside was the deep red of old blood and so thick it sponged out under Jodi's boots. She paused and looked back at the muddy footprints she'd left. She should have known to take her shoes off, she guessed, but it was too late now. She followed one side of the double staircase around to a pair of arched glass doors that framed the balcony and the woman, swaying under her layers of silk.

"Joanie, I'll be honest with you," she said as Jodi pushed open the glass doors. "This is not my place, not my ancestry, but it fascinates me." She waved her arm toward the row of mountains on the far side of town.

Jodi studied the back of her head, the dark buzzed haircut and sharp tendons running down her neck. So this was Lynn. She looked nothing like Jodi had imagined when Dunham spoke of her. She was so delicate and attractive, like some dark butterfly. Jodi had been sure she was on her way to meet with a hiking-boot-wearing Greenpeace activist.

"I don't know, maybe it's not permanent, this emanation, but I feel it *right now.*" Lynn turned. Her eyes were bright and wet. "This is the battleground. The raw core. The Iapetus Ocean trapped under the Appalachians for six hundred million years! You know there are still places here where freshly dug wells fill with salt brine?" She stepped forward and rested her hand on Jodi's shoulder. Jodi flinched and stepped back. She wondered if Lynn were drunk.

"I'm sorry." Lynn laughed and her laughter echoed in with the music. "Ethan must have told you I get emotional about this whole thing."

The fabric of Lynn's outfit was so thin that the movements of her breasts were clearly visible beneath. Jodi looked off toward the bright line of sky and the rust-orange sunset just above Skinner's Peak.

"You mean Dunham?" she said.

"Yeah, you know I never know what Ethan really thinks of me." Her silver bracelets clacked around her wrists. "I worry too much about what people think of me, though." Her back was facing Jodi again and the white silk of her panties glowed under her shifting dress.

"So, um," Jodi said, "you're interested in buying land that's in danger of being fracked?"

Lynn turned to her and the intensity of her gaze startled Jodi. "Yes, there's nowhere else on earth quite like this place, right? I mean, I don't even know how to describe it but you know what I'm talking about." She smiled. "Ethan told me your story and I called immediately. You're not easy to get ahold of."

Jodi nodded. "We don't have electricity up there yet or anything, no phone. But, uh, I wanted to say, it's important to me to know . . ." She'd had the whole thing rehearsed but now the words would not come out right. "I want to buy the land back from you eventually. My family and I are living on the land now." Her voice steadied and her confidence grew as she pronounced the word *family*. "We don't have a lot of money but it's important for me to know that I'm working toward owning the land again."

Lynn cocked her head. The wind blew her dress and she seemed to be moving even when she stood still. "Ownership is . . ." She opened both hands and spread her fingers wide. "I mean, what does ownership really even *mean* anyway?"

Jodi wanted to reach out and strangle that skinny neck, squeeze it until all Lynn's words stopped. She waited for her to say something about Native Americans not having any concepts for ownership of land or some bullshit.

"You'll be stewards." She stepped toward Jodi and grabbed her hand. Her skin was surprisingly warm. "We'll make a trust of it."

Jodi pulled her hand free. If I leave now, she thought, but—what? If I leave now, Effie's land will most likely be stripped and pumped and left a shriveled carcass. And maybe it didn't have to matter so much that she wouldn't personally own it as long as the land was safe. She remembered, as a child, going to visit Effie's brother, Elbert, who'd been in and out of jail for years but had finally gotten a job managing a cattle operation over in Monroe County. Elbert had lived alone in an Airstream trailer on the edge of the hundred acres, caring for the heifers that were owned by an out-of-state man who rarely visited. The farm hadn't belonged to Elbert but he'd seemed happy enough there.

"You hate me."

Jodi looked up. It didn't seem to be a question really.

"I'm not blaming you," Lynn said. "I'm just saying you all hate me. I don't know why I fell in love with a place that nobody seems to want me to be in love with. I stop at the gas station and everybody looks at me like I've been out killing babies. And it's not even about my money, I don't think. I'm used to being hated for having money; it's something different here, though."

Music drifted through the doorway, a range of piano keys like a spattering of raindrops, singular and then flowing.

"But we're not so different, I don't think. I mean, I know I'm just a big tree hugger and this is not my ancestry here but I was cut once, my skin laid open to the bone, and in the time it took them to find me, I saw something there." Lynn closed her eyes and her face shifted, drew in as tight as a fist. "It's the same stuff they pull from the earth and it's inside everything and all of us but we cover it up."

The music had stopped but the last notes hung, nearly visible in the air.

"Do you have anything to drink?" Jodi asked, and on second thought she added, "Ma'am."

"Don't call me 'ma'am,'" Lynn snapped, but her eyes were still smiling.

Jodi followed her through the living room where the walls were hung with enormous paintings of stone-faced women, hair piled high, bodiced dresses laced tight. Lynn poured two glasses of ruby wine from a decanter.

"You like Philip Glass?"

"Who?"

"The music that was playing when you came in."

Jodi nodded and took one of the wineglasses. She thought of Andy out in the car, smoking cigarettes alone.

"I'm thinking we can have a showing of the new dance I choreographed. There's this guy, Jay Praxley. He can play the Glass piece." Lynn swallowed a large mouthful of wine. "Maybe a silent auction, some hors d'oeuvres and wine—that should be enough, don't you think?"

"Enough?"

"Well, enough to get us started, at least. There are also some private donors who could pitch in if the land is in immediate danger."

The wine was acrid. Jodi drank it anyway, swallowing small mouthfuls. There was a feeling in the pit of her stomach, the bitter-penny taste of self-pity, just like she'd felt each time she met with the therapist at Jaxton. These women got something out of helping her, a self-satisfaction that Jodi begrudged.

"You know this was all caused by water." Lynn paced behind the couch. "All of the riches here, the coal, the shale—they must have taught you this in school?"

Jodi remembered reading once about peat bogs and seabeds but she was too exhausted now to follow Lynn's leaping conversation.

"An ocean from here to California! And the waters filled up with dying plants. The great inland sea." Lynn flung her arms wide and her bracelets clacked. "So rich in death, hundreds of feet of dying plants, and then the seabed drops and the Appalachians thrust up as tall as the Alps. Imagine it."

She walked to the window as if she might be able to see the mountains shift again out there and Jodi thought of the moment four weeks before when she herself had stepped out of Jaxton and seen the mountains, so strong and green, and all the hope they had filled her with. She could not think about them now without thinking also of everything else she had not known—Ricky's past, the loss of the land, everything she could not see from inside those concrete walls.

"With limestone too, it's the water. It's so strong, you know, the water and the gravity, it will dig through anything to get down and move on. If we cut open the mountains, we'd see rivers like veins carving out those magnificent uterine caverns." Lynn turned back toward Jodi. "They're so womb-like, don't you think? So feminine."

ANDY'S CAR WAS dark when Jodi got in.

"Well," he said, cranking the ignition. "I nearly run out of smokes."

The dashboard lights blinked on and the motor purred.

"That lawyer gonna help you keep the land?"

Jodi looked back at the buttery glow of lit windows. "I don't think it's that simple," she said.

When they arrived home there was a pickup truck parked beside Miranda's car. Not old man Farren's pickup either, this one was bright red and looking shiny new. Andy turned his headlights on it then pulled up beside.

"That's A.J.'s new truck," he said. "You expecting him?"

Jodi shook her head.

As she walked up the front steps she could hear the pitch of men's voices and Miranda's tipsy giggle. She pushed the door open, blinking into the bright room.

"How many hippies did you hit?"

It was Dennis. She recognized his voice even before her eyes adjusted. He was sitting in one of the kitchen chairs, tipped back against the far wall, a can of PBR balanced on his knee. A.J. sat beside him and Miranda perched on the edge of the table, swinging her legs.

"Dad give you a ride over to Lewisville?" Dennis said.

Jodi nodded.

"It's always been weird up there," Dennis went on, "but it's fucking thick with them now, huh?"

"Them hippie chicks are okay with me," A.J. said, grinning. "Hell, they don't care if you can see their titties." He laughed.

"Yeah, that's cool," Dennis said. "If you like your girls hairy." He pulled a can from the plastic loops and held it out to Jodi. "Me and A.J. here was wondering what you two ladies are up to tonight."

Jodi took the beer and went to lean against the chimney. From the back bedroom she could hear Rosalba and the boys' voices. "Nothing much," she said.

"Come out and have a beer with us."

"We've got beer here." Jodi pointed at the remainder of the six-pack.

"Shit, that's gone in two seconds," A.J. said. "Come on, y'all ain't come down and hung out in town since the first night you got here."

Between the wine at Lynn's and now the beer, Jodi was starting to get a buzz that she didn't exactly want to let go of and refusing A.J. seemed to take more energy than she had.

In the bedroom, she found Ricky, Rosalba, and the boys spread out on Ricky's mattress reading his Bible.

"The beast has horns like a lamb but he speaks like a dragon," Kaleb explained.

"Lamb-dragon!" Donnie chanted, crawling across the mattress.

Rosalba reached out and ran her fingers through his hair. "*You* are a lamb-dragon," she said.

Donnie reared up, giggling and pawing the air.

Jodi pressed herself closer in against the doorframe, tensing her fingers against the wood as a sadness spread through her. She did not show her love enough, she thought. She held back, every time, and then it was too late; someone else had moved in and taken her place.

"Hey, Rosalba," she said, hating the emotion so audible in her words. "We're going into town to hang out for a little bit. You want us to drop off the boys at my parents'?"

"Oh, no, I will watch them," Rosalba said, looking around, as if for confirmation from the boys and Ricky. "You go, have fun, we will be here."

STEERING HIS TRUCK with one hand, A.J. wormed the other into his pocket and came out with a palmful of little white pills. "Take a couple," he said, offering them to Miranda, Dennis, and Jodi. "Wake you right up."

Jodi took two and stared down at them there in her sweaty palm.

"I can sell you some clean piss if Ballard ever acts like he's wanting to test you," A.J. said.

"Well, I hope not." Jodi glanced from A.J. to Miranda. She knew she ought give the pills back and tell Miranda not to take hers either but the truth was she wanted them bad, wanted anything to wash away the taint of self-pity from her visit with Lynn.

"Miranda told us you've been hanging out with old man Farren," Dennis said.

Jodi looked up. "He gave us some plywood for the roof," she said, swallowing her two tablets quickly, trying to convince herself that coming out with Dennis and A.J. was not the worst idea she'd ever agreed to.

"I'd be careful if I was you, seems like a fucking creep. Ginny Highlander used to rent that trailer down the road from him and she says she and Buster were getting it on one night and she looks up and sees the old man's face peeking in the window." Dennis laughed. "Freaky," he said, leaning over to roll down the window. "Tim Jenkins saw him in Lewisville too, at one of those protests against mountaintop mining. Says he saw Farren holding an anticoal sign."

Jodi kept her eyes on the road ahead. "I don't know nothing about that," she said.

They stopped in at the Gas 'N Go for beer and then drove to the other side of town, down by the river. Half a dozen pickup trucks sat parked at various angles along the mud bank and the stabbing light of a campfire flickered down below.

"Moose!" A.J. called out as a skinny, leather-jacketed man hopped down from the truck beside them. The man's left leg ended midthigh and his jeans were rolled up and clipped like a half-used toothpaste tube.

"Now this guy," A.J. said, pointing at Dennis, "they turned away." He looked back to be sure that Miranda was listening. "But *this* guy saw Fallujah." He clapped Moose on the shoulder. "Purple Heart."

Dennis had suffered from occasional seizures as a child. The armed forces had refused him and he had never gotten over the insult despite the evidence of the awfulness of Iraq.

Jodi watched Moose make his way down the trail in front of them and thought of that West Virginia girl in those sickening pictures at Abu Ghraib. That twenty-one-year-old from Short Gap with her pink grinning, grotesque face. The images had scrolled across the TV screen at Jaxton and the girls had ribbed Jodi about it, said her home state was getting famous. Didn't you know, somebody commented, Charles Manson was from West Virginia too?

"This is my sister, Jodi, and her friend Miranda," A.J. said to the crowd around the fire. "Y'all remember Jodi, don't you?" A few people wobbled their heads but none of the faces looked familiar. "Jodi just got out of medium, so y'all better watch out." He winked and set the twelve-pack of PBR down beside a plastic chair.

The fire leapt and sparked. It seemed brighter and perkier than any other fire Jodi could ever remember seeing. The light grew and shrank as the wind blew and whenever anybody moved their shadows multiplied and scattered under them in a million different pieces.

Miranda handed her a beer. On the other side of the fire the river went speeding by, making a nice long rush of sound. This had, after all, been a good idea.

"Did you hang out down here when you were a kid?" Miranda asked.

Jodi looked at the ring of faces around the fire, still young but growing fleshy with age, eyes glazed, yellow dirt stains on the knees of their jeans.

"No," she said. "I hung out up on the mountain mostly."

Miranda paused, lighter raised halfway to her cigarette. "Your parents moved to town and just kinda left you up there, huh?"

"No." Jodi took a drink from her beer. Her head had started to hurt, a bright spot of pain like a bull's eye in the center of her forehead. "No, I wanted to stay up there," she said, but her words sounded a little hollow and even she had to admit there was a limit to the amount of free will you could attribute to a seven-year-old.

"Hey, this is Tiffany," Moose said, coming toward Jodi and holding out a pint of Evan Williams. Behind him walked a blonde woman with a dollar bill safety-pinned to her T-shirt, just above her left tit.

"It's her birthday." Moose passed the bottle.

Tiffany took a swig and then tipped the bottle down, pouring a bit of whiskey onto the ground. "For Danny," she said.

"Hey now." Moose recovered his bottle. "It's not like he's dead."

"Wait, is Danny in jail?" Dennis came around to their side of the fire.

"It should have worked, it always worked," Tiffany said. "But they had those goddamn dogs and they were jumping and biting at him. They tore his shirt and he gave in."

Jodi looked at Dennis and he smiled. "You won't believe this shit," he said.

Danny had attempted to conceal a quarter pound of weed under the voluptuous folds of his belly fat. He'd done it before and gotten away with it—no one wanted to look up under that sweaty girth—but the dogs had done him in this time.

"Possession?" Dennis said.

Tiffany shook her head and took another swig of whiskey. "Possession *and* intent to distribute."

Jodi felt a jolt of fear. She pictured Dennis's duffel bag up in the rafters. There was certainly enough in there to land a distribution charge. She caught Dennis's eye and he smiled.

"Hey, I know what you're thinking." He inhaled and held the joint out to Jodi. "But just relax, you ain't muling that shit, you're just storing it and nothing bad's gonna happen, okay?"

He came in close and grabbed both Jodi and Miranda by their shoulders, the weight of his body thrown against their backs.

"You ladies must get lonely up there on the mountain."

Miranda looked first to Jodi and then over her shoulder at Dennis. "We keep busy."

"Oh, sure, sure." Dennis wobbled, his fingernails pressing into Jodi's skin. "I was just thinking I'd give you all the opportunity to meet some folks." He lifted his right hand, waved at the ring of people around the fire, and then brought it to rest on the back of Miranda's neck. He had both hands on her now. "But ain't neither one of you said hardly two words since you got here."

Jodi gripped her can of beer, the metal cool and too thin, crumpling under her grip.

"You're all tense, honey." He was massaging Miranda's shoulders.

Jodi stared off across the river toward Randolph Mountain, its buckled ridge barely visible in the moonlight. "Nothing much has changed around here, has it?" she said.

Dennis let go of Miranda with his right hand and turned to face Jodi. "Sure it has. For one thing we're all more attractive than we used to be, don't you think?" His laughter shot out too fast, loud and lonely in the night air.

"Hey, Dennis, come piss on this fire," A.J. said. It seemed he'd taken more of his pills and now he was rallying the crowd back toward the trucks.

Dennis and two other men pissed away the remaining flames in a hissing cloud of rank steam and then the group of them scrambled back up the clay bank together, their voices ricocheting and mixing in with the gurgling river. At the trucks there seemed to be some sort of confusion. Jodi and Miranda moved toward A.J.'s pickup but then Dennis grabbed Miranda's arm and said, "Hey, let Tiffany ride with him," and in the drunk dark they were separated: Jodi up in the cab with A.J. and Tiffany, and Miranda off in another truck.

"All right, you two ready?" A.J. crowed, passing Jodi and Tiffany fresh beers.

They drove around the back way toward town again, the headlights tunneling along the empty road.

"I think old Dennis has taken a shine to your friend," A.J. said.

Jodi gripped her beer can, the cold liquid spilling across her knuckles as they rounded a sharp curve.

"What?" A.J. leaned up past Tiffany. "Y'all too busy up there homesteading to have a little fun every now and then?"

Jodi looked away and downed the rest of her can in one long swallow. "You got any more of those pills?" she said.

A.J. laughed. "All right, that's more like it." He lifted up out of his seat to rummage through his pocket. "You know these don't grow on fuckin' trees, though."

"I can give you some money." Jodi nodded. "You got me coming and going though, huh? Sell me pills and then sell me the piss to cover it up with."

"Hey," A.J. said, "I got whatever you need."

They drove through town and out the other side, toward the old strip mine where A.J. veered off the pavement, the truck engine ripping through the quiet night. They bounced along the gravel berm in total darkness until the floodlights of a CSX freight spilled suddenly into the truck cab, the engine rumbling low but steady alongside them as the pieces came together in Jodi's head.

"No fucking way," she said as a dry terror shivered through her. "No, wait—stop—"

A.J. grinned and pushed the truck up into fourth gear and the train let out a long whistle blast. On the left the shadow of an old warehouse flashed by. On the right there was nothing but the metal tracks and light and the sound of the train keeping pace. The wail of the whistle caught in Jodi's chest and stayed on, clanging there.

"Stop."

Adrenaline had released into her veins now and mixed with the pills and beer and began to multiply.

The truck lurched and sped up. Tiffany grabbed Jodi's hand. Her nails dug into Jodi's flesh. The train was panting, close behind them. Jodi freed her hand and craned her neck. She spotted two of the other pickups, closing in on their tail, headlights bouncing in the rearview mirror.

A.J. turned the wheel and pressed the gas. They rolled up onto the tracks. Jodi felt a loosening in her gut. There was no more air anywhere. She closed her eyes. Nothing but the scream of the truck's motor and the throb of the train, the window beside her jittering in its frame. She was watching it all from outside somewhere, watching herself drift. Utterly aware now of how helpless she was, not just in this moment but in all of it. Out of orbit, untethered, and spinning off into some unknown galaxy.

The truck bucked up, mounting the wave of sound, the thrumming engine, shrill whistle scream. *Fuck*, a voice called. *Fuck . . . fuck . . . fuck.* Jodi curled for the blow.

And then she was shaking, almost crying, and the sound was all behind them, leaking away.

May 1989

The gas station is way out at the edge of Mineola where the two-lane road fades into a single strip of cracked pavement. The brown-haired woman works from five to midnight. Jodi and Paula have cased it enough to see that she is always there alone.

"I don't know." Jodi paces in front of the motel room window; through the curtains she can see across the railroad tracks to the yellow-and-red gas station and the movements of the woman inside behind the counter.

Paula is measuring out a line of coke on top of the dresser. "They're trained to cut their losses. You show the weapon and she'll hand it over so fast."

Even from inside their room Jodi can feel the heat. The railroad tracks shimmer with late-day sunlight, and dusty spikes of dried plants poke up out of the parking lot. She hates how the heat comes on so dead and flat every morning, as huge and uniform as the sky. In the dips and gulleys of West Virginia, the days always started off cool and sleepy with a thin green mist lifting up from the river.

"I'd do it myself." Paula tilts her head and presses the back of her hand against her nose.

There is a cluster of industrial tanks back beyond the gas station with metal staircases curving up the sides, and the setting sun paints strips of light across them like the jars of colored sand Jodi saw for sale in Mexico.

"But when *you* hold the gun it's clear you're not afraid to use it."

Jodi turns away from the window and walks to the dresser for her line. The truth is, she loves to hear those words and her blood picks up at the thought of holding the gun like that again, showing its power to some stranger so that they see her, really, truly see her, deeply outlined forever in their brain.

PAULA PARKS THE car in the alley between the Elko Motel and Oasis Liquors but keeps the motor running. Jodi gets out and heads up the street, her purse with the pistol inside hitting her hip with every step. As she walks by the liquor store she notes the neon glow of the alcohol advertisements, the way the warm light expands in the not-quite-dark air and makes her feel that she's in a scene from some movie. Across the street a pregnant woman is folding towels inside the Thrifty Bundle Launderette and Jodi likes that, the familiarity of it. The world has not stopped spinning just because she is on her way to hold up a gas station. If that woman can just keep folding her laundry, Jodi figures, everything will turn out all right.

She pulls the pistol out of her purse as she passes the gas pumps, the little pools of oil and fuel reflecting the yellow-green parking-lot lights. The gas station lot is empty but she can hear the wheels of a car out on the road. She tenses but it goes on past, the swoosh of a slow-driving sedan. She walks to the front door and the brown-haired woman behind the counter looks up briefly, then glances back down at the magazine she is reading.

If no one believes that she—a seventeen-year-old girl in blue jeans and a halter top—will do this, if no one believes this will happen, on this warm early evening on the edge of a quiet town, then maybe, Jodi thinks, she can do it—go on in there and demand the money—and be gone before anything gets disturbed. She and Paula will leave town fast and the woman folding towels at the launderette can stop by the gas station for cigarettes. The gas station attendant can go on with her night, get done with her shift, and drive home.

The bell on the door clangs. Jodi has the pistol pressed flat against her leg, hidden behind her purse, but the woman is not even watching.

When she does look up there is a level of simple and obvious disgust in her eyes. What do you want? the eyes seem to say. I hate you already because you're young and stupid and not yet burdened by compromises and wrinkle lines.

"Yes?"

Jodi lifts her right arm slowly. "I need you to empty the register."

A bit of color flushes the woman's cheeks but her eyes are still dull and annoyed. "Is it loaded?"

Anger floods Jodi's veins, she fights to keep from saying anything, knowing her voice will come out squeaky. She steps closer and clicks the safety off instead.

The woman winces and looks toward the register. "You know this won't change anything," she says.

It seems to Jodi that the woman is speaking to her from some other dimension, this bored, motherly voice, undeterred by the cocked gun.

"Give me the fucking money," Jodi says. Things needed to start happening faster now, much, much faster.

The woman presses a button with her coral-colored nail and the drawer slides out.

"We make a bank deposit at three p.m. so there's not much in here." The woman slips out a slim stack of twenties, fives, and ones. "You know this kinda thing won't change much." She looks directly at Jodi as she hands over the cash. "You'll still end up like me."

Jodi bucks a little at the words. The money in her hand seems tainted now with this heavy inevitability and it sticks to Jodi as she runs up the street toward Paula's car, lungs burning, the feeling of it on her skin the way the sensation of a spiderweb stays long after you wipe it away.

They drive out of Texas and stay in the first motel they can find that doesn't ask for any ID.

"Don't be hard on yourself, we'll try again someplace else," Paula says as Jodi counts out $108.00. But it is not the disappointment over the money that bothers Jodi. She cannot figure out how to explain the woman and now, when she thinks about it, she is not even sure that their interaction was not a dream.

August 2007

It was after eleven when Jodi woke in the back bedroom at her parents' place. Sunlight covered the end of the bed and Jim Morrison stared down at her with his sexy-moody face. Through the open window she could hear the buzz of conversation.

Andy and Irene did not look up from the TV when she passed through the living room. The others were all out on the front porch drinking coffee. Jodi watched them through the kitchen window. She couldn't remember if Dennis and A.J. had slept there too or just shown up in the morning. Seated behind them, on the stairs, was a wiry, mustached man.

As Jodi opened the door Miranda pushed herself off the railing and walked toward her, holding out a cup of coffee.

"Your cousin got me a job," she said, smiling. "I'm gonna bartend down at Slattery's Girl."

Jodi caught the flicker of flirty excitement in Miranda's eyes.

"You remember Justin, don't you?" Dennis said.

Jodi took the cup of coffee from Miranda and looked again at the man on the stairs. He looked like an aged version of nearly every kid she'd gone to high school with.

"Phillip's youngest boy," Dennis prompted.

Jodi squinted. She couldn't remember the last time she'd seen any of her cousins, but sure, she thought, that could be him, same small-muscled frame as all the men in her family.

"You don't want to work in a place like that," Jodi said, passing the coffee back to Miranda.

Miranda laughed, brushing her hair from her face. "A place like what?"

Jodi stepped closer, focusing on the freckles scattered across Miranda's cheeks. "A place that expects you to be a slut."

Miranda paused, cup halfway to her mouth. The front legs of Dennis's chair thumped down onto the porch boards.

"Not all the girls that work there is like that," Justin said.

Jodi glanced back at him where he sat, mouth slack.

"He works as a bouncer," Miranda explained.

Jodi nodded. Miranda was already moving ahead, sloughing off her life like snakeskin. So easy, Jodi thought, you take it all so easy—this is my new best friend now, my new job.

"You don't need to be working in a bar. You've got kids to take care of."

"I know I do. That's why I want this job. I can make good tips."

"But if you're working at the bar, you'll sleep days and work nights and you won't even see them."

"I'm always *not* thinking about the boys, right? Is that it? You ever think that maybe one time I'm making a decision 'cause I *am* thinking about them?" Miranda turned away. "It'll only be a few nights a week."

Jodi watched the tendons in Miranda's neck. She looked so fragile, that thin, pale skin and those tiny bones, but she seemed positive that she was bulletproof. Or at least that she could dust herself off after the bullets were removed and that something better would be coming along soon.

WHEN JODI AND Miranda pulled up in the yard, Ricky was standing on the front porch of the cabin, hands in his pockets. He said nothing but watched closely as they climbed out of the car. The yard was marked with fresh tire ruts, the loamy topsoil churned up in great gashes among the green grass.

"What all happened here?" Jodi called.

His shirt was untucked and only half-buttoned, his hair sticking up wild, and as she got closer she could see that his hands were shaking.

"Ricky, what—"

"Rosa. They got her." He looked at Jodi. "I tried. I . . . I . . . they had two guns and—"

"What are you talking about?" Jodi's face felt too hot, ears pounding with blood as she ran up the front steps. "Where are the boys? Ricky?"

"I told the boys to stay quiet for their own lives."

Jodi stood so close she could smell Ricky's sour sweat and see the tiny blue-black whiskers on his chin.

"What's going on?" Miranda called from behind them.

Jodi stepped in closer. She could see the stains under the armpits of Ricky's cream-colored shirt, the streaks of dirt in the folds of his neck, and the red veins skittering across the whites of his eyes. "Ricky. Where are the boys?"

He jerked his head back toward the cabin door.

"Everything's all right?" Miranda said as Jodi ran, pushed past Ricky and on inside, blinking against the shadows, seeing only the outline of the cookstove, the sink, and then the bedroom door, closed, with a ladder-back chair wedged up against it.

"Kaleb? Donnie?"

She shoved aside the chair.

They were curled up on the floor, heads poking around the corner of the mattress, pupils dilated huge.

"Oh, no, come here." She knelt but they did not move toward her. "What happened, babies, what happened?"

Ross began to cry, quietly, his shoulders shaking and his wet face resting on the corner of the mattress. Jodi crawled across the floor, pulled Donnie in close, and then reached out for Ross, and though he held his body stiff, she hugged him and laid his head down on her lap. His pants were damp and stank of piss.

Kaleb reached up and ran his fingers across Jodi's cheek and she realized then that she was crying too, the salty tears running down and stinging her chapped lips.

"I'm sorry. I'm so sorry," she whispered, bending over to kiss Kaleb's head.

Ricky could not stop stuttering and pacing. Miranda got the boys settled down with her in the back bedroom and Jodi sat with him on the porch until he could get the story out straight.

He said the men had come in the early-morning hours, in a jacked-up truck, carrying shotguns.

"She gone on out there when she seen them coming." Ricky brought his fingers into a fist and then released them. "I tried to say no, tell them we wouldn't trade her. I would have done more but the boys. She told me to go back and keep the boys safe." He looked over at the churned-up yard. "I told them we wouldn't trade. Tried to give the money back but—"

"The money?"

"The money they give. They took a bag out of the shed and left money."

"What are you talking about?"

He heaved himself up and started across the porch and Jodi followed around the back of the house to the woodshed. From the highest branches of the trees the cicadas called out, a spiraling scream that sounded to Jodi like a soundtrack to true insanity. Ricky stepped around a wheelbarrow with a deflated tire and stood on tiptoe to peer up into the woodshed rafters. "Here," he said, then moved aside for Jodi to see.

The bag of sinsemilla was gone but a small brown suitcase sat in its place.

Jodi pulled and it landed at her feet, throwing up a cloud of cocoa-colored dust. She bent close, the air around her full of the smell of wood shavings and machine oil. The little gold latches sprang at her touch and the lid lifted to reveal an even bed of crisp green money. Jodi's head pulsed and she let the lid fall down.

"I told them we wouldn't trade Rosa. Told them—"

"Hush, Ricky."

She stared off past his darkened silhouette. On the far side of the fence, in what used to be the Caulfield's pasture, a Hereford lowed discontentedly, calling out to the herd that moved ahead of her. The heifer raised her head and turned her slack gaze toward Jodi, her hide rippling under a haze of horseflies. Jodi looked again at the little suitcase. She lifted the lid and pulled out a packet, flipping the bills between her fingers, stiff as playing cards. Ten packets of five hundred each.

WHEN SHE FOUND him, out back of the Gas 'N Go, Dennis was seated on an empty milk crate, talking to a shirtless man with a bald sunburned head.

"Dennis," Jodi said, walking toward him across the cement lot.

He glanced her way and held up one finger. The bald man was telling a story about a bear hunt on Randolph Mountain.

A brown dog loped out of the shade of the building and into the empty street, his bones slinking under his skin. The outside wall of the gas station was painted with big blue letters—WE SUPPORT COAL—and in the oily puddles around the pumps little sparrows dove and rose, shivering water off their backs.

"Hey, Dennis, what the fuck happened up at my place last night?" Jodi moved in closer.

"Hold on," Dennis said to the bald man. He looked over at Jodi, his eyes loose and distant. He lifted his beer bottle and sunlight caught in the liquid and turned the brown glass to shimmering. "What do you mean?" he said, and Jodi could smell the yeasty alcohol on his breath.

"Where's Rosalba?"

"She went back home."

"*Went* back home?" Jodi glanced over at the bald man but he'd gone inside. "You mean an armed posse came and took her away?"

Dennis's laughter rang out like buckshot. "Man, Jodi, you sure got—"

"I've got kids living up there is what I got. I've got a family I've got to think about and I can't have—"

"Why, what happened?"

"I get home and the boys are locked in the bedroom pissing their pants."

"Look, I'm sorry, Jo." Dennis shook his head and lifted his beer bottle to his lips. "Cruz told me yesterday that the state cops have quit prowling. He said he'd be coming to pick up Rosa soon."

"Where is she now?"

"You don't have to worry about Cruz and his boys."

"But where is she?"

"Rosa? She's back where she's been living."

"And where's that?"

Dennis jerked his chin toward the mountains. "Look, just forget about her. Sorry I had to bring her up there but . . . just don't worry about her."

Jodi looked at him standing there, the sun silhouetting his head, and she wanted to shake him, tell him she needed control over some part of her life.

"You're sticking your nose in where it don't need to go," he said. "Sorry about the way it went down but—"

"What about the suitcase?"

Dennis looked straight at Jodi. "That's for that weed you've been storing. Cruz took it off my hands for me. I'm gonna find all the cash in there? Right?"

Jodi nodded. "I'm gonna need you to take it away."

He raised an eyebrow.

"I should never have let you keep nothing up there in the first place and I—"

"Hold on. I'm trying to help you out here. I don't see you making money any other way." He stepped closer to her. "You know what, though? If you don't wanna look at it that way, I got something else you oughta know." He pointed his beer bottle at her and there was something dark in his face now. "I know about you and Miranda. Don't matter how much you lie." He took a long drink. "I think it's sick but I ain't gonna do nothing to you. Some folks around here, though"—he drew a circle in the air with his bottle—"wouldn't handle it so kindly. Might wanna see those boys raised up in a different, more Christian home."

A film of sweat settled on Jodi's neck.

"You remember those girls over in Shawnee County," Dennis said.

Jodi looked away. She felt faint and dry mouthed as the images rushed across her mind, the story of those Yankee girls who'd traveled through West Virginia back in the mideighties. They'd gotten lost and begged a place to stay off a farmer in Shawnee County. He'd let them sleep the night in his hay barn but folks said when he went to check on them in the morning he'd found something happening there that made him raise his rifle to their heads. State police had come snooping but by then the car and bodies were gone and all the neighbors there stood by the old man, whose character, they said, was impeccable.

"You keep something for me and I'll keep something for you."

Jodi looked up and Dennis's mouth was moving but she could barely hear his words over the sound of her own blood as she stood there, breathless and gutted by her own silence.

"All righty?" Dennis turned and pitched his beer bottle high into the thin blue sky.

June 1989

The parking lot outside the hotel room is empty except for a Ford pickup and a broken bicycle chained to the fence by the pool. Jodi wears her black bra and polka-dot panties, the ones that have almost no holes. She carries in her purse the .38, the room key, and a pack of cigarettes. Under her bare feet, the stairway is hot, all the green paint worn away so that the sun shines too brightly on the bare metal.

The water is moving, sloshing, and flashing, jumping just for her. She takes her time finding the right seat, testing the deck chairs to find one that sits up straight. Later, when her skin feels like a paper flame, she will slide into the water and stay under as long as she can. But for now she will wait.

Jodi wakes sweaty, stretched sideways across a bed and wrapped in yellow-brown sheets.

It was you, she tells the wall where Paula's shadow hangs even after she is gone. *You convinced me I was better than my shitty little past. You convinced me we were part of something brighter than a ten-watt life and I have to believe you.*

She wakes to birdcalls, roosters, and the radio-announcer voice of fruit vendors in the street. *Melón, papaya, manzana, muy bonita, las manzanas, los melones. Venga! Venga!* Leaping from the bed, she pulls the curtains open but the parking lot is bare. It is America here. No fruit vendors, no fifty-cent tacos. Just the bleach-blue swimming pool.

Jodi stands naked, palms against the cool glass of the window, but there is no one there to see her.

August 2007

It was almost eight o'clock by the time Miranda left for her first shift at Slattery's Girl. Out in the yard the shadows were softening and Jodi watched from the porch, Ricky standing in the doorway behind her. She could feel his restlessness, feel his eyes scanning the yard and that gashed-up ground. For the past three days he had not stopped obsessing over his failure to save Rosalba. No matter how many times Jodi explained that she had just gone back home, Ricky was unconvinced and Dennis's sporadic visits to the cabin seemed to agitate him even more.

Two days after Rosalba left, Dennis had come to retrieve the cash but in its place he'd stored another smooth leather case, this one full of little white bundles. He'd tugged one of the squares loose and held it up for Jodi to see.

"Now ain't that beautiful?"

The packet of wax paper was stamped with a picture of a skull and the words MASTER MIND.

Jodi shook her head. "What—"

"Straight from NYC. I shouldn't even be showing you this but this is the shit that's gonna make us the real money." His face had glowed with the same grin he'd worn when talking about the bunny ranch. "I just gotta wait until I find the right buyer. People around here are used to that Mexican black tar shit—they don't even know what something this pure is worth."

"Where the hell did you—"

"Let's just call it a gift from the gods." Dennis snapped the suitcase shut and stood up. His shadow stretched out behind him across the chalky earth, marking a black path straight toward the wood-splitting block.

Jodi's pulse quickened and again she heard Officer Ballard's voice: *You shall not associate with persons engaged in criminal activity.* She was due to meet with him again in two weeks.

"You know why I'm bringing you into this?" Dennis had smiled at Jodi, all balmy and brotherly, as if he'd never threatened her. He winked and then turned away, seeking out a new hiding place, up at the corner of the roof at the other end of the shed. "You know if this works out right, after a while I'll have the kind of cash to where I could give you a loan for the land." "Bye!" Miranda waved out the window as she turned the car around in the yard. Jodi waved back, and watching the Chevette's taillights flare in the tall grass, she thought she'd allowed herself to become more attached to Miranda than she'd really meant to. From the beginning she'd known that Miranda was flighty and irrational but she'd come to depend on her laughter and quick smile and the way she was always adding some spark, setting up a makeshift bar and painting stars across the tarp roof. Somehow even her volatility seemed essential, an important ingredient in this strange new life of theirs, and now just this small change, this loss of their evenings together, felt irreparable.

"She'll be back?" Kaleb said. Jodi turned to face him.

He was leaned against the doorframe, there beside Ricky, the two of them staring out into the yard.

"She's just going to work," Jodi said, but the words sounded to her too much like a hope or a prayer.

"And you'll help her?"

"Hmm? How's that?" Jodi knelt beside Kaleb.

His eyes were huge and serious. "Sometimes Mom needs help," he said.

Jodi let out a long breath. "She'll be fine," she said, but she had to squeeze her eyes closed to keep back the emotion. A kid like this never ought to have to say a sentence like that. She leaned forward and kissed the top of his head. "She'll be okay," she repeated, and as the sound of the motor faded down the lane she took his hand and led him back inside.

It was a hot night and when she approached the cookstove Jodi could see the flames still leaping there, slivers of orange light visible around the edges of the cast-iron eyes. Rosalba's absence rang loudly throughout the house. As much as Jodi had hated Dennis suddenly dropping her there, she hated her disappearance even more; it was a constant reminder that she could trust nothing to remain the same for long.

The cabin smelled of burnt beans and wood smoke and as she poked at the dying coals Jodi remembered the heat on heat of Effie's summer canning and the batch of black raspberries she put up the day before her first stroke.

They'd spent the morning out in the canes together, the vines pricking blood tattoos all up and down their arms. In the afternoon Effie had prepared the canning jars and fed the cookstove with quartered rounds of ash, good for a fast flame. The kitchen was transformed into a syrup swamp of sugar heat. Standing over her biggest cast iron, Effie had cooked the berries down. The tin thermometer tacked to the side of the woodshed read eighty-seven that day but the temperature in that kitchen must have passed over a hundred. Effie had ignored it. She'd stepped with precise movements, dabbing the sweat from her eyes with a handkerchief and lowering the shiny jars of fruit down into the boiling water.

"She's lonely at night, I *know* it," Kaleb whined.

"Who's lonely?" Jodi said.

"Butter."

He had not quit talking about that dog all week.

Jodi moved through the cluttered shadows to the table where she lit up the oil lamp. The light formed an oval that enclosed them: Ricky smoking quietly at the end of the table, Kaleb and Ross sharing a chair, with the

Farmer's Almanac spread before them, and Donnie sitting on the floor playing with jacks.

"Miranda says no pet dogs allowed," Ricky reminded them. "She says you
can't buy dog food on food stamps."

Jodi pictured Miranda's face, her green eyes shining with the delight she
sometimes took in telling her boys no—her way of acting grown up—and
Jodi kicked herself again for getting attached to such a whimsical child-mom.
The more she thought about it, the more she felt a pull to go, to borrow
Farren's truck and fetch the dog to spite Miranda for taking the bar job. She
needed to get out of that quiet, overheated cabin anyway, needed to do something, go anywhere, just move.

IN HIS DOORWAY, Farren stood silently, staring at the crowd of them
there in the dark yard. He brought his cigarette to his lips and the cherry
flared with his breath. The gray dog stuck his nose out between the old man's
knees.

"Well," he said finally, "I'll come down there with you, I guess, but I've
got to finish my dinner first."

He turned and headed back toward the kitchen. The others followed him
into a living room dwarfed by a giant La-Z-Boy. In the blue light of the TV
the whole place looked like it had sunk under water. It smelled old and familiar to Jodi, the earthy scent of home-rolled cigarettes and the tang of whiskey.

Farren opened the refrigerator and the yellow light pooled around him.
He pulled out a carton of milk and then grabbed a bottle of Jim Beam off the
counter. At the far end of the table a CB radio sat, burbling quietly.

As Jodi's eyes adjusted to the grainy light she saw that all the walls of the
narrow kitchen were plastered with magazine pictures. Photos of horses glued
up beside pictures of cathedrals and photos of John Kennedy—lots and lots
of photos of Kennedy—Bugs Bunny, the state flag, and there, in the corner,
three pictures of Princess Diana with her blinding smile.

The boys pushed past Jodi and crowded around the table, watching closely
as Farren opened a packet of American cheese. He left the thin plastic wrappers in a pile beside his plate and laid out the pieces of cheese like a puzzle,

coupling each one with a slice of baloney and topping them off with dollops of mayonnaise. When the spread was complete, he leaned back in his chair and surveyed it, sipping at his glass of milk-whiskey. The boys' faces followed Farren's every movement.

"They've eaten already," Jodi said, leaning against the doorframe. "They don't need to be begging like that."

Farren smiled and held out pieces of cheese for each of them to take. "I come from a big family, bunch of always hungry boys," he said. "Mama used to give us leather strings to chew on, said we just needed something between the teeth."

THEY PARKED THE truck in the gravel pull-off beside the river, across the road from a gas station and convenience store called Good Stuff. The boys tore out of the cab, shouting, and Farren opened a cooler he kept in the back and pulled out a bag, heavy with the scent of blood and meat.

"Don't go down there," Jodi shouted, trying to keep an eye on all three boys, though all she could really see were morse code blinks of lightning bugs. "Stay up here, don't go down by the water."

The river murmured in the blackness below, a wet whisper.

There came the sound of clattering rocks and little feet.

"Ouch," one of the boys cried. "Don't push me."

"Quieten down," Farren called, coming around the side of the truck. "You want a skittish dog to come, you've got to quieten down and let her smell."

He dropped the contents of his sack in a trail, leading up to the open door of the truck.

Across the road, the Good Stuff store glowed, a small pod of greenish-yellow fluorescence, giving off a warmth that reached a few feet out into the night. Inside, a black-haired woman perched on a stool behind the register, holding an unlit cigarette. The store looked so cozy. Jodi thought of Miranda in her little pink dress, standing behind a counter in a loud and low-lit bar.

Farren watched the boys on the edge of the embankment, pinching and shoving each other. "Where's their father?" he said.

"They don't have a father no more," Jodi said quietly. "Just Miranda and, well, Ricky and me."

"But she ain't your kin, though, no? Just a friend?"

Jodi felt her heart kick at the phrase. She tried to catch the look in Farren's eyes but it was too dark to see. Everything had seemed so safe, so secluded, back there on Effie's land. But certainly Farren had been watching them, before they even knew him, and what all might he have seen?

"Butter!" Kaleb cried, and Jodi looked over, in relief, to see a yellow shadow dodge toward the cab of the pickup truck.

Farren fetched them a length of rope and dropped them all back at the house. The dog was docile until the truck pulled away and then she leapt, dancing at the end of her tether, barking after the taillights.

"I'm gonna sleep out here with Butter," Kaleb announced.

"No," Jodi said, "you sleep in the house with your brothers."

"But Butter's *alone*," he said, pressing his hands together.

"No," Ricky said, "she's here with us."

Kaleb looked up at him and nodded, his face so serious.

Such a big heart, Jodi thought, ruffling his hair. Sometimes he reminded her so much of young Ricky, up in that oak tree with his rescued bird, and it was for that reason, she guessed, that she'd agreed to follow his whim and save Butter. She'd never quite thought it through before this moment but sometimes, with Kaleb at her side, she felt as if she had young Ricky there, pulled up through the years to complete this dream world.

"*Rosalba's* the one we oughta be worrying about."

Ricky was staring out at the yard.

"That dog'll be fine," he shouted. "We need to find Rosalba, though. She's the one that's lonely."

Jodi let all the air out of her lungs. There was nothing more she could say, she guessed. She had said it all to him too many times now. If Rosalba had carved out a distance between Jodi and Ricky, her absence was gouging an even huger hole.

Jodi led the boys to bed and then carried the lantern back toward the kitchen. The moths at the windows moved with her from room to room, thudding against the cheesecloth screens until she blew out the lamp.

"Hey, Ricky," she called, grabbing the bottle of whiskey and heading outside.

She feared the silence, the empty porch and even emptier bed. She feared her thoughts, swarming like moths inside her brain.

"You want a drink?" She held out the bottle, desperate now for some point of connection.

He took a swig and passed it back. Down at the end of the mountain, the fire of the fracking tower was visible, an orange haze that pulsed through the trees. This town, Jodi thought, no, this whole state, had been trying for so long to find a way. A way to survive and still keep some things safe. *Just mineral rights is all you're selling*, the company men had been saying as far back as the Civil War. *You keep the land and we take out from under it what you didn't even know was there anyway.* As if anything in this life could be stratified that easily.

She took a long drink and passed it back to him. In the clear silence the motors of the gas trucks were audible, a humming that rose and fell with the shifting gears. It reminded Jodi of termites, the steady chewing, so constant as to be forgettable but working their way in just the same, weakening the walls hourly.

The dog was still now, lying flat but alert in the tall grass. Her ears moved as the wind hush-hushed the oak leaves, and an owl called out in the field.

"Hey, Ricky, you like it here?" Jodi asked.

Ricky was silent and totally still and Jodi forced herself to stay quiet too, to wait it out and not fill up the empty, uncomfortable space. After a while he leaned forward and pointed up to the distance above them. Jodi saw nothing and then, in the patch of smooth sky between clouds, a sharp slash of light. A flicker, and then another and another.

"Falling stars," she cried childishly, happy for a distraction.

"Meteors," Ricky corrected her.

They both moved farther down the porch steps, leaning back to better see the trails of light that dropped here and there, and there.

Clouds blew in and obscured the sky and Jodi closed her eyes, picturing the meteor that Miranda had described, a hot light burning brilliantly as it fell, straight into a woman's house.

"Hey, Ricky," she said, with her eyes still closed. "I found your newspapers."

A breeze flapped the cloth in the window frames.

Jodi went on. "It was Dylan that killed Paula's baby, wasn't it? Or was it an accident?"

There was no sound now but the train echoing away down in the valley. Jodi opened her eyes and saw that Ricky had fallen asleep.

BY MIDNIGHT THE bottle was empty but Jodi still could not rest. She'd lain in bed momentarily but she hated the empty space, hated the distance of time and her own counting—seconds to minutes to hours. The whiskey had only fueled her anxieties, her visions of Miranda, half-naked in that shack of a bar, a ring of men surrounding her. Jodi pushed herself up to standing and headed for the door.

The air was much cooler outside, the wind picking up and shaking the trees. No rain yet but she could sense it coming. She walked through the yard and past Butter, who rose and greeted her and then barked at her back until she disappeared around the bend. The plushness of the summer night surrounded her, booming with insect noise, and then the lights of Farren's house appeared up the road and it seemed that's where she was headed.

He was in the kitchen, drinking, the rest of the house dark around him, and when she knocked on the back door he looked up as if expecting her.

"That dog giving you trouble?"

Jodi stepped inside, shaking her head. "I'm worried about Miranda. I don't like thinking about her down at that bar. I just wanna make sure she's okay."

Farren cocked his head to the side. "Well, I've got to finish my drink."

They sat at the table and he poured her a whiskey. She sipped the drink slowly, watching the light play over the wall of photos: Marilyn Monroe, Roosevelt, Donald Duck, and the Virgin Mary.

"You were the child that stayed up here with Effie," Farren said.

Jodi nodded.

"You've been gone a long time."

He seemed to want her to say something more but she was sure he knew her story, at least that she'd been in prison. Small towns always talked and then there were the newspaper stories. Jodi tried to gauge his expression but it gave away no emotion.

"You come back, though," he said.

From the end of the table, the scanner radio emitted a crackle of static, as if clearing its throat.

Seven out. . . . Go ahead . . . eighty-six, forty-one.

"Effie would've liked that." Farren stamped his cigarette into the ashtray. "She was always big on coming home. Coming home, staying home. She was dead set on keeping that land. It's how come her and my brother split."

Jodi looked up.

"Before she married McCarty, her and my brother Cecil were thick. Mama called it sinning, the way they run together all the time like that."

She leaned in, not daring to disturb whatever it was that had brought forth his stories. Effie had never talked about her own life; she told endless tales about others but when it came to herself she had saved her words.

"Cecil dreamt up that they were gonna run off to Florida together and live in the orange groves but Effie said she'd never leave this mountain." Farren flicked his Semper Fi lighter open and snapped it closed again. "It's more important to come back, though."

Jodi swallowed half her shot, letting it burn across her tongue.

"Never leave," Farren said, "and you don't rightly know what it is you're not leaving. I thought for sure the only way I'd come home was in a body bag."

"Vietnam?"

"Korea." He pronounced the word with the same balance of awe and hatred one might use to say an ex-wife's name. "Fought at the Frozen Chosin."

"Frozen chosen?"

"Winter of '50, I was fifteen, told 'em I was seventeen. My three older brothers was fighting, I thought I'd join too." Farren emptied his glass, poured another shot, and offered Jodi the bottle. "Wind come in from Siberia, dropped the temperature to thirty-five below. Got so cold the guns jammed and quit working, radio batteries dead, the medics was carrying our morphine syrettes around in their mouths to keep 'em liquid, and frostbite come on quick." He held up his right hand to show the missing fingers. "The enemies was clear over there, though. You'd shoot you a little Chinese and watch the commie bastard bleed out into the snow and it felt good."

Forty-five . . . two thirty-five . . . the radio barked from the end of the table.

. . . Need someone to go over to Ruthey Drive and get a readin' on that plate ASAP.

Three sixteen, twenty-one . . .

Farren knocked back the end of his drink. "Well, I got to go take a piss," he said, "then we'll go check on that little lady."

He made his way around Jodi and down the hall, hand pressed against his homemade wallpaper. The clock on the microwave bled a faint luminescence into the kitchen, and the radio rattled on.

Five thirty work for ya? . . . Yeah, that'll do. . . . Three twenty-one, ten sixty-one . . . three twenty-one, go ahead. . . . Ten-four.

AS THEY APPROACHED the bottom of the mountain the noise of the fracking grew, the low gurgle of trucks in motion and over it a constant hollow knocking sound. The fire at the top of the tower throbbed, a perfect Pentecostal tongue of flame, and the road clogged with traffic. Farren pulled the pickup to a stop as two tankers lumbered out of the lane.

"They're sucking it fast," he said. "Ready to move on. It ain't like the mines, the *old* type mines. I worked twenty years up at Anjean." He drummed his fingers across the steering wheel and squinted out at the frack trucks. "That was self-respectful work. We tunneled in for the minerals and left the mountains whole."

The headlights of the tanker sliced across the dashboard and into the trees. "You grew up here on Bethlehem Mountain?" Jodi asked.

Farren nodded.

"But you've had the farm to yourself a long time now?"

He stared out at the road ahead, waiting for the trucks to clear. "Cecil, Jack, and Shane didn't make it home with me, and Daddy was dead by then too. My sister, Joanie, married a Michigan fellow, took Mother up to live with her."

"You never married?"

He laughed a short bark of a laugh and pushed the gear shifter up into first. "I seen how marriage treated most folks, your granny Effie included."

Jodi smiled. She wished he would say something more, anything to help her see what he might think of her and Miranda.

THE PARKING LOT at Slattery's Girl was jammed full. Farren pulled up behind a red Pontiac and kept the engine running but pushed the gearshift into neutral.

"You want a drink?" Jodi asked.

Farren pulled out his tobacco pouch. "You know how much they charge for a beer in there?" He laid out a square of cigarette paper on his knee and sprinkled tobacco along it. "Jacked the price of everything around here when those out-of-state fracking men come in. You know they're renting trailers for two thousand a month?" He looked up at Jodi, full of disgust. "Got landlords kicking out folks who lived in Render all their lives so's they can rent to cash-happy fools."

Jodi shook her head and opened the truck door, happy for his fury at the frackers, though she wasn't sure what good it could do.

There was movement in the back of one of the cars as she passed and music blaring through the thin walls of the bar. *Black velvet and that little boy's smile.* She looked over her shoulder but couldn't see if Farren was watching. She was overcome suddenly with regret and a tongue-tied stupidness. She hadn't thought it through this far and now she was quite drunk. Her body seemed distant, her movements slow and a little too loose. What would she say to Miranda? *I was worried about you? I'm sorry, I thought . . . I think . . . I love you?* And the boys, the boys were home alone and now Miranda would know.

Black velvet, the jukebox crooned.

High above her the red blink of a satellite stitched through the patchy clouds and from down the street a woman's voice called out the name of a man, or a dog or a child.

The front door swung open and a man stumbled out, unbuttoning his pants and walking a crooked line around the side of the building. Through the open door she could see the counter, a row of baseball-capped heads, and beyond that, a red-haired girl and Miranda, head tipped back, laughing.

June 1989

The chandelier is enormous, dripping with bits of reflecting glass and so heavy that every time she looks at it, Jodi thinks: tragedy. She sees it dropping down onto the heads of the blackjack players and exploding in a wave of glass and blood. So far, though, it has held up.

She orders a Coke from the bartender and winds her way among the slot machines, back to where she can see Paula, settled in at the poker table at the far end of the room. She has been there for the past three hours playing mostly just with two men, one in a white T-shirt and too much gold jewelry and the other, the kind of man you can tell smells bad even from a distance. Through the night there have been other players but none have stayed long. Freshly shaved men whose bland faces scream of Ohio or Indiana. They wander up and stand briefly behind the chairs, shuffling their handfuls of ten- and twenty-five-dollar chips before sitting down, only to rise again after one or two rounds. And others too, men and women whose desperation precedes them, so sure of their failure that they don't even notice the few hands they do win.

Sometimes Jodi plays the slot machines, losing and then winning back twenty dollars here and there, but mostly she likes to watch Paula. It makes her feel special to be tethered to someone with that kind of power. No matter where they go, it's the same; after the first few hands, the whole room is wrapped up in her winnings, the dealer stiffens, the cocktail waitresses start bringing out unordered drinks and a manager appears and begins pacing behind Paula's chair. Her stacks of chips grow, neatly mounting towers of purple and orange, and the other players' eyes move back and forth between those stacks and their own diminishing chips.

Of course it does not always happen like this; there are nights too when Paula loses and loses and keeps on losing as if falling through the attic and then on down, down, down through every floor of a never-ending house, crashing into the basement. Her chips grow scarce and Jodi, watching, feels bloated with fear as Paula keeps pushing the tokens out onto the felt.

With enough Dex in her, Paula can keep playing all night and eventually Jodi grows too tired and goes out to the car to sleep. She curls up on the backseat and closes her eyes, the looping music of the slot machines still jingling in her ears.

She wakes to the sound of the car door opening and Paula's face in the early-morning light, cap pushed back and hair sticking out all wild underneath, hard jaw and high cheeks and that soft, full mouth. Paula lifts Jodi up into an embrace and kisses her so deeply that Jodi's breath goes away and she is all happy and wrung out—emptied—like after a good cry.

THE GAME THIS time is held in the back room of a huge steak house. Paula tells the waiter *table for two* but she leaves immediately, slipping Jodi a flask of bourbon for spiking her Coke and promising she'll be back to check on her soon.

The enormous red-leather booth feels like it might swallow Jodi whole, like she could lie down in it and be lost forever. When the waiter takes her

Coke to refill it she worries that he will smell the booze but he doesn't mention it, just folds his knees and bows a little as he places it back on the table.

"Anything to eat?"

"In a little bit," Jodi says, balancing the leather-covered menu between her fingertips, afraid that somehow, just by touching it, she might cause the terrifyingly high prices to be charged to Paula's tab. The dinners are all more than fifty dollars but down at the bottom, under the heading "Children," she finds a ten-dollar hot dog and fries.

The french fries are hot and salty and come in a paper cone but the hot dog is covered in too much mustard. Jodi pushes the dog aside and drips ketchup into the cone of fries. She eats slowly to make them last and she is still licking her fingers when Paula comes back.

"Why are you eating this crap?" she says, tipping her head toward the untouched hot dog.

Jodi knows the game is not going well. Paula would not even have come out here if she were not losing.

"It's the only thing that's not *so* expensive," Jodi whispers, eyeing the approaching waiter.

"And who told you to worry about that?" Paula flips her lighter open and brings it up to the cigarette that Jodi is lifting to her lips.

The waiter bows a little; he has a white towel laid across his right arm.

"Filet mignon, rare. And can you please get rid of this," Paula says, sliding the hot dog across the table.

After the waiter has left Jodi whispers again. "What about you, aren't you hungry?"

Paula shakes her head and says she has to go back to the game. It might be a little while, she tells Jodi, just sit tight. She is gone by the time the steak comes and Jodi is so overwhelmed by the sight of the meat she thinks she might start crying.

"Anything else?" the waiter says, and she shakes her head vigorously.

The steak tastes good but she has taken too much speed to really be hungry. She remembers the excitement of the first time she ever ate steak, with

Paula, in Dallas, before they left for Mexico. This meat seems to mock her, though, so red and oozing, and the more time that goes by, the more panicked she gets that Paula will return and see that she has not eaten.

The news comes on the television and the waiter leans back against the bar to watch. The Red Sox lead the Blue Jays 10–0 and then the reporter is announcing something about troops and protesters clashing in China. Jodi wraps the steak in her linen napkin and darts across the restaurant toward the bathroom. Safely inside the stall, she collapses onto the toilet and lets out her breath.

The steak has bled through the napkin. It sits heavy and wet in her hands until she turns and dumps it into the little metal basket with the used menstrual pads. She can't tell if she wants to laugh or cry and she is shaking now with some almost indefinable craving, a loneliness, she realizes; she wishes she had someone to tell this story to—a friend to confide in—someone she could call across all those miles and tell the truth to. Whatever that might be. Lately she feels too invisible, and though she thinks it is pathetic, a part of her wishes someone—the woman at the gas station she held up, or a hotel clerk maybe— would notice that she is really just a kid and ask her if she needs help. When she told her parents she was going they hadn't tried to stop her. She wishes now that she could at least know that they are worrying. Crossing the border back from Mexico, she'd half-expected the guard to identify her as a missing person, but no, she realizes, her family hasn't even tried to look for her.

August–September 2007

Miranda locked the front door to the bar and stepped out into the glittering night. After her shifts at Slattery's she had too much energy to go home and sleep. The sky was soaked with stars as she drove, snaking back roads far up into the hills, her mind sailing out in front of her and an electric energy radiating off her skin.

The pills Justin had started giving her were like nothing she had ever had before. Desoxyn, he called them, little tablets with a spiral on one side and ME on the other. They looked like baby aspirins but two of those buddies under her tongue and she was cut free, her mind drawn in cleanly and a blooming euphoria spreading from her chest out to her fingertips.

She hated herself for taking them. It was a distant, glass-framed kind of hate, though, and she could see a shrewish pinch-faced version of herself taunting from her haughty mount, the part of her that had never believed she was capable of staying off pills anyway. *I'll only take them at work*, she told her hateful self and then they both laughed, knowing it wouldn't stay that way.

This pill was made for her, though, she thought bitterly, holding the peachy tablets in her palm. The ME was so perfect, selfishness printed right into it: ME, Me, me, me, me. . . .

Three, four, five o'clock in the morning: she drove one-lane roads that branched off and led upward, crawling into the crevasses of the mountains and coming out on top. The movement of the car wheels felt smooth and comforting as she smoked and watched a train down in the valley, shivering in and out of the dark trees, the tracks a silver ladder stretching out eternally. The breeze through the window felt exquisite on her skin and she pulled over and closed her eyes, trying to comfort herself: everybody needs something to help them get through their days, right? At least I'm not a goddamn junkie.

She drove on and the train tracks were gone now and the river too; the view was just trees-trees-trees and the sunrise leaking up into the sky. Shockingly green trees, gratuitously green, hung thick with kudzu and ivy, and every now and then the flash of an open field.

Some nights she came home from work and stood in the bedroom, staring down at Jodi: body curled tight under the quilt, eyelids fluttering with dreams. And standing there she was suddenly overcome with a queasy feeling as if she were trespassing.

Other nights she stood in the shed and pulled Dennis's suitcase down from the shelf. The unity of those little white envelopes calmed her. She ran her finger across them, lifted one out, and put it back. She'd never been much for downers but these little packets, so pale and uniform in the moonlight, were soothingly magnetic, the power they held, there in the shed, just waiting.

MOST MORNINGS NOW, by the time Jodi woke, Ricky was gone. The first day he disappeared she'd searched and called frantically and when she couldn't find him anywhere on the land she'd piled the boys in the Chevette and drove off looking for him.

Farren's house was empty with no sign of Ricky and so they'd kept driving and found him, finally, walking along the edge of the road, almost in town.

"Ricky!" Jodi called out, the blood surging up into her face. "Oh, God, you scared me."

She pulled the car over into the gravel and told him to hop on in but Ricky just squinted and shook his head.

"We're headed to the diner," Jodi said. "Let's go eat some breakfast."

"No, I'd rather not, thank you," Ricky said. "I need to keep looking for my friend."

He turned and headed back down the road.

Jodi watched him walk off, a huge hole spiraling open inside her. There he went—the very last connection she had to Paula—moving, right now, away from her. And it was the formalness of his words that hurt, that curt distance, the way you would dismiss a stranger who had bothered you while you were busy looking for your *friend*.

"Hey," she called after him. "Hey, Ricky, I came back for you. I got out of Jaxton and that's the first thing I did."

Ricky turned to face her, cocking his head so he could look straight in the window. "Thank you," he said, and kept walking.

She watched until the brush and trees blocked him from view. She wanted to tell him she'd seen his news clippings and she understood what it was that he'd been through. But what exactly would that do?

"Jodi?"

A small hand patted her arm.

"Jodi?"

She turned toward the backseat to see three sets of big green eyes.

"Jodi's crying?" Ross said, pinching his eyebrows together with worry.

"Yeah." She nodded, her words coming out all slurred. "Yeah, it's okay, Jodi's just a little bit sad."

BACK AT THE cabin she sent the boys off to play with Butter and headed to the woodshed. Although he came up every few days to check on his "investment," Dennis had yet to retrieve the heroin and its presence pulsed constantly at the back of Jodi's brain. The sight of those packets frightened her but at the same time there was something ecstatic about their existence in her life, something a little like driving fast down a dark road with the headlights off. She might as well admit to herself that she wasn't going to get a nine-to-five-type job anytime soon and Dennis seemed to have hit upon the only possible way to make real money in this place. These methods had been here long before any of them were even born anyway: first moonshine, then later weed, and now meth and junk. The very landscape of the mountains had always supported it and in some twisted way this made Jodi feel better as she gave in, as if at least her ancestors would have approved.

A VOICE WAS screaming, hollering Jodi's name, and she surfaced slowly from a dream of rain and wind, a storm that lifted the house and tossed it away with all of them inside. She opened her eyes to Miranda's hair, beside her on the pillow, and then slowly she became aware of Butter barking and Farren's voice and the pounding of metal on metal.

Out on the porch she squinted, following the direction of Farren's outstretched arm over to a cluster of trucks. Three blue trailers and one tall crane parked, not more than half a mile away, over at the old Persinger place.

"I told you when they run the other one dry that they'd move on to a new place," Farren said. He sounded as if he blamed her personally. "They'll frack the whole mountain dry, ruin the water clear up and down it."

The noise was immense and palpable—the great thwank-thwank of the drill and all around it a sea of grinding gears and quaking machinery. Panic spiked up through her body, though she was barely awake enough to know if this was dream or reality. These frack men were hungry, she thought, hungry and moving. She'd been so worried about Ricky's wanderings and Miranda working at the bar but this was the real doom. Do something, she thought—call Lynn, call the lawyer, do something, *do* something.

IN HER PARENTS' kitchen, she sat with a can of Bud in one hand and the phone pressed to her head, trying to concentrate sufficiently. She needed just a little beer before making this pleading phone call to Lynn. She'd been taught never to ask for handouts but now it seemed there was nothing left to do but beg for help.

"I've never sorted darks and lights in my life and my loads come out just fine."

Irene and Miranda's voices rang out from the laundry room. There was something different about Miranda lately, manic mood swoops that sent her zipping high and then crashing down exhausted. The more she thought about it, the more Jodi felt sure she was taking pills again. She'd tried to bring it up twice but each time Miranda denied, almost crying as she screamed, *How could you say that? How dare you?*

Jodi had been too distracted lately by Ricky and Rosalba and Dennis and now she was losing Miranda and losing the land. Back in that hotel room in Delray she'd promised Miranda that she could do it, *they* could do it, start new, stay clean, and make a good life for the boys. It had seemed so simple then; all they had to do was make it to West Virginia and find some kind of job and then the six of them could live there, sheltered and healing. Now, though, it seemed to Jodi that she'd failed to provide a life interesting enough to make the pills unnecessary.

In the living room the TV emitted explosion sounds:—*and then, I'm gonna gouge your eyes out.*

Jodi squinted at the paper in her hand and read Lynn's number aloud to herself before dialing. The beers she'd drunk, combined with a couple of hits off the joint Dennis was currently smoking, were making this phone call exceedingly slow and difficult.

Yeah, I'm gonna gouge your eyes out, that's what I'm gonna do.

Lynn's phone rang. Jodi watched her fingers slide up and down the red beer can.

"If you'd put peroxide on it in the moment," Irene said, "there'd be some hope. It's not gonna come out now, though."

"Hello," the phone spoke.

Jodi pulled the earpiece away from her face.

"I can't answer the phone right now but if you'll leave your name and number I'll call you back."

"Hey, Lynn, it's Jodi here." She stopped and took a sip of beer. "They're putting a frack well in, right now, just this morning, on the property just over from mine and I wanted to see . . . uh, I'm worried my land could be next."

She placed the phone back in its cradle and moved her chair to the doorway where she could watch the TV without having to talk to Dennis who was sprawled across the couch, head in his wife's lap, the smoke from his joint rising above him in a straight line. His wife appeared to be sleeping but her hands kept moving, crochet needles tapping out a tick-tick tune. On the screen a cartoon animal with huge neon-pink eyes leapt up and down on top of a fat red-and-white animal with a blue nose.

Jodi finished her beer and fetched another. The fridge was full of beer. It was the first week of a new month. She stood there, the cool yellow air swimming around her, enjoying the weight of the can in her hand and the view of all those other unopened beers. She found a pack of Marlboros beside the sink and tried to determine by the number of smokes inside if the pack was her father's or hers. She gave up after a minute and lit one. *Happy, happy, joy, joy,* the television sang.

In the yard there was a rustle of movement and then Dennis's girls began shrieking. The children stood in a ring beside the empty birdbath and in the center Ross lay flat on his back, blood flowing thickly from his nose. As the adults poured out into the yard the girls stopped screaming and stood, pressed forward on their tiptoes. Ross was not moving but his eyes were wide open.

"Hey, what happened here?" Dennis said, and his girls turned to him.

"He fell," Dana said. "Tripped and fell and starting bleeding in his nose."

Jodi pushed past and ran down the steps, gathering Ross up and carrying him toward the house. He closed his eyes. The blood had almost stopped running but berry-bright drops of it still clung to his nose and chin and the lobes of his ears.

Miranda was in the doorway as Jodi came up the stairs. She reached for Ross and Jodi looked up at her. Her pupils were tiny dots and the tendons along her neck stood out as if they'd been wound too tight.

"Give him some room. He needs room to breathe," Jodi said, carrying

Ross inside to the kitchen sink. Even as she said the words, though, she wished that Miranda would act like a normal mother for once and take Ross from her but Miranda just stayed there with Irene on the porch.

Jodi stared down at Ross's face and let the water run until it came out warm. The blood had begun to crust and dry in swirled patterns, red-brown rust rivers crossing his cheeks. He seemed not to want to open his eyes, even after his face was clean, and so Jodi held him tight, rocking him, the thin legs of the kitchen chair wobbling. They rocked to the sloshing rhythms of the washing machine and the hum of a mower droning somewhere down the street. Through the window above the sink she could see the peak of Palmer's Knob, and beyond that, the mountains that gave way to more mountains. Traffic glimmered on the hill road that twisted north and junctioned in with other single-lane roads, all of them squiggling up over those ridges, deeper into coal country. She reached her hand out and, with her fingers stretched, managed to block the window, but when she took her hand away the mountains were still there, beautiful, ancient, and suffocating. She could see a small strip of blue sky above the peaks but it seemed the mountain was compressing all the air, setting itself smugly between her and everything easy. To get anything, you've got to cross me, it said. She thought of the old settlers traveling the mountains for days, only to come to the End, the unfordable split of the New River gorge.

BACK AT EFFIE'S a long black foreign car was parked in the yard, gleaming like a single patent-leather shoe. The sight of it started something buzzing in Jodi. Every time she came home lately there was trouble waiting.

"Stay here a minute," she said, but Kaleb, Donnie, and Ross spilled out of the Chevette before she could shut the engine off.

"Hold on," Ricky called, and when they did not listen he followed them.

On the porch a short-haired woman in a cranberry-colored dress stood up and walked down the steps, followed by Butter. It was Lynn, Jodi realized, dressed in an asymmetrically cut dress, the deep redness of which made her skin look pearly.

Donnie and Ross rushed across the grass and tackled Butter around the neck while Ricky and Kaleb stood back, staring at Lynn. She stepped around them and walked toward the car.

"I got your message."

Jodi closed the driver's-side door and walked around the front. "Thank you, thanks for coming up, I—"

"It's incredible here." Lynn spread her arms and stared off over Jodi's head, her eyes sparking.

"Yeah, it's a little wild still, we haven't got to clear the field out yet but, you know—"

"No, no, it only just goes to show how much more beautiful a place can be without human intrusion."

Miranda came around the front of the car. "Is this your lawyer friend?" she said.

Lynn's lips broke open into a smile. "I don't have any law degrees," she said, walking past them across the yard. "I'm just a concerned party."

Miranda looked at Jodi and Jodi brushed past her, following Lynn.

"I see we lost the land there." Lynn pointed toward the field and the frack tower on the hill.

"We?" Jodi walked up beside her.

"Well, yeah, the we who care about the land."

They'd reached the edge of the yard and the rusted barbed-wire fence that separated Effie's land from the Persinger place. The white frack tower stood out brilliantly against the trees.

"It makes so much sense seeing you here," Lynn said, turning to face Jodi. "I mean, *you* make so much more sense in this place." She smiled. "But you don't really know who you are yet, do you?"

Jodi glanced at Lynn and then off toward the frack pad where the trucks were parked for the evening but the sound of the drilling kept on. Even without looking, Jodi could feel Lynn's eyes on her.

"It's kind of beautiful. The unknowing," she said. "There's some magic about you. You're unalloyed."

"Un-what?" Jodi looked back at her.

"It's the sort of energy one usually gets from a child. The wild trust in the universe."

Jodi laughed, unsure if she should take offense. "How old are you?" she said.

Lynn's face twitched. "How old do you *think* I am?" she said, and when Jodi did not respond immediately she brought her hand up to her hair. "And yes, I do color it, if that's what you were wondering."

"No, I was just thinking we're probably the same age. Thirty-five?"

"Thirty-nine." Lynn smiled. "I feel so old, though. You've got so much hopeful energy. For me, everywhere I look now it's just . . . Did you know we're at the precipice of a sixth extinction? Probably not a precipice, I think we're past that. By the end of the century we'll have lost fifty percent. And with almost no fossil record left."

The leaps and jumps of Lynn's conversation unnerved Jodi. She turned to walk back toward the house.

"I'm sorry, I'm boring you." Lynn reached out and tucked a strand of hair behind Jodi's ear.

Jodi stepped back. "No," she said, "no, I just don't know what—"

"Don't worry." Lynn grabbed her hand again. "I just need to find one or two more donors for the silent auction. We'll set the date this week."

THE NEXT MORNING Farren met Jodi, Ricky, and the boys at the head of the lane and they walked out silently, the sound of the machines rising all around them. The little hillside that once held the Persinger house had been clear cut and flattened on top, molded and graveled until it resembled a landing pad. They stood in the shade of the sycamores and watched as the white metal tower climbed higher into the cloudless sky and hoses spilled like loose intestines across the muddy ground. A permanent line of tanker trucks inched around the well.

Even with Lynn's assurances of help, the sound of the drill hammered a doom rhythm into Jodi's brain. The hollow gong-gong-gong of it echoed on through even the deepest hours of the night. She thought of Rosalba's words, *Everything was gone, the farm I grew up on, the way we used to live,* and she

could see them, the huge mechanical god-hands of the frackers and the car-
tels, coming down from the pure blue sky and lifting, scooping away.

"Somebody was to strike a match in the wrong place," Farren said, "this
whole operation would fire up and blow to hell."

"Where are they digging to?" Donnie yelled.

Farren said something but his words were lost under all the sounds and
all Jodi could hear was a mumble about layers and openings and radium. She
remembered Lynn's words about the fracking and tried to imagine Farren and
Lynn conversing and laughter rose in her throat. She turned and looked back
at the small, dark shape of Effie's house.

When the mines had slowed and the coal companies had pulled out, Effie
said they would be back to take more eventually, so sure had she been that
the future was only a parallel of the past.

June 1989

It is a slow night at the Crystal Club and the air conditioner is barely working. The girls sit around in clumps at the cocktail tables, fanning themselves with newspapers and smoking. Jodi and Paula have been here for the better part of an hour, trying to sell some of the coke that Paula bought from a man down in New Orleans. The bouncer at the Crystal is an old acquaintance and he said he'd let the girls know what Paula has. They've been doing this, hopping from club to club like traveling salesmen, since New Orleans. The allure of the clubs has worn thin. Jodi wishes she could just go out to the car and sleep but she's supposed to be Paula's security.

Legs walk by, smooth brown skin arching up to a plump butt and tits pointing down, the purple areolas stretched by hungry baby mouths. You see this much skin for too long, Jodi thinks, and it stops meaning anything. A part of her wants to tell the girl that if she covered her pussy until partway through the show, then maybe there would be a bit more excitement.

Paula gets up and goes over to the table full of strippers. They are too far away for Jodi to hear what they're saying but Paula's mouth moves and then all the girls laugh.

Jodi leans back in the booth, slides her hand inside her purse and fondles the pistol, the metal smooth against her skin. She can feel herself loosening, the Valium she swallowed half an hour ago burning away the connections between words and what they mean, between here and now and yesterday.

A stripper comes out of the bathroom, glances around the almost empty club, then sits in the booth with Jodi. She calls herself Gabby and she's got braces, which, she explains, she thought would be a big turnoff to men but actually they think it's exciting.

"Jonno, he paid for them. Said my dad should have paid for them a long time ago." Gabby bares her teeth and runs her index finger along the lines of metal. She has little gold rings on every one of her chubby fingers.

"Jonno?" Jodi is watching Paula at the table of strippers. All evening the girls have refused to do stage shows because there is almost no audience. When the DJ cues their music and calls out their names they heckle him and lean back, propping their heels up on the table. But now, a new song comes on and a frizzy-haired girl stands, winks at Paula, and shows her how she can move each butt cheek individually.

"He owns this place." Gabby taps her pink-painted nails against her braces. "You could make a lot of money working here."

Watching Paula, Jodi feels a lick of jealousy rise inside her. The strippers are all turned around in their seats, a ring of faces angled up toward Paula, and Paula is beaming with that same look she gets when she's on a great run at the card table. The more of an audience she gets, the better she performs. She's probably off on some tangent now, already forgotten what she is here for, or maybe not; maybe she is leading them all around to the subject of coke, priming them so they'll buy it off her whether or not they ever wanted any to begin with.

"You look so young. You could make a lot of money." Gabby reaches out and touches Jodi's cheek and Jodi wishes she found this girl even a little bit attractive.

"I am young," she says, then pushes up out of the booth.

Paula is gone.

Jodi scans the room. They are supposed to be a team. Paula sells the coke and Jodi is there with the pistol to make sure no one messes with them.

The rhinestoned velvet curtain beside the stage is swaying. Jodi moves toward it, gripping her purse. Behind the curtain there is a hallway with a yellow rectangle of light at the end. There are voices in the room beyond. Paula's voice: *Yeah, here, try a line.*

The girl is bent over a narrow counter that extends the length of the room, crowded with coffee cups, cans of hairspray, tissue boxes, and strappy lingerie. In the mirror Jodi can see Paula eyeing the girl's back, which is branded on the left side with a sickle-shaped scar. As the girl inhales, Paula places her hand on the girl's ass and squeezes it.

"Hey." The girl straightens up and looks at Paula.

Paula does not remove her hand. "I figured, you get a free bump, I should get a feel."

The girl laughs, then turns and sees Jodi in the doorway. Her mouth puckers and then flattens out into a smile. "Your girlfriend's pretty cute," she says, tilting her face back toward Paula.

Paula's shoulders tighten and she spins around, her expression blank.

Something unfurls in Jodi's chest, a fury of shock. She slides her hand into her purse and grips the cool metal of the pistol.

"Let's get out of here," she says, and surprisingly her voice comes out loud and steady. She has never spoken to Paula like this before.

Paula twists her mouth. "Wait for me out there," she says.

Anger hooks Jodi's stomach and pulls it up toward her heart. "No," she says, sliding the pistol out of her purse.

September 2007

They were wilting before they'd even left the parking lot. Ross kept begging to be carried, Donnie cried out that he was *thirsty!*, and Kaleb was stone silent but looked like he was about to pass out. At the bottom of the gravel hill was a football field's worth of tables of junk. From where they stood it looked like a model, Jodi thought, a little cross-section displaying the constant and useless movements of humanity.

Miranda had wanted to go by herself to the Sunday morning flea market but Jodi had insisted that they all come along and do something together on Miranda's rare day off. And so there they were, in the ninety-degree heat, strung out across the parking lot in a weary hand-holding line, all of them except for Ricky, who had refused the invitation.

The flea market was ringed with produce stands offering the same goods that most folks had overflowing in their gardens at home—string beans, squash, and boxes upon boxes of tomatoes—red, yellow, stripy pink and green. A few enterprising stands offered Georgia peaches and Florida melons. An old woman bent her ear to each watermelon, thumping and listening.

"They're all ripe, ma'am," the flush-flaced man behind the table said. "Fresh from Florida and sweeter than a newborn baby."

Miranda led the way past a snow cone stand and a table filled with baseball cards, assorted wrenches, and six naked Barbies.

"What do you want to look for?" She glanced back at Jodi, her eyes puffy from lack of sleep.

Jodi shrugged. "A chain saw maybe."

"We'll meet back up at the donut stand in half an hour?"

"Where are you going?" Jodi stepped closer to her.

Miranda waved her hand at the rows of tables. "Around," she said. "I'll take Donnie, you take Kaleb and Ross?"

She moved off down the aisle, leading Donnie by his hand as she passed by tables full of costume jewelry and frosted-glass dishes.

Jodi stood with Ross on her hip and Kaleb at her side. The air tasted of dirty sugar and gasoline. A loudspeaker voice crackled intermittently. *Miss Pauleena Hutchins would like to announce . . . Tupperware sale . . .* From somewhere down at the end of the field a chorus of dog barks rose and fell.

Kaleb grabbed Jodi's hand and pointed toward a red Chevy truck with a man sitting on the hood playing a guitar. The cardboard box at his feet was filled with spotted kittens, a roiling mess of orange-and-white fur. The man smiled at Kaleb and called out to him in song.

"Have a kitten, sweet little kitten, best little kitten that you ever did see."

In the truck window the faces of two girls appeared, freckle nosed, brown haired, and blue eyed.

"Come on," Jodi said, staring down the aisle where Miranda had disappeared.

"I'm *tired*," Kaleb said.

"I know." Jodi nodded. "Me too. We'll get some ice cream in a minute. Let's just see where your mama's headed."

As they neared the end of the field the barking of the dogs grew louder and just past a stand of baby clothes Jodi saw them, chained to a blue pickup, in the shade of two tall pines. There were ten of them, little beagles and black-and-tans and a few tall redbones, and as Jodi watched, Miranda emerged from a row of antiques sellers and walked toward the dogs.

Jodi pulled Kaleb and Ross back as she ducked behind a fireworks stand.

"Hey!" Miranda waved to the baseball-capped man leaned up against the truck.

The line of dogs leapt, pawing the air and choking against their chains as Miranda and Donnie approached them.

The man spat a line of tobacco. His face looked familiar but Jodi couldn't quite place it. He lifted off his cap, scratched his head, and put the cap back. Jason—that was it—Jason or Justin or whatever—her cousin, the bouncer, Phillip's boy. Jodi eyed the man's dirty jeans, Harley-Davidson T-shirt, and the bright glint of his belt buckle printed with HERITAGE and a billowing Confederate flag.

"Hey, gorgeous," he said to Miranda. "This your little boy?"

"Yeah, you weren't at Slattery's last night. You not working there no more?"

"Not every weekend," the man said.

Miranda nodded. "Sheila told me you'd be here today." She reached down to pet the beagle. "What's this one's name?"

Justin laughed. "I don't name them."

"Why not?" Miranda knelt and her shorts rode up, cupping the bottom of her ass. "She's so cute, why wouldn't you name her?"

Jodi watched Justin watch Miranda's ass. A poison was forming inside her, making her blood move all sluggish. It seems you're not gonna do anything, she thought, but just stand here and watch them flirt. She was losing the land and she was losing Miranda. She squeezed Kaleb's hand harder.

"Wait, it *is* a girl, right?" Miranda looked up at Justin.

"You don't see a pecker, do you?"

She patted the beagle and stood up and the other dogs all jumped again, their bugle barks scrambling out loud through the dry air.

"You got something you could spare to give me?" she said.

Justin smiled and shook his head but motioned her toward the cab of the truck. "I shoulda known you wasn't just stopping by to say hi," he said.

They huddled there beside the truck for a moment and then Miranda stepped away, the bulge of a pill bottle visible now in her back pocket.

"Thanks," she said, grabbing Donnie's hand. "I'll see you at Slattery's?"

As she came down the aisle Jodi stepped from behind the fireworks stand.

"Miranda," she called, pulling Kaleb along with her.

Miranda stopped, an expression on her face that Jodi couldn't quite read.

"So that's why you've been so keen to come here?" Jodi dropped Kaleb's hand and reached out to grab Miranda's arm.

"You fucking followed me?" Miranda freed herself from Jodi's grasp and walked off fast and angry up the aisle.

Watching her, Jodi marveled at how much of a space this woman had carved out in her heart, how quickly she'd gone from being a distraction from the plan to being an integral part, and she hated herself for letting it happen that way, for going weak and letting her emotions run her life. Again. The tattered beast perked up its head.

"At least you could have told me you've been taking that shit," she called out at Miranda's back.

Miranda kept walking.

Jodi caught up and gripped Miranda's arm again. She leaned in close to her ear. "How many times have you fucked him?"

Miranda flicked her eyes over to Jodi. "No, never, it isn't like that," she said.

"Sweet corn, sweet corn," a woman called in a singsong voice as she held a long green ear toward them, peeling back the husk to show the flossy strands and bright gold kernels as yellow as Miranda's hair.

"You fuck him at work? Or in his truck?"

"You better quit that." Miranda pulled away and turned, looking back down the aisle for her boys, but Jodi leaned in close again and brought her hand up to clasp Miranda's soft, soap-smelling neck.

. . .

Through the bar windows the late-evening sun angled in and hit the rack of bottles like an explosion. Miranda could not stop staring at the warm glow of the bourbon and the way the light spilled through the vodka bottle, sending out strings of tiny, shivering rainbows. The pills did that to her sometimes—stopped all time while she narrowed the universe to one single moment. The first kick was always like a hand against her back, pushing the swing higher and higher, and then she'd settle into the buzz and move through the night happy, trundling along in her own little train car, separate but connected, pulled forward through the shift. Lately she'd started snorting the pills, now that her body was adjusted to them. She comforted herself with the fact that if she snorted them it meant she used fewer.

"What is it with this place, really?" Sheila was saying. Sheila was always saying large, clouded things. "It's this whole entire state. People keep talking about how the frackers are coming in here and then moving on so fast but it's not just that. It's like the whole state is in fast-forward."

Sheila was nestling bottles of warm beer into the open ice chest. A joint rested, smoldering in the ashtray on the counter before her, inking its dark smell out into the room. Miranda took a hit and moved over to look out the back window.

"Did you ever notice how everybody here blooms and busts so quick?" Sheila said.

The sun was notched in the gap between two green mountain peaks.

"How old are you?"

"Twenty-five," Miranda said.

"You know how many people I know who are younger than you and already dead?" Sheila lifted the joint to her lips. "Dead or in prison."

The last sunlight leaked out across the brown river.

"You know how old I was when I got pregnant?" Sheila said. "Fifteen."

Miranda thought to tell her that she herself had been only seventeen but her voice was unlocatable at the moment and, besides, it was not really a conversation.

"It's like we're all pressing up so fast, we cash out and then there are years and years still left. There's so much time but none of us know it till it's too late and we already died or ruined our lives trying to grow up and get out quick."

Dots of pollen and dust hung in the light, drifting slowly down toward the water. Fairies, Miranda used to call them. When she was little she would lie on her back and watch the dust motes dancing, watch and watch until she was really seeing nothing but the tiny imperfections in her own vision. Even then, that young, she had been trying to float away from her present reality. She could remember spinning and spinning in the front yard until she fell down in the grass, happy to feel nothing but dizzy, gleefully disconnected from the sick-death smell of her mother's bedroom and the oppressiveness of her father's smothering love.

THE BAR FILLED up earlier now that the truckers were on break. While the new frack well was being built the men who drove the gas shipments got a few free days and none of them knew what to do besides drink. Miranda lined up beers and Jim Beam shots before the men even made it through the door. They grinned and nodded, their movements reminding her of her sons, a kind of timid exuberance.

The room swelled with more and more men as the night continued and Miranda rocketed back and forth behind the bar. She liked the fast-paced energy and as she took orders, her mind ticking off Bud, Michelob, Jim Beam, she felt that she was hovering somewhere just above herself, watching her own bony legs in cutoff jeans pacing up and down the bar and her hands flying efficiently. But other thoughts came too, an image of Ross's little blood-covered face and Jodi's smile. She felt a sweet-sad shiver pass through her as she thought of Jodi, up on the mountain, curled asleep and dreaming in their bed.

Justin showed up to work the door and Miranda begged him for more pills. She'd been holding back, telling herself she'd wait till the end of her shift, but at the sight of his face she knew she couldn't wait. *Speed-freak*, he said, laughing, his hand moving down her leg, fingers sliding up under the denim to squeeze the soft rise of her ass cheek. *Please*, she said, the noise of the room bashing loud around her. He slid his fingers up higher under her shorts and told her to stick out her tongue real quick.

She shook her head and he laughed. "Wait, you're snorting 'em already?"

Miranda shrugged.

"Be careful, baby." He pressed two tablets into her sweaty palm.

Time slowed and sped up simultaneously. Miranda's movements turned liquid again and the night went rattling along nicely, all the nauseating thoughts of failed motherhood and failed relationships beautifully buried.

Delta Dawn, what's that flower you have on? the jukebox cried, and behind the bar the radio bubbled a different tune, something with a lot of saxophone. Sheila liked to keep the radio on even when the jukebox was playing; late at night she could pick up stations you couldn't hear during the day.

"I'll take another." A bushy-bearded man pushed his shot glass forward and Miranda filled it, glancing up at his whiskered face.

These men were the enemy, according to Jodi and Farren, but Miranda couldn't see the devil in them. They just looked anxious and lonely. She understood that there would be more fracking to come up on Bethlehem, and more than likely on Jodi's land, but even that did not exactly seem so frightening. She'd been looking for a place to lose herself in and this had seemed like it, but lately she found herself thinking more and more about Lee. Maybe she'd thrown away her life with him too fast. Sure, he was gone on tour too much but Nina's house didn't seem so bad to her now: hazy days of soft carpet, endless television, and never having to worry where food and money would come from. Maybe it was not too late to get that life back. This here was not the life for her, not this moldering bar or the tumble-down cabin. Even as she stood there, stocking warm beers in the ice chest, a part of her had already moved on ahead.

WHEN DENNIS'S PICKUP drove into the yard, Jodi was out back, planting the carrot and turnip seeds that Farren had brought over. She stood there, one hand clutching weeds, the other held up over her eyes as she squinted against the late sun. The truck doors opened with a rusted squawk and three men piled out, dim silhouettes against the wavering green of the grass and the trees. It took her a moment to see that it was her two brothers and Ricky.

"Lookee what we found," Dennis crowed. He held a beer bottle in one hand and his baseball cap in the other. He waved his cap in Ricky's direction and laughed. "Out searching for his ladylove again!"

Ricky stood on the far side of the pickup, holding a bottle of Jack Daniel's and staring off toward the frack tower, where it rose, skeletal through the leafy trees.

Jodi wiped her hands on her thighs as she crossed the grass. "What's going on?"

A.J. was giggling and holding up to his mouth a thin half-smoked joint.

"Ricky," Jodi said, "is everything okay?"

He took the top off the bottle of Jack and lifted it to his lips.

"I saw her," he said.

Jodi stepped closer to him. "What are you talking about?"

"We found him walking out Snake Run Road, babbling about finding Rosalba." Dennis took a swig from his own bottle. "I figured he was just a little brokenhearted, hell, sometimes we all just need a drink."

"I saw her." Ricky turned his back to them and hunched over, holding the open whiskey bottle between his knees. "I did see her too in the back of a—"

"Ricky," Jodi said. "Rosalba's gone, you ain't gonna see her nowhere." She reached a hand down to rub his shoulder and he sprang at her, lunging.

"I *did* see her," he thundered, dropping the bottle and bringing both hands down onto Jodi's shoulders. His hands were heavy and his voice, raging loud, sounded just like Dylan's. "I saw her riding in the back of a pickup, went up Snake Run Road."

Jodi closed her eyes and held her body stiff. "Okay, Ricky, okay. You saw her," she said, and as she stood there, eyes closed, steadying her breath, the *her* got all tangled up somehow so that she pictured a mountain road winding along and the familiar figure of Paula just around the bend.

THREE

September 2007

The Chevette was gone when Jodi woke. She stood in the kitchen, coffeepot in one hand, staring out the window and listening to the grinding-gear rhythms of the frack trucks in the field. She registered the absence in the front yard slowly and then all of a sudden: Miranda was asleep, the boys were still in their bedroom, and the car was gone.

She wanted to shout Ricky's name but what was the point? She was the one who had set it all in motion, back in Georgia with her grand idea: *Hey, Ricky, let me teach you to drive.*

She set the coffeepot back on the counter and walked out the door. He couldn't have gone far yet. Farren could drive her around until they found him but there was one more thing she knew she needed to check before leaving. As she crossed the yard she wished there were some sort of prayer she believed in, some incantation like the one the Catholic priests chanted, something to say to oneself in times like these, but all she could think was No, please, no.

Butter came out from under the porch and tried to rub herself up against Jodi's leg but Jodi kept walking. *No, please, no.* She ducked under the shed roof and pressed onto her tiptoes, reaching up, wanting so badly to feel the firm leather handle, those little metal clasps, but there was nothing at all to feel, nothing but hot, empty air.

"Fuck," she said, rocking back onto her heels. "Fuck, fuck, fuck."

BY THE TIME she arrived at Farren's, her T-shirt was soaked through and sweat dripped down the back of her neck. His pickup was not in the yard but she approached the house anyhow, calling out his name and then Ricky's too.

From the corn patch out back half a dozen crows rose up, a cluster of black splotches against the hot blue sky. She stepped onto the porch and pressed her face against the front window. The glass was thin and bubbled in places, covered in a yellow-brown dust. She didn't know why she was wasting time here except that she kept hoping for one of them to show up, for something to change. Peering in at the darkened living room, she felt the panic settle fully in her veins, a deep cold followed by a flush of heat. *Fuck you, Ricky. What the fuck have you done?*

She turned and fled, out of the tin shade and into the yellow sun, knowing the road to town was five miles. She was out of shape but filled up with adrenaline. She watched her own feet move across the cracked black pavement and then looked up to the shivery green of the trees all around her. She ran past trailers with yards full of fading plastics—old car seats, lawn ornaments, boots, and coolers—a strew of forgotten items, abandoned midtransit on their way somewhere. In scrappy patches of porch shade dogs lay, raising their heads slowly at her passing, too heat dazed to bother barking.

Jodi ran until she couldn't run anymore and then stopped, doubled over the gravel ditch, heaving. She felt a surge of self-pity rise inside her like bile and she reached to greet it but it didn't work as well out here. In

Jaxton she'd had so little control that she'd been able to blame every misfortune on something far outside herself but here the self-pity was not as purely, sadly sweet. It was too tinged with regret and embarrassment and she felt the weight of all her bad decisions caving in on top of her. Why the hell had she let Rosalba stay with them in the first place? She felt fear, yes, but rage too. Rage at herself, at things not working out the way she had imagined. Rage at Ricky. What the fuck had she been thinking bringing him here?

The heat and the rage mixed until she felt she was moving through it all physically, the emotions and bad decisions, the weather, and all of it. Was it always headed this way? Everything in her life? She thought back to her younger self, back before she ever met Paula, before Effie passed away. She was never too good in school but never too bad either, unsure of what she could expect from life, unsure even of what she wanted, knowing only that she loved that farm and the simple seasonal movements of it. She had pictured that as Effie grew older, she and someone else, a boyfriend or husband—for, before Paula, she had never imagined loving a woman outside of the dreams in her head—would harvest hay and raise cattle in the back pasture. It would never have been an easy life, there was no real money to be made there, but with part-time jobs it could have worked. And that was all she had been trying to find her way back to all this time, the future that had been lost the moment she followed Paula out of that Wheeling casino.

Her legs were wobbly by the time she reached town. The Chevette was not at the Gas 'N Go and the man at the register said he hadn't seen anyone who looked like Ricky. Jodi splashed cold water on her sweat-red face and headed out the back door toward her parents' house.

The little blue bungalow had the blinds tightly drawn. Approaching it, Jodi felt the same unease she had as a child. Ever since her parents moved there she had felt that it was such a separate sphere, the whole thing as private as a closed-up bedroom.

It took Andy a long time to come to the door and when he did he looked like he might have just woken up. No, he said, they had not seen Ricky.

Jodi nodded and pushed inside toward the phone on the kitchen wall. Andy stood in the doorway, scratching his crotch as Jodi dialed Dennis's number. His lethargy angered Jodi. All of it, Farren's absence, the Gas 'N Go cashier's flippancy, and Andy's sleepiness, seemed to mock Jodi's urgency. She wiped sweat from her upper lip and gripped the phone.

"'ello?"

"Veeda, hey, is Dennis there?"

"No, huh-uh, who is this?"

"Jodi. Is he at work?"

"Everything's okay?"

"Is he at work, Veeda, you think he's at work?"

"Well, should be. You got his cell number?"

She dialed the cell but got no answer and placing the phone back in its cradle she felt the slurring of the moment, the way that house trapped time: Andy slowly opening his Marlboro pack and lighting a cigarette, shuffling over to turn on the TV and crack the first beer of the day. If she stayed a moment longer, she would get stuck in all that slowed-down time and so she sprang for the door.

After the closed-down hopelessness of the house, the heat felt good and she struck out across town, over the railroad tracks and on down toward the river where the katydids chitted in the trees. Ricky had spoken of seeing Rosalba in a pickup going up Snake Run Road, and though she could barely remember where it was, that, Jodi decided, was where she was headed.

The particulars of the roads and directions eluded her but the buildings she passed were riddled with memory-scars: the diner where she'd washed dishes the summer that she met Paula, the football-field concession stand that she was not cool enough to get a job at, the high-school gymnasium where, at age fourteen, she'd decided to enter the talent show by reciting her beloved Tennyson. Even now she was not sure exactly what reaction she'd hoped for, awe or respect perhaps. She'd traipsed up on the stage in Effie's old wedding gown and closed her eyes to better articulate and project her carefully memorized "Lady of Shalott" lines and in her reverie—the warmth of the stage lights on her silky dress, those beautiful lines flowing from her lips—she had failed to notice the gym teacher–cum–master of ceremony until he was grabbing the microphone from her hands, pointing to his watch and shouting *time's up!* The spattering of applause for her was nothing compared to the thunderous ovation for the following act, a spunky lip-synced version of George Strait's "It Ain't Cool to Be Crazy about You."

IT WAS EVENING by the time Dennis caught up with Jodi, still walking, in the waning heat, out along Route 3. The sound of his engine flared at her back. He honked and pulled over into the weeds, head hanging out the window.

"Dad said you been calling me. Said you come by looking for Ricky."

"He took the car this time," Jodi said.

The cab of Dennis's pickup smelled of chewing tobacco and stale beer. Jodi pushed aside a pile of chip bags and plastic soda bottles and climbed in. Dennis looked dirty and tired; his work uniform was still on and his blue shirt with the Sunrise Poultry logo was splattered with bits of dried chicken blood.

"Where you headed?" he said, pushing the gearshift out of neutral. "I been driving around for the past hour, looking for you."

"Snake Run Road. Yesterday Ricky said—"

"Snake Run ain't out this way. You're headed smack-damn in the wrong direction."

Jodi stared out the window. She felt exhausted. She kept on forgetting just how much she had forgotten about this place, how much of a stranger she was here.

"Is she really staying up Snake Run?" she asked as Dennis turned the truck around.

"Up in the back of Saw Mill Holler but you get there by going on Snake Run."

She knew she should mention the suitcase but she feared Dennis's reaction.

By the time they had reached the narrowing chasm of Saw Mill Holler, night had set in with lightning bugs luminescing along the edges of the steep curves. Jodi had no memory of this road and no idea where it led. They wove on, deep into the split of the mountains, the blacktop looping around itself, and from far below, down the hillside, came the sound of a fast-churning creek.

Dennis was uncharacteristically silent. Just tired, Jodi told herself, hoping he was not frightened, pushing back her own fears. They wound around a hairpin curve and the truck's headlights splashed onto the maroon bumper of the Chevette, slanting up out of the ditch.

"Shit," Jodi said, all the air going out of her as Dennis slammed on the brakes and jerked the truck over onto the gravel.

They were out of the truck and moving fast through the double beams of the headlights.

"Ricky?"

"Hey, Ricky?"

Their voices bounced off each other and for a moment, before she remembered that it was mostly his fault they were even in this situation, Jodi felt a surge of gratitude toward Dennis for being there.

The back tires were up in the air and the nose of the car wedged neatly down in the ditch. The pickup's lights illuminated only the back half of the vehicle so Jodi had to feel her way, blind and groping, digging her heels into the soft dirt bank as she worked to open the front passenger's door.

"He ain't in here," Dennis called from the far side of the car, and Jodi could see, as her eyes adjusted, that it was true.

She cursed him as she climbed back up the mud bank. Now that she knew he wasn't dead inside the car or badly wounded, anger spiraled up inside her.

"You got your cell phone?" she asked Dennis. "We should call and see if the cops picked him up."

Dennis shook his head. "If he kept walking from here, he could be up at Cruz's place by now."

They drove on, curving deeper back in the holler until Dennis pointed off to the right and Jodi looked to see the lights of half a dozen trailers up ahead, their front porches glowing through the knotty pine trees. Dennis turned onto a rutted dirt road and drove until they reached a chain-link fence with a tall metal gate. A floodlight blinked and Dennis shut the truck off and stepped out. Jodi moved to open her door but Dennis shook his head.

"Just give me a minute," he said.

A dog barked, its voice bobbing down the hill ahead of its body, and a bearded man appeared out of the field beyond the gate, an AR-15 held tight in his right hand.

"McCarty," he called, and Jodi, sitting there in the empty truck, felt herself lurch. Of course McCarty was Dennis's name too but to her that singular word was the language of Jaxton, of penalty and authority and roll calls.

"Yeah, Cruz will wanna talk to you," the bearded man said, shaking his head at Dennis as he pushed the gate wide and held back the panting dog.

Dennis climbed back into the truck and drove on up the dark road.

"Ricky's here?" Jodi said, her words sounding too loud and breathless.

Dennis nodded. He said nothing but the veins in the side of his neck were jumping and Jodi suddenly felt nauseated. She balled her hands into fists and stared up the hill toward the porches where two women sat smoking, their bare legs crossed, pale skin bright against the night.

Dennis pulled up beside the first trailer and the front door opened. A man shuffled down the porch steps. Dennis opened his door and Jodi reached for hers but again Dennis told her to stay put.

"But—"

"I'll be right back."

"Ricky doesn't really know you. I should come."

"Stay *right* here."

Jodi watched him disappear behind the second trailer. The night was cooler back here in the crook of the holler and she could see, high above, in the sliver of sky between mountain peaks, a scattering of stars spread like tossed salt. She thought of herself and Ricky on the cabin porch watching falling stars.

Music started up in the nearest trailer, a man's voice crooning, and for a moment Jodi was sure it was Ricky singing and she gripped the door handle, but just as quickly the voice faded. Someone changed the radio station and it fizzled to static and then a pink bubbly voice sang out something about first kisses. The women on the porch put out their cigarettes and went back inside.

Jodi pushed the truck door open as quietly as she could and stepped out. The grass was wet with dew and the night air buzzed full of mosquitoes. She crossed into the darkness between the first and second trailers. Around back she could hear men's voices and through the trees the lights of a tall, pillared house shone faintly.

Through the curtainless windows Jodi could see into the front room; paint and plaster peeled off the walls and a tilted chandelier hung over a huddle of men: Ricky, arms folded across his chest, staring off toward the boarded-up fireplace; Dennis, his face red as he shouted at a short brown man with tattoos on his neck; and two other men, skinny, cracked-out white dudes, flanking each side of the tattooed man. In the middle of them all was a black-and-white pit bull whose scarred head looked too heavy for its bony body and, beside it, the leather suitcase.

Jodi brushed the fuzz of mosquitoes off her arms and moved slowly up onto the porch, keeping her feet quiet as she headed for the open front door.

"I had no fucking clue," Dennis screamed. "*No* fucking clue, dude. I did not send him up here."

Jodi slipped into the hallway.

"He threatened me, threatened my girls—"

"I have a really fucking hard time believing that you felt threatened by—"

"Okay, okay, *annoyed*. He took up all of my afternoon with his yelling about Rosalba and . . . and then he gives me the skag, so I see this is fair. For my time wasted I keep the skag and you can have your friend." Cruz smiled. "And maybe it is that he is smarter than you? That is why he brings it to me? Because what in fuck are you doing trying to sell this shit around here?"

They were close, just through that doorway, close enough that Jodi could smell them, the dog scent and beer and weed.

"I won't sell it around here." Dennis glanced between Cruz and the suitcase. "I'll move it out, down in Atlanta."

"You think anyone wants to buy this shit anyway?" He motioned toward the suitcase with his foot. "You thought this powder shit was pure, huh? Fancy? Because it's not sticky and dark like my black tar?" Cruz was smiling wide now, flashing silver teeth and wet gums. "You know how many times this shit has been stepped on?"

Dennis looked like he might cry.

"Still, a nice gift, though."

"Come on, Cruz, you know that shit wasn't his to give."

"Well, let's say you should keep a little better track of your friends."

The man beside Cruz laughed. The laughter echoed in the huge high-ceilinged room. The dog looked up at the men and barked. Cruz kicked the dog and it bobbed its head and whimpered. Ricky bent suddenly. He held his hand out to stroke the dog's head and then the room erupted: dog flying at Ricky's face, Cruz stumbling backward, the suitcase tipping over, and the two men backing away.

"No," Jodi screamed. She was running toward Ricky who lay sprawled now, the dog on his chest, his screams mixing in with Jodi's and bouncing all around the room.

"Who the fuck?" Even as he asked the question Cruz was turning from Jodi toward Ricky and kicking the dog with a sick whump.

He bent to catch his breath. "Who the fuck is this?"

Jodi opened her mouth to explain herself but stopped. The suitcase was no longer on the floor.

"Dan-ees," Cruz said.

Dennis paused in the doorway, both hands grasping the suitcase.

Jodi looked beyond Cruz and over to Ricky whose neck was scratched and red but not bloody.

"Dan-ees, put the suitcase on the floor," Cruz said, pulling a small silver pistol from the back of his pants.

Jodi crawled past Cruz toward Ricky, sitting now and looking stunned as he watched the dog lift its head slowly. She felt numb and bloodless and had to push herself to crawl, arm, leg, arm, until she reached him.

"You know this ain't yours," Dennis said, and then the sound of the pistol ripped through the room.

Dennis dropped the suitcase, stuttering backward, the sleeve of his blue shirt flushing dark as he fell against the wall.

"Oh," Jodi said, surprised at the sound of her own voice so loud there in the silence after the shot.

Cruz picked up the suitcase and stepped over Dennis. He waved his men to him and spoke in a voice too low for Jodi to understand. The men nodded and flanked out, one on each side of the room. Cruz walked out the front door.

Jodi stood and looked at the man closest to her. His eyes were glazed but his rifle barrel pointed straight at her brother, finger resting on the trigger. She looked at the other man, a twitchy twin of the first, rifle leveled at Dennis's head.

Dennis moaned and Jodi stepped toward him and then glanced again at Cruz's men. They did not stir. Their faces wore the calm look of trained animals waiting to be called upon. Jodi bent over Dennis. The shot seemed to have hit only his upper arm but he was shaking, breathing all stuttery and losing blood quickly.

"Oh, fuck," Jodi said, propping him up against the wall. His head lolled. She pulled at his undershirt and ripped it with her teeth. Even here, inside, the mosquitoes were thick, buzzing and landing on Dennis's neck and arms. "Shit," Jodi said, keeping her voice quiet as if louder words might awaken Cruz's men to action. "I'm gonna make a tourniquet, okay? You're not gonna die."

Dennis's eyes were all jittery. His arm was slick and warm with blood.

"Just bandage the wound," Ricky said.

Jodi looked up to see him standing just behind her. Cruz's men moved their rifles from Dennis to him. Unaware, he bent and took the ragged cloth in his hands, pressing it firmly against Dennis's arm and wrapping it three times tight.

"Let's get him to the truck." Ricky grabbed Dennis's shoulders and lifted him.

Jodi turned to the men. "We're taking him to the hospital."

Neither man said anything but their rifles were still fixed on Ricky.

"We won't tell anyone who shot him," Jodi said, and when no response came she bent and grabbed Dennis's legs.

They carried him slowly through the front door and Jodi held her breath, waiting for the crack of rifle fire.

"Go on and get the truck," Ricky said. "I'll wait here with him."

Jodi lowered her brother into the grass, wiped her blood-gummed hands on her pants, and took off running. The night was loud with the static of crickets and tree frogs. She could hear laughter from inside one of the trailers and the sound of her own feet swishing through the tall grass. Clouds were blowing in, covering up the pinprick stars and everything was so still. She shook her head as if to wake herself. The beauty of the summer night, the fucked-upness of the situation—she could not see how to straighten it all out and understand everything.

In the truck, they propped up Dennis with his head on Ricky's lap and legs across Jodi's thighs. In the dark of the cab Jodi could barely see his face but she could hear him moaning and smell his blood and she felt sick.

"Where's Rosalba?"

Ricky jerked his head toward the trailers. "She said I shouldn't have come looking for her."

Jodi jammed the gearshift into reverse, then up into first, the engine screaming. She took the dirt road too fast and they bucked over the ruts so hard she feared they'd bust a tire, and then there, at the bottom of the hill, the headlights leapt up bright against the metal fence.

"Fuck," Jodi said, "fuck, fuck, the gate."

She pushed Dennis's feet off her lap and jumped out. "Somebody open the fucking gate!"

A car approached down on the blacktop road, its lights swinging like a tide across the trees. She ran toward the gate but the car drove on, deeper into the holler, and when the light and noise had passed all she could hear was the fast drum of her own blood.

"Hey, anybody there?" she yelled, her throat dry and painful.

There was a rustle of footsteps back beyond the truck, the clink of metal, and the man with the AR-15 appeared. He said nothing to Jodi, just pulled out a clutch of keys.

She drove faster than she'd ever believed she could, whipping the curves in one long motion, her stomach up in her throat.

"You fucking idiots," Dennis said suddenly. "Shit. Fuck. I'm gonna kill you."

They rounded a curve and the headlights spun onto the maroon metal of the Chevette and she glanced at Ricky but he had his head down, staring at Dennis's arm.

Rain began to fall as they reached the edge of town, big drops that sounded out against the windshield and blurred the stoplights and streetlamps. Jodi ran a red light on Front Street and turned onto the river road. She pushed the truck up to ninety, the wet blacktop glistening on the dips and rises of the hills. She looked over at Dennis's pale face and glassy eyes and remembered the way he had looked as a baby, when he first arrived home, tucked inside a wicker laundry basket with A.J., two little hairless beings. *Defenseless*, Effie had called them, explaining to five-year-old Jodi that they were too tiny to make it on their own. *You've got to protect them*, she said.

IN THE BRIGHT lights of the ER lobby, she gave Dennis's name and her parents' phone number to the nurse.

"He'll be all right?"

The nurse stared at Jodi, working a piece of chewing gum fast between her teeth.

"I mean, it just hit his arm, he won't die, right?"

"Well," the nurse said, moving her gum to the other side of her mouth. "It don't *sound* like he's in danger of dying, honey."

Jodi nodded. "I'm just gonna go right outside and smoke, okay?"

She found Ricky out front, watching the rain. Jodi studied his face, the fuzz of untrimmed whiskers and deep wrinkles around his eyes. Back in the truck, after he'd bandaged and carried Dennis, she'd felt something that was almost gratitude toward him but now as she watched his moody face she felt an anger rise again.

"So Rosalba told you that you shouldn't have gone looking for her?"

Ricky shrugged and looked down at his feet.

Out on the highway an ambulance siren began to scream.

Jodi sucked hard on her cigarette. She was sick with a wild vertigo, and though she tried not to think about it, she could suddenly see all her messy loyalties unspooling and coiling down the hillside before her, all the links and chains of mistakes, and she pictured the lines of Ricky's desire crisscrossing and snarling in with hers, him so bent on rescuing Rosalba and her so bent on saving him.

"You almost got my fucking brother killed. You know that?"

Ricky glanced up but his face was blank and he did not say anything.

"I loved Paula," Jodi went on. "I really did and I thought I owed it to her to save you."

Ricky wrinkled his eyebrows. "Rosalba told me you can't save somebody," he said.

He pulled out his pack of Winstons and lit one, cupping the flame out of the rain. She felt a kick of fury at him for being so fucking calm and taking it all so easy.

"I found your newspaper story," she said. "The one about you being a murderer."

Ricky paused, cigarette halfway to his mouth, and stared down the hill toward the highway where a pair of taillights blinked and disappeared.

"But it was Dylan, right?" She'd thrown the words like arrows, expecting that they'd hit his heart and turn him vulnerable, but he showed no emotion.

"You've been digging through my personal things?" He cut his eyes over to Jodi.

"I . . . It was raining on your papers and . . ." She could not meet his stare. "I don't understand why Paula never told me."

Ricky brought his cigarette to his lips and inhaled. "Well, we need to focus on Miranda's boys now," he said. "Need to watch over those boys."

IT WAS NOT until after midnight that Jodi and Ricky could head home, after Irene and Andy and Veeda arrived, frantic and crying, after Jodi mumbled an explanation of the "bar fight" Dennis had gotten into, after they'd smoked two whole packs of cigarettes, and finally the nurses had come out and proclaimed Dennis stable.

On the drive home Ricky explained to Jodi how Rosalba had told him that he needed to watch out for Miranda's boys.

"She said there was a man come out there to the trailers and was asking around about Miranda and her boys."

Jodi felt a trap door swing open inside her and she was floating, almost plummeting. "What?"

"A man with black hair and a mustache, asking did she know Miranda Golden?"

"Fuck," Jodi said as the last of the adrenaline energy left her body, her hands barely guiding the steering wheel. "You think it was Lee?"

"Lee don't have black hair."

Jodi exhaled a long breath. "When was he there?"

Ricky brought his hands together in front of his face, as if praying. "Rosalba says I'm to take care of those boys, watch over them." He turned toward the window, staring out at the roadside where the glow of animal eyes reflected in the headlights.

AT THE HOUSE Miranda came out onto the porch carrying an oil lamp. "Where have you been?" she said. "What the hell's going on?"

Ricky walked past her inside and Jodi came slowly up the front steps, petting Butter on the head. She was too tired to even open her mouth.

"Jo, baby, you look awful." Miranda grabbed her arm and pulled her close. "Why are you driving Dennis's truck? Are you hurt? You're hurt."

Jodi brought her head down to rest on Miranda's shoulder, nuzzling her face in against her neck. She thought suddenly that if she could just feel the warm weight of Miranda's body in her hands, then everything would be okay. "We might have to go on a little vacation," she said.

"Where have you and Ricky been?" Miranda pulled Jodi inside.

"I mean, we might have to get out of town for a minute. Don't you think the boys would like to go camping?"

Miranda's blonde hair was flashing in the lamplight, her eyes bright as she bent close to Jodi. "Baby, what are you talking about?"

"There's a man in town asking around about you, Miranda, looking for you and the boys."

Miranda looked away.

"We just need to lay low, get out of town for a little bit, okay?" Jodi gripped the sweet warmth of Miranda's fingers and her eyes ached. She really did love this woman, she thought—funny, because for so long she'd been sure it was only lust.

"Everything'll be all right. We'll just go on a little vacation," she said, "and when we come back Lynn will have her gala and pay for the land and we can start for real here, get some chickens, a couple of yearlings, get the boys signed up for school." Jodi could hear the frantic cadence of her own voice but she wanted to believe the words too.

IN THE MORNING Jodi walked to Farren's house and asked him to help get the Chevette out of the ditch on Snake Run. She'd figured they might have to call a tow truck but when they got there only the front right tire was flat and the nose a little buckled in. They eased it up out of the ditch with Farren's truck and put on the spare tire and then Jodi followed Farren back through Render. A gauzy fog hung over the river, lit here and there by spears of sunlight, and the town was coming awake now, cars backing out of driveways and a waitress at the Bantam Chef turning the sign on the door to OPEN. As she drove, Jodi let herself be lulled into an optimistic attitude. She and Miranda had stayed up the night before, talking until Jodi could not keep herself awake. They'd decided to head for Moncove Lake and now, she thought, with the car functioning, everything really would work out okay. But as she followed Farren around the last bend of the lane she saw that Dennis's truck was gone from the yard.

"Miranda?" she hollered, jerking up the emergency brake. "Ricky?"

The front door hung open and the house was empty. There were half-eaten sandwiches on the table and Miranda's pink dress drying on the back of a chair and when Farren's truck motor cut off she heard voices in the woods behind the shed.

They found Ricky and the boys in the back field, standing in a semicircle around a midsize copperhead snake.

"Everybody back up," Farren said, grabbing Ross and carrying him a good ten feet away.

"Look, it's swimming in the grass!" Donnie said.

Farren found a chunk of limestone and followed the snake until he could drop it, square on that reddish head. The body bunched and twisted even after the rock was in place.

"Why'd you kill him?" Kaleb cried, tugging on Farren's pant leg.

"Poison," Farren said. "You can't have the poison ones around."

"But what about his soul?" Kaleb said. The skin along his arms, where he'd been pinching it, was covered in a trail of bruised-blue half-moons. "Neenee says all God's creatures have mighty souls."

Farren's lips twitched. "I don't know about a snake soul." He sucked hard on his cigarette, then threw it down and ground it out.

"Hey." Jodi turned to Ricky. "Where's Miranda?"

"We come out here for blackberries," he said, "but we found that snake."

"How long's Miranda been gone?"

"Justin come by and she said she had to go to work for a little bit."

"She doesn't work in the morning," Jodi snapped.

Ricky shrugged and looked down at Butter who was sniffing the air and staring at the now still snake. Jodi wanted badly to blame Ricky for Miranda's disappearance—it seemed easiest just to blame him for everything—and a part of her, though she hated to admit it, wanted to forge a new plan with Miranda and the boys and leave Ricky out of it. He seemed now like a heavy, tangled weight.

WHEN THEY CAME out of the woods Dennis's rusty pickup was parked in the yard and, beside it, a shiny black car that had to be Lynn's.

"Somebody's visiting," Ricky said, and Jodi felt a lunge of annoyance at the obviousness of his words.

"Yeah, no shit," she said, walking walked faster until she was up beside Kaleb. She grabbed his right hand and he squirmed but she held tight. Over the past week he had grown more quiet and fidgety, picking at his own arms until they bled and scabbed. Jodi looked down at him as he fondled the dimpled indents in his skin, and she thought of his words: *Sometimes Mom needs help.*

"Don't pick at yourself," she said.

He stopped walking and stared up at her, a wave of anger crowding his face. Jodi looked away, toward the house, and squeezed his fingers too tightly.

Lynn and Miranda stood side by side on the porch, Lynn in a floor-length purple dress and Miranda wearing tiny cutoff shorts and a baggy black T-shirt. She was so skinny. How, Jodi wondered, had she not noticed before just how skinny Miranda had gotten?

"You never told me your girlfriend was a concert pianist." Lynn caught Jodi's eye as they walked up.

"No, no, no, that's not what I said." Miranda shook her head.

"Maybe she should play at our gala." Lynn smiled, her teeth flashing between her red lips.

"I don't perform anymore." Miranda sat down on the edge of the porch and lit a cigarette. Her hand shook as she raised it to her lips and her pupils were wildly dilated.

"When is it?" Jodi said, glancing from Miranda to Lynn. "The gala."

Lynn moved to the porch steps, her high heel catching in a gap between two boards. She grabbed the side of the house to steady herself and her face flushed and in that moment of lost composure she looked suddenly sweet to Jodi.

"Tomorrow evening," she said.

"Tomorrow?"

"I'm sorry I didn't tell you sooner. I kept meaning to come here and let you know but I figured you'd be free."

She walked down into the yard.

"I'm thinking of making a documentary." Her eyes moved over Jodi's shoulder and out across the pasture. "I'm just not sure what medium would best express . . . You know, it's not just fracking and mining that threaten this place. There are people who have land here who . . . well, who just don't even know how to care." She walked past Jodi, off toward the boundary fence and the Persinger place. "They put up those old asbestos trailers and then they abandon them or they so overburden the land, so many people living on one piece of land. You know I acquired ten acres off this family last month—"

"And what do *you* do with the land?" Jodi followed behind, her pulse jumping.

"Preserve it."

"Free of people?"

"Well, no, not necessarily." Lynn looked back over her shoulder. Her eyes were bright and lips almost smiling. "Hey, look, we're on the same team here. I'm not trying to take your land from you. I'm trying to get it back."

Jodi dropped her gaze and nodded.

"Mom?" a voice cried from behind them. "Mawwm-mom!"

Jodi turned to see Ross tearing across the yard, a snarl of bees swirling around his tiny legs.

"Oh, shit." She lunged after him as he ran toward the porch with Butter close behind, yelping and snapping.

"Owww!" Ross screamed, flapping his hands at his sides.

Miranda rose from the porch and ran to him, gathering him up into her arms and brushing the bees away as she moved toward the cabin.

"Miranda, here, let me see," Jodi called, but by the time she made it to the porch Miranda was already inside, the screen door slapping closed behind her.

"Yellow jackets," Ricky said, moving past Jodi. "We'll put tobacco on it."

"Toothpaste," Farren called from the yard, and Ricky turned to him. "Toothpaste?"

"And garlic." Farren nodded. "But tobacco won't hurt none either."

Lynn looked from Ricky to Farren. "Folk remedies?"

Farren headed off toward his truck.

Lynn looked up at Jodi. "Tomorrow evening," she said. "Can you come around five? I'd love it if you could say something too, you know, nothing formal, just something heartfelt about growing up on this land."

Jodi nodded but she could not wipe away the mental image of an organ grinder's monkey with his little cup of money.

MIRANDA AND ROSS struggled beside the kitchen sink, Miranda gripping Ross's legs as he bucked and cried.

"Is he allergic?" Jodi asked. Miranda shook her head.

Jodi pressed in beside them. "We'll put tobacco on it."

"Gotta get the stingers out first." Miranda jerked his leg up toward the light from the window.

"No, no, don't do that." Jodi lifted Ross into her own arms. "Yellow jackets don't leave stingers."

Miranda looked up, her face full of ugly hate. "Don't fucking tell me how to take care of my own kid," she said.

Jodi stepped back, stunned, and then moved to lay Ross down on the counter. He'd been stung three times on one leg and twice on the other. "Hand me a cigarette, please," she said.

"You think you know so much."

Jodi glanced at Miranda. She was sweating and breathing heavily.

"Miranda," she said. "Where'd you go this morning?"

Miranda looked away out the window.

Jodi pulled a cigarette from her own pocket and broke it open, turning back to Ross. His cries had subsided to whimpers and his body relaxed a little as she pressed the tobacco against his shins.

Behind her Miranda laughed, or maybe cried.

"Hey," Jodi said. "I tell you there's a man in town looking for you and the boys and this is what you do? You just take off and leave them alone here?" She turned to look at Miranda. She *was* crying.

"You shot her," she said slowly. "It wasn't an accident. Justin told me."

Neither of them moved. The pitcher pump dripped into the sink. Out the window the clouds had shifted and a darkness settled over the room.

Jodi pulled Ross up into her arms again. She brushed past Miranda without looking at her. "You'll be all right, you just need to lie down and rest now," she whispered, carrying Ross into the bedroom.

He looked so small in the big bed in that shadowed room, that same room that Jodi had slept in every night of her childhood, in this house that only seven weeks before she had believed she would never see again.

"What's wrong with Mama? Why's she crying?" Ross whispered.

Jodi straightened his pillow. "She's fine. It'll be fine," she said.

MIRANDA WAS HUDDLED on the front porch, knees tucked up under her chin.

"What kind of shit are you on?" Jodi said, lowering herself onto the step beside her.

Miranda barked out a quick laugh. "It's not that. I'm coming down now, I'm fine, it's just . . ." Her pale hands flapped frantically in front of her face. "You know, I'm glad somebody finally told me the truth."

Jodi gripped the edge of the wooden stair. Her limbs were leaden and the white fear was creeping in again, blank and too thick to move through.

"Did you do some crystal? Is that what you were doing with Justin this morning?"

Miranda took a deep drag on her cigarette. "Everybody thought I already knew. Here I am, so stupid I believed your gun accident lies and nobody told me any different 'cause they all thought I knew."

Jodi sat silently. She felt powerless to speak or to move.

"I did know there was something on you, though." Miranda looked over at Jodi. "Something dark all over you and I think I liked it. It's like a . . . What do they call it when you know you've been somewhere before?" She looked down at her palm and blinked. "Déjà vu!" she said. "First time I saw you, it was like that. I knew it. It's like that thing you can't say but it's in the back of your mind all the time and then somebody says it and it's like a bell, right out loud."

Miranda's hands seemed unconnected to her, they flapped in an odd rhythm, swirling her cigarette against the sky and grabbing at her own hair.

"You know how sometimes your mind is such a big, lonely place?" Miranda said. "I mean, it's really small, actually, I mean, I think sometimes about the space inside my skull and it's really small but it gets so lonely."

Jodi still could not move but she felt herself thawing just a little. She's going to let it go, she thought. Maybe it was the meth but Miranda couldn't seem to keep her mind focused and Jodi felt herself relaxing a little now that the conversation seemed to be twisting away from Paula. She exhaled and Miranda turned and looked right through her.

"Why'd you kill her?"

"No." Jodi closed her eyes. Her heart was beating too fast. "No, it wasn't like that." Breathe, she told herself, breathe. Maybe it was better that they just get this conversation over with. No more secrets. No more lies. She should have told Miranda already. If she loved her, she should have told her.

"I was messed up in the head," Jodi said. "I didn't mean to."

Her words hung there, weak and ugly, and Jodi felt suddenly angry that Miranda had forced her to say them.

"Your boys were playing with a copperhead snake," she said, opening her eyes.

"What?" Miranda sat up straight. "Wait, what happened?"

"Farren killed it. But you left those boys here alone. They could have been bit."

"I was only gone for a minute," Miranda said. "They were playing out back with Ricky when Justin come by and I was only gonna be gone . . ." She held her hands up in front of her face and stared at them, brought her index finger to her lips and licked it, then inspected it again. "I was only gonna be gone for a minute."

"You abandoned them before?" Jodi said. She knew that if she took hold of the conversation now and steered it right, they wouldn't have to talk about Paula again. "That's how come Lee didn't want you near them?"

Miranda was still sweating despite the cool wind, her hair plastered to her forehead.

"What else was I supposed to do?" Her eyes were wild with emotion. "After we left Nina's it was just me and them in the hotel room and I had to leave them there when I went to work." She stuck her fingers in her mouth, then took them out and kept talking. "I guess they got tired of waiting for me. I guess maybe they run out of snacks. Donnie pulled the TV down off the stand and busted it. I'd told Kaleb to keep the door locked so nobody would come and hurt them." Miranda took a deep breath. "I told him never to open that door, so he climbed out a window on the second floor."

She started crying then, big ferocious sobs, and Jodi gathered her in her arms, rocking gently. She could hear the wind in the grass and the motor of a car wending away somewhere down the mountain.

June 1989

If Jodi closes her left eye the stripper girl disappears. But when she blinks the girl is there again, in the corner near the bathroom, leaned up against that folding contraption that's supposed to hold your suitcase. They don't have suitcases. The girl's got nothing but her minidress and six-and-a-half-inch heels. Paula and Jodi have everything they need in a ratty orange Mexican carpetbag.

The girl tucks her head down into her arms, and her shoulders shake. She cries in a practiced, showy sort of way and when she pulls her knees up to her chest the triangle of her pink panties is visible between her legs. Jodi leans back against the plywood headboard and runs her finger down the barrel of her .38. The girl's been cooperative the whole time and she hasn't had to hold the pistol on her since they jumped her, out back of the Crystal Club, but she likes to keep it out to remind her that this is serious.

Paula scoots down to the end of the bed and leans toward the girl.

"Look, honey, we ain't gonna hurt you," she says. "As soon as Jonno's ready to make the drop, this'll all be over."

The room is dim and crowded, rust-colored carpet, a nicotine-yellow lamp and wallpaper with big purple flowers blooming like mildew stains all across the walls. Paula improvised a trash can cooler beside the bed for their beers. It leaks slowly, making a wet trail toward the TV where a muted Roseanne Barr waddles back and forth, mouthing off silently.

"Aren't we supposed to be the ones who call the shots?" Jodi says, looking at Paula's hunched back. "Aren't *we* supposed to tell Jonno when to make the drop?"

Paula doesn't move, doesn't say anything, just keeps staring into the corner at the girl's tousled blonde head with brown roots showing through. It was supposed to go fast, just one-two-three: grab the girl, call the guy, trade, and go.

Jodi wipes the pistol with the edge of her daisy-print tank top until it shines in the dull lamplight. "Aren't we supposed to threaten he'll never see his favorite little stripper ever again?"

The girl's head jerks up. Her eyes are dry, eyebrows arched like thick spider legs. "Dancer," she says. "I'm a *dancer*."

Paula stands and walks into the bathroom, cigarette smoke trailing behind.

"You might as well just fucking call him up and tell him where we are," Jodi says. "Tell him not to worry about paying us, just come on over to the Mariann Motel and blow our brains out."

"Jodi, get in here," Paula hollers in her best gruff-husband voice.

The girl has her head tucked down in her arms again. Jodi unplugs the phone and carries it with her, pistol in one hand, phone in the other. The bathroom smells heavily of piss and sulfur water. She sets the phone down on the cracked counter beside the sink.

"What the fuck did you bring that in here for?" Paula's got her face all scrunched up, blue eyes angry, mouth like a pink bruise.

"Are you fucking serious?" Jodi kicks the door halfway closed.

The fluorescent light makes a constant buzz. Taking Paula's cigarette, she places it between her lips, inhales and blows out a stream of smoke and tequila breath. She never did think this hostage thing was a good idea. Paula plays it cool but Jodi sees the tremor behind the hard jaw. They need to get Ricky away from Dylan and once they do that, Paula insists, they're going to need more money than she can make at the card tables.

Jodi drops the cigarette into the toilet bowl and they both watch it bob.

"Paula," she hisses, beginning to feel now the shiny softness of the Seconal she swallowed with her last beer. "That girl's a stripper but she's not stupid. She—"

"Dancer." The girl's voice floats in. "I'm a dancer."

Paula and Jodi lock eyes. Jodi reaches up to smack the smile off Paula's face but Paula grabs her wrist, pins it to the counter, and whispers, "Shut the fuck up." She leans close, hip grinding into Jodi's crotch. "You hold the gun. That's all you gotta do, baby, I got the rest."

They move out into the room, Paula's arm around Jodi's shoulders, a united front. Jodi holds the gun out toward the stripper but the girl's not even looking so she settles onto the bed and turns up the volume on the TV. *So first*, Roseanne says, *you gotta get rid of all the stuff his mom did to him. And then you gotta get rid of all that macho crap that they pick up from beer commercials.*

Paula bends to plug the phone back in and the soft mounds of her hips show over the hem of her jeans. The Seconal shimmers in Jodi's veins and she reaches out and wraps her arm around Paula's waist. She pulls her toward the bed but Paula pushes her hand away. Touching is always on Paula's terms. She flips up Jodi's skirt, rips off her top anytime she likes, but in the ten months she's known her Jodi's never seen Paula all naked.

"I gotta go pee," the girl says, and Jodi jumps up, her legs faltering under her, knees bending together. She pulls herself straight. "All right," she says, nodding toward the bathroom and holding the pistol out, admiring how, with the gun in her hands, her arms seem so strong and tight.

Paula says *calm down* but Jodi's having fun. The girl hovers over the toilet seat, her little pussy shaved bare, a lollipop inked on her skinny thigh. Away from the stage lights she's not all that pretty, not even that young.

Jodi marches her back to her corner.

"You want a beer, baby?" Paula waves the gun aside and passes Jodi a Budweiser. She lights her a cigarette and the room is warm again, glowing with the fact that everything is going to be all right. Settling back on the bed, Jodi closes her eyes and exhales a thin stream of smoke up toward the ceiling.

"What about you, honey? You want one too?" Paula walks over to the girl.

Jodi turns to watch Paula. "We don't have that many beers," she says. "I don't want you sharing with that fucking stripper."

"Shut up," Paula says.

"Oh, I'm sorry, I mean *dancer.*"

The girl glances past Paula and her eyes jolt Jodi. Raccoon ringed with makeup but solid and unafraid. Jodi lifts the pistol, cocks it.

"Don't fucking look at me," she says.

Roseanne goes off and Jodi flips past *Married with Children*, animals in Africa, a Mexican soap opera, and then there's that song—*far through the heart*—and the Gemini on some bright stage, Lee Golden up front with his white jeans and gold guitar—*Our land, our land is far through the heart of this snow. . . .*

"Paula," Jodi calls. It's their song but Paula is in the bathroom again, fixing up a shot.

JODI WAKES TO laughter in a dark room. She surfaces out of dreams of mountains, wet green ridges under banks of morning clouds, and the lamp beside the bed is off, the clock blinking 4:43 a.m. Over the hum of the TV talk-show host Jodi hears bubbling laughter and through the half-closed bathroom door a path of light spills across the floor.

She sits there, blinking and staring at that light, trying to unscramble the events of the past few hours. At some point she remembers the beers were gone and she felt drowsy and had fixed herself a little wakeup shot just to keep alert but then she and Paula were arguing, Paula telling her she was too amped and anxious, and so she'd swallowed a few more of those little red dream-time pills.

"Paula?" Her sleep-soaked voice barely cracks a whisper.

In the sheets she finds the pistol, cocks it, and crosses the carpet. There in the bathroom mirror, she sees skin. The shower is running and the girl is naked, blonde hair frizzed out wildly and her ass beautifully firm. Pinned between her and the wall is Paula.

The buzz of the fluorescent light mixes with the hiss of the shower and scratches around inside Jodi's brain.

"Come on," the girl says. "Didn't your mama ever tell you? You gotta take your clothes off to get in the shower."

Paula laughs. The laughter is Paula's. Paula is the laughter.

Jodi strains to turn up the noise in her brain. The buzzing has morphed into shaking now. Cold. It's cold in there. The air conditioner chugs and Jodi tries to concentrate on the hiss, tick, buzz but the girl's voice slices right through.

"Here, I'll help you."

She reaches for the top button on Paula's shirt. Jodi grips the pistol. There's not enough air. Pepto-Bismol pink nails fumble open the button on Paula's shirt. Glossy nails on button number two and Paula puts her hand on the girl's ass, fingers resting on the brown mole right there above the crack. Buttons three and four fall open and the girl looks up at Paula's face. Jodi raises the pistol; she needs to feel that taut-arm strength again. She remembers the look on Paula's face the night they were supposed to rescue Ricky, the vacant stare and promises of *soon, soon, soon*.

The fluorescent light keeps on buzzing, bouncing bright. The girl bends to unbuckle Paula's belt and her ass jiggles. Paula looks at the reflection of that ass in the mirror. Her eyes move up to the door. She sees Jodi there. She tilts her head back. She smiles, those full, dark lips opening wide. Jodi's heartbeat thrums up and she's not cold anymore, not shaking. She's not there. She stares straight into Paula's mouth and pulls the trigger.

September 2007

The backseat of the Chevette was loaded with groceries but Miranda could not go back to the cabin. Not yet. She circled the IGA parking lot slowly, the heat crackling up from the pavement in great waves. It was September but still so hot. She couldn't sleep at night; no electricity at the cabin obviously meant no air-conditioning, no fan, nothing to stir the heat. She couldn't stand that unbroken heat. She'd lie there in bed with this heavy panic, a feeling like she was on a bus going who the hell knows where and had missed her stop long ago but just gone on pretending everything was okay.

Lately she'd taken on extra shifts at the bar, working almost every night now, and afterward she drove down the river past little clusters of trailers and then on beyond into the deep woods. She arrived back at the cabin at dawn, exhausted and anxious, and crashed there, restless in the bed for a few hours, the boys' voices scratching into her thin sleep.

She'd lost weight too, she thought, looking down at the sagging skin on her legs. She fidgeted, slowed the car, and lit a new cigarette, then circled the parking lot again. Back beyond the loading dock a field opened up, a swath of brittle grass and a cluster of trees. In the shade a group of cattle stood dumbly waiting. Everywhere she looked there was this heavy waiting.

She pitched her cigarette and cut the wheel sharply; a gallon of milk slid off the backseat and bounced onto the floor. She pictured the milk spilling up under the seat but did not stop to check.

It was hot inside Slattery's Girl, dry and yeasty smelling but comfortingly dark. She'd been told never to come here during off hours but she had a key and the bar had a phone.

She poured herself a glass of whiskey, drained it, and poured another. She took the phone from its cradle and watched her fingers as they punched those familiar numbers.

The phone was ringing.

Miranda paced the bar.

It was twenty-three steps one way but always twenty-four steps on the way back. She let her mind play with the curiousness of that fact while the phone rang. Fifteen, sixteen, seventeen, she reached for her drink.

"Yeah?"

That voice.

"Hello?"

Miranda heard herself laughing.

"Lee, it's me."

She lowered herself to the floor.

"Miranda, baby."

She lay down across the dusty floor and balanced her glass of whiskey on her stomach. "Lee."

"He found you?"

"I'm tired Lee, I—"

"Where'd he find you?"

"I, I've got . . ." She closed her eyes to try to make the words come out right. "I mean, I came down to town to get groceries."

"Valez finally fucking found you. I sent him looking for you like—"

"No, I want *you* to find me."

She was crying.

"I'm tired, Lee, I'm tired all the time. I need to come home."

The glass of whiskey was rocking, sloshing in great waves inside the little glass while her body shook.

"Hey, stay with me, baby."

"I'm here," she said. His voice was coming out of the phone and mixing in with her own and in it she heard a solidness. In their fucked-upness they completed each other, she thought. Alone they were both too wobbly but together they could balance each other out.

"Just keep talking to me, baby, tell me more," he said. "Where are you? I'll be there, just keep talking to me."

LYNN'S GARDEN WAS draped in gauzy silk, the bushes cocooned in white and strips of chiffon dangling from the trees. The lawn was bustling with uniformed women carrying silver chafing dishes and men unfolding long wooden tables.

Jodi wandered into the house and found Lynn in the living room, bent over the floor. Sharp dashes of light leapt up as she moved and it took Jodi a moment to realize that she was picking up pieces of a fractured mirror.

"I can't decide," she said, holding up a palm-size fragment. "I love the *idea* but I don't want to go too rococo."

Jodi shivered at the sight of the broken mirror and its cold, watery light.

"Besides, how would we hang them? Drill little holes? Wrap the whole piece in wire?" She turned and looked at Jodi. "It's too much, probably, right?" She stood and walked over to the far side of the room. She held the mirror fragment and the light followed her, bouncing out of her hand. "I always like preparing for a party better than I like the party itself."

She wore a feathery dress, long in the back and short in the front, layers of cream and white under a thin top shift of deep blue. Her black shoes were high and blocky, all sharp angles in contrast to the frothy dress.

"Sit down," she said, setting the piece of mirror on the mantel and picking up a white-and-gold pack of cigarettes.

Jodi did not move.

"What's wrong?" Lynn held out her hand.

Jodi let Lynn lead her over to a long white couch. They settled into the cushions, Lynn's leg pressed close, her skirt spilling over onto Jodi's lap. Her cigarette smelled like cinnamon.

"I have a gift for you," she said, and from the bosom of her dress she retrieved a tiny metal box that sprang open to reveal six pills. "Have one."

Jodi shook her head and reached into her own pocket for her cigarettes. "What are they?"

Lynn smiled. "Part of the experience."

Jodi laughed and lit her Marlboro but then reached out and took a pill. A small blue circle with a tiny crown printed on one side.

Lynn slipped off her shoes and leaned back. She pressed her bare feet up against Jodi's leg and her dress shifted around her with a shushing sound. There was a breeze coming in through the windows and it played with the edges of the thin fabric, lifting it up to expose her white-blue thigh.

"They're sweet kids?" Lynn said. "Your girlfriend's boys?"

Jodi looked away. She set the blue pill carefully on the back of her tongue and swallowed. "Your party's starting." She pointed out toward the garden, which had begun to fill with guests.

"It's good to make them wait," Lynn said. "And besides, I really actually hate parties." Jodi looked back at her and Lynn smiled. "You're surprised?" she said. "You keep insisting that we're so different but I don't think so really. I mean, these parties are useful but it's not like I enjoy hanging out with those people." She waved her hand at the glass doors.

In the garden the men pumped one another's hands and smiled broadly while the women hung together in small herds, the heels of their shoes sinking into the soft earth.

"Sometime I'd like to have a whole party and never join," Lynn said. "Just watch from in here. Watch them being watched. A panopticon party."

Jodi thought to say something but then it seemed unnecessary. She felt a liquid building, a rush that started in the deepest part of her and reached out in a glittering sheet to the edges of her body. A bell was ringing somewhere and the rhythm of it matched her ripples of pleasure.

"I'm in the mood for white," Lynn said, standing and floating across the room toward the bar.

It was not a bell but a piano and the sound of it was breaking open something, pressing insistently in under her skin.

"Jodi?" Lynn lifted a sweating bottle of white wine.

Jodi shook her head.

"You want bourbon," Lynn said, bending to retrieve a cut-glass decanter from a lower shelf. "Did you always know you were gay?"

Jodi snapped her head up. Lynn was smiling and blinking, her pupils like tiny, dark stains inside the white lakes of her eyes.

"Ethan told me about you. He said he looked you up and read about your trial and when he told me the story all I could think was, it's so sad and beautiful."

Lynn walked toward Jodi, the glass of bourbon held high as she twisted the story, turning it around into something pretty. Jodi thought of the priest at Jaxton, begging to absolve her. *In the blood of the lamb you shall be redeemed.* But how, she had wondered, could blood absolve blood? No, there would be no absolving, only building upward and away, like a grafted branch, growing into something new.

"It's you and your girl against the world," Lynn said, "and then everything spills out of your hands and it's all unwarranted chaos and—"

"No, no, it's not like that at all. It was simple, simple and evil," Jodi said.

THE SHOT CANCELS out all other noise and separates time into two distinct spaces. Jodi stands between them. The wall is dripping red. Below the bright spray Paula is moving, her body unspooling across the linoleum.

The air smells of the rank heat of doe season: backyards strung with stiffening bodies and clouded with that mineral smell, the oily scent that erupts when the knife slits the white fur belly.

Jodi drops the gun and it bounces and falls again, this time facing the doorway.

The stripper is perched on the toilet bowl, her head tucked between her knees. Naked. It seems she is weeping.

Paula's shirt hangs open, the last button almost undone. Her chest is pale and unmoving.

Gravity is reaching, growing up toward Jodi, but she hangs in that moment between the before and after, a scream building steady like a pulse inside her.

LYNN DID NOT join the party until it was nearly dark. Heat lightning was breaking out over the western ridges and the wind had torn the silk from the trees. Jodi watched Lynn walk outside and then she stood, sick and in need of a bathroom.

She vomited into the spotless toilet bowl, half-enjoying the raw intensity, and then lay with her face against the cool tile floor and thought of Miranda in the cabin painting her nails and smoking cigarettes, Ricky and the boys sprawled across the bed.

She left through the front door, grateful that she'd parked far enough away not to be blocked in. As she drove out of Lewisville the houses dropped away and a deep and total blackness set in. She watched the road sweep under her and the movement felt good. It was still possible, she thought. More than possible. With the land in Lynn's name it would be safe and she and Miranda could take the boys camping and buy themselves a little time to figure out what they needed to do to get full custody. Then she'd come back and own up to it, tell anyone who cared to know that she loved Miranda, and they'd get the boys enrolled in school and buy some chickens. She would put Ricky in charge of the chickens, she thought, he'd like that, although another part of her mind still kept cutting him out of all her plans. Where he would go, she didn't know, but with all the complications he'd caused she couldn't quite fit him into her image of a perfect future.

Just past the first steep curve of the mountain the car's headlights flashed onto a young deer. Jodi jerked the Chevette to a stop. The doe's eyes were enormous and mirror smooth and she stared straight ahead, so close, her face vacant with fear. The forest breathed huge around them, the hillside scurrying with unseen movement, and when Jodi rolled down the window there was a tang of smoke. The deer bolted into the trees and she drove on.

Near the crest of Bethlehem the siren started—a far-off wailing that pulsed closer as Jodi drove up over the top of the mountain. The sky was on fire. Spiking forks of orange flame flared out of the tall white frack tower.

Through the open window the smell of smoke and fear filled the air. There came a movement from along the roadside, a flap of wings in the trees. Jodi jerked the gearshift and sped up.

Half a mile from the lane the sirens overtook her, the sickening volume swelling up behind her until the trucks forced her off onto the shoulder and streamed by in coils of red-and-white lights. She ducked instinctively, then cranked up the window, but already the car was thick with smoke and the road barely visible before her. She wished she hadn't taken that pill from Lynn. Her eyes watered as she edged on and came to a stop just short of a hazy figure silhouetted against a second pair of headlights. The fire was shockingly beautiful, a deep orange that made the night blacker around it. Jodi closed her eyes as a white wall of fear overtook her.

When she surfaced Ricky was standing at the car window. She pushed open the door and stepped out.

"What's happening?"

Ricky's face was strange, as still as the deer's. In his right hand he held a plastic gas canister.

"Where are Miranda and the boys?" Jodi leaned in toward Ricky.

The air shuddered orange all around him, full of a sharp almost gunpowder smell.

"Hurry up and get in the truck," a voice called.

Jodi squinted over Ricky's shoulder. It was Farren.

"Come on." She stepped closer to Ricky and reached out for his hand but he turned away.

The air seemed to be thickening by the minute, a hot wind pressing in on them.

Jodi ran to the truck and slid in next to Farren. "Where are Miranda and the boys?"

"Get him in the truck now," Farren said.

It took both of them working together, though, under the soaring smoke and shaking sirens, and as they struggled with Ricky, Farren explained what he could understand. He'd seen Miranda go by around five, riding toward town with some man in a blue truck. Next time he came out on the porch, he said, it was near dusk and a big white bus was parked at the end of the lane. By the time he made it down there the bus had pulled away and the smell of smoke was on the wind. He found Ricky out by the frack tower with a lighter and can of gasoline babbling about how the evil came up from that well and was wrecking everything.

Jodi turned to Ricky where he sat beside her with his head leaned against the passenger's window, and a fury scorched across her brain. His face was empty as he stared straight ahead. Outside the trees moaned and split under the heat with great popping sounds and Jodi wondered suddenly if this wasn't retaliation, if he hadn't somehow known that she'd fantasized about making plans with Miranda and leaving him out. "What the fuck?" She leaned toward him, spitting into his face. "What the fuck were you thinking?"

A hand gripped her shoulder. "There are two problems here," Farren said, "but only one we can do anything about right now. A bus like that can't get too far too fast on roads like this. We go now and we can get those little boys back safely." He did not let go of Jodi's shoulder until she had relaxed against the seat and then he reached inside his jacket and handed her a small pistol.

"Just in case," he said. "They need to see that we're serious."

Jodi's fingers reached for it but her stomach dropped at the touch of the cold metal. She set it on the dashboard and looked away but she could still feel the presence of the gun and Ricky there beside her.

The speedometer leapt—thirty-five, forty-five, fifty—and Farren leaned close to the wheel. Snatches of their life flashed in Jodi's mind and then were sucked away out the window: the kids in the yard with sparklers, the ballooning tarpaulin roof and Miranda's smooth legs up in the high branches of the sweet gum tree. Jodi felt dizzy in the swirl of images and in that moment it wouldn't have surprised her at all if she'd woken suddenly in her Jaxton cell to realize it was all of it just a fever dream.

At the bottom of the mountain the smoke thinned. They passed the blinking sign for Slattery's Girl and Jodi imagined Miranda, head thrown back, laughing behind the bar, and her blood jumped.

Then they were out of town and back into the density of the woods. The moon came out from behind a bank of clouds and spilled silver over the trunks of the trees. It looked, Jodi realized, quite beautiful and the beauty of it made it hard for her to breathe. She saw her terror stretching, bright and long, as they moved moment by moment farther away both from the boys— out there in front of them somewhere, out of reach—and the cabin, behind them, alone and unguarded against the hurtling blaze.

The road took a hairpin turn and the three of them leaned into one another, Jodi in the middle, her shoulders knocking against both men as the road reeled before them. And then, unbelievably, on the rise just ahead: the red taillights and tall tinted windows of a white tour bus.

A spike of electricity zipped up Jodi. She kept waiting for the bus to disappear. A communal hallucination, a wish dream, she thought, but it stayed there, bright and sleek with a giant painting across the side of Lee Golden's grinning face.

They overtook it on the next straight stretch. Farren laid on the horn, flashing his blinkers and pressing hard on the gas, the truck fairly panting from the strain as they pulled out in front. Up ahead the blacktop curved into a blind but Farren mashed on the brake and cut the wheel. The truck spun and then halted, blocking the road. Jodi turned to watch as the bus shuddered to a stop too, brakes squealing. It sat about fifty feet back and tilted so that the passenger's side of the bus was visible through the window of the pickup.

Everything was still for a moment. Nothing but the motors ticking and the dust swirling in the twin pairs of headlights. Then Farren opened his door and Jodi scrambled after him.

"I promised Miss Rosalba," Ricky said, sliding across the seat.

Farren turned. "You stay here, inside the truck," he said, pushing the door closed.

Jodi hovered behind Farren as he leaned against the front tire. The lights inside the bus had gone black.

"How many people in there, do you think?" Farren asked.

Jodi shook her head. She wanted to ask what Farren's plan was but suddenly there came the sound of metal hinging and then a rustle of footsteps. Jodi could just barely make out the silhouette of a man in a white T-shirt walking from the driver's side around the front of the bus, his slicked black hair shining a little in the thin light. For what seemed like several full minutes no one moved or spoke. The wind slid through the tall trees.

"That him?" Farren finally whispered, and Jodi opened her mouth to say no when a shot blasted out.

It took a moment for her to realize that the noise came from inside the pickup.

Farren turned, eyes big, as the sound blew around them and then everything went still.

The dust in the beams of the headlights.

Frozen.

Then fluid.

The man in front of the bus door crouched and Jodi rose and saw Ricky, silhouetted in the pickup truck window, pistol outstretched. She was shocked he even knew how to use a gun.

"Ricky," she screamed, but her voice was covered over by the bark of another shot and then a return greeting from the bus.

Farren grabbed Jodi and pulled her down against the tire as the shots rang by. There was a shattering of glass and the windshield exploded above them. Farren lunged up and shouted Ricky's name and then ducked again as the other pistol answered, a staccato, repeating. Bullets scudded across the dirt and rang against the blacktop, rattling into the metal of the bus and the truck with a tremendous clattering.

No, Jodi thought, no. It was beyond anger now, beyond anything. She could hear nothing but the enormous ringing inside her head. Her lungs felt small and shallow, incapable of drawing a full breath. She pictured the three little boys and Miranda just on the other side of those bus doors. She pictured Kaleb's eyes big with fear.

From around the edge of the truck tire she could see a pair of shadowed legs approaching. She squeezed Farren's arm. *Shit, fuck.* Why had she left the pistol in there? Why had he given it to her in the first place?

Noise and the movement came almost simultaneously, a blast and then the slap and push of air as a body hit the ground with a gargled cry.

"Ricky?" Jodi screamed, and she rose up to standing.

But Ricky was still in the window, and in the dirt on the far side of the truck the slick-haired man lay squirming. His leg twitched and Jodi could see the blood.

The man moaned and his gun went off again but this time pinging in the opposite direction.

Jodi could feel herself trembling. She thought again of the shuddering wall of flames up on the mountain and she could feel it all, the jagged moments of this night all inside her.

A slice of yellow light appeared in the doorway of the bus.

"Cease-fire," a voice called, "or whatever the fucking hell. Don't shoot me in front of my sons. I'm unarmed."

The slice of light grew wider and Lee Golden walked down and around the front of the bus. "Who the hell's out there?" He stood, hips squared and shoulders pulled back, calling his questions into the night.

"Take my pistol, Lee." The man on the ground moved with a dragging sound.

Jodi pushed up onto her tiptoes, trying to reach in the window to Ricky but he was on the far side of the cab.

"Daddy?" a small voice called, and then another: "Daddy, be careful!"

In the doorway of the bus a blonde figure appeared with three little heads in a row behind her. Jodi felt a salt-surge of too much emotion ringing through her, emptying her out as she stared at Miranda and the boys. A part of her belonged over there with them and she could feel herself separating, raw as fresh-torn skin.

"Put the gun down, Ricky," she said.

How in the hell did they end up like this? She'd built herself around this hope and it had gone off, so wild and wrong.

"Who are you?" Lee's voice boomed into the quiet. "Who the fuck are you?"

From across the road an owl called out a single long note and Jodi pressed herself against the truck door and looked up to the arching branches over their heads and the strips of clouds and constellations above. Fixed and turning. And down below she saw this group she'd caused to gather here and she saw the line of her life, a dark seam twisting always back on itself, and she knew this moment had been coming for a long time.

She thought of the girl she was before Paula, a girl waiting for happiness to come upon her the way she had seen it happen to other girls when they grew breasts and fell in love. She'd been waiting for change to come marching toward her like a summer storm across an open field but it had not happened like that. It had come up in an unexpected rush from under her feet. And it had all kept building up into the terror and then ebbing out into the everyday gray of prison life and then just as inexplicably she'd been released and left spinning like a broken compass, seeking, with the old plan as the only way to understand anything. Now, though, she felt strangely weightless.

The land was gone and so was Miranda and she could see now how she'd laid the old pattern over her new life like the fragile tissue-paper outlines Effie had used to cut dresses. She'd carefully unfolded it and tried to fit them all inside, smothering any real chance they'd had. She thought back to her first free moment in that Jaxton parking lot with the Georgia mountains hovering over her and she saw her options drawing out from there like spokes in every direction but it was not until now, in this strange and gutted silence, that she had ever even acknowledged the possibility of other possibilities and the hugeness of the universe.

"What the fuck do you want?" Lee screamed.

Jodi breathed deeply, pulling in the silence and focusing. *We're ready now, we're building.* If she could just turn this moment around before there were any more unfixable mistakes. If she could just get that gun away from Ricky and then tell them to go . . . she'd had no right to pull them in anyway—Ricky, Miranda, Farren—no right to suck them into the twistedness of her own life.

She felt something turn in her and release and then she rose, pushing herself up and beyond. *GO, go, go.* She jerked the truck door open and was on Ricky with both arms, not breathing until she had the pistol in her fist. He roiled and turned, nearly overpowering her and she drew back, shaking, pistol held out and pointed at him. He froze. Pale face and shaggy hair outlined against the broken window.

The silence was as wide as the night sky.

Her body was empty.

This was not happening.

"Don't move," she said. She backed away from the truck, the pistol still held out and the weight of it centering her even as she shook.

"Jodi—" Ricky said.

She spun toward Farren, holding the pistol level with his face. "Get in the truck and go," she said. "Those boys aren't ours to keep."

"What—"

From this distance she could not see the expression in Farren's eyes but she could hear him breathing heavily. "Go on and get Ricky away from here. I'm not putting this gun down till you leave." She motioned toward the driver's-side door. "We gotta let them go."

She kept the pistol trained on the pickup until the motor started and the wheels turned, spitting gravel as it lurched forward. And then she was running. She did not look back at Lee. She ran across the pocked asphalt, down the embankment, and on into the blackness of the pines below.

The forest closed around her, so complete that she saw only flashes of clouded sky. There were voices on the road up above but she kept moving. Sapling branches whipped her face and her feet slid on the slippery needles until she gave in and fell, her body tumbling and the smell of the ground rising around her. The bruising weight of her body against that hard earth felt satisfying, like it might beat this wild sadness out of her for good.

Half a mile down the slope the pines opened into a small clearing and she steadied herself at the edge, her breath catching in her dry throat. She still clutched the pistol in her right hand. Her arm shook. She closed her eyes. Bits of thoughts buzzed and crackled, the darkness of the night roaring around her, but she found that in the darkness there were little pools of quiet too, not possibilities so much as realities. She had not broken parole tonight, had not been arrested, at least. She owed Ballard a visit in three weeks but if she could keep herself safe . . . Images sifted around her: her hands on the wheel of a semitruck, out on the flats of the desert, driving alone through the night, back toward the mountains. There were other pictures too, flickering at the edges of her mind: the rolling fields of some rich man's farm in the valley. She remembered the cattle operation her great-uncle had managed for some out-of-state man and that little trailer he'd lived in up until his death. She thirsted for a job like that, a place to be alone, now that the blind and awful weight of hope was gone.

She opened her eyes. The pistol glinted. She brought her arm back and then up, her fingers loosening, the weight of the gun springing away as it arced out into the night. In the silence after it landed she could hear the forest around her, the secret sound of things decaying, and the river out there, slipping on between its banks.

IN THE LATER hours of the night, rain fell and brought with it a fog that curled along the bottoms of the branches. Jodi followed the river south, back toward town, her feet steadier now on the flat expanse of low ground. After a while, a great exhaustion washed over her, exhaustion that was also a form of sweet relief. There was nothing then but the darkness, the layers of it fragmenting before her, and the steady murmur of the trees stretching over a landscape so old it was half hidden in itself, a land that had been sinking for so long its surface was only a scrim over the density that lay below. It was this, Jodi thought, this thick secrecy that haunted her, kept her coming back and wanting more, dreaming of the place even when she was in the midst of it. Like a lover who never tells all so that even in the throes of passion you cannot help but notice the melancholic taste of unknown scars and memories.

. . .

BY THE TIME she reached the caves it was early morning. The ground was wet underfoot and the air still tasted of smoke but from what Jodi could see the flames were gone. She had avoided the road and Effie's land and borrowed on some older sense of direction that in her exhaustion made a simple kind of sense.

She found the entrance and crumpled for a moment, there in the leaves. Then, pushing on, she flattened her body and pulled herself through, into the comfort of darkness and then on again, until she found the narrow channel beyond the white cake.

Out on the rock platform the wind lifted and curled around her. From there she could see the dawn paling above the dark trees and the mountains opening. Beyond the bit of land that once belonged to her, beyond the cabin and all that familiar, there was more.